THE CHRONICLES OF THE
IMAGINARIUM GEOGRAPHICA

THE SHADOW DRAGONS

Written and illustrated by

James A. Owen

SIMON & SCHUSTER BFYR

NEW YORK LONDON TORONTO SYDNEY

SIMON & SCHUSTER BFYR

An imprint of Simon & Schuster Children's Publishing Division
1230 Avenue of the Americas, New York, New York 10020

For information about special discounts for bulk purchases, please contact Simon &
Schuster Special Sales at 1-866-506-1949 or business@simonandschuster.com.
The Simon & Schuster Speakers Bureau can bring authors to your live event. For more
information or to book an event, contact the Simon & Schuster Speakers Bureau at
1-866-248-3049 or visit our website at www.simonspeakers.com.
Also available in a SIMON & SCHUSTER BFYR hardcover edition
Book design by Christopher Grassi and James A. Owen
The text for this book is set in Adobe Jenson Pro.
Manufactured in the United States of America
First SIMON & SCHUSTER BFYR paperback edition March 2011
2 4 6 8 10 9 7 5 3 1
The Library of Congress has cataloged the hardcover edition as follows:
Owen, James A.
The shadow dragons / written and illustrated by James A. Owen.
p. cm. —
(The Chronicles of the Imaginarium Geographica ; bk. 4)
Summary: The Winter King's Shadow, having gained control of the doors from the Keep
of Time and of an army of Dragon Shadows, plans to use the turmoil of World War II
to take over both worlds, but all Caretakers, past and present, come together to stop him,
using some unlikely weapons.
ISBN 978-1-4169-5879-6 (hc)
[1.Time travel—Fiction. 2. Characters in literature—Fiction. 3. World War,
1939–1945—Fiction. 4. Fantasy.] I. Title.
PZ7.O97124Shc 2009
[Fic]—dc22
2008050303
ISBN 978-1-4169-5880-2 (pbk)
ISBN 978-1-4391-6055-8 (eBook)

For James Chapple and Jeremy Owen

Contents

Contents

List of Illustrations

Acknowledgments

Writing *The Shadow Dragons* was an interesting challenge. It's a "middle book," and so brought with it both the expectations generated by the first three, as well as those anticipated by the stories to come. It was the most complex book to work on, and the easiest to understand—because the characters involved are now old friends. And so are the ones in the book itself.

Navah Wolfe and David Gale have continued to be among the most valuable supporters of my work. I believed (and still do) when I started my relationship with Simon & Schuster Books for Young Readers that I had found in David the ideal editor. He has found a perfect balance of push and pull, of encouragement and prodding, which allows me to do what I do to the best of my limits. And Navah has become an invaluable first reader. Without a doubt her queries about characters and situations has made this a tighter book—and in one specific case, allowed me to revise one character to better reflect who he was supposed to be (and in the process made the book better by far). After David and Navah are done, Dorothy Gribbin and Valerie Shea are the editing gatekeepers, who make us all look smart. I am grateful to them all for all the hard work.

Julie and Ellen at the Gotham Group, and my attorney Craig Emanuel, continue to keep the contracts pulled together and make sure that everything I need to keep doing this for a living flows smoothly and well. And Cyndee Larson at National Bank of Arizona has gone the extra mile time and again to make sure the lights are on so that I can keep doing the work I need to do. Without their support I would be hoeing a much tougher row.

It's also been gratifying to know that I've had the support of all the executives at Simon & Schuster. Rubin Pfeffer and Rick Richter have moved on, but I remain hugely appreciative for their kindness and faith in my work. And Carolyn Reidy, Justin Chanda, and Jon Anderson have all made it easy to work with this house, and I am looking forward to working with them for a long time to come.

My art directors, Laurent and Lizzy, continue to make the books shine; and over at foreign rights sales, Cecilia and Shannon have made sure that the books are shining in around two dozen other languages. My publicists, Paul and Andrea, have arranged stellar signing tours and taken very good care of me.

Friends old and new inspire me to my best work: Jim Pascoe, Daanon DeCock, Joe LeFavi, Jason Lust, Brian Henson, and Lisa Henson make me proud of my profession. And my friend Rachel Nabors (subcultureofone.com) gave me one of the best character designs (the Yoricks) I've ever had the pleasure of drawing.

My family, in particular my wife Cindy and children Sophie and Nathaniel, are the reasons that I love what I do. Watching Nathaniel and Sophie come into their own as creative individuals gives me the steam I need to keep my wheels turning, and hopefully tell the kind of stories that will inspire them throughout their lives.

My Coppervale team continues to be my base. Lon, Mary, and Jason are supportive in the best of ways; and I would not be able to keep the schedule I do without Jeremy, who is my protector and advocate in more ways than I can count.

And not least, I want to thank a friend who remains with us in spirit, and (in his brother's words) who often seemed more committed to my goals than I was: James Chapple. He was not a writer or an artist, but was a very good man who saw virtues in me I could not see for myself, and was and is one of my great friends and inspirations.

Prologue

It might be said that a mystery is simply a secret to which no one knows the answer. The answers to some mysteries may have been known, once, and then were lost as the centuries passed. But there are other secrets that are so ancient that the truth of them is impossible to discover, and they must forever remain mysteries.

No one living or dead knew the identity of the Architect of the Keep of Time.

Before Atlantis, before Ur, before any stone of any city was erected upon the Earth in the Summer Country or in the Archipelago of Dreams, the keep had stood.

The Earth was a wilder place in those early days, before the rise of man. Magic and myth mingled freely with history as all manner of creatures tried to make sense of the world around them. Some were more advanced than others, and they took it upon themselves to shape, and to organize, and to look after the welfare of the races that were developing on this young world.

Theirs was the first city, built when there was no division between the worlds, and no need for one. Their sense of wonder was unlimited, for they had no understanding at all of fear. All they knew was discovery, and challenge, and how to overcome. And so they continued to build and to explore and to expand their knowledge.

These creatures soon took note of the keep and realized that it was an anchor against the tides of time that otherwise might have ripped the world asunder. Why it was built, and who had built it, they did not know. But they chose to guard it, and they knew they could learn from it and use it to create a better world.

One among them, the eldest, discovered how to harness the flow of time by fashioning doors and fitting them into the openings that appeared throughout the ever-growing tower. This discovery came none too soon, for a new element had come into the world that threatened the destruction of all that was.

In the guise of a seeker of knowledge from the future, evil had come to their world—and slowly but surely, it was becoming stronger. In time, it would be too strong to resist.

A great council was held among the guardians of the keep to determine how they might avoid the cataclysm that seemed so inevitable, and again, it was the eldest among them who discovered the solution—but it would not be a solution without sacrifice.

Their beloved city would not survive. It would fall. And they themselves would have to accept a new calling—promotions to a new rank that would be permanent, because they would never again be able to lower their guard if the world itself was to survive.

The eldest was first to take the mantle of this new responsibility, then in turn, each of his companions, until all of them had done so. And then each of them chose a door.

To protect the future, they realized that they must also protect the past—and so one by one, they entered the doors of the Keep of Time, until there was no point in the past that did not have, somewhere behind it, its guardian.

The last of them remained behind, watching, waiting, until one among the new races could produce a king worthy of becoming a guardian himself. Only then could he rest, and lay down the seemingly eternal burden.

The world did change; empires rose and fell. Only the keep remained as it was. The great mystery of the Architect's identity might never see an answer; and the secrets of the keep that were known were closely held.

But even so, only two things were sure: first, that to walk through a door was to cross over from the present to some point in the past; and second, that somewhere on the other side, there would be a Dragon.

THE SHADOW DRAGONS

PART ONE

Inklings and Mysteries

. . . a man was standing as if he were waiting . . .

CHAPTER ONE

Ransom

"*We are definitely lost,*" John said with decisive authority. "I haven't the faintest idea where we are."

"How can you be lost?" his friend Jack asked with a barely concealed grin. "You're the Principal Caretaker of the *Imaginarium Geographica*. You're probably the foremost authority on maps in the entire world. How is it you've managed to get us lost not two hours' walk from Oxford?"

"I wasn't paying attention," John said irritably. "I was enjoying the conversation and the company. After all, this is the first time in almost twenty years that the three of us have been able to come together as friends out in the open. I like secret societies as much as the next man, but actually having Charles participate as a formal member of the Inklings is going to be delightful."

"Agreed," said Jack, clapping Charles on the back. "The ability to share things with Hugo has been a blessing, but I've been itching to discuss your work at length with Arthur Greeves and Owen Barfield."

"It was fortuitous that Greeves sent you a copy of my new book," Charles agreed, "at the same time that you sent your own to the Oxford University Press. It was just the sort of coincidental happening that's interesting enough to sound truthful."

"That's because it *is* true," Jack insisted, "and all the more significant for it. Although we're going to have to work on our timing for these private walkabouts—I had to bow out of a walking tour with Barfield and Cecil Harwood to come out today."

"And I suppose *you* never get lost?" John said, raising a skeptical eyebrow.

Jack made a dismissive motion with his hands. "Never," he said primly. "We always bring a map, and I am, after all, the best map reader. Honestly, it's a mystery to me why I wasn't made the Caretaker Principia in your place."

John laughed. "I'll gladly give you the job right now," he said, pretending to remove his pack as Jack whistled and looked the other way, pretending to ignore him, "unless we can find someone better qualified, like a badger or a faun."

"I think you're both looney," said Charles, "and it's starting to rain."

They all looked up at the overcast sky, and as one, had the same thought. It had been raining on the night they first met in London—the night their lives were irrevocably changed.

It had been nearly two decades since the three men were brought together at the scene of a terrible crime. John's mentor, a professor of ancient literature named Stellan Sigurdsson, had been killed by a man called the Winter King, who was searching for the book known as the *Imaginarium Geographica*. John was being trained to become the next Caretaker of the great book, and Jack and Charles, as much through circumstance as by design, became Caretakers as well. With the help of another Caretaker called Bert, who became their trusted mentor, they managed to keep the

Winter King from using the book to conquer the Archipelago of Dreams, the great chain of islands for which the atlas was the only guide—but at great cost. Friends and allies were lost, hard lessons were learned; and even then, their nemesis returned again and again like a persistent nightmare at the edge of the waking world.

At the end of their first conflict, a great Dragon called Samaranth had dropped the Winter King over the edge of an endless waterfall. But nine years after that adventure, the three companions returned to the Archipelago to search for the great Dragonships that had vanished—along with all the children— only to discover that his Shadow had survived and was as deadly as the real Winter King himself.

Five years after that, they found themselves drawn into yet another crisis, when rogue Caretakers who had allied themselves with the Winter King tricked their friend Hugo Dyson into going through a door to the past—where he changed history itself.

Only by traveling through the events of two millennia and discovering the identity of the Cartographer of Lost Places, who created the *Geographica*, were they at last able to set things right. But what they discovered was disturbing: The Cartographer, who was once Merlin, was in large part responsible for the Winter King— his twin, Mordred—becoming the twisted, evil man he was. And the Caretakers would not have succeeded at all without the help of a young girl, Mordred's daughter Rose, also called the Grail Child, who returned with them to the present as Hugo's niece.

That was five years ago, and other than a few flurries that necessitated the counsel of the Caretakers—usually just John— there had been no reason to return to the Archipelago. The rogue Caretakers, led by the adventurer Richard Burton, had remained hidden, and there was no sign of the Winter King's Shadow. There were still difficult problems to deal with: The Keep of Time, where the Cartographer resided, had been crumbling apart since their first trip to the Archipelago; and the king, Artus, had tried to replace the monarchy with a republic, to only limited success. But the years of the Great War were far behind them, and all was right enough with the worlds here and beyond to set aside duty and responsibilities for a few hours to better enjoy a pleasant spring walk in the English countryside.

"It's a shame that Hugo could not join us," Jack said. "We've had too few occasions as of late to catch up with him."

"Uncle Hugo wanted to be here," came a voice from somewhere above them, "but he had some obligations to attend to in Reading that could not be delegated elsewhere. He sent me along anyway, because he knew you needed to discuss the Problem."

Rose Dyson dropped down from the birch tree she'd been climbing and dusted herself off, then moved to stand next to Jack.

The "Problem" she referred to was evident to all three Caretakers. When she returned with them to the present from the sixth century, she was barely an adolescent. Tall, perhaps, but the auburn-haired Rose was still obviously a child—and that was, as Hugo put it, the "Problem."

He had placed her in a boardinghouse near his teaching post in Reading, where she was enrolled in school as his niece. And over the course of five years, she had not visibly aged a day.

"It's a natural law without a demonstrable basis," Bert had told them once. "Denizens of the Archipelago age more slowly than we do in the Summer Country. Days and nights are the same as those here, but they're often out of sync."

This much they had witnessed for themselves on numerous occasions. Night in Oxford turned to day upon crossing the Frontier, and vice versa. And once, even the seasons had been reversed: Jack had traveled from Oxford in late summer, only to find the Archipelago in the grip of a terrible winter. So it wasn't just a matter of slight temporal differences—there were rules of time at work between the worlds that no one had as yet been able to decipher.

"Is the fact that she was born there, and brought here, the reason she hasn't aged?" Jack proposed.

"Not necessarily," offered Charles. "She hadn't aged normally on Avalon, either. But given her peculiar lineage, there may be no precedent for the kind of person she'll become."

"I'm a conundrum," Rose said from a few feet up the path, where she was using a branch to lever up a large stone. "Or an enigma. I forget which."

John nodded in agreement. "That's for certain. I've been thinking of contacting Aven and Artus about continuing her schooling on Paralon. At least there she'll not be questioned, no matter her age."

"Plus, she's family," said Jack. "She and Arthur were cousins, so that would make her an aunt, or second cousin, or some such."

"Twenty generations removed," added Charles.

"All of which doesn't change the fact that you've managed to get yourselves lost," came an irritated voice from above. "Of course, I know exactly where we are."

John rolled his eyes. "Of course," he said drolly, looking sideways at the others. "Having him up there is like having a conscience that won't shut up and won't take suggestions."

Complicating matters further was the other teacher the companions had brought forward from the past as a companion for Rose—the great owl Archimedes. That he was in fact a clockwork construct was the least of the problems he caused Hugo Dyson in Reading. He wasn't a predator; he wasn't dangerous; but he was irredeemably sarcastic and wickedly smart—and more than one local had been surprised by an encounter with a talking owl that could insult them while spouting jokes about Plato's Cave.

Archimedes, called Archie for short, stayed in Hugo's rooms, mostly—but it was inevitable that he and Rose would be seen together, and a talking owl combined with a girl who wasn't getting older was a recipe for disaster.

A month earlier they had transported the bird to the Kilns, the residence near Oxford that Jack shared with his brother Warnie and adopted mother Mrs. Moore. Warnie had already been initiated into some of the mysteries of the Caretakers, but it was a more delicate process with Mrs. Moore. However, once she recovered from the initial shock, and once she had accepted the need for secrecy, she and the owl became affable companions. Archie apparently got on very well with females.

Warnie was another matter entirely. The first hour they met, he had made a sudden move that startled the bird, and Archie bit his arm. It left a nasty welt, and thereafter Warnie persisted in referring to the bird as "Lucifer," which didn't endear him to the owl once Jack had explained the reference. The pairing made for a very lively household.

Moving Rose to the Kilns was a second option—but again, they would be risking the same kind of exposure there as they had in Reading. And keeping all knowledge of the *Geographica*, the

Archipelago, and the denizens within a secret was the prime rule of the Caretakers—the very rule that caused Burton and others to rebel. There would be no easy answers—which was why it was important for all three Caretakers to discuss the move as soon as they were able.

Archimedes lit atop a shrub next to where Rose was digging a hole and cast a disdainful eye at John. "Don't you have the atlas with you, Caretaker Principia?" the bird asked. "Isn't it full of maps?"

"Yes, I have it, and yes, it is," John said irritably. "But I don't have any maps of England in it."

The owl hooted in derision. "Only a scholar would go on a hike with a book of maps that are of absolutely no use."

"It's immensely useful!" John shot back. "Just, ah, just not here and now."

It was not all that unusual for a professor to carry books with him wherever he went—even on a walkabout holiday such as this one—so John simply carried the *Imaginarium Geographica* around with him. Too many times in the past circumstances had called for its use, and through misfortune, or lack of preparation, he had found himself without it.

Even after the badger Tummeler had begun publishing an abridged and annotated edition in the Archipelago, and copies were freely available, John still preferred to keep a light hand on the actual atlas. It was impossibly old, and had been written in by some of the greatest creative minds in human history. There were notations that were to be read only by the Caretakers or their apprentices, and so were not available to Tummeler. And there were maps that were left out of the popular edition because the little mammal saw them as unimportant.

What Tummeler didn't realize was that it was often those out-of-the-way places where the turning points of history occurred, in the same way that the men and women who changed the world were not always the ones who seemed to have the power to do so. No one understood this principle quite so well as two professors from Oxford and their editor friend from London.

The owl launched himself back into the air as a stone tumbled into the hole Rose had been digging.

"There," she said, dusting her hands. "That's much better."

"What's better?" Charles asked.

"The stone," Rose replied. "It was in the wrong place. I put it back."

John and Jack blinked at each other in consternation. They couldn't decide if the girl was too simple or too complex to really understand.

"Are you certain he's not going to, ah, rust?" Charles said, casting a glance upward at the bird circling overhead. "Hugo would be quite put out if something befell the owl."

"He hasn't rusted so far," said Jack, looking around the small clearing, "but we're going to be soaked to the skin if we don't find a place to bed down for the evening. We'd best be going, and quickly. It's getting dark."

"Any suggestions?" said John.

Jack indicated a faint footpath to the northwest, which veered off the main walking trail. "There's a faint glow coming from over there. With any luck, it's an inn—or at least a farmhouse where we can get directions and our bearings."

There was indeed a light emanating from somewhere behind a grove of trees. The roadway must have been on the other side, as the path was sparse enough that it could not have seen many travelers. Nevertheless, the companions followed Jack's lead and pressed their way through the trees.

As they walked, the path opened up into a proper road which crossed another going east-west, and there, at the junction, stood the source of the light—a tall streetlamp, which looked as if it had been plucked out of Oxford and dropped here in the countryside.

Underneath it, dressed in a battered topcoat, a man was standing as if he were waiting for a bus, or unwary passersby. Moving closer, John was startled to realize that he recognized him. Or at least, he thought he did.

Jack had the same flash of memory, and both looked back to note that Charles was right behind them.

At first glance, it looked as if Charles—*another* Charles—was standing at the crossroads, waiting for them. The man was tall and had Charles's bearing—but as they walked closer, it was apparent that he was a stranger to them. The three men and the girl nodded politely and began to move past, taking the path to the right and away from the lamp's comforting glow.

"Pardon me," the man said, raising a hand in greeting, "but do you have the time?"

"What?" said John. "Oh, uh, yes, of course," and he turned, pulling his watch from his vest pocket. It was a distinctive sort of watch: silver, untarnished, with a red Chinese dragon on the cover. "It's half past five," he said, snapping the watch closed, "or half past drenched, depending on your point of view."

"Mmm," the stranger mused. "Well put, John. But actually, I also need to know the year, if you don't mind."

At the mention of John's name, he and the others froze in

place. Had the man merely overheard them talking? Had one of them uttered John's name? Or was something more sinister afoot?

"Why do you need to know the year?" John asked cautiously, as Jack and Charles moved protectively closer to Rose.

"Because," replied the man stiffly, "I've come a long way, and I seem to have lost track."

"Lost track of the years?" Charles exclaimed. "If you don't even know what year it is, should you be out and about in the woods all alone?"

"Actually," the man replied, "I came here to protect you, Charles. The year, if you please?"

"It's 1936," said Jack. "April, if you couldn't tell."

The man surprised them by slumping against the waypost in obvious relief. "Thank God," he said, running a hand across his head. "1936. Then I've not arrived too late after all."

"What year did you think it was?" asked John. "And pardon my asking, but how is it that you know our names? Have we met, perchance?"

"You are the Caretakers of the *Imaginarium Geographica*, are you not?" the man replied. "Let's just say we are in service of the same causes. And I was fully expecting to arrive here in 1943."

"You were expecting to arrive in the future?" said Charles. "That's not really possible, is it? I mean, not unless the circumstances are extraordinary."

"You've been in such a circumstance, I believe," the man said. "And it wasn't the future I was aiming for, but the past. I just seem to have overshot my mark, to our benefit, I hope."

John and Jack exchanged worried glances. The man knew

enough to be dangerous to them—but he had so far done nothing more than talk while leaning against the post. And he did say he was there to help them.

"Forgive our hesitation," John said mildly, "but we've heard credible stories of every stripe and color from the best of them. How are we to know you are indeed on, ah, our side, so to speak?"

In answer, the man reached into his pocket and pulled out a silver pocket watch. On the back was the clear image of a red dragon. It was identical to the watch John had just pulled from his own pocket. "It was given to me by Jules Verne," the man said, "as, I suspect, he gave yours to you."

"Good enough," John said as he and the stranger compared timepieces. "I've only ever seen one other like it."

"That would probably be Hank Morgan's," said the man. "His is used a bit more frequently, I'm afraid."

"So are you also a time traveler?" asked John.

"Not so much a traveler in time, as in space," the man said, "although thanks to the watch, I have the ability to do so when the need is dire. My mentor has a different set of goals for me than he had for Hank."

"Verne," said Charles. "So he's the one who sent you?"

"Indeed," the man replied. He pulled at his collar and looked around. "We should find a place more suitable to talk, unless you have an objection."

"That was our plan anyway," Jack said, offering his hand. "Do you have some place in mind?"

"I do," said the stranger, shaking Jack's hand, then John's and Charles's in turn. To Rose he gave only a long, appraising glance.

"You know all of us," Charles said amicably, "but you've not yet introduced yourself."

"Ransom," the man said as he turned and began leading them down the path to the left. "My name is Alvin Ransom."

Chapter Two
The Inn of the Flying Dragon

"I'm a great admirer of all your works," Ransom said as they walked briskly along, "especially your latest, John. That book about the little fellows with the hairy feet, and wizards, and whatnot. I particularly liked the part where the giants turned into stone. Very moving."

"Actually, those were trolls," John said. "And . . ." He stopped walking. "Hang on there," he exclaimed. "How could you have read that? I haven't even finished that book yet—and I've barely touched it in years!"

Ransom slapped his forehead. "Apologies, my good fellow. I forgot it's not due to be published until next year. That's what I get for trying to curry favor with you by coming up with compliments."

"Oh," said John. "So, ah, you didn't really like it after all?"

"I haven't finished it," Ransom admitted. "But it is on my nightstand, and I fully intend to, as soon as I have the opportunity."

"What is your profession, Mr. Ransom, if I may ask?" said Charles.

The lamps were ... moving with the light of active flame.

"I'm a philologist," he answered evenly, "at the University of Cambridge."

"A philologist?" said John. "Really? A languages specialist? How odd that we haven't met before."

"Not particularly," said Ransom. "The Cambridge that I come from isn't the Cambridge you're familiar with."

"Different country?" asked Jack.

"Different dimension," replied Ransom.

"That sounds *exactly* like Cambridge," said Charles.

"Bert has alluded to the concept of different dimensions once or twice," John said, "but we never got into specifics. Charles is our resident expert in that particular field."

Charles beamed with pleasure at the compliment. "I've actually devoted quite a bit of attention to the topic," he said brightly, "even wrote a book about it."

"I know," Ransom replied, his voice suddenly somber with respect. "It's one of our most important theses on the subject of multidimensionality."

Charles blinked at him. "It was, ah, a work of fiction, actually."

Now it was Ransom's turn to be surprised. He started to make a comment, then paused, his expression softening. "I keep forgetting what year I've come to," he said mildly. "There are things I take for granted that you won't actually know about for a few years yet, God willing."

Jack and John exchanged a glance of concern. God willing? Just what was that supposed to mean? That they wouldn't discover the knowledge Ransom referred to too soon, or that they might not have the opportunity at all?

"You seem to know a great deal more about us than we know

about you," Jack said. "I don't know how comfortable I am with that discrepancy."

"That's one reason my Anabasis Machine—I mean, my pocket watch—was fashioned in the manner it was," said Ransom. "There are too many double agents afoot in the lands, and too many allegiances built on the sand. It's difficult to know whom to trust—and so Verne made certain to give those of us who are loyal to the Caretakers' trust an unmistakable symbol."

"A silver pocket watch," John asserted, "with a depiction of Samaranth on the casing."

Ransom nodded. "Exactly."

"Couldn't that be easily duplicated, though?" Charles opined. "I mean, it's a very nice watch, but there are a hundred watchmakers in London who could make a replica in a day."

Ransom almost stumbled as he spun about to frown at Charles. "Haven't you realized by now just how deep a game Verne, and Bert, and the others are playing?" he said with some astonishment. "When the Dyson incident occurred, didn't you think it significant that Verne had already prepared for the eventuality by arranging the Lanterna Magica for you to find, fifteen centuries before it was needed?

"These are the people who *invented* the idea of a secret society," Ransom continued, "so of course there would be safeguards." He snapped open his watch. "The first is the engraved inscription."

Jack and Charles moved closer to peer at the watch cover, which bore two words: *Apprentice Caretaker*, and the Greek letter *omega*.

"Only the Caretakers themselves, their apprentices, and those like myself who have been recruited to the cause know that Bert chose that letter as the Caretaker's mark," said Ransom. "That's the first safeguard."

"And the second?" asked Jack.

Ransom glanced at him in surprise before grinning broadly and turning to resume walking down the path. "I'm surprised that you don't know, considering you are one of the actual Caretakers," he said with a trace of amused smugness, "but then again, the use of the watches and the safeguards didn't really become critical until nearly 1938."

He looked over his other shoulder at John and tipped his chin. "But *you* know, don't you?"

John glanced around to make certain they were alone, then rolled his eyes heavenward. Of course they were alone. They were lost in the English woods following someone from another dimension. If there were anyone lurking about to hear them, it would have to be a stroke of remarkable luck and accidental timing.

"Yes," he said quietly, arching an eyebrow at Ransom. "Bert told me just a few months ago. 'Believing is seeing.'"

"Believe," the philologist replied.

"That's it?" said Charles. "That's a bit simple for a secret code."

"Simplicity is best in cooking, personal combat, and secret codes," said Ransom. "And that statement and response are both more simple and infinitely more complex than you can possibly imagine."

"I can imagine a great deal," Charles huffed.

"Oh, I meant no offense," Ransom said quickly. "That was just a turn of phrase. Of the three of you—"

"Four of us," said John, nodding his head deferentially toward Rose, who smiled.

"Five," came a voice from somewhere above them in the gloom. "Couldn't count in Alexandria, can't count now. Some scholar you turned out to be."

"Sorry," Ransom said, peering up at the owl that circled overhead. "Uh, sorry," he repeated to Rose, with slightly less enthusiasm.

"As I was saying," he continued, "of all of you here, Charles is the one most likely to be able to comprehend what we're about to do. Because, strictly speaking, the place I'm taking you to isn't *in* our dimension."

Without explaining further, Ransom removed a small leather case from inside his coat. It was thick, and about as tall and broad as two decks of playing cards placed side by side. He untied the binding, and inside the companions could see a sheaf of thick, handmade paper with scrawled notes and sketches.

"These pages are for practice," Ransom said as he removed a dozen loose cards from the back of the case, "but these are the real cat's pajamas."

The cards were yellowed with age, and more akin to parchment than paper. Most of the sheets had intricate, nearly photographic drawings on them; only the last few were blank. All of them bore a remarkable pattern on the reverse side: an interweaving series of lines that formed an elaborate labyrinth, at the center of which was the symbol for eternity. Along the borders were symbols of a more familiar nature.

"Elizabethan?" asked John. "These appear to be some kind of . . . I don't know. Royal stationery?"

Ransom smirked. "That's a closer guess than you realize, John," he said, nodding. "Queen Elizabeth commissioned them, but hers was certainly not the hand that made them."

"John Dee," Charles intoned, drawing in a breath. "It had to have been Dee. We know he was an early Caretaker, but his books are missing from the official Histories, and Bert will not speak of him."

Ransom nodded again. "One of the dark secrets of the Caretakers," he said somberly. "Burton was not the only one of your order to betray his oaths of secrecy."

Before the companions could inquire further into what that meant, Ransom fanned the cards out in his hand. "As the Anabasis Machines—the pocket watches—can be used to travel in time, so can these cards be used to travel in space.

"We don't know enough about time travel to do more than journey to what Verne called 'zero points,'" the philologist continued. "We can make educated guesses, but anything outside the zero points is basically gambling without seeing our own hand of cards, so to speak."

"That's how you miss a target date by seven years," said Jack.

"Yes," said Ransom, "although seven isn't bad. If you have the chance, you should ask Hank Morgan about the time he tried jumping to 1905 and accidentally ended up becoming the sixteenth-century Indian emperor Akbar the Great."

"You mean *meeting* the emperor?" asked John.

"No," said Ransom. "*Becoming* the emperor. Like I said, it's a really good tale to dine out on."

"So I'm inferring from what you've said that these cards allow for a bit more precision?" asked Charles.

"Exactly. We actually call them 'Trumps' in honor of your book, Charles," said Ransom. "Dee made them as some kind of literal otherworldly tarot—at least, that's what Verne believes. Only a hundred of the original sheets were discovered intact, and we realized their usefulness when Verne found two with drawings on them."

"And what are they used for?" said Jack.

"Simply put, they are used to travel between places," Ransom replied. "Whatever place is drawn on a Trump can be traveled to."

"Without limitation?" asked Charles.

"As far as we know," said Ransom. "Distance is no barrier, and neither is the ether that separates dimensions. In fact, the only limitation we know of is the number of blank Trumps that can be drawn on. We don't know the process Dee used to make them, and so Verne parceled out the ones we did have with a stern instruction to use them sparingly. Of the dozen given to me, I made nine that I use most frequently, and have three that can be created in case of grave emergency."

"Nine, ah, portals isn't very many," said John. "It seems like a much bigger limitation than you imply."

"Not so," said Ransom. "Verne recruited several agents like myself, and we all have at least six Trumps that are completely unique. The other three are points of conjunction, where we may meet up and then travel together when necessary. They can also be used to communicate—although that risks detection, so we try to do so sparingly."

"Does Hank Morgan have a set?" asked John. "That would explain how he was able to send messages to Jules Verne when we were stuck in the past with Hugo."

"Well deduced, John," Ransom said with a smile of approval. "He does indeed, although we had not worked out all the mechanics of using them at that point."

"Wait a moment," said Jack, confused. "If Hank had these

Trumps with him in Camelot, why didn't he just use them to get us out of there as soon as he realized who we were?"

"Two reasons," said Ransom, with slightly less approval. "First, if he had been able to use them to take you out of Camelot, it would not have helped your situation. Trumps don't traverse time, only space. So you'd still have been in the sixth century—just somewhere less useful."

"I'm betting the second reason has to do with time travel," said Charles. "There was already enough damage done by them just being there, and events had to take the proper course to be repaired. Am I right?"

"Eminently so," Ransom replied. He selected one of the cards, then replaced the others in the book, which he put back in his coat. "Everyone, now, if you please—stand behind me and give your attention to the card."

Archimedes dropped down from one of the beech trees and landed lightly on Charles's shoulder. Rose, Jack, John, and Charles moved behind Ransom and stared at the card he held in front of them.

It depicted a cozy-looking, multigabled tavern set in a wood exactly like the one that surrounded the crossroads just ahead of them. At arm's length, the drawing was nearly photographic in nature, so real and precise that it almost seemed to . . .

"Oh!" Rose exclaimed, startled and delighted at once. "The flames in the lanterns! They're flickering!"

The lamps were indeed moving with the light of active flame. The smoke from the chimneys also moved, as did the leaves stirring in the gentle breeze that blew them across the tableau . . .

. . . and onto Ransom's outstretched arm.

The philologist smiled, then concentrated all his attention on the card, which began to grow bigger.

The patterns around the border began to glow with an ethereal light, and they pulsed with a rhythm very much like a heartbeat.

In moments it was the size of an atlas, and now hung suspended in the air of its own accord. It continued to expand, and within a matter of minutes it was a life-size looking glass that could be stepped through with ease. The only thing that was different about the wood in front of them was that five minutes earlier, there had been no tavern there—but otherwise, every tree and leaf was exactly the same.

Ransom stepped through the frame of the card and beckoned to the others. "Come along," he said with a wry grin. "I assure you, it's perfectly safe."

Charles and Archie went first, with no hesitation. Rose was next, followed by Jack, and finally John, who inhaled sharply, checked his bag for the bulk of the *Imaginarium Geographica* to make sure it was secure, and stepped through.

Once on the other side, the portal shrank rapidly, until it was once more just a drawing on an old sheet of parchment, which Ransom carefully replaced in the book in his coat.

The philologist then turned about and flung out his arm as if he were the host of a party. "My friends," he said brightly, "welcome to the Inn of the Flying Dragon."

"That's fantastic," said John. "I think I like those even better than the doors in the Keep of Time."

"It takes a certain knack to get the hang of them," said Ransom as he walked toward the inn. "We've got our eye on a young fellow named Roger to become my own apprentice. He shows great promise, I think."

Charles stroked Archimedes and frowned. "I'm sorry, old fellow," he said placatingly. "I know it's a bit dreary still, but we'll need you to stay out here."

Ransom stopped on the front steps of the inn and turned around. "Why is that? Bring him in. I'm sure they can accommodate him."

The companions exchanged confused looks. "I don't know how it is in your Cambridge," said John, "but where we come from, an oversized talking mechanical owl tends to attract a lot of the wrong kind of attention."

"Really?" Ransom said as he opened the door, a knowing smile spreading across his face. "Perhaps in Oxford that's true, but it isn't the case here. Please—come inside and see for yourselves."

Stepping through the door into the Inn of the Flying Dragon was, on first glance, very similar to stepping inside one of their usual gathering places like the Eagle & Child. There was a burly proprietor tending the bar, and scattered patrons seated at the tables, with a few in the back playing a game of cards. The room was well lit and not terribly smoky. There was a scent in the air of charred spices, possibly from a curry being burned in the kitchen. The kegs of ale were stacked high, and the taps flowed freely.

A mop boy scurried over to the companions and offered to show them to a table, taking special notice of the pretty girl in their company. "May I take your owl, sirs?" he offered, trying not to look as if he had noticed Rose. "There's a good spot in the stable behind, where he'll be well looked after."

Before any of them could reply, Archie opened his mouth. "I have very particular needs, boy. Are you prepared for a guest of my composition?"

John sighed. "He means he's not a typical owl," he explained as Rose and Charles both scowled at Archie. "He doesn't really require the normal sort of food and shelter."

"Well," the boy said, "if it helps, there was a wizard here last week who brought a phoenix with him, and they seemed pretty happy when they left."

"A wizard?" asked Jack. "Really?"

The boy nodded. "I forget his name—Bumble or Humble something-or-another. But I took excellent care of his phoenix."

"This bird is, uh, not exactly natural," said John.

"Ah," the boy said. "A clockwork. We've had unusual birds before, and we'll do our best to make him comfortable."

"If that's the case," said Archie, "I want a copy of Einstein's notes on relativity, and a stuffed gopher to chew on as I read."

The boy squinted an eye and pondered this. "I can get you the Einstein notes, but only in German, unless you'll be staying the night. And the only gophers we have are in the stew—but I can get you some mechanical mice instead."

Archimedes beamed and hopped over to the boy's outstretched arm. "Lead on, MacDuff."

"Actually, my name's Flannery."

"Whatever you say, MacDuff."

"Oh, for heaven's sake," said John.

* * *

They took seats around a table near the front corner, where they could watch the door and make use of it in a pinch. A stout, ginger-haired man in a floppy hat brought several mugs of ale over to the table.

"There are several such refuges throughout the world," Ransom explained, gesturing around at the inn. "A good term for them might be 'Soft Places,' meaning places where the boundaries are not as solid as elsewhere, and where one might cross between them, with the right knowledge and training."

"Is it luck or good planning that one of your Soft Places just happens to be a tavern?" asked John. "Not that I'm complaining in any way, mind you."

"Not luck," Ransom replied. "It's essentially the power of the crossroads made manifest. A crossroads is important for what it represents, and what it in fact *is*—a junction between paths. Establishments such as the Inn of the Flying Dragon are much the same—junctions between places."

"I've completely overlooked what may be the most appealing aspect of interdimensional travel," Charles said jovially. "Are there more taverns like this, then?"

"A few," said Ransom. "I've heard of one that's supposed to be at the End of the World, but I can't seem to locate it. All that's on Terminus is a bunch of rocks and a gravestone."

"Well, yes," Jack harrumphed. "Where else?"

"There's a nice place that was once called Harrigan's Green, which is difficult to get to, but worth the trip. You can tell stories to pay for your room and board, so essentially, it's merit-based. The best stories get the best room, and the best ale."

"I'll drink to that," said Charles, rising from his chair. "I'll get the next round, gentlemen. Same for all?"

They all nodded. "And you, Rose?" Charles asked.

"I'd really like a glass of milk, thank you," said Rose.

Ransom frowned for just an instant, then started to speak before John interrupted him.

"Pardon," John said, turning to Rose. "I think Charles might need some help with the drinks. Would you be so kind as to give him a hand, Rose?"

"Of course," the girl said cheerfully as she stood, pushing back her chair. "That will also give you and Uncle Jack the chance to ask Mr. Ransom why I make him so uncomfortable."

"She's a smart girl," said Jack as Rose walked over to join Charles at the bar.

"More than smart," said Ransom.

"So, since she brought it up," said John, "why does she make you jumpy, man? Surely you know who she is."

The philologist bit his lip and thought a moment before answering. "I know who she is," he said finally, "but *what* she is is a conundrum."

"Or an enigma," Jack chimed in. "Or both."

"What I mean," said Ransom, "is that she isn't supposed to be here at *all*. In practical terms, the girl doesn't exist."

"But clearly she does," said John.

"What's clear to you and me is not so clear to others," Ransom pointed out. "Did you notice that when we entered, the barman didn't bring anything for her, or even ask?"

"I just assumed that he wasn't accustomed to dealing with children," said John.

"No," said Ransom. "There are children in here all the time, especially during the day. He didn't see her. *Couldn't* see her."

Jack sat up straighter in his seat. "This isn't the first time that's happened," he said, gripping John's arm. "Remember? After we returned to England with Rose and Hugo? At the Bird and Baby?"

John frowned, then glanced over at the bar. "That's right—Burton couldn't see her either."

"But that boy, Flannery, could," said Jack. He eyed Ransom appraisingly. "But why would you say she isn't supposed to exist?"

"Because," Ransom replied, "in the original History, she actually *did* sacrifice herself to save Arthur. It *was* a life for a life. She was *supposed* to die."

"It wasn't necessary," John said, leaning over the table. "She was willing, but that was enough."

"You know that because you were there," said Ransom, "but it wasn't the way history recorded it. And when you chose to bring her here, you somehow removed her from history altogether."

"Then why would some people see her while others can't?" Jack asked. "It doesn't make any sense."

"I can't tell you that," Ransom replied. "But since you returned, everything has been in flux—that's part of the reason I came to find you."

"What's that?" said Charles as he and Rose returned with their drinks. "Hope we haven't missed anything good."

"Just chatting," John said as he took a mug from his friend. "Seems like a fine sort of pub, doesn't it?"

"Yes," Charles agreed, sitting. "But," he added in a hushed voice, "I think the barman has a tail. And I'm all but certain that he has donkey's ears tucked in around that ginger hair under his hat."

"Oh, Lampwick's a good enough fellow," said Ransom as he took a drink, "but I wouldn't mention the ears if I were you. He's a bit touchy about them."

"To your good health," John said, lifting his glass in a toast to his companions. "May all our travels end in such favorable places."

"Hear, hear," said Jack. "This is almost like the Tuesday night meetings with the fellows back at Oxford."

"Except for the fact that we're at an inn named for a dragon, which we can only get to through a drawing on a card," said Charles, "and we're being served drinks by a barman with a tail and donkey ears."

"Well, yes," said Jack. "Except for that."

CHAPTER THREE
Pursuit of the Un-Men

Once they had settled in with their drinks, John brought the conversation back to the point. "What's so significant about 1936?" he asked. "Since you were aiming for 1943, why would it matter what year you landed in, as long as it was prior to your target?"

"It's significant," came the reply, "because it's the first time the two of you"—he indicated John and Jack—"formally met *him*," he finished, pointing at Charles.

John bristled, and his eyes narrowed. That didn't sound valid. "If Verne did send you, then you both should have been aware that we've known Charles for many years now."

"Sure," said Ransom, "in *this* dimension. But not in others. In most of them, the two of you never met him until the spring of 1936. So there were things that could not be shared with you until the natural greater course of events had occurred. Even you three have realized this at some level," he continued, gesturing at the trio of men, "else you would not have gone to such pains to keep the relationship a secret for all this time."

"Bert said we must, not for temporal or dimensional reasons," said John, "but rather to protect the knowledge of the *Imaginarium Geographica* and the Archipel—"

Their legs were those of birds, and ended . . . with wicked-looking talons.

The quick, curt shake of Ransom's head told John to stop speaking. It was a secret that needed protecting, and even here, in a small, out-of-the way tavern, sitting with an agent of Jules Verne, it was too great a risk to say some things aloud.

"Timelines must be protected as much as possible," Ransom went on, "and even when changes are made, they must be done with an eye toward the ebb and flow of events that have already occurred—past, present, and future.

"You were brought together by the murder of Professor Sigurdsson, but you were already marked as potential Caretakers." Ransom's voice dropped to a whisper with the last word. "The, ah, problem was that you weren't actually supposed to meet for a number of years. You two"—he indicated John and Jack—"in or around 1926, and you"—he pointed at Charles—"in 1936. The Winter King changed all of that. So the fact that some things have been kept from you is no commentary on your worthiness, but rather an effort by Verne to keep the fidelity of this timeline as pure as possible."

"So the me who met them isn't the me who was originally, ah, me?" said Charles. "Does that mean we changed time, or switched dimensions? I'd hate to think there's another me running around somewhere."

"There already is," Rose said. "He's you, but not the same you. I did like him quite a bit, though."

"She's right," Jack declared, his face ashen with realization. "There *is* another Charles—or was, anyway."

John nodded. "Chaz. We took him back in history, where he became the first of the Green Knights. He was from *another* dimension, but he's still in our recorded Histories in *this* dimension. So there have been, in fact, two of you, Charles."

"But not at the same time," Charles retorted. "That's impossible—isn't it?" he asked, looking at Ransom.

The companions all paused as the barman approached. "Another round of drinks?" he asked.

"Yes please, Mr. Lampwick," said Ransom. "And don't forget the milk."

Lampwick went back to the bar, and the companions again huddled closely around the table.

"Hasn't Bert explained it to you?" Ransom began, leaning in to whisper. "Surely you have had occasion to meet with H. G. Wells at one time or another, and surely you realized they were not the same man."

"I had, years ago," said Charles, "and on occasion since."

"As have I," said Jack, "but Bert told us when we first became Care—uh, when we first met, that he was not the same person as our Wells. He told us that he was the time traveler from his book, and that he'd come from eight hundred thousand years in the future."

"I'd always figured that he was exaggerating, for effect," said John.

"He wasn't," said Ransom. "Didn't you ever think it strange that Wells never mentioned you, or your group, or the book?"

"I did," said Charles, "but I assumed it was for one of two reasons: Either he was being discreet, because we were always in some public place and were not able to address those topics; or he was not yet privy to, ah, our secret society. Our Bert is quite a lot older than Wells, you know."

"So you think that his being recruited by Verne hasn't happened yet?" asked Jack.

Charles shrugged and took a long draw from his ale. "Anything is possible with time travel."

"It doesn't fit," said John. "He told us he wrote the books after having the real experiences, which he then fictionalized. So he had to have been recruited at a much younger age, as were we."

Charles and Jack looked crestfallen. "I hadn't thought of that," Jack admitted.

"So what does that mean about *our* Bert?" asked Charles. "Is he or isn't he H. G. Wells?"

"That's the point I was bringing you to," said Ransom. "He's exactly what he said—he *is* H. G. Wells, he's just not the one you know of."

"My head is spinning," said Jack.

"Think of dimensional travel as a sort of 'Othertime,'" Ransom said as Charles jumped up to bring the new tray of drinks to the table. "Not going into the past, or future, or even the present, really—just a different present."

"Or past or future as well, based on what you said," Charles remarked. "You overshot by seven years, if you thought you were going to end up in 1943."

"I was expecting to end up there, but ending up here is an accidental blessing," said Ransom. "It means I have the opportunity to help you avert a terrible event.

"In the future, it is known as the Second World War," the philologist continued, his face grave. "And unless we change events here and now, it may mean the literal end of the world for us all."

"We've been to war, before," said John, respecting the somber tone of Ransom's voice, "both here and in the Archipelago."

"Not like this," Ransom retorted. "The weapons that will be

brought to bear are effective on a continental scale. Cities will be destroyed with single explosive devices smaller than this room. Nations will crack; civilizations will be routed. And millions will die, or be forever enslaved."

"And we're to help you stop all that?" said Charles. "No pressure on us, eh, old fellow?"

"I told you that part of the reason why 1936 is so significant is because it's the first time the three of you came together, publicly, as friends."

"Yes," John said. "What's the other part?"

Ransom shifted about uncomfortably in his seat and stalled for time by sipping his ale. But he could not completely disguise the quick glances over at Rose.

"*She* is the other part of the reason," he said finally. "Her being here doesn't register as a zero point with Verne, but we think that's only because she wasn't meant to be here in this place and time at all. She is the key to everything that happens over the next seven years, which is why I was trying to reach you in 1943—so that we could try to discover alternatives."

"Alternatives to what?" said Jack.

"Alternatives to whom," replied Ransom. "She . . . is not available to us then, but there is no one else we could consult who could replace her."

"Why isn't she 'available'?"

"Sometime in the next few months," Ransom said grimly, "Rose Dyson, the Grail Child, will be murdered. And we have discovered no alternate timeline, or dimension, or world in which that does not take place."

"You might have done that a bit more diplomatically," said

Jack, scowling at the philologist and scooting protectively closer to Rose. "She's just a child, after all."

"I don't mind," Rose said, smiling reassuringly at Ransom. "Mr. Ransom was just getting straight to the point. And besides," she added, "in realistic terms, I'm actually older than all of you."

"Maybe," said John. "But I think Jack's point is that you lack the life experience to deal with many of the things an adult might encounter. That's why it's been important for you to be in school."

"And that's why you're taking me to Oxford as well, isn't it?" Rose countered. "So that I can continue to learn from you, and Uncle John, and Uncle Warnie?"

Ransom groaned. "So you've already moved her to the Kilns, then?"

"We hadn't decided," John replied. "Does that matter?"

"That's where it happens in the Histories," said Ransom, gesturing at Charles with his mug. "The ones you've yet to write."

"Is it risking anything, temporally speaking, for you to be revealing elements of the future to us?" Charles asked. "Not to be the damper of the group, especially since this is a topic of special interest to me, but I really don't want to wake up tomorrow finding everything's gone haywire."

"Verne and Bert are very cautious about what we're allowed to disclose," said Ransom, "but bear in mind, from my point of view, I'm not telling you secrets of the future—I'm relating events that have already happened in the past."

"So you expect nothing else to change?" asked Jack. "We will continue as we are, and still do what we've done, even if we know what you say will happen?"

"Yes. Nothing substantial will change."

"Except for our preventing the death of Rose, which you say would cause this 'Second World War.'"

Ransom nodded. "Except for that—which is being allowed for two reasons. Rose is an anomaly, and so her being here does not materially affect your primary timeline. But she does affect events in the Archipelago, which has a ripple effect here, and while it doesn't start the war, it makes it far worse than it might have been."

"Is there anything you can tell us about our future—um, your 'past'—that isn't dire and terrible?" Charles asked with a gloomy expression.

"You are all on the cusp of realizing great success in your careers," Ransom noted.

"Oh, thank God," said Charles. "After all those books, I was beginning to wonder if the things I've been writing about would *ever* catch on."

Ransom squirmed. "Ah, well, yours not so much, I'm afraid," he admitted. "But your association with your friends will keep your status high just the same."

"I'm sure it shall be quite the reverse," Jack said to Charles reassuringly. "Our friendship with you will be our passport to fame."

"Yes, yes," said Charles glumly. "Do you know how many stories I've published? How many poems? And still, I'm best known for works I conceived in part because of my relationship with you fellows, and the adventures we've had. And I'm a little tentative about some of those, seeing as they're little but fictionalized versions of the Histories I've been keeping."

"As have all your predecessors before you, Charles," Ransom said placatingly. "It was their way of processing the myriad experiences they had, and writing the Histories alone was a gargantuan task, assigned only to those most worthy. That you have the skill to fictionalize some of those chronicles is an achievement without peer."

"I appreciate the compliments," said Charles. He wasn't sure if the philologist was pulling his leg for decorum's sake, or if the flattery was sincere. But he wasn't going to argue. "It's just that being well known and respected for one's work has less, ah, emotional resonance when the only ones who do know and respect the work are essentially bound to keep their opinion a secret."

"It's to your advantage, though, Charles," Jack observed. "You're going to be known, in our world, for an increasingly progressive body of work, rather than for the one great book you feel has eluded you. Isn't that what every writer truly wants?"

"It would be a ghastly thing indeed," John chimed in, "to be known for only one or two significant works. That would drain the soul and temper the vinegar of any worthy writer. Don't you agree, Ransom?"

Ransom swallowed hard and waved for the barman. "I think we should get more ales before I answer that," he said, a pensive look on his face. "Several more ales."

He turned in his chair and scanned the great room of the inn, but there was no sign of Lampwick, or of the boy, Flannery—or, for that matter, anyone else.

The card players had gone, as had the three or four scattered patrons who had occupied other tables. The companions were alone in the inn.

"It's only just past seven," John said, checking his watch. "Shouldn't this place be hopping with patrons?"

Ransom pursed his lips and slowly stood up. "It should. There are always travelers seeking a moment's respite, and there is always someone tending to their drinks. Something is seriously amiss here."

Suddenly Flannery's bright face appeared at the edge of the bar, where he gestured to the companions to remain where they were. A finger to his lips told them that silence was also necessary.

"You're being watched," he whispered as he crept toward their table. "Do not let them know that you know. I was told to destroy your owl, but I hid him in my storeroom instead."

The companions sat motionless, save for Rose, who finished her mug of milk. "How do you know this?" she said quietly as she wiped the foam from her lips. "Who are you to us?"

Smart girl, John thought. *Find out if someone is on your side before you place yourself in their hands.*

"I am a friend," Flannery replied. "I'm to help you, if I can."

Charles lifted his drink to his lips to cover his words. "If you're a friend," he whispered, "then you should have a sign that proves who you're working with."

"Oh!" the boy exclaimed, before dropping back to a whisper. "I forgot! I'm supposed to give you a kiss."

Charles choked on his ale. "Pardon me?"

"A kiss," Flannery repeated as he fumbled around in his pocket. "The Valkyrie said if I gave you a kiss, you'd know I could be trusted." He held out his hand and showed them a small silver thimble.

"The kiss," Flannery repeated quietly. "From one of the novice Valkyries of Paralon—Laura Glue."

Instantly the companions' demeanor changed. "He's with us," John said to Ransom.

"What would you have us do, Flannery?" Jack whispered.

"They're outside," he replied. "They're waiting for their leader to come before they take you."

"Who is waiting, Flannery?" Jack pressed. "They who?"

"Men. Un-Men. I—I can't really say," the boy replied. "But I don't like them. They in't natural."

Ransom sat bolt upright. "Not natural? What do they look like?"

The boy scratched his head. "Big bird heads, but on thin bodies of men. And they're dressed like they're in a Shakespeare play."

Grimacing, Ransom slowly rose from his seat. "Yoricks. This will be difficult, I fear."

"Bar the door," Flannery whispered. "It will hold them back a few moments."

Together John and Ransom rose and made as if to approach the bar—then, in a single fluid motion, both men leaped to the door and threw down the large crossbeam. An instant later something slammed against it with a heavy *whump*. The creature outside the door let out a terrible shriek and threw itself against the door again and again. The crossbrace held—but only just.

"No time to waste!" cried Flannery, jumping to his feet. "Quickly! Follow me!"

Protectively shepherding Rose ahead of them, Charles and Jack dashed to the bar, followed by John and Ransom. Flannery led them around an open door to a short corridor lined with doorways. He bypassed nearly all of them, then opened the last one on the right. It showed a dark, candlelit stairway to the cellar.

"Hang on," Jack said cautiously. "If we go down there, we'll be trapped."

Flannery shook his head. "There's a secret passage hidden under a barrel of ginger beer. It leads to my secret storeroom. Even Lampwick doesn't know how to find it."

If the companions were still hesitant to follow the boy, a crashing and splintering sound from the front of the inn convinced them otherwise. The stomping of boots and an otherworldly shrieking from the creatures Ransom called Yoricks was all the motivation they needed.

They all moved down the steps, and Jack and Charles bolted the door, then moved several large crates in front of it to buy more time from their pursuers.

Flannery grabbed a lamp from one of the walls and indicated a barrel among a dozen as the one that concealed his hiding place.

"Lots of travelers come through and need something hid," he explained as Charles and Ransom moved the barrel aside. "I have a place that's secure, and I make a bit of coin on the side. Lampwick doesn't care, because it keeps the customers happy."

"And they trust you to keep the items safe?" asked Charles.

The boy nodded emphatically. "The kind of people who need things secreted away in one of the Soft Places in't the kind of people you want to betray."

"I understand completely," said Charles. "Lead the way, Flannery."

The last of the companions clambered down into the tunnel just as the Yoricks began banging on the door above.

"Won't they find this place eventually too?" asked John. "The room above isn't that large, and the entrance isn't that well concealed."

"I couldn't give a fig if they find this tunnel," Flannery said as he led them down an earthen passage. "Once they get here, they could spend a year looking and never know where we went."

The passage opened into a massive underground cavern that was literally riddled with passageways. It was a honeycomb reimagined for men, and it was a daunting thought to even consider entering one of the holes.

"Did you build this, Flannery?" asked Charles. "Most impressive."

The boy shrugged. "I had help. It's a lot like the place I used to live, so it don't scare me none, neh?"

Jack looked at him more closely. "I don't think we've ever met, but you sound like some other children I know."

Flannery nodded and flashed a brilliant smile, which was missing a tooth on the bottom. "It's nowhere near as big as Asterius's labyrinth back on Centrum Terrae, but it suits me fine," he said as he moved quickly to an opening near the left side of the cavern. "Follow me, but remember—keep turning left."

The passages were dimly lit by glowing moss embedded in the walls and a smattering of luminescent mushrooms, but Flannery was not moving so quickly that any of them ever lost sight of the flame.

Abruptly the tunnel ended, with a sharp upturn and a ladder. Flannery climbed it and threw back the trapdoor at the top.

"It's about time you came back, MacDuff," Archimedes squawked, hopping up and down on a crude wooden table. "These aren't Einstein's papers at all, just a bunch of Newtonian scribbles. And as to those mechanical mice you promised . . ."

"No time, Archie," Charles said as he and the others climbed out of the tunnel and up into the small storeroom. "There's a chase afoot."

The storeroom, which was lit warmly by several candles, was cramped and low-ceilinged. It was carved out of the space underneath a massive oak tree, as evidenced by the roots framing the walls. There were boxes and other parcels scattered around the space, obviously items left in Flannery's care. Higher up, in the trunk itself, were several windows disguised as knotholes. He scrambled up to one and peered outside.

"No one's about," he called down. "They must all be inside tearing the inn apart."

Flannery looked again. "No, wait. I see something." He motioned for the others to move to knotholes lower down. "Have a look, if you wish to see who your enemies are."

The companions clustered around the small openings and peered out into the dusky night air. The moon had come up, and it cast a wan glow over the woods. If they had not known otherwise, they would have been hard-pressed to believe that this place was not just another wood near Oxford.

A clamor from the direction of the inn drew their attention, and off to the right, they saw the glow of firelight, followed by the shadowed forms of their pursuers.

As Ransom had described, the Yoricks were both bird and man. They were seven feet tall, and their heads were the oversized skulls of birds. They had no eyes, only sockets that glowed red, and no feathers. They were garbed in Elizabethan-era clothing, including capes, and had long, skeletal arms that ended in poorly fitting gloves.

Their legs were those of birds, and ended in four-toed avian feet with wicked-looking talons. When they were not shrieking, they communicated with one another in a series of clucks and whistles.

There were nearly two dozen of them—which meant that they were prepared to overwhelm the companions by sheer numbers alone.

Curiously, they seemed to be under the command of a man, who was shorter than they, but obviously in charge. He spoke to them in a brusque tone that was too low to hear, but he was not pleased. Lampwick was also among them, although he seemed more apologetic than anything else. He said something to the man, who responded by striking him brutally across the face. The innkeeper turned and went back the way he'd come.

At the man's direction, half of the Yoricks returned to the inn, and the rest followed him into the wood, on a path that took them startlingly close to Flannery's tree.

All the companions save for Jack dropped away from the knotholes and covered the candles. Jack watched until their pursuers had passed, then joined the others, his face gone gray with fear and, oddly, shock.

"It's all right," Flannery reassured him. "The outside of my den is well concealed. They won't find us easily, and certainly not quickly."

"I don't think that's what's startled him," John said, guiding Jack to a chair. "He's seen and experienced quite a lot, so this has to be something else."

"I'm all right," said Jack. "I'm just trying to rationalize what I saw."

Charles nodded. "I was a bit surprised myself," he said. "Seven-foot-tall birds are not high on my list of expected enemies."

Jack shook his head. "That's not it. We've seen and fought worse than these fellows. But that man who was with them . . ." His voice trailed off, and he rubbed his forehead.

"You recognized him?" Ransom asked. "I couldn't at all. I've never seen the Yoricks under a human's direction before."

"I did recognize him," answered Jack. "I may be mistaken, but I would swear on my life that it was Rudyard Kipling I saw leading the charge."

CHAPTER FOUR
The Pieces of Time

"*Kipling?*" Ransom exclaimed. "That's a fine how-do-you-do. He was Bert's primary rival for the open Caretaker position after Verne took over. It's bad form for such a talented man if he's gone over to the other side."

"I never saw anything of him in the Histories, or in the *Geographica*," said John. "Bert certainly never mentioned him."

"He wouldn't have," Ransom pointed out. "After the Houdini-Doyle incident, when they nearly exposed the Archipelago to the whole world, Verne has kept any information about non-Caretakers or former Caretakers very close to the vest."

"That's just a bloody shame," said Charles. "I wouldn't ever consider putting Kipling and Magwich in the same class."

"You'll have to," Jack said, still a bit shaken. "I have no doubt that he's working with our enemies—probably Burton."

"What makes you say that?" asked John.

"You already know yourselves," Jack replied. "Didn't you see it in the papers? Rudyard Kipling *died* three months ago!"

"That would explain why we didn't recognize him at first," John reasoned, running his hand over his hair. "That man was perhaps forty at most. Kipling was seventy."

. . . they saw the miniature image of an old friend.

"That locks it," said Charles, banging a fist against the table. "Richard Burton's behind this. No one else would know how to manipulate things so as to recruit dead poets to their cause."

"I'm afraid you're right," Ransom said. "His presence here cannot be accidental."

"But yours was," said John pointedly. "If you hadn't met us on the road, then we wouldn't have ended up here, where our enemies now have us hiding under a tree. How do you explain that?"

"I can't," Ransom answered, turning to Flannery. "How did *you* know someone would be looking for them?"

Flannery shrugged. "I din't know nothing," he said. "Lampwick told me to get rid of the bird, so I hid him here. And on the way back up into the Flying Dragon, I saw those Un-Men gathering outside. That's when I knew there'd be trouble."

Jack tilted his head, appraising the boy. "But how is it you were here, today, when we needed an ally?"

"I've been here for two years," Flannery replied. "There are Lost Boys posted at all the Soft Places—the ones we know of, anyways—just in case. We all report t' the Valkyries."

"Well, God bless Laura Glue," said Jack, rising. "What do we do now, Ransom? Do we go back to Oxford?"

The philologist shook his head. "If they're here, they'll be there, too. Don't worry," he added, seeing Jack's look of concern. "They won't hurt your brother, or Mrs. Moore. They're only after Rose."

He removed the book with the Trumps from his coat and fanned out the cards in his hand. "I think it's time to consult someone with a bigger hammer," he said.

"Bigger hammer?" Charles asked.

"When you're stuck with a problem, sometimes the best

solution is to hit it with a bigger hammer. I expect he's going to try to contact Verne," said John.

John was close. Ransom held up a card that seemed to depict an ancient Egyptian village, but instead of Jules Verne, they saw the miniature image of an old friend.

"Hank Morgan!" Jack exclaimed. "What a pleasure it is to see you again!"

Hank's face broke into a wide grin, and he waved. "John, Jack. And young Rose, also, I see! And . . ." He paused. "Ah, Chaz?"

"Charles," the third Caretaker replied. "We've not had the pleasure, but I've heard many good stories about you."

Hank raised a questioning eyebrow, then turned his attention back to Ransom. "I wish we had more time to reminisce, Alvin," he said, "but there are too many events cascading together, and it's all we can do to keep track of them."

"We're at the Inn of the Flying Dragon," Ransom reported, "but we've had a bit of a complication develop. Can we come through?"

"You can't," said Hank, shaking his head for emphasis. "Not here, nor any of the Soft Places. I was here in Midian looking to acquire some manuscripts left by Saint Paul of Tarsus, and almost as soon as I arrived, I had to ask the Midians for protection. I've checked the other Trumps—every key Crossroads location is swarming with Un-Men."

"Yoricks?"

Hank nodded. "Those, and worse. Any place you bring Rose will be equally dangerous. I think they're looking for *you*."

"But how?" Ransom exclaimed. "I wasn't even supposed to end up here! It isn't even a zero point. I was aiming for—"

"For 1943, we know," Hank finished for him. "The best we can determine is that your arrival there, near Oxford in 1936, is what *made* it a zero point. And that changed the sequence of events, as well as their relative importance. Where *we* knew without doubt how crucial Rose was to the Wars of the Worlds, our enemies could only suspect."

"Until now," said Ransom, groaning in realization. "Until I confirmed it for them."

"It isn't your fault," Hank told him. "None of us could know. At least," he added with a conspiratorial look, "none of us who could share the information."

John looked askance at Jack and Charles. Was that comment in reference to Verne and his penchant for secrecy? They were the Caretakers of the *Imaginarium Geographica*, and although Verne knew everything they did, they had never so much as glimpsed the so-called Prime Caretaker.

"Have you told them yet?" Hank was asking. "About the Prophecy?"

Ransom swore under his breath and glanced sideways at the Caretakers. "I have not, but I was getting to it. I thought we had . . . well, more time."

"We don't," Hank stated. "Best get them to the Gatherum as quickly as possible."

"The Gatherum?" Ransom repeated. "But that's only possible in—"

"I know, believe me, I know," said Hank. He stepped out of frame for a moment, and the companions could hear muffled shouts and a large crash.

"I'm sorry," he said, moving back into view. "I need to go—I think the locals are about to set fire to the place."

"Anything I can do?" asked Ransom.

"I'll be fine," Hank replied. "Just whatever you do, don't take Rose to any of the Crossroads. Elsewhere she may be safe—but not here. Once you've seen to her security, get the Caretakers to the Nameless Isles, with no delay. Everything may depend on it. Fare thee well, friends."

And with that, the surface of the card blurred and went dark.

"That doesn't sound very promising," said Charles.

"Where do we take her, Ransom?" Jack said as he peered out one of the knotholes. "If the Crossroads places are off-limits, and Oxford will be watched, can we take her back to Reading? Or London?"

"I'm concerned that anywhere we go, we'll be tracked," Ransom answered. "I don't think there's anywhere in this world where she *will* be safe."

Jack snapped his fingers. "Then how about a place that's out of this world?" he said excitedly. "Do you have any Trumps that lead to the Archipelago?"

"I have just one," Ransom replied. "I've been there a few times in the recent past—*my* recent past—but it might be the only option we have left." He shuffled the cards and removed one, turning it around for the companions to see.

On the card was a drawing, precise down to the details of the stonework, intertwined staircases, and windows, of the interior of a place the companions all knew very well.

"The Keep of Time," said John with visible relief. "That will be as good a place as any, and better than most."

"Maybe, and maybe not," Ransom said with obvious

discomfort. "Coming to the Inn of the Flying Dragon is one thing, because I've been here before, and often. But I haven't been to the Keep of Time—not yet, anyway."

"What do you mean?" John demanded. "You just said you've been there several times."

"Yes, I have," Ransom replied, "but all *after* 1936. I made this card in 1943 the first time I was there, which was when I expected to meet you, anyway. I never expected that I'd end up using any of the other cards to transport you away from England to anywhere other than the Flying Dragon."

"Are you implying that if we use this Trump to escape these . . . these Un-Men," said Jack, "we'll risk going into our own future?"

"Yes," Ransom said, looking anxiously through the uppermost knothole. "That's exactly what I'm worried will happen."

"I think we've already got a solution in hand, as it were," John said, reaching into his pocket. "I have one of the watches too, remember? Once we've escaped these Yorick creatures, we can simply use it to return to our own time—as in, *this* time."

Ransom slumped in despair. "I keep forgetting—your watch isn't activated as an Anabasis Machine until 1937."

"But I'm actually a Caretaker," said John with a trace of indignation, "the Caretaker Principia, in fact, not an apprentice. Why wouldn't mine have the same properties as yours?"

"You are indeed a Caretaker," Ransom replied, "but of the *Imaginarium Geographica*, not of . . . well, it's not for me to say. To you, the watches represent badges of honor and a secret way to identify others of our creed—but long before that, they were being used by those of us chosen by Verne to help protect time itself. It was only later that he realized they could serve a dual purpose."

"Wouldn't it have been easier to make all of them time-traveling devices to begin with?" said Jack.

"Maybe on the surface," said Ransom. "It's only been recently that the scope of the Caretakers' responsibilities seems to have expanded to time as well as space, so the watches you'd been given were inert. That appears to have been a miscalculation—but then again, if they'd *all* been fully functional, that would mean your friend Hugo Dyson would also have one. Do you really want *him* meddling in time?"

"Good point," said John. He suddenly snapped his fingers. "Can we use yours, then? If you can tell me how it works quickly enough, that is."

Ransom shook his head. "If I could, I'd gladly hand it over. But it would be more dangerous for you if I did. I've been trained in its use for years by Jules Verne himself, and I still can't manage it with any degree of accuracy. If you were to miscalculate . . ."

Jack groaned. "Never mind—I think we'll take our chances with the Keep of Time. Otherwise, we might end up in the Winterland again, or worse."

"One of you might," said Ransom. "At present, the Anabasis Machine is still a single-user device."

Jack slapped his forehead. "That's right, that's right. I'd forgotten. There's also the problem of arriving naked wherever we'd go too."

Ransom snorted, then chuckled. "Hank probably told you that, didn't he? We actually worked out the mechanics of that particular problem a few years back—Verne and Mark Twain just made a special adjustment to Hank's device as a joke."

"You let him hopscotch through time naked as a *joke?*" John said, incredulous.

The philologist shrugged and chuckled again. "When you are trying to keep order in the entirety of creation, you have to take the opportunities for a moment's levity when you can."

"It *is* pretty funny," said Charles.

"Gentlemen," Flannery said, a tense pitch in his voice, "you'd best make a decision quickly. I think I may have overestimated the usefulness of our hiding place."

He gestured with his thumb for the others to look outside, and they did. About thirty yards away, Kipling and the Yoricks were standing in a clearing—and they were all looking toward Flannery's tree.

"That's it," said Jack. "Ransom, we need to use that Trump. Now. Whatever you feel the risk will be, we'll just have to sort it out when we get there."

The philologist removed the Trump of the Keep from the other cards, then paused. "Remember what I said about the rules that cannot be broken? The rules regarding time and space?"

"Uh-oh," said John. "That sounds like a very bad preamble."

Ransom scowled at him. "All I'm saying is that we don't know everything. Not yet, anyway. And there *are* rules that can't be broken—but we're discovering new rules all the time."

"What are you telling us, Ransom?" Jack asked.

"Instinct counts. Intuition counts. Not everything can be broken down into formulas. There are no equations that can prove that I am in a place where I cannot possibly be. But if I am in that place, then it must be possible—and I think some things can become possible if you just believe that they are."

"'Believing is seeing,'" said Charles.

"Yes," Ransom agreed, handing him the card. "So believe." He turned to Flannery. "I'm betting you have a secret back door to this place, don't you?"

"Three, in fact," the boy replied, pointing at a low door behind the table. "I'll show you where."

"Aren't you going with us?" John asked Ransom, surprised. "You were trying to get to 1943 anyway!"

"My first directive from Verne was to simplify, simplify, simplify," said Ransom, shaking hands with the three men. "The Trumps aren't meant for time travel. I need to find out what's happening here first. I'll try to join you later—and besides, it may not happen the way we think. Hopefully, you'll just end up safely at the Keep."

"I am so filled with confidence at the moment," said Charles. "What do you plan to do, then?"

"I'll lead them away. Don't worry—I've dealt with their kind before. I'll be fine. Just use the Trump as I showed you, and get the girl to safety. And as soon as you are able, you must go to the Nameless Isles."

A terrible screeching filled the air outside—apparently their pursuers had decided to surround the tree. "No more time to explain!" Ransom urged. "We must go!"

"I don't want to seem ungrateful . . . ," John began.

"But I got you into this mess to begin with?" said Ransom. "It's all right—I understand completely. If all goes to plan, we'll be meeting again soon, and I'll try to make it up to you."

"And just how much of your plan has worked out so far?" asked Charles.

"Forget I said anything," Ransom suggested, wincing. "Good luck to you all."

"Thank you, Ransom," said Jack, gripping the other's hand once more. "If we can ever repay the favor . . ."

The philologist winked. "Oh, you will," he said with a chuckle as he ducked into the small doorway Flannery was holding open. "You and I are destined to become great friends, Jack. In one dimension or another, anyway. And Jack," he called back over his shoulder, "call me Alvin."

And with that, he clambered into the tunnel and vanished.

Trying to ignore the clamor of the Yoricks outside, Charles held up the Trump and focused his considerable attention on it. And, as before, it started to expand—but this time, as it grew, the image of the Keep of Time began to lighten and fade.

"Uh-oh," said Jack. "It looks like one of the burned-out slides from the Lanterna Magica."

John agreed. The frame of the Trump was filling the small storeroom now, and the image was almost completely white. "We may be better off trying to negotiate with Kipling," he said just as something massively strong struck the side of the tree. "Or not."

"I'll go first," Charles offered, and he stepped through. Jack and Rose were next, followed by John.

"Archie?" said John. "Are you coming?"

"Coming where?" the owl retorted. "There's nothing *there*."

Another *whump* hit the tree. Archimedes hopped off the table and through the portal. The bird sighed. "Oh, very well.

It's obvious you're afraid to go anywhere without my guidance."

The sounds of the Yoricks faded as the portal began to shrink, and in moments it had closed completely. The Trump still bore the illustration of the Keep, but that was not where the companions were.

It was an endless expanse of whiteness. There was no distance, no perspective. Just infinite space. Except for the old man.

"Hello," he said, his voice flat. "Can I help you with something?"

He was slender rather than thin, but hunched with age. He was dressed in a white tunic and cloak, which were embroidered with infinity symbols. His cold eyes were expressionless, and he looked at the companions with all the interest of an architect examining a grain of sand.

Before any of them could speak, Jack grabbed John's elbow and nodded at what the old man held in his hand.

It was a pocket watch. A silver pocket watch.

"You aren't supposed to be here," the old man said dismissively. "You aren't members of the Quorum. You can't be here."

"Begging your pardon," said Charles, "but we didn't plan to be. We had every intention of being elsewhere."

"Then do so, and go," he answered with a wave of his hand. "I have work to do."

"We would if we could," John put in, "but we don't know where—or when—we are."

The old man didn't reply, but merely regarded them with disdain—until his eyes fell on Rose.

To the companions' great surprise, his mouth dropped open in shock and his eyes, cold a moment before, suddenly filled with tears.

"Rose," he said, his voice barely a whisper. "How can you be . . . ?"

Barely taking his eyes off her, he opened the pocket watch, which bore no dragon on the cover, and was festooned with several more dials and buttons than John's own watch.

The old man's forehead wrinkled in confusion. "Most unusual," he murmured to himself. "A new zero point, and here, in Platonia! This must be brought before the Quorum."

He snapped it shut and looked at Rose. His expression had completely changed—he was watching her with a rapt intensity that bespoke familiarity. Somehow, he knew her.

John looked at the girl. Her face was placid. She was observing, and nothing more. She didn't know—couldn't know—who the man was in this strange, infinite space.

"We're trying to reach a place called the Keep of Time," Rose said. "Can you help us?"

"The keep?" he replied in surprise. "Interesting." He consulted his watch again and adjusted a dial. Then he looked up and actually smiled.

"By what means did you come here?" he asked.

Charles showed him the Trump. "Ah," said the old man. "Primitive, but useful in its own way." He moved closer and regarded the companions more carefully, taking furtive, emotion-laden glances at Rose.

"So you're the three," he said rhetorically. "The Prophecy had something to it, after all, did it?"

"We don't know anything about a prophecy," Charles said. "We just need to get Rose somewhere she'll be safe."

"And so you shall," said the old man, abruptly wheeling away.

He stood some distance off, with his back to them. "Use your card once more," he said at length. "It will take you where and when you are meant to be."

Charles did as instructed and held up the Trump, which was already beginning to expand—but this time there was no fading of the image. In moments the frame displayed a perfect, rich picture of the interior stairwell of the Keep.

"Thank you," John called out to the old man as the companions moved through.

He responded with little more than a shrug, and didn't turn around until the frame began to shrink. Tears streaked his cheeks, and he was clutching the watch with hands that trembled.

"I am . . . glad to have seen you, all of you," he said in a shaky voice. "And Rose," he added, "try to think well of me in the future— and in the past."

And with that, the infinite whiteness vanished as the Trump closed, and the companions found themselves standing within the Keep of Time.

PART TWO

Abandoned Houses

"All set. . . . What is our destination?"

CHAPTER FIVE
The Spanish Prisoner

It was not in the Magician's nature to wait for anything, so it was boredom, rather than the arduous journey or noxious atmosphere, that finally caused him to lose his temper. Fortunately, his companion, whom he had drolly dubbed "The Detective," was accustomed to such outbursts and took them in stride.

"This was not what I signed up for," the Magician grumbled. "I was the toast of Europe. America was at my feet. I had the run of the finest hotels, and the best restaurants valued my opinion of their fare more than they did the critics'. But mostly, I was enjoying myself. And I gave all that up for what? To sit here, in a leaky boat, ticking off the seconds that pass as the stench eats away at my topcoat. I've had it, I tell you."

His companion nodded in understanding. "I don't want to be here any more than you do, Ehrich. But we can't exactly let our attention flag—not at this juncture. You know as well as I do how crucial it is that we are here doing what we're doing."

"I told you, *Ignatius*, don't call me Ehrich," the Magician shot back before settling down, as his look of indignation was slowly replaced by one of resignation. "I know we agreed to do this, and I still believe in our cause. It just feels as if our talents are being wasted. You and I represent the finest in our fields—and yet we have committed ourselves to the role of errand boys."

"Errand boys in the service of a greater calling," the Detective pointed out. "After all, Columbus discovered the Americas, but someone still had to row him ashore."

"Do you remember his name?" the Magician retorted. "Does anyone? I want my own place in the history books, thank you very much. I don't want to change the world by proxy."

"You do have your own place in the history books," said the Detective. "That accomplishment cannot be erased, merely added to."

"It would have been easier to add to before I died," the Magician grumbled. "At least then I was visible on the world's stage."

"You still are," said his companion. "It's just a different world."

The Magician was about to say something in reply, when both men were suddenly silenced by a deep rumbling sound emanating from the sky.

They shaded their eyes from the sunlight and peered upward to a floating structure so distant it appeared to be a dark smudge against the sky. Suddenly several small objects appeared and grew swiftly larger as they fell.

"Row!" shouted the Magician, grabbing an oar. "They're dropping straight for us!"

The two men hastily moved the boat several feet south just as the first stones and part of an archway struck the water where they'd been sitting. A few moments later another object, larger this time, hit the water with a violent splash.

"That's it!" said the Detective, reaching out with a pole that ended in a hook. "I've got it—grab your end, will you?"

"I have it," said the Magician, pulling the object into the small boat, which sank several inches into the water with the added weight. "When do you think it is? Are we up to Victorian yet?"

"I have no idea," said the Detective. "He doesn't let us go through them anymore, remember?"

"That's not my fault, Arthur," said the Magician, using a less provocative name. "I'm sure we'll be allowed to use them again sooner or later."

"I could care less, Harry," Arthur said as he took up an oar and began to row. "As far as I'm concerned, the only value in opening doors to the past is what they can do for our future—whatever world we end up in."

The Magician did not reply, but merely took up rowing with the other oar, and in moments the two men, the leaky rowboat, and a door into time had vanished into the fog.

"What was *that* all about?" John asked Rose. "Who was that man?"

"I have no idea," Rose answered. "But he certainly seemed to know me. And he did help us."

"I'd've thought to try the card again eventually," Charles huffed. "It was only a matter of time before it occurred to one of us."

"Of course, Uncle Charles," said Rose. "He just helped move the process along."

"Well," Charles said, blushing.

"The Trump couldn't have been better placed," said Jack, pointing down. "Have a look, fellows."

There was, in point of fact, almost no floor at all. They had stepped onto one of the landings where the stairways crisscrossed, but just a few steps below there was only open sky. A few yards below, the jagged bottom edge of the tower's stones hung over clouds higher than a mountain, and the stairways' supports had been twisted into chaotic shapes from the weight of the falling stones.

"Another level lower, and we'd have been treading air," said Jack. "We ought to tell Ransom he needs to redraw his card from a higher vantage point."

"I'm not sure he can," John said, pointing in the opposite direction. As one, the Caretakers gasped. They could see the ceiling. That meant there were perhaps forty or so doors left in the tower before the ongoing entropy reached the room where the Cartographer was. And after that . . .

"I say," Charles mused, looking downward. "Is that a boat down there, below us? It's too far to make out properly."

Jack wrapped his arm around a twisted piece of railing and looked to where Charles was pointing. "I think it is," he said, puzzled. "What would a boat that small be doing in the Chamenos Liber?"

Before any of them could venture an answer, the tower began to rumble and shake. A thunderous noise filled the air, and before their eyes the stones in the walls began to separate.

"It's coming apart!" John yelled, scrambling for the landing. "Up the steps, quickly!"

Together the three men raced up the stairs, pushing Rose ahead of them for safety. If one of them fell, as their friend Aven once had, there was no *Indigo Dragon* to catch them before they hit the surface of the water below.

An entire section of stones and steps fell away just before the frame of the lowest door also peeled off and dropped, as, finally, did the door. Abruptly the tower stopped trembling, and the four companions could once again catch their breath.

"That was close," John breathed.

"Too close," Jack agreed.

"I can't see the door," said Charles, peering over the edge of the steps. "Or the boat. I hope it didn't sink the poor devils."

"They probably just left," Jack offered. "It's a terrible place to be fishing, anyway. It stinks of sulfur, and stones are always unexpectedly dropping out of the sky."

"Yes, but anyone in the vicinity would already know that," said John. "Who would come here to fish?"

"Trolls," said Charles. "Or Cambridge scholars."

"Never mind," said Jack, trying to hide a smile at his friend's joke. "Everyone all right? Rose? Archie?"

"I'm fine," Rose replied, looking at the owl. "This is the most fun I've had in ages."

"They're not very bright," Archimedes commented to her, "but they do have a way of keeping things stirred up. Good for the vim and vigor."

"If we could find a way to stir things up less," said Jack, "we'd be very happy men, eh, John? I say, John—are you listening?"

The Caretaker Principia slowly shook his head.

"What's the matter?" Charles asked.

"That door," John said, pointing across the landing. "It's *open*."

"So it is," said Jack. "The last tremor probably shook it loose."

"I've never seen that happen before," John observed. "Remember, the doors are anchored on the reverse by the time they open to. I don't think they *can* be jarred open."

"Should we close it?" asked Charles.

"I'm wondering if we shouldn't have a look," John replied. "So much of what's happening has to do with the Time Storms caused by the collapse of the keep—and Burton is obviously playing at a game we haven't seen yet. I say we have a look."

"We should discuss this," said Jack.

"I agree," said Charles.

"You scholars are worse than three Scots with a match," said Archimedes, "if you have to have a referendum and debate over something as elementary as whether to open or close a door."

Rose did not voice an opinion, but simply walked across the landing and pulled the door open.

"Oh Lord," said Charles. "It's done, fellows. Let's have a look— if it's some prehistoric beastie, we can close it quick."

"Agreed," John said, turning to Rose. "Just don't step over the—"

Rose stepped over the threshold and through the door.

It took a few moments for the frail-seeming, bearded old man to realize that the light falling across the goosedown quilts of his bed was not from the window.

The oil lamps in the room provided enough light for him to read and write. But mostly, he slept. The perpetual twilight kept him in a constant state of drowsiness, and besides, he was tired. Tired to the bone. He'd had a lifetime of adventuring, and this, such as it was, was his reward.

He might have been happier on some island in the outer reaches of the Archipelago, but he would not have lived nearly as long. Here, in this room, Time itself had stopped—or so he'd been told.

And so he waited.

Waited to discover if the so-called Prophecy might indeed come true. Waited, because if it were true, then he would once again be needed. And as often as he had done great deeds and had remarkable adventures, it was all only for the reason that someone had needed him. This, and the love of a beautiful woman, were all the motivation he needed. And so he waited, because the Frenchman had promised that someday he would be needed again.

In his half-drowsy state, he barely noted the new streamers of light in the room, and only then when a shadowy form approached his bed and leaned in closely to speak to him.

"Is it you?" he asked, eyes blinking with tears. "Is it my Dulcinea?"

"My name is Rose Dyson," the girl said as the old man rubbed the sleep goblins from his eyes and propped himself up onto his elbows, "but Dulcinea is a beautiful name, especially with your accent."

"Ah," the old man demurred, "it is in the nature of old Spaniards to speak the name of their one true love as if she were the only woman on earth."

"And how should I call you?" asked Rose.

The old man sat up straighter in his bed and adjusted his nightshirt, then preened his mustache and beard before answering.

"My name, dear girl," he said with gravity and panache, "is Don Quixote de la Mancha. And I have been waiting for you for a very long time."

The three Caretakers and the owl entered the room, but only John paused to examine the door. Any other door in the keep could be opened with a touch, save for the Cartographer's door, which had been sealed by the mark of the king: the Greek letter *alpha*.

Next to the handle on this door was a small Greek letter *pi*—the mark of the Caretaker Principia. John's mark—which he had never made.

John filed the observation away in the back of his head to be addressed later. For now, he wanted to discover the identity of the strange man who was conversing so easily with young Rose.

The man who had introduced himself to Rose as Don Quixote was now making similar introductions to Jack and Charles. Archimedes was ignoring them altogether and had instead focused on the books to one side of the great bed.

The room was almost identical in size to the one farther up where the Cartographer resided. But rather than a clutter-filled workplace, this room had been appointed for comfort. The elaborate four-poster bed was covered in goosedown quilts and draped with finely embroidered heavy silk curtains. There was a tall window with lead-lined panes of milky glass, and several beautiful oil lamps. The books were scattered about, as were the habiliments of a knight: a lance, a sword and scabbard, and authentic—if tarnished—sixteenth-century Spanish armor.

If this is not the real Don Quixote, John thought, *he has certainly made the effort to play the part.*

The old man rose from the bed and straightened his nightshirt. He was impossibly thin and wore a thick beard that pointed in two directions. His hair was more gray than black, and more white than gray.

"If the lady will shield her eyes," Quixote said diplomatically, "I should like to dress."

Rose obediently stood in the corner, looking over Archimedes' shoulder as Charles and Jack helped the old knight dress. His clothing and armor were humble but fit him well. Once he was dressed, he again sat on the bed, and Rose sat beside him.

"You said you were waiting for us," she asked. "Why?"

"Because of the Prophecy, of course," Quixote replied. "You do know about the Prophecy, do you not?"

"We've heard rumors," said Jack, "but we've been a little too pressed for time to ask anyone about specifics."

"Well then, I shall tell you," Quixote declared. "After all, it is your Prophecy."

"Ours?" said John. "How do you know?"

"Because," replied Quixote, "you are the only ones, other than the Frenchman, who have come through that door in nearly four centuries. He said that I would meet three Caretakers, and it would be my honor to aid them in their quest."

The Frenchman. Obviously Verne, thought John, whose interest was suddenly piqued. "You called us Caretakers," he said. "Do you know about the *Imaginarium Geographica?*"

"Know of it?" said Quixote in surprise and mock chagrin. "Why, in all modesty, if it had not been for me, there would be no *Imaginarium Geographica* to take care of. It is one of the greatest, most important books in history—but even great books may, on occasion, be lost. And when that happens, it falls to heroes such as myself to find them again."

"It's hard to imagine a Caretaker losing the *Geographica,*" said Jack, winking at John. "The height of irresponsibility, if you ask me."

"Accidents happen," John said, reddening. "People do misplace things, you know."

"Exactly so," said Quixote. "That's one of the reasons there are three of you, did you know?

"The book known as the *Imaginarium Geographica* has passed through a number of Caretakers," he went on. "Dante, and Chaucer; Giovanni Boccaccio; Petrarch. But sometime in the sixteenth century—my century," he added with a bit of wistful pride, "a Caretaker managed to *lose* the *Geographica*—and at the precise time when a terrible conflict was brewing in the Archipelago."

"What kind of conflict?" asked Jack.

"Let me ask you this," replied Quixote. "Have you ever read about a tyrant who called himself the Winter King?"

"Once or twice," John deadpanned. "So to speak."

"At that time, there were rumors of his arrival in the Archipelago," said Quixote. "The first concern was that the *Geographica* be kept safe, and there seemed no safer place than within the halls of Paralon itself. So it had always been kept in the Archipelago. But somehow the book was stolen, and the worlds were plunged into a shadow of fear. No one knew where it had gone, nor what use the thief would put it to. All that was known was that it had been taken across the Frontier, into the real world.

"The Caretaker, Miguel de Cervantes, was summoned to a meeting of the Parliament in Paralon, where all the races of the Archipelago had come together to debate the matter. His guide and messenger, a tall, thin Spaniard, agreed to venture out into the real world to search for the *Geographica*."

"You," said Charles. "That was you."

"Just so," the knight said, bowing his head in acknowledgment. "In my search, I encountered a scholarly detective named Edmund Spenser, who helped me to discover that the *Geographica* was not lost, but had indeed been stolen. The thief was Tycho Brahe, who was a scholar of Ptolemaic geography and had heard of a marvelous book that contained maps said to be created by Ptolemy himself."

"That's mostly true," Archie piped up from the corner, "although he did have some help—and some of his students actually did all the *real* work."

"While Spenser and I pursued the *Geographica*, Cervantes had an adventure of his own, wherein he met an ethereal creature called the Lady of the Lake. He gave her a kiss, and she gave him a bracelet in return and also the secret of passage between the worlds.

"On Cervantes's return to England, he was reunited with myself, Spenser, and Brahe, whom I'd brought to London. I had found the *Geographica* once more, and it was determined that there must always be three Caretakers, to avoid such a catastrophe ever happening again."

"We know about that," John said, opening the book and turning to the endpapers. Below the names of those who had come before, Cervantes, Brahe, and Spenser had signed their names in the front of the Geographica with the same quill and the same ink.

The old knight nodded and beamed at the sight of the book. "I witnessed the signing myself," he said proudly. "It was one of the great moments in a life full of such moments."

"Why didn't you sign?" Charles asked. "You had every right to become a Caretaker, and more than enough reason to justify it."

Quixote shook his head. "I am a messenger at worst, and a knight with noble ambitions at best. I am inquisitive, but it was not my destiny. Also, I asked, but was not chosen."

"Chosen by whom?" wondered Jack.

"By the Prime Caretaker," Quixote replied. "He said that at that time, those three must needs be the Caretakers—that I had had my role to play, and perhaps would again.

"As to the three who were chosen, the *Geographica*, together with the bracelet given to Cervantes, was passed from one to the other, the better to keep it secret and safe. When one of the three died, another would have been in preparation to take his place. And as Geoffrey of Monmouth did before them, the Caretakers, often writers as much as geographers or scholars, shared a fictitious version of their adventures with the world. I know that Miguel did as much with regards to my stories, if not with his own adventures.

"Spenser went on to write *The Faerie Queen*, and that feckless thief, Brahe, passed on the *Geographica* to Johannes Kepler."

"Few men of science have been chosen to become Caretakers," said John, "but it makes sense that Brahe passed it to Kepler. Scientist to scientist, as it were."

"In those bygone days," said Quixote, "science was about explaining things, and thus was as much an art as anything else. But in later years science became about *proving* things—when all that was ever really required of science *or* art was to simply believe."

"Spenser and a later Caretaker—Wordsworth, I believe—both wrote of Arthur's sons, Artigel and Eligure," said Charles. "It's one of the better volumes in the Histories."

"You mentioned a Prophecy," Jack interjected, "and you said it relates to us. How is that? What is the Prophecy?"

Quixote sighed heavily and began again. "As you know, the *Imaginarium Geographica* was passed on year to year to new

Caretakers. It was in the care of one of the most recent of their number, a Frenchman called Jules Verne, in the first years of the twentieth century, when mysteriously, the bracelet of the Lady of the Lake was stolen. For a brief time, the *Geographica* itself was also lost.

"Soon after, stories of a dark, evil presence that lingered on the edges of the Archipelago, not quite living, yet not dead, began to reappear. An evil waiting for its opportunity to seize power. An evil referred to in veiled whispers only as 'the Winter King.' For years the stories had persisted, almost fading away into myth and fable, but now the stories began anew. And this time, the whispers went, the Winter King was not waiting and watching—he was at work. He was building a ship called the *Black Dragon*, which he intended to use to cross the Frontier and conquer all of the Archipelago of Dreams.

"It was only then that the Frenchman, Verne, realized that the Winter King was no new villain, but an old threat, who had before plunged the worlds into war. And he recalled a Prophecy, made centuries earlier, that should such an evil once again appear, he would be defeated only by three scholars from your world. And from that day forward, Verne devoted all his time and resources to finding and preparing the three for the battle that was to come."

"What?" declared Jack. "Do you mean us? We're the three?"

"We *were* the Caretakers when the Winter King was defeated," said John, "so it's possible."

"But we *already* defeated him," Jack exclaimed, "so what does that mean?"

The Caretakers looked to one another in resignation. They all knew it could mean only one of two things: Either the Prophecy

Quixote spoke of was wrong, and they hadn't needed him to defeat the Winter King at all; or he was right, and a final conflict with their greatest enemy was still to come. The old man in the white place had also referred to a prophecy—and that was too unlikely to be a simple coincidence.

"We must take him with us," Jack suddenly said. "Don Quixote, come with us, please."

At first John was surprised by the urgent tone in Jack's voice, but a moment later he realized what his friend's motive was.

The Keep was still crumbling. And the next tremor would destroy Quixote's room.

The knight needed no further prompting. He, Rose, and Archimedes gathered a few items in a small knapsack, while the Caretakers conversed near the door, which Jack had propped open.

"His story does make sense," Jack whispered. "Cervantes *was* a Caretaker, after all. And we all know Caretakers have fictionalized real events and peoples from the Archipelago in their stories. We've done it ourselves!"

"I can't recall the generalities of his story, much less the specifics," said John. "Did we overlook it, Charles?"

"That's just it," Charles protested. "It's not that I might have overlooked his story in one of the Histories—it isn't in the Histories *at all*. I've been very thorough, especially after the Dyson incident—and I'm telling you, the story he's related to us is nowhere to be found."

"And what was that about Jules Verne losing the *Geographica*?" said John. "I can't believe that. He's always too many moves ahead of any adversary. I can't believe he'd ever countenance such a blow."

"Then again," said Jack, "we were once young and stupid—or at least, younger and stupider than we are now. We learned to become the men we are in part because of the mistakes we made. Couldn't the same be possible for Verne?"

"We've overlooked something else," said Charles. "Hank Morgan also mentioned a Prophecy. So it isn't just Quixote. Something larger is afoot, I'm sure of it. But do we believe him or not?"

"Either way," said Jack, "I don't think we have a choice—we have to take him with us, or he'll perish with the next tremor."

The three companions silently agreed. On that point, there was not—could not—be a debate. Every other door in the keep, save for the Cartographer's, opened into an entire world at a particular point in the past—and when the doors fell, the passageway was simply severed. But this room was actually part of the keep—and to stay within it would be too great a risk.

"All set," Quixote said, having also loaded himself down with a considerable array of weaponry. "What is our destination?"

"Up," said John, pointing. "We go up."

The company, which now numbered six, stepped from the room and closed the door. John felt the small click of a lock under his fingertips, and the *pi* symbol seemed to glow faintly as the door closed.

"What has happened to the tower?" Quixote asked as he looked worriedly over the railing at the damaged keep and the nausea-inducing drop. "It is eternal, is it not?"

"Everything ends," said Jack. "Eventually."

The old knight shook his head sadly. "I fear you are right. But still, it is a fearsome sight."

"Look up, old fellow," said Charles. "That's my answer. Always look up."

Quixote nodded, then took a position behind Jack as together, the companions and their new acquaintance began to climb.

As the group ascended the stairway, the Caretakers explained to the knight whom it was they were going to see.

"I have heard stories of this man, if a man he truly is," said Quixote, "but I have never seen him with my own eyes. Only in stories, and from the things the Frenchman says, do I know him at all."

"He's a difficult man to understand," John said, "but then again, he's also two millennia old. We've all spent time with him in our calling as Caretakers, but we also had the chance to know him at various points in his youth. I regret to say that if we had been more perceptive, or simply better examples and less fearful, he might have become a better man than he is."

"You knew him in his youth?" said Quixote. "Two millennia ago?"

"It was under unusual circumstances," said John.

"Those were indeed unusual circumstances," said Quixote, "if you could manage such a journey through time."

"It was an accident," Jack put in, "involving a scholar and two badgers."

"That would probably be enough," said Quixote. He looked down at Rose. "And you, young Rose? Do you also know this Cartographer of Lost Places?"

Rose smiled. "I've only met him once," she replied, "but in a way I'm closer to him than the Caretakers are. I'm his niece."

"His niece?" Quixote said in surprise, wondering at her obvious youth. "If that is so, then either you have also slept for many years in a tower, so that the days pass you by, untouched—or you have a remarkable parentage."

"You have no idea," said Charles.

It took very little time, relative to their previous visits, for the companions to reach the top of the stairway and the second to last door. John and Jack took furtive glances at the last door a bit higher in the keep—the door that opened onto the future.

Rose had already guessed her role in this visit. The door was locked, to be opened only by one of the descendants of Arthur— but as had been proven once before, being Arthur's cousin was authority enough. Rose reached out and opened the door.

It swung into the room on silent hinges, revealing what could only be described as organized clutter. Maps and globes and parchment and books filled the space, making it seem smaller than Quixote's room some forty doors below. In the center of the cartological maelstrom sat a familiar figure, who was busy at work.

"Oh, drat," the Cartographer said without looking up from his desk. "Is it already the end of the world again?"

. . . on the edge of the uppermost shelf was a small glass bottle . . .

Chapter Six
The Last Map

Rose entered the room first, followed by Archie, the three Caretakers, and Quixote, who was still trying to take stock of what was going on—as well as when and where, for that matter.

"Hello, Uncle," Rose said. "You're looking well."

"What?" the Cartographer said, tilting his head and peering over the top of his glasses. His expression softened when he saw the girl. "Looking well for my age, you mean," he went on, putting down his quill and standing to better appraise his visitors. "It feels like a thousand years since I last saw you, child."

"Nearly that, Uncle," said Rose as she moved forward and embraced the old man. After a moment's hesitation, he returned the hug and even kissed the top of her head.

"What do you mean, the end of the world?" John asked, closing the door. "Which world are you talking about?"

The Cartographer sighed. "Your first question is ripe with stupidity, but your second redeems you," he said with a snort. "To make maps, or assist with annotations, or sign autographs for a badger requires only one or two of you to come see me, but for"—he paused and counted heads—"five of you, plus my niece, to come means some kind of disaster is imminent, and at the rate this tower has been crumbling, my guess is that the world is ending."

"So when the tower is destroyed, the world will end?" asked Charles.

"My world will, at any rate," said the Cartographer, "so I don't really make a distinction."

"I've apologized before," Charles offered, "but repairing the keep really is something that's beyond my abilities—or anyone else's, for that matter."

The old mapmaker waved his hands dismissively. "I wasn't chiding you, boy," he said with a huff. "We've all known what the inevitable end would be. But still, it would have been nice if you'd dropped in more often to chat. Brought me some cookies, a comic book or two. A better television would have been nice. You can imagine what the reception is like here in the Archipelago."

"We've come as frequently as we've been needed," John started to protest, "and more often in recent years."

"More often?" said the Cartographer. "You haven't been back at all in at least seven years, if not more."

John glanced around at his companions with a dark expression. Ransom had been correct: Going through a card created in their future had *transported* them to that future. They were in 1943.

"Don't be so sour about it," the Cartographer said, noting the expressions on the Caretakers' faces. "I'm only having a go at you."

"It's not that," John began. "When Ransom sent us here, he—"

"Ransom sent you?" the Cartographer said in surprise. "Alvin Ransom? I thought he'd gotten himself lost in the Southern Isles along with Arthur Pym."

"Ah, that would be me," Quixote said, raising his hand. "And I was not lost—not precisely, in any regard."

"He sent us here through this," Charles said, holding up the Trump. "It worked a bit differently than we'd expected it to, but it did work."

"That's very interesting," the Cartographer said, in a way that indicated he was not used to being interested. He folded his hands behind him and paced across the braided carpet. "Ransom . . . he's Verne's apprentice now, is he not? A very quick study in many ways. In point of fact, he was here very recently, making that selfsame card. But he does have his drawbacks, you know." He stopped and looked at Jack. "Cambridge man, you see."

Jack started. "Why point that out to me?"

"You'll find out in around a decade or so, if there's still a Cambridge by then," the Cartographer replied with a wink. "Just don't let the badgers know."

"What do you know about him?" asked John. "We've only spent a few hours with him, and we only went along because he had one of the pocket watches."

"Ah, he did, did he?" said the Cartographer. "That was one of my ideas, I'll have you know. Something we used to do in the old days of the Mystery Schools, although I'm not really given to joining secret societies—not ones that would have me as a member, at any rate."

He held out his hands and waggled his eyebrows, but got only puzzled looks in return. "Does no one in Oxford watch the Marx Brothers? Never mind," he said with a wave. "Ransom. Bright lad. Unusually adept with spatial perceptions, as you've no doubt noticed. I had him training with me here for a few months before he was seduced by the Frenchman. Not sure if it's a loss or a gain, overall."

"What were you training him for?" asked John. "To be a Caretaker?"

"To be a Cartographer, actually," came the reply. "You don't think I want this job forever, do you?"

"I wasn't aware that you could resign," Charles said mildly.

The Cartographer grinned wryly. "Resign, no, but retire, probably, and whether I like it or not, thanks to you," he said, wagging a finger at Charles, who blushed. "Or hadn't you noticed? I don't have a retirement plan in place, but it would be nice to have a successor.

"I don't hold out much hope for that happening, though," he continued, with a heavy exhalation of breath. "I understand that something's been stirred up back in the Summer Country, and that's causing chaos here in the Archipelago. No one really bothers to keep me updated on things unless they need something from me—but if it's as bad as the wind seems to indicate, I won't be useful to them for much longer anyway. All I do is make maps, and with that," he finished, pointing to the *Geographica* sticking out of John's pack, "you have all the maps anyone needs in this world."

"I think that's part of why we're here," said John. "We have to get Rose to a place that isn't in the *Geographica*."

The Cartographer made a sputtering noise, and his eyes bugged out. "If it isn't in the *Imaginarium Geographica*, boy, then it wasn't worth noting, or no longer exists. And there are even maps of places in the latter category still in it, so—"

Jack interrupted him. "Ransom told us we needed to make our way to someplace called the Nameless Isles. Do you know anything about them?"

"The Nameless Isles!" the old man exclaimed, eyes blazing

with anger. In an unusual show of physicality, he actually stepped forward and grabbed Jack by the lapels. "Are you certain that's what he called them? The Nameless Isles? Tell me, boy! Tell me now!"

All three Caretakers were taken aback at this sudden flaring of emotion. They had seen the man known as the Cartographer at many periods throughout his life—but during his tenure in the Keep of Time, they'd never seen him express anything more than annoyance.

"That's precisely what he called them," said Jack. "We don't mean to upset you, Myrddyn."

At the mention of his true name, the old man was startled out of his anger. He let go of Jack, and with a few deep breaths, he composed himself once more.

"I apologize," he said haltingly. "It's become somewhat of a joke, this 'end of the world' business, especially with the tower crumbling more each day. But the Nameless Isles were something to be hidden away, not named, not discussed, not shown, until and unless the actual end of the world was imminent.

"Far to the north of the Archipelago of Dreams, past the domains of the Troll King, past the islands of the Christmas Saint, lies a circlet of islands that have never been named. No map has been drawn to locate them—well, none that could be duplicated, that is. And certainly none that could be included in the *Imaginarium Geographica.*"

"Why couldn't they?" John asked.

"Because the islands themselves are alive," came the response, "or at least as close to living creatures as large masses of stone are likely to get. They have a form of consciousness, and they have will. They are constantly on the move, so they can never be found in the same way twice. A map on paper or parchment would be useless."

John grimaced. "How can we find them if they're always moving?"

Archimedes let out a snort and sidled over to the Cartographer. "He really doesn't listen well, does he?"

"It's been a constant problem," the Cartographer admitted. "I told you the maps could not be included in the *Imaginarium Geographica*," he said to John, "not that the islands couldn't be mapped at all.

"Finding the route to a living island that is constantly moving," the Cartographer went on, "requires a living map that may constantly change—and so every map I have ever drawn for the Nameless Isles has been drawn on the seekers themselves."

"You're going to draw the maps on *us*?" Jack exclaimed.

"Not all of you," the Cartographer said in exasperation. "I do have other deadlines to meet, you know, and drawing one on each of you would take all day and then some. No, just one of you will do. So," he finished, rubbing his hands together, "whose strong back shall we transform into a map?"

John's face took on a dour expression, and Jack stammered a moment, trying to decide what to say. In his younger days, he would have been the first to volunteer, but age and seasoning had made him much less rash. Still, one of them was going to have to do it if they were to make any progress at all.

Quixote suddenly stepped forward and removed his helmet as he dropped to one knee. "If I may serve yet again in this humble way," he said in his high baritone, "then I shall offer myself as the canvas for your quill."

The Cartographer looked startled for a moment, then made a clucking sound with his tongue and helped the knight to his feet.

"Your self-sacrificing gesture is appreciated, and your honor and nobility are without question," the old mapmaker said, "but to be most frank, while your spirit is willing, your flesh is wrinkled. I could do it, no question, but it would be akin to projecting a movie reel onto a shar-pei."

"Uncle Merlin," Rose began as the others comforted the crestfallen Quixote, "I would be willing—"

"Absolutely not," he replied, holding his hands up defiantly. "For all I know you've already got a tattoo or three, and I'm not going to be accused of adding to your delinquency. Also, you're still quite small, and an island is likely to slide off your back altogether.

"No," he said with finality, "If it's to be any of you, it must be one of the Caretakers three."

"We could draw straws," Jack began, when Charles let out a loud noise of exasperation.

"Oh, for heaven's sake," he said as he began pulling off his shirt. "I'll do it, but when my wife starts asking prickly questions, I'm deferring to you fellows."

The Cartographer instructed Charles to lean himself over the drafting table to allow as even a working surface as possible. It was set low to the floor, so Charles's legs dangled at an awkward angle until his companions propped them up with pillows.

"Uncle Charles," Rose said, hiding a giggle, "you look like a bear rug, stretched out to dry."

"More like a bare rug," said John. "The press doesn't let you out to get much sun, does it, old fellow?"

"Do you want to trade places?" Charles shot back.

"Looking good," John said quickly. "Carry on."

The Cartographer rummaged around in the overladen shelves in the back corner of the room, muttering to himself, until he finally emerged with a long, gleaming black quill and a stoppered bottle of ink.

"The quill is made from the tail feather of one of Odin's ravens," he explained as he took his seat behind Charles. "Hugin . . . or maybe it was Munin. I forget. It doesn't matter, anyway. What makes this process work is the ink."

He set the quill aside and gently removed the stopper from the bottle, which appeared to be half-full. The cloudy liquid inside swirled about lazily in the glass and seemed to emanate a faint glow and a familiar scent.

"Apple cider?" John said, sniffing. "The ink you use is apple cider? Will that even work?"

"An unusual map requires an unusual medium," the old mapmaker replied. "It only smells like cider because of its extreme age."

"Did it come from one of the apples on Haven?" Jack asked. "Those trees were quite old, I believe."

"Oh, it's far, far older than that," said the Cartographer as he dipped the quill point into the bottle. "If it didn't come from one of the oldest trees that ever was, it certainly was in their forest. You who subscribe to these newfangled modern religions have a name for it: the Tree of Knowledge of Good and Evil."

Charles nearly bolted upright. "Do you mean the juice you're using to draw with may have come from an apple off the same tree Adam and Eve took an apple from in the Garden of Eden?"

"Same *tree?*" the Cartographer said indignantly. "Pish-tosh. It's from the same *apple*. They only took two bites from it, after all.

"Now," he said, adjusting his glasses. "Hold still—I want to get this right the first time."

Slowly, with deft and deliberate strokes, the ancient man once called Myrddyn, then Meridian, and then Merlin, before at last becoming known only by his trade, began drawing the map that would guide the companions to the Nameless Isles.

He began at the lower left, just under Charles's rib cage, with a vast island large enough to have continental aspirations. Then, pausing only to dip the quill, he quickly worked his way upward, adding smaller islands in a variety of shapes and putting in navigational notations as he sketched. Another sizeable island was situated between the shoulder blades, followed by two half-moon isles that were obviously volcanic in nature.

As he drew, the lines of the cloudy apple ink left only a shiny, moist indication that quill had touched skin; but as he sketched his way down the right side of Charles's back, a curious transformation began to happen on the left.

The lines wavered, faded, then solidified into a rich, reddish-brown color, much like the lines in the older maps of the *Geographica*.

As the map was being created before the companions, all of them were transfixed by the mapmaker's work—except for Rose. While the others watched the line work magically appearing, she remained focused on the maker.

They had only ever met once before, in this very room, but she had known who he was instantly.

She knew because her mother and grandfather had told her stories about him and about her father, who was called Madoc before he took the name Mordred, and through the stories she came to know them. She knew everything about them, including— or perhaps especially—the flaws that had made them who they became. And she learned something else: that when you know everything about a person, it becomes very difficult to hate them, and very easy to love them.

And so there, in that small stone room near the top of a floating tower made of time, six personages watched the old mapmaker create his work on his living canvas. Two, the clockwork owl and the ancient knight, watched with a sense of duty for what was to come. Three, the Caretakers, watched with awe, reverence, and a small inkling of fear for what the map portended. But only one, the Grail Child Rose, watched with love—because she was the only one there who was more concerned with seeing the mapmaker himself than with obtaining what he might provide to them.

The Cartographer halted to consider his work, then again leaned close and completed the circlet of islands that ringed Charles's back. "Now," he said softly, "for the final three."

He dipped the quill one last time, then stoppered the bottle. "Waste not, et cetera," he breathed to no one in particular. Swiftly he drew one final island in the center and added several notations above and below.

The old man leaned back and closed one eye, examining, appraising. Then, with a nod that indicated he was satisfied, he stood up and replaced the quill and bottle where he'd found them.

"One of my better works, all told," he said, wiping his hands on a cloth. "You're quite a good canvas, young Charles. Patient, not fidgety, very few moles to work around. If I'd had a hundred of you I could have done the entire *Geographica* on the backs of scholars and done away with the parchment altogether. We could have kept you in a village somewhere, growing fat and happy on tea and cakes. Then, whenever a captain needed to go somewhere, we'd just call out your particular island and send you off with him."

"An interesting idea," John said as Charles groaned and straightened up. "But what happens when you lose one of the, uh, maps?"

"Interesting doesn't always equal practical," came the reply, "but being practical is always less interesting."

"How do you feel, Charles?" Jack asked as he helped his friend slip his shirt back on. "Does it itch?"

"It's not really too bad," said Charles as he tucked his shirt into his trousers. "It does tingle a bit, but not unpleasantly so. A little like having some friendly ants roaming around searching for a picnic."

"Better you than me," said John. "When you get back to London, you'll just have to remember to sleep on your back to avoid explaining it to your wife."

"No worries there," said the Cartographer. "The map isn't visible in the Summer Country—only here, in the Archipelago."

"Well, if I'd known *that*," Jack huffed, "I'd have volunteered myself."

"Mmm-hmm," Charles hummed skeptically. "I'm sure you would have, Jack."

"Thank you, for . . . for everything," said John, offering his hand to the Cartographer, who paused, then took it at the wrist, in the old fashion. "We should leave. There's no, ah, time to waste."

"We've overlooked one thing," Jack said mildly. "We're still stuck in the Keep of Time."

"It gets easier after the first thousand years or so," said the Cartographer.

"That is a problem," John agreed, realizing they'd come via a one-way passage. "And we don't have a Compass Rose with which to contact anyone either."

"Isolation clears the mind and sharpens the senses," said the Cartographer.

"Perhaps we could fashion some sort of rope and lower ourselves down," Charles suggested.

"And then what?" said Jack. "We swim to the Nameless Isles?"

"We could use the Opening to access the Underneath, and the islands below," John suggested, rubbing his chin. "Autunno is the closest source of allies we have."

"That just creates a whirlpool," Jack countered. "We'd only drop *farther*."

"Why are they arguing about this?" Quixote asked the Cartographer. "Aren't we just going to take the boat?"

The Cartographer shrugged. "I think it's the process they have to go through. They are somehow required to argue pointlessly about things that are completely irrelevant before deciding to do what was staring them in the face all along."

John looked at the old men. "You have a boat?"

"Of course I have a boat," the Cartographer shot back. "You yourselves sent me here in it. It hasn't gone anywhere else since." He jerked a thumb over his shoulder at the chaotic shelves behind his chair.

Sitting there on the edge of the uppermost shelf was a small glass bottle that contained a miniature Dragonship.

"The *Scarlet Dragon*," John said in realization. "I've never given it another thought."

"I'm not surprised in the least," Archimedes said, preening.

"So it turns into a boat when we break the glass," Jack said. "We still have no way to escape the tower."

"I'm suddenly beginning to see why you're professors," said the Cartographer as he handed Jack the ship in the bottle. "Arguing about the problem instead of asking if anyone has a solution is the best way to ensure tenure. Cambridge is lucky to have you."

"I teach at Oxford," said Jack.

"That's right," the old mapmaker murmured. "I keep forgetting what year it is."

He rustled around in the far corner of the room, where things seemed to be organized in piles rather than piled on shelves. After a minute he uttered a triumphant "Aha!" and turned back to the companions with a wry gleam in his eyes. He was clasping several sheets of parchment as if they were fragile china dolls.

"Here," the Cartographer said, proffering the pages to John. "See what you can make of these."

The old sheets of parchment looked very much like those in the *Imaginarium Geographica*, and John said as much, wondering aloud if they might have come from the same milling.

"Identical, in point of fact," the old mapmaker said with a hint of derision in his voice. "I'm surprised you even questioned it."

John and Jack examined the pages, which were ragged along one edge. "Torn out?" Jack asked. "Were these removed on purpose?"

The Cartographer nodded. "There are secrets hidden within those pages that were too much to handle for some of the

Caretakers-in-training," he said blithely. "De Bergerac in particular made unorthodox use of them, and when that idiot Houdini was recruited, the Far Traveler and I were vindicated in our decision to tear them out."

"I thought the *Geographica* couldn't be destroyed," said Charles. "Wasn't that actually a problem when we started all this?"

The Cartographer sighed like a schoolmarm with a worn-out dunce cap. "For one thing, boy, I am the Cartographer. I made the atlas. So I can take out whatever I wish. And for another thing, I wasn't destroying them, merely hiding them. The ones that have been drawn on are dangerous enough—but four or five centuries ago a rogue Caretaker actually stole a stack of blank sheets."

"Is this the moon?" John asked, looking through the pages. "And . . . Mars?"

"Don't get distracted from your goals," the Cartographer said, grabbing the pages and riffling through them. "This here is what you need right now."

The page bore an unfinished drawing of a familiar place that was as comforting in its own way as Ransom's card of the keep had been.

"That's home!" Rose exclaimed. "I would so love to go there, Uncle John!"

"Avalon," said John, nodding. "That would be the perfect place to start the journey to the Nameless Isles. But," he continued, "the drawing is incomplete. Will it still work in the same way as Ransom's card?"

"What Ransom does by practice and instinct, you'll have to do paint-by-numbers," the Cartographer replied in a tone that was only slightly condescending. "I've seen you draw, Caretaker.

You should be able to finish what Roger Bacon started."

"If you have the means to travel out of this place," remarked Charles, "then why didn't you leave ages ago? Why don't you come with us now?"

The Cartographer hesitated, and a hard look crossed his features, then softened. "I am bound, if you'll remember, to stay here in Solitude, until such time as Arthur chooses to release me."

"Arthur is dead," Charles said bluntly.

"Charles," chided Jack. "His heirs are able to open the door," he said, turning to the old mapmaker. "I'm sure it is within their power to free you as well."

"When and if they choose," the Cartographer said. He clapped his hands together. "But that is a discussion for a different day. For now, you need to finish the drawing and be on your way."

He provided a pencil and several crayons to John, who quickly began to draw on the sheet, sketching in details of the ruins that existed there now, blurring out the unblemished portrait that Bacon had begun of the structures that were new and unfallen. John had seen the island in both states—pristine and ruined— and he didn't want to take the risk that a drawing of Avalon as it once was would take them further back in time. Better that it take them to the place as he knew it best, even if it was only a shadow of its former glory.

In less than an hour the drawing was completed.

"Simply use it in the same way Ransom used the Trump," the Cartographer instructed them. "Hold the picture in your mind, then merge what you see there with the picture before you. It will expand, and you should then be able to step through.

"I would prefer not to watch, if you don't mind," he said dismissively. "You've distracted me enough today as it is, and I really must get back to work."

The Caretakers each thanked him and bade him good-bye. Don Quixote gave him a stiff and formal bow, which they were surprised to see returned. Rose gave the old mapmaker a hug, then kissed him on the cheek.

"Thank you, Uncle Merlin," she said. "I'm sure we'll see each other again very soon."

"Yes, yes," he said, pressing her away. "Be about your business. I must return to mine."

He turned away from the companions and took up his quill, then began to sketch on the parchment at his desk as if they weren't even in the room.

"Well enough," said John. "Let's take another trip, shall we?"

As they had done with the Trump of the keep, John held up the parchment so they could all concentrate on it. In seconds the soft susurrations of the breezes of Avalon began to swirl through the picture and into the chamber.

The image began to grow, until it filled the entire wall next to the door. Charles, Jack, and Rose moved through, followed by Archimedes and Quixote. John stepped through last, but only after one final glance at the Cartographer. The old man never looked up or ceased sketching with his quill.

The picture began to shrink rapidly, and in moments, it had vanished altogether.

For the rest of the day, the Cartographer sketched random lines across the parchment, creating the illusion of working, but in reality he was making motions at his desk for their own sake. He continued to do so until the point of his quill snapped, splattering ink across the sheet.

In frustration the old mapmaker crumpled up the page and threw it across the room. His lip quivered, and his eyes welled with moisture. Only a single tear escaped and trailed down his cheek to his chin, dropping to the floor, before he took out another sheet of parchment and a fresh pen and once more began to draw.

Attending to the various globes were three women . . .

CHAPTER SEVEN
The Grotto

The island of Avalon occupies an unusual place within the wonder of creation, as it is the only island that exists equally in both the natural world and in that of the Archipelago of Dreams.

As such, it became the first true crossing place between the worlds. In the past there had been other points of passage—usually accidental—but experiments in recent years using dragon feathers and vehicles other than the Dragonships had proven that connections between the worlds are *everywhere*. With the proper preparation, it was possible to cross from any point along the Frontier, the great barrier of storms that protected the Archipelago, into any corresponding point in the natural world.

The steam-powered vehicles called principles had been used on occasion, but most frequently, Bert and other travelers had crossed over in the Dragonships, which Prince Stephen had refashioned into airships. So there was little need to sail on the waters through the traditional crossing point that was Avalon.

A shame, John thought as he stepped through the parchment, *especially considering the glory that this island once was.*

In their journey through the past to rescue Hugo Dyson, John and Jack had been able to see Avalon in its pristine state: alabaster columns supporting high stone arches; glistening temples of marble and mother-of-pearl; walkways and walls of stone inlaid with jade. It was the Golden Age of the gods made manifest in a single ethereal vision. Only the vision was real, as were the goddesses who inhabited it.

"Well," Charles said once they had all moved through the parchment, "it's a bit more crumbly around the edges, but otherwise, it actually feels good to see this shabby old island again."

John chuckled to himself and winked at Jack. Of course Charles would see it differently than they did. He hadn't been with them on that adventure—not this Charles, at any rate. The "Charles" they'd had with them was from another timeline and was called Chaz. And he made a sacrifice of his own, becoming the first protector of Avalon—the first Green Knight.

"I wonder," said Charles in what was practically a continuation of John's thinking, "where the devil that scoundrel Magwich is? Shouldn't he have appeared by now, waving around a spear and asking us to state our allegiances, or some such?"

"Hmm," Jack mused, looking around the low embankment. "He's probably off taking a nap."

"Well, let's go," John began, turning to instruct the others on a plan of action, when he saw Rose and stopped.

She had dropped to her knees in the sand, and her eyes were full of tears. Quixote had knelt beside her and was gently trying to console her. Archie too was doing his best to make supportive gestures.

"We're all idiots," muttered Jack under his breath to John. "We were so intent on getting out of the tower that it never occurred to us how she would take coming here."

He's right, John thought as they moved over to the girl, *on both counts*.

Rose had been born on Avalon. She was conceived in the city of Alexandria, but her mother, Gwynhfar, had fled the Summer Country and come here. Gwynhfar joined the other two women on the island, the enchantress Circe and the sea-witch Calypso, in becoming the Morgaine—the three supernatural women who may have been the Fates, or goddesses, or simply beings of incomprehensible power.

Sometimes they changed personalities, if not personages— Gwynhfar was not among them when John, Jack, and Charles first met them—but there were always three, and they always reflected aspects of who they truly were. Sometimes they appeared as beautiful women; sometimes, harried old hags. Often the advice they gave was useful, but in John's experience, they were more manipulative than helpful. But whatever else they were, the original Morgaine had been Rose's mother and surrogate aunts. And whatever else Avalon represented, it had been the only home she had known, until John and Jack arrived there centuries earlier and took her with them to resurrect a dead king.

From that experience, she went to England and into a boarding school—and she had never come back to the place of her birth until now. So she had no memories of Avalon except from when it was full of gleaming, glorious edifices fit to rival the finest Greek temples. To come here now and see the island in such a state of disrepair had to be shattering.

"What happened?" Rose was asking as the other men knelt beside her. "What happened to my home? How did it get this way?"

"It's been almost five centuries," John said softly. "Many things change in that much time."

"But wasn't the knight here?" she asked, clutching Charles's hands. "You were here, Uncle Charles. Why did you let this happen?"

Charles stammered a bit under the directness of the question. "I . . . uh, I wish I could tell you, my dear child," he said, looking to John and Jack for support. "It wasn't I who came here, but I know he did the best he could."

"No one lives forever," Jack said, nodding in agreement. "Chaz did everything he could, I'm sure—but when he died, another took his place."

"And another after that," added John. "There have been twenty-six Green Knights, in fact, and I'm sure they all did the best they could. But nothing lasts forever."

"Well, something should," Rose said, still sniffling but calmer now. Quixote produced a beautiful if faded silk handkerchief for her to wipe her face and blow her nose. "Some things should last forever, especially when they exist on an island like Avalon."

"Tell you what," said John. "We'll find the Green Knight, the one who is the Guardian now, and we'll ask him what happened here."

"That sounds like a plan to me," Charles said, rising to his feet and cracking his knuckles. "I'd like to know where Maggot is myself."

The companions searched the island for the better part of an hour, but to no avail. There was no sign of Magwich.

He'd originally been forced to take the role of protector of

Avalon by the Dragons, who offered him the choice of service or slow roasting on a spit. Others had become the Green Knight as a form of penance—but only Magwich, who had been a failed apprentice Caretaker, actually saw the role as a means to do as little as possible. He was lazier than he was stupid, but he was not completely irresponsible. If he was not on the island, then he was either dead, or worse.

"Maggot being dead wouldn't break my heart," said Charles with a touch of rancor.

"Whatever else Magwich was," John reminded him, "he also had Caretaker training. Perhaps not much, but enough to be dangerous. We must find where he's gone to."

"But he couldn't just leave the island, could he?" asked Jack. "Wouldn't he turn into dust, or at least set off alarms with the Dragons?"

"Artus sent the Dragons away, remember?" John said. "When he set up his republic, and dissolved the monarchy. If they weren't looking after the welfare of the king, they probably would have cared less about watching the goings-on of a third-rate knight on Avalon."

As they discussed the Magwich issue, Rose, Archie, and Quixote rejoined them from the short walk they'd taken to the western side of the island. Rose used to spend time there fishing with her paternal grandfather—or at least, that was who John and Jack had assumed the old man was—and she wanted to see if he, at least, was still there.

The expression on her face gave them the answer. Rose was still visibly upset, but she seemed to have mostly regained control of her emotions, and she was back to her usual mode of absorbing the information around her.

Rose was unusual in many ways—this had always been evident. But John realized that today was the first time in a long time that they perceived her as what she really was: a child, trying to learn the lessons she needed to become an adult. And finding that some lessons are harder than others.

"Let's go look around the cottages and the cave," Jack suggested. "He's going to be there, if anywhere."

"He's supposed to be here, among the temples," Charles countered.

"That's what I mean," said Jack. "This *is* Magwich, after all. We've just wasted time looking for him where he's supposed to be."

"Good point," said Charles.

The narrow path along the western edge was a bit difficult to traverse for Quixote, and the crosswinds were strong enough that Archimedes stayed well inland. But the companions made quick enough time that they arrived in the clearing where the Morgaine lived while the sun was still high above the horizon.

It was a scene of greater entropy than the temple had been. Where three cottages had once stood, there was only scattered rubble and straw. Nothing remained of the cooking pit, and even the old well had been all but destroyed.

Worse still, all the rare and dangerous artifacts that had also been left there for safekeeping were also missing.

"Pandora's Kettle," said Charles. "It's gone!"

"And the shield of Perseus," Jack added. "And the wands, and armor, and jewels . . . all of it."

"Damn his eyes," said Charles. "Magwich was supposed to

guard everything on this island. When I find him . . ." He didn't need to finish the sentence.

"When was the last time we actually saw him here?" John asked. "I can't really recall."

"Whenever it was," said Charles, "remember we're missing seven years. A lot of things may have happened in that time alone."

John nodded in agreement. "The Cartographer said as much. If so many things are going poorly in both worlds, it stands to reason that Avalon would be involved."

"It's the fact that the kettle is gone that worries me," Jack noted, "as well as the only means of capping it—Perseus's shield. Either Artus and Aven took it to Paralon for safekeeping, or else someone else came to get it—to use it. Only a handful of people ever knew what it could do."

John's eyes flicked over to Rose, who was looking down the well and not listening in on the discussion.

"And one in particular who *did* use it," said John, his voice low, "but he's dead."

"His Shadow is still out there somewhere," Charles reminded them, "and the Trolls and Goblins also knew how the kettle was used. The field of suspects is wide open."

"Shall we check the cave?" Quixote asked, peering into the dark cavern. On entering the clearing, he had ignored the cottages altogether in favor of the cave, which seemed to have completely entranced him.

"He's not going to be there," said Charles dismissively. "He never liked it in there to begin with, and after the Morgaine left, I doubt he had any reason to go in at all."

"Where did they go?" asked Rose, obviously crestfallen. She was hoping that some aspect of her memories had survived on the island, but it was becoming more and more clear that the place was completely abandoned.

"I don't know where they went," Charles said. "After the, ah, accident that caused all the trouble at the keep where your Uncle Merlin resides, the Morgaine told us we had unraveled time itself—and we thought we had put things right, but the next time we came here, they were gone. No one knows where."

"Most intriguing," said Quixote. "And no one in the castle could tell you where they went?"

Charles looked at John, then Jack in confusion. "You mean on Paralon?" he said. "No, no one there had any clue, not even Samaranth."

The old knight shook his head and pointed into the cave. "Not on Paralon," he said plaintively. "The *castle*. The castle in the *cave*."

"We've been in there, more than once," Jack said, grimacing slightly at the hint of condescension he heard in his own voice, "and there's nothing in there but dust and cobwebs. Hasn't been for over a decade."

"Pardon," said Quixote, bowing slightly. If he'd taken offense at Jack's tone, it didn't show. "I would not presume to teach such esteemed scholars as yourselves, but I have a special knowledge of this cave. You see, I have been in it before. There is a wondrous meadow there, and a great castle made of crystal. Inside the castle there are wondrous halls of alabaster marble, where the great heroes of history are interred. It is my hope to one day rest among them.

"And," he said in conclusion, "in that place, sometimes, it is possible to commune with the dead. So if we choose to enter, it may very well be there that we shall find the answers you seek."

John blinked, then blinked again. "I'm sure we don't know what you're talking about, my good knight."

Quixote sighed, then smiled knowingly. "I am well used to those around me not believing the stories I tell," he said, gesturing broadly with his hands. "My tales of the adventures in the Archipelago saw me painted with the brush of a teller of falsehoods, never mind that to tell a lie would be ignoble of a knight. So I understand and I tell you with no rancor that it was prophesied that I would sleep until the call came to serve once more. And I believe that I was destined to be here, now, to aid you on your quest."

John pondered the knight's words silently for a moment. In the keep, he had told them that he possessed special knowledge that would be needed by them on their journey. None of them had really believed him, and they had taken him with them out of compassion more than anything else. To do otherwise would have meant his death. But they had never actually considered that he might have been sincere all along.

"Don Quixote de la Mancha," John said, bowing, "I have spoken in haste, and we have not availed ourselves of the counsel you might offer. If you have a special knowledge of this place, I beg you share it with us."

Quixote bowed gravely and blushed at John's respectful speech. He was not accustomed to being spoken to so well, and it took him a few seconds to compose himself.

"To enter the meadow where the castle stands, we must first fall asleep. . . ."

"Fall asleep?" Charles said. "All of us?"

Quixote nodded. "It is through the realm of dreams that we may cross through to the castle."

Charles and Jack each sighed heavily and slumped against the stones lining the entrance of the cave.

"You mean, you dreamed it all," Charles began.

"I'm so glad you understand," said the old knight in obvious relief. "Most people regard it as insanity."

Jack's brow furrowed. "Uh, begging your pardon, but I'm on the fence regarding that myself."

"To be fair," Charles pointed out, "he has been sleeping in the keep for the better part of four centuries. To him, all of this might seem as if it were a dream."

"You're starting to get the hang of it," said Quixote, clapping Charles on the back. "You'd make a fine knight yourself, you know."

"I really don't think we have time for all of us to take a nap," John said diplomatically.

"Oh," Quixote said, deflating. "I suppose we could try the door, if only we had access to a king or queen of the Archipelago. But that's probably too much to ask."

As one, the Caretakers looked down at Rose. "It's worth a try," she said. "After all, I was able to open the Cartographer's door."

Quixote looked from the girl to the companions and back again, gradually realizing what they were talking about. He wheeled around and strode to the remnants of the cooking pit, where he found a solid piece of charcoal, which he handed to Rose.

On the old knight's instruction, the companions all entered the cave. Archie remained behind to be, as John put it, their "canary in the coal mine."

"Isn't the canary supposed to go first, to make certain the air is clear?" asked Jack.

"I didn't say it was a perfect analogy," John replied, "but it's good enough in a pinch."

"If anything happens here," Archie huffed, "your canary will be sure to sing out loud and long."

"Thank you, Archie," said John.

"Humph," said Archie.

Quixote showed Rose what she must do, and the companions watched as she used the charcoal to sketch a broad, high door on the back of the cave wall.

"Very good," said Quixote. "Now, if you'll just recite the poem that opens the door."

Rose blinked. "I don't know what that is."

John stepped forward and opened his pack. "I think I do," he said. He unwrapped the *Geographica*, flipped to a particular page, and held it out for Rose to read.

The girl took the book in her hands and began to recite the verses John had indicated:

> *By knowledge paid*
> *For riddles wrought*
> *I open thee*
> *I open thee*

> *By bones bound*
> *By honor taken*
> *I open thee*
> *I open thee*

For life eternal and liberty gain'd
To sleep and dream, as kings we reign'd
I open thee
I open thee

As she finished speaking, a cracking sound reverberated throughout the cave, and a seam of pure, radiant light appeared along the inside of the charcoal lines. Quixote leaned forward and pushed against the wall—which swung outward, away from his touch.

The light from the other side was blinding after the gloomy twilight of the cave. It took a few seconds for the companions' eyes to adjust, then, cautiously, they all moved forward and through the doorway.

As Quixote had promised, the door opened to a vast meadow of nearly indescribable beauty. There were fields of wildflowers that ended in gently sloping hills of wild wheat and clover. The scents of the flowers and grasses were almost overwhelming, and a sharp, loamy tang permeated the air, as if a thunderstorm had just passed. But the sky was clear and deeply blue, and it appeared to be morning, although there was no sun in the sky.

In the distance, past the golden fields, rose the towers and crenellations of the crystal castle. The blue light, reflected up from the fields, caused the castle to appear bright green, as if it were constructed of emeralds.

Charles gave a low whistle in admiration, and Jack could only continue to stare, slack-jawed in amazement at the sights, as Rose knelt to gather a bundle of clover to press to her face.

As for John, he looked in wonderment at the beauty that surrounded them, then at Quixote, then back again. The old knight had been not only truthful, but extremely precise in his accounting as well.

"Lead on," John said, gesturing for Quixote to take them to the castle. "Your word is good."

Quixote bowed his head and took off at a brisk pace down a well-worn path through the meadow.

The companions followed after, with occasional digressions by Rose and Charles to examine some new patch of flowers that appeared along the way. At first it had appeared that the castle was very close, but as they continued to walk, it became evident that that was not the case. The castle grew taller and more broad the closer they came, but it took nearly an hour to reach the high red gates.

"I had almost thought we'd discovered Macdonald's Fairy Land," Jack said to the others, "but the markings on these gates are Greek."

"This isn't Fairy Land," John agreed. "I don't know what it is."

Quixote said nothing, but instead reached for a corded rope that hung to one side of the gates. He gave it a pull, and a low chime sounded from within.

In short order a gatekeeper appeared, unlocked the gate, and swung it open.

He was aged without seeming old, and more weary than aged. He looked over at Rose with a flicker of surprised recognition, then composed himself. He next regarded Quixote with a cautious eye, before giving his full attention to Charles, John, and Jack.

"I have not seen you before," he said in a voice thick with a French accent. His tone indicated that he was used to speaking with authority. "Why have you come here?"

"Avalon is deserted," John told him. "We're looking to discover why, and what may have happened to the Guardian."

The gatekeeper snorted. "That fool? He has been gone from the isle for many years. Where he went, I cannot say—but the one who might tell you the rest resides here, in the castle."

"Are you the new Green Knight?" Charles asked.

The gatekeeper rolled his eyes. "Do I appear to be made of wood?" he said. "As a knight, I guarded milady, and I guard her still, as well as the others within. What happens outside these walls is no longer my concern."

"May we pass?" asked Jack.

"On what authority do you ask to enter?" said the gatekeeper.

John unwrapped the *Geographica* on a hunch and showed the cover to the old man. "On the authority of the heirs of Arthur, King of the Silver Throne."

The gatekeeper looked as if he had been struck across the face with a hammer. He staggered back a moment, then pulled himself against the gate to stand steady.

"Enter and be welcomed," he said, his voice shaking with barely controlled emotion.

As the companions passed by, they were able to look at the gatekeeper more closely. He had the bearing of a knight but would not meet their eyes, lifting his head only to glance at Rose. There were scars on his arms and face, which had once been handsome. But the sorrow in his eyes and on his countenance was the deepest any of them had ever seen. More surprisingly, under his cloak they could see his own armor, which also bore the mark of the king.

"Who is this?" Quixote asked Charles behind his hand. "He never bothered to say three words to me when I was here before."

"I can't say for certain," Charles replied as they walked into the castle grounds, "but if I were to hazard a guess, I'd say we just met Lancelot himself."

The gatekeeper pointed the companions down a broad avenue between the gleaming green towers, to a pair of white doors. "I must go no farther," he said, "but I will see you on your return. May the gods grant you the knowledge you seek."

"Lancelot?" said Quixote, when they reached the doors and passed between them. "Really? I always thought he was a monk. I—"

The knight stopped talking as the doors closed behind them, leaving them in an expansive room that aspired to be a world, and that rendered them all speechless.

A thousand architectural styles were represented by the miniature buildings that were ensconced in transparent globes placed on gleaming pedestals throughout the room. On closer examination, the Caretakers realized that each miniature city was a world unto itself and contained tiny people and other creatures.

All along the walls were doorways interspersed with crypts, and at the far end of the hall was a bowl of blue fire, set into the floor in front of a massive wall.

Jack clutched at John's coat and pointed. "Look!" he whispered. "I think we've found them!"

Attending to the various globes were three women who floated above the surface of the floor in gossamer robes. One, the closest, was clothed in blue; the next, a short distance away, who was looking into a globe containing a Norse village, wore green; and the most distant of them wore pink.

It wasn't until the woman in blue moved to a globe closer to the doors that John realized he knew her. "Do you know us?" he called out. "Are you of the Morgaine?"

"When one has been a part of the Morgaine," the apparition said, "a part of the three who are one remains ever after. But I am still myself, especially here, in this place."

"And what should we call you?" asked Charles, before John could whisper to him that they already knew this woman. They had met her long ago.

"Call me Guinevere," the apparition said, opening her arms wide to embrace Rose. "Welcome home, daughter."

Chapter Eight
The Nameless Isles

Guinevere, with her ethereal presence and turquoise hair, seemed more like a fairy than one of the Morgaine—but enough of who she was remained that Rose knew her and recognized her, and it gladdened the companions' hearts to see the girl so fulfilled and happy.

"What is this place?" said John.

"Call it the Elysian fields, or Valhalla, or Vanaheim," replied Guinevere. "It is all and none. But it is a place where the dead heroes of the past may come to rest, before they go on to their afterlife or are needed again."

"Why is Avalon deserted?" John asked. "The Morgaine are gone, and the Green Knight is as well."

"The Morgaine keep their own counsel and left of their own choice," Guinevere intoned. "The Guardian was enticed and easily gave up his post."

"As I thought," Charles fumed. "Once a Maggot, always a Maggot."

"What are you doing here, Mother?" Rose asked. "I've missed you, very much."

Guinevere looked down at her daughter. "As I have missed you.

"I expect you must be the Caretakers," the cat said . . .

But we each have our paths to follow, and mine has ended here."

"Ended?" said Charles bluntly. "Are—are you dead?"

She looked up at him and raised an eyebrow. "That would depend on your point of view, Caretaker," she answered. "I left the Morgaine to marry, and saw the downfall of a kingdom. But from the ashes of that tragedy, my children built a kingdom anew— you are its guardians now, and one of you may yet earn your place among the heroes here."

She turned and glided away, gesturing for the companions to follow. She led them to the great marble wall, next to the blue flame.

The marble wall contained three crypts. Guinevere passed the first of them and then paused at the second, resting her hand lightly, almost reverently, on its surface. "Here rests he who was my husband, who breathed his last in my arms," she said, the sorrow in her voice unconcealed. "The first King of the Silver Throne, the first king of Camelot. Here lies Arthur, who will sleep until he is needed again."

"We know a little of his death from the Histories," said Charles, "but Geoffrey of Monmouth was incomplete as a chronicler and fictionalized some things to make his stories more interesting. I didn't realize you had been with him when he died."

She looked pained at hearing this. "I—I wasn't, but I was near," she said, "and I have remained with him ever since.

"Mordred returned to Camelot and brought war with him," she continued. "I had abandoned my duties on Avalon to become Arthur's queen, to protect and watch over him. And I failed. I failed him, in every way. And so it is my penance to stay with him here, to watch over his body and wait for the time when he might rise again to protect all the lands that are, and the people who reside there."

"That's very, ah, loyal," said Jack.

"And optimistic," said Charles.

"It is prophesied," stated Guinevere, "that in the time of greatest need, he will rise once more to defend and protect his kingdom. But," she added before any of the companions could ask, "now is not that time."

"How do you know?" asked Jack.

"There is a Prophecy," Guinevere began.

"I'm starting to get weary of hearing about prophecies," said Charles.

"Does he need me again, Mother?" Rose asked, moving around Charles to take Guinevere's hands. "Does he need my blood to save him, as it did before?"

Guinevere shook her head. "That is not written for you," she said to her daughter in a voice both gentle and firm. "You gave your sacrifice once. In time, it will be for another to do so."

She held her daughter's hands for a moment more, then let them go and crossed her hands in front of her. "What else would you ask of me?"

"Who are in the other two crypts?" Charles asked. "If you don't mind my inquiring."

"In the crypt on the left is the first of the heroes," said Guinevere. "The original, the archetype, the one who inspired all those who came after."

"Hercules?" Jack guessed, only to be slightly embarrassed when the lady responded with a laugh.

"Little mortal, I forget how short a time you have lived, and how little you know of the history of the world. The first hero, who sleeps here next to Arthur, was the one called Gilgamesh."

"And in the third?" said John, whose curiosity had overwhelmed his need for decorum. He really wanted to know: Who could possibly merit being interred next to Gilgamesh and Arthur Pendragon?

Instead of answering, Guinevere glanced almost imperceptibly at Rose, then shook her head. "It is not for me to say," she replied. "Not at this time."

"Guinevere," Jack said suddenly, "may I ask a boon?"

She looked at him curiously, but could not disguise her amusement at the request. "You may ask."

"We first came into the Archipelago to protect your daughter," said Jack. "There are those roaming about, in both this world and in the Summer Country, who seek to harm her. Perhaps even kill her. We don't know of any place where we might take her that will be as safe as she'll be here. Could she stay?"

John and Charles both started to say something, but held their tongues as they realized the truth of Jack's words. If this place was as difficult to enter as it seemed, it really might be the safest place for the girl.

But Guinevere shook her head. "She cannot. This is not a place where the living can long stay. In time she would become as transparent as I. I have lived a full lifetime—more than one, in fact. And so I can accept this ghostly existence. But it is not for her. There is a—"

"Prophecy," said Charles.

"A destiny," Guinevere said, giving Charles a stern look, "that she must seek out. She has an extraordinary life ahead of her, and should not dismiss it so easily by staying here with phantasms.

And this is only the beginning. You will need her if your worlds are to survive."

"Why did the Morgaine abandon the Archipelago?" asked John. "Why did they leave?"

"There is nothing gained but futility in weaving a tapestry whose picture changes at a whim," Guinevere said plainly. "Elements of creation are changing, even now, as we speak. Events in history are being made and unmade with every passing moment."

"Is there anything you can tell us?" John pleaded. "For your daughter's sake, if nothing else?"

"A great weapon is being brought to bear against the forces of the Light," Guinevere said, "which you will not be able to withstand. Only by wielding a weapon of equal power will you have the chance to prevail."

"How do we find such a weapon?" said Jack.

"Summon the Lady," the apparition said as she began to shimmer and fade. "The Lady of the Lake. Only she can return what was given. . . ."

Rose leaped forward, but it was too late. Her mother was gone. As the companions watched, the woman in green also faded and vanished, and then, more slowly, the woman in pink, who raised a tentative hand to wave—at Quixote.

"Do you know her?" Charles asked.

Quixote didn't reply for a long moment, then turned to the Caretaker. "It is not yet my time to be here," he said, his voice heavy with emotion. "I must see through this quest and fulfill the Prophecy. And then, perhaps . . ." He glanced back once more, then quickly turned away. "Perhaps I will have earned the right to join her here. But now is not that time."

All around them, the crystal castle had begun to fade, as if it had been a mirage. The globes vanished, then the walls, and finally the doors. All that remained was the lone figure of the gatekeeper, standing in the expansive meadow.

"Did you find the answers you seek?" he asked the companions as they approached. "Did you speak to her?"

"The fairy with the turquoise hair?" said Charles. "We spoke, and she told us a few things that might prove useful, yes."

"And how did she look?" he asked, trying to mask the eagerness in his voice. "Was she well?"

"As beautiful as ever," said John.

The gatekeeper slumped his shoulders and sighed heavily with relief. "Thank you for that," he said quietly. "It has been too long since I saw her."

"You *are* Lancelot, aren't you?" Charles asked.

The gatekeeper nodded wistfully. "I was. Now I am simply the gatekeeper. Much like your Green Knight, it is my way of doing penance—and part of the agreement is that I may be close, but can never again see her."

"That's awful," said John.

"No," said Quixote, nodding in understanding. "It is the price that must be paid for an unpayable debt. And it is the only choice a noble knight would make."

The gatekeeper lowered his head. "Not noble enough, I fear."

Quixote reached out and lifted Lancelot's chin. "The most noble acts," he said sternly, "are those performed when there is nothing left to be gained. You are not merely a gatekeeper. You are a brother knight. So speaks Don Quixote de la Mancha."

The doorway to the cave lay open in front of them. "Farewell,

Lancelot," John said as the companions walked through it.

"May God go with you," replied the gatekeeper.

Rose looked back, just once, in the direction where the green castle had been, as did Quixote.

"Good-bye, Mother," she said.

"Good-bye," Quixote whispered. "Good-bye, my beloved Dulcinea."

And with that last farewell, the door swung closed and was a cave wall once more.

The sun was just beginning to set as the companions reached the eastern beach. Either a full day—or more—had passed while they were in the castle with Guinevere, or their journey had taken scarcely any time at all.

"It had to have been a few hours," John said as he checked on the *Geographica* in his pack. "I'd swear to it."

"I think that grotto, or whatever—wherever—it was that the meadow and castle sit, functions much like Quixote's room in the keep," said Charles. "I don't think time there passes in the same way as it does for us."

"You're probably right," said Jack. "It's frozen, or at the least, passes much more slowly. How much worse would it be if we were to emerge and find out the reverse were true? That while we chatted with a long-lost queen for a few hours, centuries were passing by outside?"

"Brr," John replied. "That would be a bit much. I've already been rather preoccupied with just the idea that we may have lost seven years of our lives by stepping through a drawing."

"That's one reason we should be underway as quickly as

possible," said Jack. "We've literally no time to waste."

Jack reached into his pocket where he'd kept the bottle and pulled out their ship. With curt nods of approval from his companions, he windmilled his arm and dashed the bottle against the rocks in the shallow tidepools.

In moments the ship had grown to its full size, much to the companions' great relief. It was much smaller than every other Dragonship, but it was large enough for the four men, the girl, and the owl to be comfortably seated within.

"There's no sail," Charles pointed out, "nor any oars. How do we move her about?"

"I think this is one of Ordo Maas's special ships," said Jack, stroking the Dragon's head. "I think we just need to tell her where we want to go, and she'll get us there. Right, girl?"

There was no audible response from the masthead, but for a few seconds, the Dragon's eyes seemed to glow more brightly, and her neck grew warm under Jack's hand.

With a crunching sound, the boat pulled itself out of the shallows, then glided swiftly through the water at the edge of the storm clouds of the Frontier. A few hundred yards from the island, she stopped and waited.

"Well," John said, standing. "I'd say that's our signal to start navigating." He turned to Charles with a broad grin on his face. "All right, Sir Charles. Strip. It's time to have a look at the map."

"Well?" Charles asked, once he was naked to the waist. "Which way do we go first?"

"First and last," John said, "we need to go north. Due north. That's where we'll find the Nameless Isles."

♦   ♦   ♦

Traveling so directly north, the only islands they passed that were familiar to them were Prydain and a small group of islands called the Capa Blanca. Prydain was one of the greater islands, second only to the capital island of Paralon, but the Caretakers had never actually traveled to the Capa Blanca islands before.

"I understood from the Histories Bert wrote that they were originally settled by shipwrecked sailors from Spain," Charles remarked, feeling a chill now that the sun was setting. "The sailors built several very lovely towns and had quite a nice culture developing until some British doctor showed up and taught the animals there how to talk. After that it was all downhill. The animals wanted better working conditions and higher wages. You know how it goes."

"Spanish, eh?" said Quixote. "Perhaps we could stop in on our way home. It's been too long since I heard my native tongue."

"Doesn't Verne speak Spanish?" asked Jack.

"Dreadfully," said Quixote. "I made him promise to never again make the attempt."

The last island they passed, the easternmost and most northerly island in the *Geographica*, was a midsize round island called Gondour.

"They're quite the democracy, according to Mark Twain's notes," said John, "although I never did care for his spelling of the name. Always have to catch myself when I mispronounce it 'dour' instead of 'door.'"

"Aren't they assisting Artus with his new republic?" asked Jack.

"I think so. The one oddity is that they are a republic ruled over by an impeachable caliph. I'd imagine it makes for some very lively debates."

After Gondour, there was going to be very little to see for a long while, so the companions made themselves as comfortable as they could in the *Scarlet Dragon*, and took turns sleeping. Jack and Quixote volunteered for the first watch and took up positions at the fore of the boat.

"Jack, may I ask you something?" said Quixote.

"Certainly."

"Have you ever known failure?"

Jack turned to the knight in surprise. "Of course I have. Everyone does, at one time or another."

The knight chewed on his lip as he pondered Jack's reply. "I thought I had failed, once," he said at length, "but I am wondering if that event was not part of my own destiny, Prophecy or no."

"How do you mean?"

"I think I know why I am here, with you," said Quixote. "I think I understand, at least in part, my role. I am owed a debt—and my claiming it may be a key to all that we are experiencing."

"Who owes you the debt?" asked Jack.

"The Lady," Quixote replied. "The Lady of the Lake."

He turned away and said no more, and Jack was reluctant to press him. The rest of the night passed without incident.

In the morning John again instructed Charles to sprawl himself against the masthead so that they could better read the map.

"This is not very dignified, you know," Charles pouted. "Can't you just sketch out a copy in the *Geographica*, so I can keep my shirt on?"

"Sorry, old boy," said John. "Some of the islands have already changed position."

It was true—the locations of several of the Nameless Isles had moved during the night. John made some corrections and adjusted the tiller on the *Scarlet Dragon* to communicate the changes to the boat.

"If all goes as I hope it shall," John said, "we ought to be there by nightfall."

The course the map took them on led them safely distant from the kingdom of the Trolls, farther to the west—which was for the best, as none of the companions had ever liked Arawn, the former prince who was now king of the Trolls. He had been a rabble-rouser during their first encounter with the Winter King, and later allied with him against them. Arawn had been as ungracious in defeat as Artus had been gracious in his victory, and so the Northlands had been a place to avoid ever since—if they could help it.

The islands of the Christmas Saint, past the Troll Kingdom, were the absolute northernmost chronicled in the *Geographica*. All three companions had read the annotations thoroughly, and very early on in their role as Caretakers had conspired to find reasons to correspond with and eventually visit the principal resident. John had even gone so far as to persuade him to write letters to his children, which was one of the great delights of fatherhood. To know beyond a doubt that Father Christmas existed was spectacular enough; to be considered worthy of corresponding with him was a childhood dream made manifest.

Beyond the isles of Father Christmas, there was nothing. Nothing in the *Geographica*, and nothing as far as the companions could see. None of the previous Caretakers had ever made the effort to sail so far—they had simply assumed that what had been documented was all there was to see. Of them all, only John's mentor, Professor Sigurdsson, had ever taken an active liking to the actual adventuring, the discovery of new lands. He had ventured deep into the Southlands on a fabled voyage, and more than once into the deep west—although John had no clue what he could have been searching for, or what else could be discovered that way, since Terminus and the endless waterfall marked the true End of the World as he knew it.

Charles, when he was not putting on his shirt and taking it off again so the others could check their position, spent his time talking about multiple dimensions with Archimedes, who had proven to be a worthy adversary in a debate.

Quixote preferred to talk to Rose when he could, asking her about the more mundane aspects of boarding school in Reading, with an occasional digression to tales of Odysseus on Avalon.

Jack, for his part, spent the better part of an hour scanning the horizon with a spyglass provided to him by Quixote, until he finally realized that there was no actual glass in the spyglass.

"I never really needed it." Quixote shrugged. "It doesn't help if you're lost, and if you aren't lost, why do you need to see a place you'll soon arrive at anyway?"

Eventually, as the Cartographer had promised, a smudge of land appeared off in the distance, then grew larger at an alarming speed. The Nameless Isles were far closer than they had appeared to be, and had the appearance of a mirage. It took effort to focus on them—a moment of drifting attention found the islands sliding from one's field of vision.

At close range the illusion dropped, and the islands came into sharp relief. There were thirteen all told: a massive island to the south and east of the others, which served as a shield of stone; a small cluster of islands to the west; two larger, half-moon islands to the east and north; and directly ahead of them, a broad, dune-colored island that sloped up from a short beach to a flat expanse of sand, black crystals, and short, blocky trees.

All of the smaller islands had been built up with columns and arches that were all but prehistoric. From their appearance, their construction, and their apparent great age, John surmised that they may have been built in the earliest years of prehistory—contemporary with the first cities, such as Ur and Untapishim. The structures on these outer isles formed a kind of massive arena enclosing the three inner islands. There was no mistaking the purpose: They were defensive, or at least protective, in nature.

On the center island was the unmistakable shape of a house in the distance—and from all appearances it was immense. Directly ahead was a dock, a small boathouse, and a sight that made the companions cheer in joy and relief.

The *White Dragon*, the airship piloted by their mentor Bert, was moored to the north side of the dock, where it floated calmly in the shallows.

"I suddenly feel much better about the prospects of this trip," Charles admitted. "Nothing against you fellows, but Bert always seems to know the score."

"I'm with you there," said John. He guided the *Scarlet Dragon* alongside the larger ship and leaped to the dock to tie a mooring line.

A large orange cat was sitting just past the dock, idly cleaning itself while keeping a watchful eye on the new arrivals to the island.

"I expect you must be the Caretakers," the cat said at length. "Come ashore. You're expected."

"Are you the welcoming committee?" Charles asked as he jumped to the dock and looped the mooring ties to a pylon. "If so, I'm pleased to meet you."

"I am what I am," the cat said, "and if that pleases you, so be it."

"What does that mean?" asked Jack.

"It means," the cat replied, tipping its head toward Rose, "that I am like her. Here, and not here, all at once."

"A riddle?" said John.

"An enigma," said Rose.

"A conundrum," said the cat, which tilted its head, then began to disappear.

"My word," said Charles. "The cat! It's vanishing!"

"No," said the cat, which by now was nothing more than a head, floating in the air. "I'm simply going to a place you aren't looking."

"That makes perfect sense," said Rose.

"It's very confusing," said Jack.

"Thank you very much," said the broad smile that was once a whole cat. "You may call me Grimalkin. Welcome to Tamerlane House."

PART THREE

The League of Poets

The walls were covered with paintings . . . large enough to step through.

Chapter Nine
The House of Tamerlane

The Magician and the Detective pulled the door out of the ship's hold and dragged it across the field to where the construction was taking place. There were carpenters and bricklayers and all manner of roustabouts scattered across the worksite who were carrying materials and banging on things and generally trying to look busy. But everything always stopped when they delivered a door.

Just so, the Magician thought. *The rabble should stop and take notice when I'm onstage.* It might not be a formal performance as such, but he and the Detective were performing the job that could only be trusted to the betters of these rabble.

"Are you two idiots going to take all day dragging that door over here?" said a brusque voice.

At the top of the rise, holding the project blueprints, stood a solid man whose eyes glittered with purpose and whose scarred cheeks testified to his will. Richard Burton was not one to suffer fools or layabouts—not for long, anyway.

"Bring it up here," Burton instructed them, pointing to a frame that had been erected on a patch of clover. "Carefully, now. The Chancellor will not be pleased if we lose another one. Nor will I."

A few months earlier they had been bringing another door up the rise when some of the workers dropped a wheelbarrow load of bricks from the scaffolding high above. The bricks had struck the door with enough force to shatter it, and splinters were all that was left. Burton had examined them with an Infinite Loupe—a modified set of eyeglasses that could be used to see through time—and proclaimed it to have been linked to the ninth century.

"And to Persia, unless I miss my guess," Burton had said. "That could have been useful—but it isn't a time or place that is wholly unknown to me, so we'll let it go, for now."

Of course, Burton's idea of "letting it go" meant beheading the workers who had spilled the bricks, but since it was also useful in motivating the rest of the workers to be more careful, he didn't see it as a complete waste of effort and resources.

The Detective and the Magician stood the door in place and fitted it to the frame, then stepped back.

Burton wiped his hands on his leather apron and stepped up to the door. Cautiously he reached for the handle and slowly pulled the door open, careful not to step over the threshold.

A bright light emanated from within, giving Burton's harsh features a demonic cast. Baroque-period music could be heard from somewhere deep in whatever place the door had opened to. "Excellent," he said as he closed the door. "The Chancellor will be very pleased. A few more, and we'll be able to give the order to move forward. A few more doors . . .

". . . and we'll be able to conquer all of creation."

The central island of the Nameless Isles was practically barren of vegetation, save for a number of massive stumps of petrified wood, and the black obsidian crystals that were scattered among the dunes.

At the end of the dock, a path formed of obsidian pieces wound its way up the slope to the front door of the extraordinary dwelling Grimalkin had called Tamerlane House.

It was a Persian palace, both ancient and exotically new all at once. It was massive in an organic way, wings spreading out across the rise like the branches of an enormous tree. There was very little in their experience that it could be compared to, but John had heard stories of the fabled Winchester House in California, which had been built by an heiress to the Winchester rifle fortune to house the spirits of those who had been killed by the rifles. She built endless rooms, and stairways, and closets, and alcoves, and on and on and on. For decades the hammers never stopped. And for the first time, John was looking at a similar structure born of a similar obsession. He wondered with a mixture of curiosity and fear just what kind of spirits were meant to be housed in Tamerlane House.

In answer to his unspoken question, a familiar figure, looking only slightly more presentable than his usual charmingly bedraggled self, appeared at the top of the steps. It was Bert.

The three Caretakers rushed forward to shake hands and embrace their mentor, who appeared equally glad to see them. Rose hugged him tightly as he kissed the top of her head, and even Archimedes restrained himself to a polite greeting that was hardly sarcastic at all.

"You're a tall drink of water," Bert said, shielding his eyes from the sun as he looked up at Quixote, who bowed in greeting. "How did you get pulled into joining this motley crew?"

"He pretty much had to come," explained Jack. "His room was about to fall into the Chamenos Liber."

"His room . . . ?" Bert said. He blinked a few times, then moved closer to the old knight. "Are you Don Quixote?"

A deeper bow this time. "I *am* Don Quixote de la Mancha," he said with a flourish, "and I am your humble servant."

"Does he have to do that every time he meets someone?" Jack asked John.

"It certainly makes him memorable," John replied. "Maybe you should try it with your next reading class."

"Har har har," said Jack.

"I know all about you," Bert said to Quixote with a gleam in his eye, as his old familiar twinkle began to reappear. "Jules has told me many things—and while your presence is a surprise, it is not wholly unexpected.

"Come," he went on, gesturing for them to follow as he turned to enter the house. "There is much to talk about, now that you've finally arrived."

"We were expected?" exclaimed Jack.

Bert grinned wryly. "Of course. Ransom told us what happened seven years ago, so we've been waiting. Otherwise, you wouldn't have gotten past Grimalkin."

"The Cheshire?" said John. "He seemed pretty harmless to me."

"He may look like a simple Cheshire cat," said Bert, looking around cautiously to see if Grimalkin was listening, "but in reality, he's one of those Elder Gods that fellow Lovecraft has been writing about."

"You're kidding, right?" said Charles. "It's a joke."

"Laugh if you like," Bert called over his shoulder, "but if I were you, I wouldn't take off his collar. For *any* reason."

"As I was saying, we had an idea what had happened to you when Ransom reported in," Bert said as he served the companions tea and Leprechaun crackers in an elaborate parlor, "so we hoped you'd make your way to the Nameless Isles, as Hank had suggested."

"I must admit, Bert," said John, trying not to sound as if he were chiding the older man, "as the Caretaker Principia, I was a bit put out to find there were islands I was unaware of—indeed, islands I was not *allowed* to know of."

"I am sorry about that, John," Bert replied. "Had it been up to me, I'd have said something to you much sooner. It's been a matter of some debate, my position being that if you had been aware, you could have come here directly from Oxford, and not skipped over seven vital years."

"Debate with whom?"

"The Prime Caretaker. But we will discuss that shortly." Bert stood up. "For now, we should make some accommodations for Rose and the good sir knight."

"You rang?" Grimalkin said, appearing on the back of a couch.

"Ah, Grimalkin," said Bert. "Yes, please. If you would be so kind as to show the lady and her gentleman escort to their rooms?"

"Certainly," said Grimalkin, eyeing Archimedes. "Do I get the bird to play with?"

"Define 'play,'" said Bert.

"Oh, never mind," said the cat as his body faded out to nothingness. "Come this way."

"He'll take care of you," said Bert. "Just follow his head."

"I could use a rest, I think," Quixote said. "Thank you, master Caretaker."

As the two companions and the reluctant owl followed the bobbing cat's head down a corridor, Bert turned back to the Caretakers. "Now we can talk as men do, about things of import and consequence."

"Will she be safe here, Bert?" asked John.

"Safe as houses," Bert replied, "or at least, as safe houses. She has nothing to fear here. Grimalkin will look after her, and no one may come here who wasn't invited. That's one of the reasons these islands have remained nameless, and why no map of them exists in the *Geographica*. This place is our own version of Haven, to withdraw to when we must, or when circumstances are most dire."

"Well, we've certainly got a map now," Charles said, scratching at his side. "Does it keep moving even when we've arrived here?"

"The Cartographer cornered you for the duty, eh, Charles?" said Bert with a grin. "It's easier when you're traveling with friends. My first trip here was solo, and I had to use a mirror."

Suddenly a flock of birds barreled down the hallway, each carrying silverware and china place settings. As in the Great Whatsit on Paralon, the servants of the house were large black birds, who were dressed nattily in vests and waistcoats.

"Crows?" Jack asked as the last of the birds flew out of the hallway.

"Ravens," Bert corrected him. "A full unkindness."

"I'll take an unkindness of ravens over a murder of crows any day," said Charles.

"Your jokes are still both literate and unfunny," said Bert, hugging Charles around the shoulders. "It's so good to see you again, lad!"

Bert led the three friends through room after room, but other than the ravens, the house appeared empty.

"Is there anyone here?" Jack asked, peering up at a stairwell that ended, inexplicably, at the high ceiling. "The place seems to be abandoned."

"The master of the house is indeed here in residence," said Bert, "but he seldom chooses to appear. You may meet him after the Gatherum."

"The what?" asked John.

"Better I simply show you than try to explain," Bert said with deliberate mystery and a touch of glee. "Here—I want to show you the Pygmalion Gallery," he continued, waving them down another long corridor. "In fact, I've wanted to bring you here for a very long time."

"What prevented you?" asked John.

"Those evil stepsisters, Necessity and Planning," Bert replied as they approached a set of tall polished doors. "One always gets too little attention, and the other too much—and they never seem to balance out."

The doors were covered with cherubs, and angels, and all manner of ornate and byzantine carvings. In the center, where the doors met, were three locks. Bert removed a large iron ring with two heavy skeleton keys from his pocket. He unlocked the first lock, then the next.

"Three locks," Charles said, "but only two keys?"

"The third key is imaginary," explained Bert. "It's a safety feature." He made the motions of choosing a key and inserting it into the third lock, and the companions were all surprised to hear a loud click.

"It's always the most difficult," said Bert. "You have to turn it just so."

The gas lamps came up as they entered an anteroom. Beyond was a spacious gallery, with velvet-lined walls, lush oriental carpets, and high ceilings that irised to a circular skylight. The walls were covered with paintings—portraits, John noted, that were almost life-size and large enough to step through.

"An astute observation, young John," Bert said. "Do you recognize any of the portraits?"

"Any of them?" said Charles excitedly. "I recognize them all!"

In the center of the north wall was a full-figured portrait of Geoffrey Chaucer, and slightly smaller portraits of Sir Thomas Malory and Goethe hung to the right and left of it. On the south wall, directly across from Malory's portrait, was an equally large painting of Miguel de Cervantes, flanked by portraits of Franz Schubert and Jonathan Swift. Next to Swift, the companions each noted with barely concealed surprise, was a portrait of Rudyard Kipling, appearing exactly as he had at the Flying Dragon.

Kepler was there, as were William Shakespeare and Nathaniel Hawthorne. Jack was almost as good as Charles at identifying the portraits, but John was having a harder time of it.

"I recognize Twain, and Dickens," he said to Bert, "but I'm really at a loss for several of the others."

"Surely you know Daniel Defoe"—Bert indicated an exceptional portrait set in a rather ordinary frame—"and of course Alexandre Dumas *père*.

"This is where the most important debates about the Archipelago of Dreams take place," he went on somberly, his voice hushed as the four men walked deeper into the gallery proper. "Within this room is the greatest collection of knowledge and wisdom to be found in any world."

"I thought that was the Great Whatsit, on Paralon," said Charles.

"That is a great repository of learning, yes," said Bert, "but you cannot have a discussion with a book, or debate with a parchment."

"And we're supposed to fare better talking to paintings?" Jack said as he leaned close to examine a portrait of Washington Irving.

"That may depend more on your own skills," Bert replied mysteriously, "than on the conversational skills of any particular painting.

"Gentlemen," he announced with a flourish, "I'd like you to meet your predecessors, those who have gone before you in the most important job in creation: Behold the Caretakers Emeritis of the *Imaginarium Geographica*."

"All of them?" John said in unvarnished awe.

"Mostly, yes," answered Bert. "The only ones we don't actually have here are Wace, Bacon, and Dante. We do have a picture of Geoffrey of Monmouth, but when we told him what it was for he panicked and fled, and so the portrait remains unfinished and cannot be used to bring him through."

"Bring him through what?" Jack exclaimed.

"Through to here—into Tamerlane House," said Bert with a twinkle in his eye. "Watch and learn."

Bert removed his silver pocket watch and walked to the portrait of Hans Christian Andersen, where he inserted the watch into a small, semicircular indentation at the bottom of the frame. He pressed a button on the side of the watch, and a jet of eldritch light shot around the frame. Then, as the astonished companions looked on . . .

. . . Andersen stepped out of the frame and into the gallery.

"Very nice to be out," he said, stretching his arms. "Not that I mind hanging around in here with the rest of the brethren, but in the picture, it's impossible to scratch if you get an itch."

"I imagine it is," Bert said as he inserted the watch into the next frame, and Cervantes joined them on the floor. "Don't frown so, Nathaniel," he called to the painting of Hawthorne. "I'm getting to you next."

As Bert continued the process of liberating the former Caretakers from their frames, Charles commented on the fact that several portraits were turned to the wall, and one even appeared to have been scorched in a fire.

"You already know why," Bert said in answer. "Those are portraits of Caretakers who either failed their duties badly, or betrayed them, or both."

"So, Houdini and Conan Doyle—," Jack began.

"No," Bert replied quickly, cutting him off. "Their portraits are *not* here. And we don't speak of them, not here in this house."

"If their portraits aren't here," said John, "then how is it possible that they exist past the dates of their death?"

"And the burned one?" asked Charles.

"If you get a moment, you might ask Percy Shelley about that one," said Bert. He turned to Jack. "Better yet, you should do the asking."

"What?" Jack said, confused. "I—" He stopped with a lurch. "Oh, dear Lord above," he whispered. The blood drained from his face as he pointed to one they'd overlooked. "Is that . . . ?"

On the far end of the northern wall was a portrait of James Barrie.

"As I told you, a lot has happened in seven years," said Bert, "but now you'll have a chance to catch up. Hello, Jamie."

"Greetings, Bert!" Barrie answered cheerfully. "Boys, it's good to see you again!"

"If you don't mind," a stately, bearded portrait sniffed, "I believe my seniority should dictate that I be released sooner rather than later."

"Very well, Leo," Bert said with a frown, "although technically speaking, Chaucer has seniority here."

"Leonardo da Vinci?" Jack asked behind his hand. "Didn't he steal a lot of things from Roger Bacon?"

"Practically everything." Bert sighed. "If Geoff Chaucer could have done it over again, he'd have picked Michelangelo. But we were still learning the process then, and Leo became a Caretaker instead, mostly because he was older. We've been going after younger apprentices ever since."

"We're not going to let him out, are we?" Jack whispered.

"If we don't," Bert replied, inserting his watch into the frame, "we're all going to hear about it for years."

"Rude," said da Vinci. "I can hear you, you know."

"The effort would have been wasted if you couldn't," said Bert.

In short order, centuries' worth of Caretakers had filled the gallery and were milling about, chatting, arguing, pouring drinks, and getting reacquainted with old discussions, which they were conducting in a variety of languages. John, Jack, and Charles were doing their best just to hold their own in the dialogues. It was hard enough just to keep their composure.

Bert pulled John aside. "There's one more, lad," he said with a smile and a hint of melancholy. "I thought you'd like to summon him yourself."

They stepped over to the last portrait, and John felt his breath catch in his throat. He realized, as he stood there looking at it, that it was the most obvious thing in the world to expect—but he had never even considered the possibility that his mentor, Professor Stellan Sigurdsson, would be included among the throng of Caretakers who were defying space and time to come together at Tamerlane House.

"May I use my own watch?"

Bert nodded his assent. "You may indeed."

With trembling hands, John placed the watch into the frame and watched the light race around the edges. An instant later he could smell that familiar chocolate-tobacco mixture, as his old mentor and teacher stepped down from the frame.

"Hello, my dear boy," said Professor Sigurdsson. "I am very, very happy to see you again."

They shook hands, then embraced.

"I'm . . . very happy to see you again too, Professor," John said. "Perhaps this reunion will last longer than our previous one."

"I hope so, John. I truly do."

While the professor and his understudy became reacquainted, Jack and Charles steered Bert back into the anteroom. "Bert," Jack said quietly, "I wonder if I might have a word with you about Kipling."

They had noticed only at the end, after Barrie had been liberated, that among the crowd of Caretakers were several famous personages who were not, in point of fact, official Caretakers.

"I'd wondered when that would come up," said Bert. "There are a few here in the gallery who were not official Caretakers, but who were loyal to the cause. The practice of naming three Caretakers at a time was a practice born of necessity, and so there are some from days past who were, ah, 'spares,' you might say."

"We're spares?" Charles said, faintly mortified.

"No, not at all," Bert said, comforting him. "You are a Caretaker—but there are those among us who were able to contribute in other ways, but whose, shall we say, temperaments were not well suited to the task. Oscar Wilde, for example. Or Chesterton."

"G. K. Chesterton's dead?" Jack exclaimed.

"Sorry for the surprise," said Bert mildly, "but if it helps, he's pouring a brandy over there with Kepler."

"It's one of those 'apprentice' Caretakers I want to speak to you about, Bert," said Jack. "How well do you know Kipling?"

Before his mentor could answer, Rudyard Kipling stepped around his chair and stuck his hand out in front of Jack. "The name's Kipling, my boy. A pleasure to make your acquaintance."

"Er—um—ah," Jack stammered as he shook the other fellow's hand. "Likewise."

He waved John over from where he was chatting with the professor and introduced him and Charles in turn, each of whom, with some visible reluctance, shook Kipling's hand.

"Wonderful time for a Gatherum, wouldn't you say, Bert?" Kipling said brightly, as he clapped John on the shoulder. "And it's so nice to see the new blood here too, rather than just the usual roster of fuddy-duddies."

"Pardon me, sir," said Jack politely, "but have we seen each other? Recently? In England?"

"Mmm," Kipling murmured, looking inquisitively at Jack. "I don't believe so, unless you were at my funeral, which was the last time I was in England—in which case, I was definitely preoccupied."

"Sorry, I missed it," said Jack.

"No worries, old fellow," Kipling said, smiling. He clapped Jack on the back, then Charles. "After all, that's what we have Tamerlane House for, isn't it?"

John was about to ask something else when Kipling spied another acquaintance among the group and strode away.

"I'm sorry," said Bert. "What did you mean to ask, Jack?"

"I don't think it's important right now," Jack replied. "Don't worry about it."

Bert moved into the next room, and John swiftly pulled Jack and Charles aside. "What do you think that was all about?"

"I've no idea," said Jack, "but he didn't act like a man who had just been hunting us."

"He wasn't, remember?" Charles said. "That was seven years ago."

"Does it really matter to these people?" John asked as Bert reappeared at his side. "They treat things like time, and space, and life and death as if they were playthings."

"Not playthings," said Bert, interjecting himself back into the discussion, "but certainly more flexible than the men of science would have us believe. Come along now, lads. We're about to take our places for dinner."

There were many . . . the companions knew by name and reputation . . .

Chapter Ten
The Cuckoo

Everything in Tamerlane House was evidence of two philosophies: that of excess, and that of quality. Whatever there was of any given category of object, be it china or clocks, was represented by hundreds of examples of the highest caliber. Room after room was filled to overflowing with rare and exquisite objects and items that might have been the plunder from a hundred very cultured pirates. It was, with no embellishment needed, a veritable treasure trove. But the most valued among its contents were just sitting down to what John, Jack, and Charles were certain was destined to be the most extraordinary dinner in the history of history.

The great banquet hall was lit by brass lamps hung high in the air, and had been decorated with silk tapestries that seemed to be a visual representation of every story from every culture that had ever existed, living or dead. The details were such that an entire tale, start to finish, could be depicted in a few square inches, and the stories themselves frequently overlapped.

The table was oak and ash, and fully sixty feet long and ten feet wide. It was set with flawless silver trays and crystal bowls, which promised a great feast to come.

There were many Caretakers the companions knew by name

and reputation, if not for their work, but several were entirely
unfamiliar to them by appearance. Bert gladly acted the part of
host and made sure that introductions were given all around while
the preparations were being finished for the feast.

On the left, Mark Twain and Daniel Defoe sat in deep
discussion with Nathaniel Hawthorne and Washington Irving.
Charles Dickens, Mary and Percy Shelley, and Alexandre Dumas
père sat directly across from them, arguing about some arcane
poem and the meaning of life.

Next to Dickens, on his left, sat Jakob Grimm, who was
pouring wine for Jonathan Swift and, disconcertingly, a smiling
Rudyard Kipling.

At the far end of the table were those Bert referred to as the
Elder Caretakers—which basically meant everyone who had
performed in the role prior to the seventeenth century.

Da Vinci had taken the first chair on the left, opposite Chaucer.
Next to them were Sir Thomas Malory, who was dirtier than the
companions would have imagined, and the Frenchman Chrétien
de Troyes, whom Bert said had to be kept a distance away from
Malory.

Tycho Brahe, Miguel de Cervantes, and Edmund Spenser,
the first trio of Caretakers, sat together on one side, and across
from them, ravishing the fruit plates, were William Shakespeare,
Kepler, and the philosopher Goethe. Next to him, Franz Schubert
sat with his head down, talking to no one and just twisting his
napkin into knots.

"Schubert doesn't socialize," whispered Bert. "There aren't
enough women here to suit his tastes, and confident men make
him uncomfortable."

"Are there *any* women here other than Mary Shelley?" John asked, looking up and down the table as he and his companions took seats adjacent to Mark Twain. "We certainly are a boys' club, aren't we?"

"There have been one or two considered as apprentices," Twain offered as he gestured at John with his cigar, "but Mary alone was chosen, I'm afraid."

The Feast Beasts, which were identical to the ones the Lost Boys had imagined on Haven, entered the room with silver trays laden with roasts, and dumplings, and all manner of exotic delicacies. The companions had seldom seen such a repast, and it was only then that they realized how hungry they were.

"I suppose it's been days," said Charles, "although in more practical terms you might say we haven't eaten in years."

As they ate, Jack kept a wary eye on Kipling, whom he was still certain he'd seen at the Inn of the Flying Dragon. John, for his part, was itching to know why no one had taken the chair at the head of the table. He'd come to the conclusion that it had been reserved for the Prime Caretaker, and he knew without a doubt that Jules Verne was that man.

Bert excused himself to go move Malory to a different chair. He'd been making comments about the French spices, and de Troyes was getting red in the face.

After Bert got up, John realized that there was an uneasy truce being negotiated at this end of the table as well. Professor Sigurdsson had not looked up from his plate except to ask for the gravy boat; and across from him, James Barrie was trying desperately to look in any other direction. John decided that if anyone were to break the ice, it would have to be one of the current Caretakers.

He elbowed Charles. "Say something," John hissed.

"What?" Charles hissed back. "I don't want to be stuck in the middle."

"Anything. Just get one of them talking."

"So, Jamie," said Charles jovially, "what happened to your dog? When you died, that is."

"Oh, for heaven's sake," said John.

"What?" said Charles. "You said anything."

The professor and Jamie looked at each other, then burst out laughing. When they caught their breath again, the two old colleagues regarded each other with baleful looks and held them, unblinking, until finally Jamie broke the trance and lowered his head.

"You didn't have to cross out my name," he said without looking up. "In the *Geographica*. That was quite painful to me, Stellan."

"As your choice was painful to me, Jamie," the professor noted. "Of them all, you had the most open mind. You understood the Archipelago better than any of us before or since—no offense, John," he added quickly.

"That may have been the problem, Stellan," Jamie admitted, looking up again. "I would have given myself over to it too fully. And I knew that I had to make a choice, so I did."

"If it will help, yours wasn't the only one, Jamie," said the professor. "We crossed out Houdini and Conan Doyle's names too, and one or two others as well."

"That doesn't really help, no," said Jamie.

"So what *did* happen to your dog?" asked Charles.

"The boys are taking care of him," Jamie answered. "He's in good hands."

"What?" Charles said again as he noticed Jack and John's expressions of exasperation. "I was really worried about the dog, is all."

From the front of the table, Bert signaled for silence by tapping a spoon against one of the crystal glasses. "We've supped and feasted, and had more than a few drinks," he announced with a conspiratorial wink at Percy Shelley, "among other things. And now it is time to call the Gatherum of Caretakers to order. We have business that urgently needs our attention."

He bowed to Chaucer and returned to his seat as the older man rose. "The floor is yours, Geoff."

"As Senior Caretaker," Chaucer began.

"Humph," snorted da Vinci, who then muttered a curse in Latin.

"*As Senior Caretaker,*" Chaucer repeated more solidly, "it falls to me to present the dilemma presently facing the two worlds. It is only the gravest of circumstances that require us to meet, in the flesh, to determine a course of action.

"Centuries ago, an evil man called the Winter King attempted to conquer the Archipelago by slaying his nephew Thorn, also called the Arthur, and in doing so, he nearly destroyed our world.

"Our world and the Archipelago are inseparably linked. What happens in one influences the other. And the Winter King's war in the Archipelago plunged our world into the Dark Ages."

"They weren't all *that* dark," said Malory.

"Now, Tom," said Spenser.

"After a terrible battle," Chaucer continued, "the Winter King was defeated and went into hiding, somewhere on the edges of the world. A new High King, Artigel, was crowned, and the *Imaginarium Geographica* was made available to him to help unify his rule of the Archipelago.

"The strength of Artigel and of all the High Kings who followed came from the Ring of Power, which allowed them to summon the great Dragons, who have always been the guardians of the Archipelago and all who reside within. But there was also a Prophecy that one day the Winter King would return, and bring darkness to both worlds."

"Oh, dear," said Charles.

"Shush," said Jack. "He's just getting to the interesting part."

"That's what I was afraid of," said Charles.

Chaucer went on. "The Prophecy said he could be defeated only by three scholars, men of imagination from our world. But as the years passed, the Prophecy, and the warning, was forgotten.

"Then, after centuries of hiding, the Winter King reemerged just as the Prophecy said, leading an army of terrible creatures from all the dark corners of the world. He once again sought to wreak havoc on the two worlds, and would very nearly have succeeded, had it not been for the three Caretakers of Prophecy: the successors of Bert and Stellan."

He gestured to John, Jack, and Charles, and as one the Caretakers Emeritus began a round of vigorous table thumping, punctuated by cheers, whistles, and "Well done's."

John beamed, as did Charles. Jack, however, had learned to be more cautious, and he suspected that the story was not yet finished.

"If we are the three of Prophecy," Jack said when the applause died down, "then why was it necessary to keep it a secret for so long? Especially from us? Why not tell us, before all those events had become history?"

"There are Histories, and then there are Prophecies," Professor Sigurdsson explained. "Histories tell us of what was, and are dangerous only in that they contain secrets that might be cautiously shared. Prophecies tell us of what may be, and thus are full of mysteries that may be spoiled in the sharing."

Several of the others nodded and thumped on the table in agreement.

"A History shared only expands knowledge," said Chaucer, "which may then be used for good or evil. But to share a Prophecy too soon, or in the wrong company, risks a cascade of complications that may change the Histories themselves."

John, Jack, and Charles reddened with shame, each thinking of different situations but with the same cause: Are we here to be reprimanded? Did we do too poor a job?

"Every one of us has made mistakes," Bert said, correctly reading the expressions on his friends' faces, "but that wasn't why we couldn't tell you."

"We didn't tell you," the professor continued, "because that would have compromised what was most important to your performance as Caretakers—your own point of view and natural judgment. If you knew there was a Prophecy about you, then you might start tailoring your responses to fit what you thought was supposed to happen, rather than doing what you believed in your hearts was the best course of action."

"If it helps," added Bert, "we never knew which three Caretakers would be the ones referred to in the Prophecy—not until it came to pass. We realized you were the right three, because you were the ones on the job when the Winter King reemerged."

"Excuse me," Charles said, raising his hand. "May I ask a question?"

Chaucer smiled. "No need to raise your hand, Caretaker. We are all equals here."

"Some of us are just more equal than others," said Defoe.

"Hear, hear," said da Vinci.

"I was just wondering," Charles continued, "what the point is of revealing the Prophecy to us now, when we battled the Winter King so many years ago?"

"Ah," said Chaucer. "So we get to the meat of it. Do you want to answer that, Samuel?"

"Certainly," Twain said, tapping out his cigar on a plate. "You are, of course, referring to your *first* encounter with the Winter King, are you not?"

Charles gulped. "I suppose so."

"We discovered after the crisis wherein all the children and Dragonships were taken that the King of Crickets was actually the Winter King's Shadow in disguise," said Twain, "and for his Shadow to survive, he must also still be alive."

"That constituted your second conflict with him," said Chaucer. "We believe the third is yet to come; the Prophecy speaks of three battles with the Winter King—who, despite your victories, remains our great adversary."

"But we destroyed the Shadow," said John, "or at least, Peter Pan did. And we've come to believe in recent years that our true enemy is actually Richard Burton."

"Where choosing new apprentices was concerned, I had a very shallow learning curve," Dickens said apologetically. "First Burton, then Magwich. We'd all have been better off if I'd never been chosen at all."

"That isn't so," said Kipling. "You yourself were a stellar Caretaker, and other than those two nonstarters, you've demonstrated exceptional judgment."

"Well, thank you, old fellow," Dickens replied, "but when Burton is one of our primary adversaries, I can't but regret all the training I *did* impart to him."

"Should we say anything about Kipling?" Jack whispered.

"And look like idiots?" answered John. "He's not said a foul word since we got here and hasn't so much as looked cross-eyed at any of us. If he's playing for the other side, he's hiding it well. But if he isn't, we'll have just made a new enemy in our own camp."

"On the whole," said Chaucer, "our record has been one with more victories than defeats, and we have more allies than enemies. And while our enemies are resourceful, and have much knowledge, they do not have it all. We have the Histories, and the prophecies, and the *Imaginarium Geographica*. And most vital to our cause, we also have the Grail Child. The odds are in our favor, regardless of those who chose to turn traitor."

There was more table thumping—but disturbingly, several pairs of eyes flickered toward Jamie as Chaucer spoke. Rather than ignore the glances, Jamie stood.

"I may be unique among this gathering as the only one among us who was once a full Caretaker, and then resigned," he said amidst an undercurrent of grumbles. "But I think my presence here is proof of where my loyalties lie. I have never, nor will I ever, betray our secrets to Burton or any other enemy of the Archipelago."

"That's the problem, isn't it?" asked John. "Burton feels exactly the same way. He believes he's more loyal to the Archipelago by trying to bring all its secrets to light. He truly doesn't understand what kind of havoc will be wrought."

"The Imperial Cartological Society," Dickens said darkly. "They have been a thorn in our side for too long, and Burton has seduced many of our former allies."

"Have *you* been approached, Barrie?" Kipling asked. "Has Burton tried to recruit you?"

Jamie blushed and fumbled with his buttons. "I must admit that he has tried, but not in years," he replied with a glance at the companions. "He believed I might be eager to join him because of my choice to abdicate my responsibilities, but after I explained that my reasons were not the same as his, and that I intended to keep my oaths, he left me alone. And then I died, and it became a moot point."

"Good man," said Kipling. "Would that others of our order had been as strong."

"We should be looking to Jakob," Hawthorne said brusquely. "After all, his own brother was a washout as a Caretaker, and we know he's already sworn allegiance to Burton."

"That's a lie!" Jakob Grimm shouted, standing and placing his fists on the table. "He would not betray us, and never would he betray me!"

"What about Alexandre Dumas *fils*?" asked Defoe. "He made quite a show of leaving us, and was quite loud about his intentions to betray us all."

"Forgive me," Alexandre Dumas *père* said, "and my son. I hope that he would not have sold us out to Burton and his ilk, but I cannot say with certainty."

"And would you betray us, for his sake, if he had?" Kipling asked.

"Never."

"I'd be willing to give you both the benefit of the doubt, Jakob, Alexandre," said Dickens. "I've been through similar situations myself, and I know how your loyalties have been tested."

"Ah, yes," said Charles. "Maggot."

"Pardon?" said Dickens.

"He means Magwich," Jack corrected. "We've had more than our share of difficulties with him."

"I'm very sorry about that," Dickens said. "It was an awful judgment call on my part to bring him in the first place. He was a very strange sort of fellow, but he had a good core—or so I believed."

"It's well and truly rotten now," said Charles. "He betrayed us once to the Winter King, and I have no doubt that he would do so again."

"I think he should be flogged," said Shakespeare. "Posthaste. That will teach him the error of his ways, I think." He looked around at the others, beaming, as if he'd just solved the world's problems with a single remark—then deflated a little when he realized that no one was paying attention.

"Magwich has already been made the Green Knight," Bert said mildly. "He's paying his dues."

"That's just it," said Charles. "He isn't. The Green Knight isn't on Avalon."

There was a chorus of disbelieving remarks and more than a little grumbling at that.

"Charles," Chaucer said skeptically, "the Green Knight cannot leave Avalon. It's a binding of the Old Magic. Only the Dragons themselves might break such a binding, and they would hardly be inclined, since it was they who bound him in the first place."

"What if he's just faded into dust?" suggested Jack. "That's what happened to his predecessor, isn't it?"

"Charles Darnay had fulfilled his calling and was therefore released," said Dickens. "Do you really think Magwich has fulfilled *anything?*"

"You make a good point," said Jack. "He did prove helpful once, uh, in his own fashion. I don't know that I'd say he could be trusted, but I'd begun to think better of him."

"Extending trust to those who have already proven themselves untrustworthy," Twain remarked, "is a bit like cutting off the end of a rope and sewing it to the other end to make it longer."

John explained briefly the circumstances that had resulted in their arrival in the Nameless Isles, omitting only their suspicion of Kipling as an ally of their still unknown adversary.

"So Quixote is here?" Spenser said with a joyous expression. "My old partner! I would love to see him!"

"I'll pass, if it's all the same to you," Tycho Brahe muttered. "I'm sure he feels the same."

"It's all right," said Cervantes. "The past is the past—I'm sure he's forgiven you by now."

"I would hope so," said Brahe. "If you can't get some leniency after you've died, when can you get it?"

"Hank told us what had happened," said Twain, "and Ransom filled in the holes after. So we knew that seven years hence, you'd try to make your way here."

"That was the plan," said John. "It was a risk to use Ransom's Trump, but we felt that once we had removed Rose from danger and had moved past Verne's zero points, we'd have a better chance of preventing the war."

"Prevent the war?" a quiet voice said. It was Franz Schubert— and it was the first words he had spoken all evening. "Prevent? I'm sure I misunderstand you, young man. You cannot prevent something that has already begun."

"Already begun!" John exclaimed. "You can't be serious!"

One look at Bert's face confirmed that it was true. "The war in the Summer Country has been raging for four years now," the old traveler said, "exactly the same length of time we've been preparing for it here, although they may have fared the worse for it, since our war in the Archipelago has not yet begun."

"But I thought taking Rose away from danger was supposed to stop the war from happening!"

"Stop? No," said Chaucer. "Protecting the Grail Child was of the highest priority, and we are all grateful for your wisdom and diligence in doing so. But her survival was never meant to stop the wars—our adversary was going to see those begun regardless of the safeguards we put into place.

"Her survival was important, because it was the only way to ensure that the wars would *end*."

Chaucer signaled to one of the ravens, who flew across the room and removed a book from a nearby bookcase. The raven laid it on the table and snuck a grape from one of the platters before it flew off again.

The book was roughly the size and shape of one of the Histories. The covers and binding were steel gray leather, and the pages themselves were so white as to appear cold. For leather and parchment to be so bereft of color, the book had to be ancient. More ancient than anything else the Caretakers had ever seen.

In contrast to the *Geographica*, which bore the Greek letter *alpha* on the cover, this book was embossed with an *omega*—the same letter Bert used as his personal emblem.

"This is the only book more dangerous than the *Imaginarium Geographica*," he said, his voice heavy with responsibility. "It is filled with notations, and formulas, and stories, and even maps. But it is also as close a record as a book can be to a History of the Dragons. It has notes on the first time any dragon has ever appeared in any land, and it lists every one of their True Names. But even more importantly, it contains the prophecies that may yet save the Archipelago.

"In the past, it has been called the *Telos Biblos*, according to the Greek. We simply refer to it as the Last Book. It is one of a set of books—we don't know how many. It was obtained only through great sacrifice, and it is the reason why we have come together today."

"It was taken from the library of the first Caretaker to go rogue," Chaucer continued. "John Dee. Very little is known about him save for rumors and whisperings, but we know that he recorded the True Names of the dragons—and he also planted the seeds for the Imperial Cartological Society, which blossomed under Burton.

"Because of this book, we know many of our enemies who

were once friends. Milton. Kit Marlowe. De Bergerac. William Blake. Coleridge. Lord Byron."

"I almost took him out of the game," Percy Shelley commented, "if Mary hadn't thrown the portrait into the tide pool to put out the flames."

"What separates us from them is our belief in order," Bert said sternly. "George Gordon, Lord Byron, was a Caretaker, and his portrait still hangs here, albeit turned over. He'll never participate in a Gatherum, but he'll not aid the enemy, either."

"I knew Kit Marlowe," put in Shakespeare. "He was quite a fair writer—for a traitor, that is."

"The Last Book has remained here in the care of the Prime Caretaker for many years," said Chaucer, "and through it we have learned many things about time, and space, and our own Histories. We also know that our adversaries have gleaned enough knowledge from this, and other books like it, to develop their own methods of moving in time and space, and that makes them more dangerous than ever.

"Because of this book, we know that there is going to be one last great conflict with the Winter King, but not what guise he will take. It may be his Shadow in disguise again, or Mordred himself risen from the endless deep, or both. We know that the three current Caretakers are the key to defeating him. And we know that he has acquired a terrible weapon with which to defeat us."

"How does Rose figure into this?" asked John. "Why was she so important that she was to be killed? And how does her being here now help our cause?"

"Verne can answer you more fully as to the destiny we suspect is ahead of the girl," Edmund Spenser said, leaning over the table to better be heard. "But what little we do know also comes from the Prophecy."

Chaucer turned to a page near the front of the Last Book and scanned it until he found the passage he wanted. "It said that in the final conflict with the King of Shadows, three scholars from the Summer Country will stand united against him. An ageless knight will deliver to them the means to defeat the Shadow King, which will be wielded by a daughter of the Houses of Troy and Aramathea. Rose Dyson, the Grail Child, is the only person in all of history who has that specific heritage. And we believe that she is the key to his final defeat."

"Dear God," said Charles.

"It's a lot to take in, isn't it?" asked Twain.

"That's why we've taken the steps we have," said Bert. "We needed to make sure you were here, now, under the right circumstances, to see that Prophecy fulfilled."

"I think I need a drink," said Jack. "Or five."

"We should adjourn for brandy and a bit of air," suggested Irving. "We've been at this so long it might be a good time for a break." He looked at his watch and frowned. "Drat. I think my watch is running a bit fast. What time do you have, Rudyard?"

Kipling blanched. "I'm not sure," he said, craning his neck. "Do we have a clock in here, Bert?"

"Just check your watch," said Irving. "You *do* have a watch, don't you?"

Kipling went pale. "I, uh, I seem to have left it elsewhere," he said with a weak laugh. "Sorry—no watch."

The room went still.

"A Caretaker is never without his watch," Spenser said coolly. "Where is yours, Kipling?"

In response, Kipling turned out his pockets like a circus clown and grinned sheepishly—then shoved Irving off his chair and leaped onto the table.

"Hell's bells!" Twain exclaimed. "What the devil are you doing, Rudyard?"

Kipling ignored the question and the shouts of the others and instead threw over the candles on the table. Then, amidst the confusion, he bolted from the room.

"Someone stop him!" Irving shouted. "He's heading for the gallery!"

Jack was closest to the doors, and the most able-bodied of the Caretakers—or so he thought. He had exited the room and was racing after Kipling when Jakob Grimm passed him by.

Kipling wheeled about and pushed open the doors to the gallery anteroom, then threw them shut just as Jakob caught up to him. Jakob was struggling with the doors as Jack and then the rest of the Caretakers ran down the corridor.

"He's locked it!" Jakob exclaimed. "I can't get it open!"

"Stand back," said Hawthorne. He took the measure of the doors, and then smashed into them with a powerful, well-placed kick. They didn't budge.

"You thought one kick would do it?" asked Jack.

"Well, I *am* Nathaniel Hawthorne," he answered, gesturing to the others. "All together now!"

Hawthorne, Jack, Irving, and Jakob threw themselves against the doors, which cracked open in a shower of splintered wood.

"There!" said Jack. "He's going back inside the painting!"

At first glance, that seemed to be precisely what Kipling was doing—until the Caretakers rushed forward to capture their colleague and suddenly realized that the portrait of Kipling . . .

. . . was *shrinking*.

"What kind of enchantment is this?" Irving declared.

Whatever was happening, it was too late to catch the Caretaker-gone-wild. The image was the size of a playing card now, and there was no way to reverse or halt the process. In seconds the image would disappear completely.

"Be seeing you," Kipling said with a wink. And then he was gone.

CHAPTER ELEVEN
The Master

"*It wasn't a portrait* at all!" John exclaimed. "It was a Trump, just like the ones Hank and Ransom use!"

"You're right, young man," Twain said, examining the painting. "A rather ingenious ploy—creating a Trump that opens on top of a painting of the same image."

"He must have used a similar one to come into the gallery," said Jamie, "and merely pretended he was being summoned from his portrait as the rest of us were."

Bert moved over to the painting and tapped on it lightly with his fingertips. "No," he said. "This was an actual portrait done with Pygmalion resins, as all the rest have been. He only needed a means of escape that we couldn't easily duplicate."

"Can we follow him?" asked John. "Through the painting?"

Bert grimaced and shook his head. "They're meant to be one way, and they don't actually go to a place," he said resignedly. "When the Caretakers go back, they aren't somewhere—they're just in a painting."

"He's going to report to his masters," Jakob cried. "We've got to do something! He must be stopped!"

"I left the doors to the gallery unlocked," said Bert. "How was

"The place you're seeking . . . isn't there."

it that Kipling locked them so quickly, since I have the only three keys, and one of *those* is imaginary?"

"I don't know," Jakob said. "He closed them behind him, and as I caught up, I found I couldn't get them open. But believe me, I was pushing as hard as I could."

Defoe stood behind Jakob and closed his hands into fists. "Perhaps we have another turncoat in our midst," he said with obvious menace in his tone. "Where's *your* watch, Jakob?"

With a few fumbles born of fear and haste, Jakob rummaged around in his pockets and finally, with a great sigh of relief, produced his watch.

"You're good, then," Defoe said. "I'm sorry I doubted you, Brother Grimm."

"Thanks," said Jakob, still visibly shaken. "I'm sorry about the doors. Wilhelm would have been smart enough to do it the right way."

"So Kipling knows all our secrets," said Defoe.

"Not all of them," Bert said in admonishment. "He was only a part of the whole. We have the books, and we have the three Caretakers of Prophecy. They will see this through, regardless of Kipling's betrayal."

"This may be the worst possible time to bring this up," said John, "but we had already suspected Kipling was a traitor. We just didn't tell anyone."

Quickly he related the rest of the details about their flight from the Inn of the Flying Dragon, and the fact that Jack believed Kipling had been leading their pursuers.

"Why didn't you tell us this before?" asked Hawthorne. "We might have found him out all the sooner."

"He didn't tell," Twain said, lighting up a fresh cigar, "because he is not an ass, and neither are his two compatriots. They came here today and have listened to a great many impossible things without blinking. But they also saw us turning on our own like a pack of hungry dogs.

"We questioned Charles Dickens' loyalty because two of those he trained turned out to be traitors themselves—never mind the fact that he also trained our Prime Caretaker. We questioned Alexandre Dumas, not for what he chose to do, but because of the choices of his son. And we were one minute away from lynching poor Jakob because we know his brother to be allied with Burton, and he couldn't produce his watch quickly enough.

"No," Twain said with finality. "Young John did exactly the right thing. He watched, and waited, and when it was time to act, he used his best judgment. And that's all anyone can ask of a Caretaker."

"Thank you, Mr. Clemens," said John.

"You don't have to thank me, boy," said Twain as he stepped out into the corridor, puffing on his cigar. "I'm deceased, remember? At this point, I'm just here for the entertainment."

"I am sorry," Jakob said again. "Not just for myself, but for . . . for my brother."

"He made his own choices," said Bert, "but of the two of you, we got the better man. Come," he called to the others, gesturing broadly. "Let us retire to the conservatory for drinks and more discussion. Our schedule has just taken an unexpected leap forward."

The conservatory was in the very center of Tamerlane House, and the ceiling inside the room rose to an impossible height.

It had to be ten stories high and was capped by a glittering, translucent dome.

Windows rose along two sides, above a second-floor landing and stairway, with massive tapestries hanging in between. Below were a walk-in fireplace and several shelves lined with busts and sculptures amid a number of chairs, which surrounded a long table much like the one in the dining room. As before, John noted that none of the Caretakers took the seat at the head of the table.

"There's nothing outside that's this tall," John said wonderingly as he looked up at the dome. "Have we gone down somehow, below ground?"

"Oh, no," said Bert. "The earth here is impossibly hard. Just putting in a basement was a trial and a tribulation. This room was built specifically to house the tapestries"—he pointed at the explosions of color that were draped on the walls—"but Marco Polo had underestimated their size when we acquired them from him, and we had a dilemma. So we installed a tesseract, and that's made all the difference. Isn't the dome lovely?"

"Nice, very nice," said Charles. "Egyptian?"

"Hittite," said Bert. "But you were close."

Once drinks were poured and all of them had again settled down from the commotion Kipling had caused, Bert called for silence, and Chaucer stood to address them.

"It has been many years since one of our number has turned," he began, "but we must press forward. Kipling's betrayal changes nothing."

"Perhaps he should be flogged," put in Shakespeare.

"Changes nothing?" Hawthorne exclaimed. "He knows about the girl!"

"They already knew about Rose," Twain corrected. "What they didn't know was that there were other players in the game. They didn't know that John, Jack, and Charles are to play a key role in the final defeat of the Winter King. And they didn't know that Quixote would deliver the weapon of his downfall. So in my opinion, our mission has not changed—we must protect the girl. She is the endgame."

"They may not have known all those things," said Charles, "but we've given them something else: We've confirmed that we know who our adversary is. The Prophecy itself has confirmed it. In some form, we will be facing the Winter King."

"And now that they know we know," said Jack, "he will be making his move."

"I concur," said John. "The war in the Archipelago begins right now."

"I think, given this turn of events," Chaucer said, "we should bring in the Grail Child and her guardian. We need to have all the players on the board, and we all need to know what everyone else knows."

Bert signaled to the ravens, and they flew out of the conservatory, returning a few minutes later with Rose, Quixote, and Archimedes in tow.

It took most of an hour to make introductions. Rose was unusually timid, but polite. Quixote was typically formal in his greetings, except when he got to Edmund Spenser. The two men gripped each other's forearms and laughed. It was a reunion of true friends and colleagues.

"It has been far too long, you old Riddle Master," said Spenser. "How are you?"

"Riddle Master?" answered Quixote. "Pish-tosh. Without your detective skills, the Sphinx would have defeated me."

"Hello, Quixote," said Cervantes.

"Miguel!" Quixote said, shaking his hand. "How goes the new book?"

"I'm almost finished," Cervantes told him.

"Which new book is that?" John whispered to Bert.

"It doesn't really matter," Bert replied. "He always says he's almost finished."

When Quixote came to Tycho Brahe, the best they could manage were polite, if curt, nods at each other. Room was made for Quixote to sit next to Spenser, and Rose went to sit between Jack and Charles. A raven flew in and placed a glass of milk in front of her.

"Thank you, Warren," she said.

"Welcome, miss," said the bird, bowing its head.

They began by having Quixote relate the tale of the cave on Avalon, and what the Lady Guinevere had said to him regarding their enemies.

"She said a great weapon was being brought to bear against the forces of the light," he said somberly, "and that we would need a weapon of equal power to combat it. I asked where such a weapon could be found, and in reply she said to seek the Lady, that she may return what was given."

"The Lady of the Lake," said Malory. "She cannot be summoned on a whim."

"Ah," said Quixote, "that point of fact is exactly the reason I believe I am to play a role in this matter, and why the Frenchman believed I was the knight of the Prophecy.

"Many years ago I was called upon to perform a service for the Caretakers."

"And a job well done," said Cervantes. "You traveled to the Summer Country and to the edges of the Archipelago itself, and you brought back the *Geographica*."

"Indeed," said Quixote, "but what none of you knew, save for my partner Edmund, was that in the course of events I performed a service for the Lady of the Lake. And to this day, she owes me a boon."

"This wasn't in any of the Histories," Irving said with an irritated glance at Spenser. "Where was it chronicled, Caretaker?"

"It's in one of the appendices," replied Spenser, "under the title 'The Thin Man and the Queen of Stars.'"

"Ah," said Irving. "Your pardon, Edmund."

"If you are able to summon the lady," said Chaucer, "what weapon do you believe she will give you?"

"'Return what was given,'" Jack said suddenly. "That can only mean one weapon. We saw it given to her ourselves, John."

"That's right," said John. "It's in one of the, ah, less accurate chronicles written by Geoffrey of Monmouth. After the first battle with Mordred in Camelot, when we brought Rose to restore Arthur's life, he called on the Lady of the Lake—his mother—and gave the shattered pieces of his sword to her.

"The weapon we need to defeat the Winter King is the weapon he wanted for himself," John finished, now visibly excited. "It's the sword of Aeneas! It's Caliburn!"

"I concur," Chaucer said, after all the murmuring and table thumping that had followed John's statement had died down.

"That *must* be the weapon mentioned in the Prophecy. But that still leaves us with many unknown pieces on the board. Even if Quixote should succeed in obtaining Caliburn from the Lady, it must still be repaired—and there is no one living who knows how it was forged."

"The Cartographer," said John. "It may be worth consulting him."

"A possibility," allowed Chaucer. "A better one may be the Ancient of Days—the shipbuilder Ordo Maas. He has knowledge of techniques long lost to the rest of the two worlds. He might be willing to help."

"And then what?" said John. "We wait for our adversary to make his plays and then respond in kind? You said the war had not yet begun in the Archipelago, while it's been raging along in the Summer Country. What if he's there already? What if he's planning on turning it into the Winterland first—and then returning here?"

"He hasn't been in the real world," Bert said. "We'd have known, or seen some aspect of his movements there. But we've seen nothing."

"He has to be operating somewhere," said Jack. "Burton and the others of the Imperial Cartological Society are operating in both worlds—why can't he?"

"You've hit the problem on the head, boy," said Twain. "They must have a base of operations, but we just haven't been able to locate it. And believe me," he added, tapping out his cigar, "we've looked. In *both* worlds."

"It isn't there," a soft, slight voice said from somewhere above them. "The place you're seeking—it isn't there."

As one, the assembly looked up to the figure standing at the railing above and gasped in unison.

It was the master of the house.

He stood to the right side of the landing, which was still steeped in shadows. His smallish frame seemed to implode upon itself as he stood there, moving his hands nervously, trying to decide what to do with them. His eyes glittered from under a deep brow and his hair was strewn about as if he'd just risen from a long nap.

He finally gripped the railing to steady himself, then repeated the words he'd spoken: "The place you're seeking isn't there."

Edgar Allan Poe quietly descended the staircase and moved around the table to take his place at the head—a place John had assumed was reserved for Jules Verne.

"Is Poe the Prime Caretaker?" he whispered.

"You've already guessed that Verne has that title," Bert whispered back, "but we can discuss that another time. Poe is something else altogether. He may have a mild manner and bearing, but believe you me—he functions on an entirely different level from the rest of us."

The regard the Caretakers Emeritis held for Poe was evident in their treatment of him. Not a one among them stirred or spoke. The slight man sat and moved some stray strands of hair out of his eyes; then he leaned back, clasping his hands together.

"One of the reasons I shared my discovery of the Soft Places," he began, "is because they are not just places of sanctuary, but may also be used as beachheads against us in the war. We have sent our agents out among the myriad dimensions not only to act as our messengers, but to serve as our spies. The enemy's refuge must be somewhere."

"But most of the Crossroads end at taverns or inns," said Jamie. "Even accounting for a portion of the lands around them, they just aren't large enough. It would have to be a hidden village, like Brigadoon."

"Brigadoon is simply a story from the Encyclopedia Mythica," Poe said, "but in principle, you are correct. There must be a township, or a village, or an island somewhere among the Soft Places large enough to contain the armies of the Winter King and his allies. If we are to gain an advantage, we must find that place."

"Whom do we have out?" Chaucer asked.

"Hank Morgan, Alvin Ransom, and the Rappaccini girl," said Twain. "And Dr. Raven. You know what happened to Arthur Pym."

"Yes," said Poe. "Most unfortunate."

"They should be reporting in soon," said Twain. "I've sent them messages via the Trumps, and their information may prove very useful, especially now that all the major players are here."

"I agree," said Poe. "We shall adjourn for the evening, to rest and recharge, so that we are prepared for what is to come."

The Caretakers all stood up from the table with Poe and moved to various parts of the house to commiserate in small groups. Quixote sat with Spenser, Cervantes, and Brahe by the great fireplace, and in one of the anterooms, Defoe and Swift were showing Rose how to make treasure maps. "You see," Defoe explained as he drew on a sheet of parchment, "you make any shape that seems right. Then you use the names of anyone around you to name the geographical details, like marshes, and rivers, and mountains. And then you make an *X* where you want the treasure to be. And I promise you, if you find an island that matches the map, you'll also find the treasure."

"Or you'll be shot by tiny people with tiny arrows," said Swift. "And you don't want to know about the talking horses."

"I swear, I thought they were centaurs," protested Defoe.

"Daniel, Jonathan," Twain said in warning. "Watch your tongues when there's a lady present."

"Sorry," Defoe and Swift said together.

Professor Sigurdsson was fascinated by Archimedes and retreated with the owl to the library for a game of chess before John could pull him aside.

He had wanted to speak to the professor at length, but Bert tugged on his arm before he could follow them. "There'll be plenty of time to speak to Stellan later," Bert said. "The master of the house would like a private audience with the three of you upstairs in his quarters."

"Poe wants to talk to us?" Charles exclaimed. "Wonderful!"

"Just be careful," Bert cautioned as they ascended the stairs. "He is most trusted, but he is very eccentric. He doesn't always make sense—not at first, anyway. But he is always worth listening to, and he is responsible for everything we have. Even Jules defers to him."

"Lead on, MacDuff," said Jack.

"That bird is a bad influence," Bert said. "On *all* of you."

Four flights up, Poe's own space in Tamerlane House was a room barely sixty feet square. In one corner was a shabby little camp bed, under which a pair of shoes were neatly placed. In the opposite corner were a writing desk and a simple tallow candle. There was no other furniture, or indeed, decoration of any kind in the room. It was the one place in that entire exceptionally colorful house that seemed to have had the color leached from it. John thought it was the most melancholy room he'd ever seen.

Poe was sitting at the desk, writing.

"What do you think of utopias?" he asked without turning around.

"I'm for them, myself," said Charles.

"It would depend," said Jack. "I worry that we'd grow stagnant as a civilization if we truly lived in a utopia."

"Your mentor, Master Wells, had the same worry," said Poe. He turned around and looked at John, his eyes huge in the dim light of the candle. "Do you know what kind of problem I have with utopias?"

John blinked. "I'm sure I have no idea," he said.

"Pistachio nuts," Poe said. "None of them mention pistachio nuts. I love them myself—but they seem to get left out of all of the perfect societies. Would you like a pistachio nut?"

Without waiting for an answer, he held out his hand and dropped a nut into each of the companions' hands. He popped one into his mouth and crunched on it, so the others did the same.

"Follow me," Poe said, rising from the chair, still chewing. "I'd like to show you something."

He led John, Jack, Charles, and Bert down a long hallway that became taller and narrower as they went. Near the end, they found they had to turn sideways just to squeeze through.

"You all right, Jack?" asked John.

"Yes," Jack grunted. "Just regretting eating so many of Mrs. Moore's meat pies."

At the end of the hall was a wide atelier lit by a massive chandelier, and at the far side of the room, near a window, sat a man, painting.

"Basil Hallward, our resident artist," Poe said in introduction. "Oscar Wilde discovered the young man at Magdalen and found he had a remarkable gift for portraiture. We brought him here and commissioned him to create the portraits of past Caretakers."

Hallward glanced over at the companions and nodded distractedly, then did an abrupt double take. He jumped to his feet and threw a sheet over the canvas in progress.

"I say," Charles remarked, "were you by chance painting a portrait of *me?*"

Hallward choked, then looked to Poe, who calmly returned the artist's gaze before looking up at Charles.

"Ransom," Poe said simply. "He was painting Alvin Ransom."

"You do look quite similar, Charles," said Jack.

"My word," Charles exclaimed. "I hope nothing's happened to the poor fellow."

"Oh, no, not at all," Poe answered. "It's just a precaution. What's useful for us Caretakers is also useful for our apprentices."

Hallward nodded. "Useful, yeah. Useful."

"I agree," a voice said behind them. It was Defoe. "Nothing like having someone handy who can—literally—paint the illusion of life," he said cheerfully.

Poe looked askance at Hallward. "You've painted pictures for some of the others?"

"I've considered availing myself of his services once or twice," Defoe said, smirking.

"Now, Daniel," said Bert, wagging a finger in warning, "we've cautioned you about that before. Caretakers only. It's too dangerous to have others hanging around the gallery who might overhear our secrets without the oath of secrecy to bind them.

"And you," he finished, pointing at Hallward. "No freelancing."

"Yes, sir," the painter said, chagrined.

"Caretakers only?" Jack whispered to Charles. "But didn't he just say that Hallward was completing a painting of Ransom?"

"Poe said apprentices, too," Charles reminded him.

"May I have a word?" Defoe said to Poe. "I'd like to discuss the Kipling situation."

"Don't worry," said Bert. "I'll see the lads to their rooms."

He led the companions back out of the atelier and closed the door. "Defoe and Kipling were close," he explained. "This has got to be quite a blow for him."

"For us all," said Jack. "I just wish we'd said something earlier."

"Not everything can be forecast," said Bert. "Not even the things we already know will happen."

"Isn't it risky that so many future events are known and being acted on?" asked Jack. "Won't that disrupt the future—or worse, corrupt the prophecies?"

"Jules and I decided some time ago to view everything as being the past," said Bert. "That's one advantage of having lived eight hundred thousand years in the future. If I view it all as history, then all we're doing is trying to shape the best history possible. Sometimes that means keeping information, such as the prophecies, a secret. And other times it means sharing as much information as possible about the immediate future so that the right preparations can be made."

"Or so that you can pinch books of American presidential quotations from thirty years hence, so you can sound erudite and wise," John said, winking.

"Will you let that go?" said Bert irritably. "I tell you, if Milton had heard Kennedy speak, he'd have swiped it himself."

"What do you mean by 'immediate future'?" asked Charles.

"No more than a century or two," said Bert, "but that's one of the reasons we do use the knowledge. My own chronicle warned of that."

"*The Shape of Things to Come*," said John. "I read it, but it came out in the thirties and was written by *our* Wells, wasn't it?"

"Yes," said Bert. "It was based on my own version, but with two major differences. While both predicted World War II, and both saw it as lasting for two decades and ending with a plague that nearly destroys the world, his ends with an eventual utopian society, and mine does not."

"What's the other difference?"

"His was fiction," said Bert, "and mine is not; it is occurring as we speak."

"So the Winter King is trying to create the Winterland," said Jack.

"That's why we hoped to start our countermeasures in 1943," said Bert. "I fear he already *has*."

Chapter Twelve
The Adversary

The night passed quickly, and when the Caretakers all gathered again in the conservatory for breakfast, the sun was still low on the horizon.

"The Caretakers keep Oxford hours, it seems," Jack said, yawning. "Early to bed, early to rise. I can't believe we're the last ones awake."

"I don't think they have to sleep when they're in the paintings," said Charles. "Or if they do, it's not because of exhaustion."

"Maybe we'll be paintings here someday," said John. "Won't that be a nice thing to look forward to in our old age? The chance to do it all again?"

Jack started to respond, but Charles scowled and walked away, waving a hand in greeting at some of the other Caretakers.

"What's gotten under his hat?" said John.

"I think he's just worried," Jack replied. "There's a lot to process, even for someone of Charles's perception."

The Feast Beasts had once again served an extraordinary repast. Fresh fruit, of varieties both identified and not; vegetables of unusual shapes and colors, which nevertheless exuded fantastically saliva-inducing aromas; eggs Benedict; milk from eight kinds of cows, three kinds of goats, and one more animal—the pitcher

Three . . . glided close, then landed smoothly on the deck.

of which no one would touch. There were green eggs and ham, hashed brown potatoes, and country-style omelets.

"I'm normally as carnivorous as the next man," Jack said to Bert, "but we have lots of friends here in the Archipelago who are talking animals, and there are at least three dishes on the table featuring ham. It's making me a little uncomfortable."

"Worry not," Bert said as he sat at the table and tucked a napkin into his collar. "For one thing, there are certain dishes, such as my beloved eggs Benedict, that just aren't the same without meat. And for another thing, it's no one you know."

"Very comforting," said Jack.

The Caretakers were just finishing up the breakfast feast when Charles, Jack, and John pulled Bert into the corridor for a word in private.

"I hesitate to bring this up too loudly," Charles said, looking around almost guiltily, "but you'll understand, considering the reaction everyone had when Kipling couldn't produce a pocket watch."

Bert grinned. "You're worried because you and Jack don't have watches."

"Precisely."

"Understandable, my boy, totally understandable," said Bert. "But you needn't have worried. For one thing, you are current Caretakers. If we didn't trust you, you would not have kept the job this long, especially given some of the, ah, hiccups of your tenure.

"For another, we believe you three to be the scholars mentioned in the Prophecy. No amount of precaution would prepare us if you chose to cross over to the other side.

"And lastly, it wasn't until after 1936 that we realized we had to discover some way to identify our own agents—and we'd already used the watches to do so in a limited capacity. So in short, the reason you don't have watches yet is because you disappeared for seven years, and we hadn't had the chance to give them to you yet."

"Whew," said Charles. "I'm very relieved."

"So am I," said Jack. "Everyone here seems fairly civilized, but for an instant I flashed on the distressing notion that I might have to go toe to toe with Hawthorne."

Bert led the three companions up a winding flight of stairs to a hallway that was so cramped and tiny that they had to crouch to make their way down to the door at the end, which was even smaller.

"Is this where the watches are made?" asked John. "The Watchmaker must be a very compact fellow."

"This is just our storeroom," Bert replied as he knelt on the floor. "The Watchmaker is a very secretive creature. Verne has met him more often than I, and the only other thing I know about him is that he's an old friend of Samaranth."

"So he's a Dragon?" asked Jack.

"I asked the same question," said Bert, "and all he would say was that he had declined the promotion."

"What are you doing down there?" said Charles. "I don't think we can even get through that door."

"It's a voice-released lock," Bert explained, leaning low to the small wooden door. "Who knows what evil lurks in the hearts of men?" he said in a baritone voice. A pause. Then he added, "The Shadow knows!"

There was a click, and then the wall—not the door, but the entire wall—swung open into a stone-lined room.

"The Shadow knows?" said John.

"I got the idea from some radio dramas I gave to the Cartographer," said Bert. "It's a safety feature."

Inside, the walls were lined with small drawers and shelves laden with silver watches.

"Many of them resemble my own," Bert said, "but it was an earlier model. Most of the rest look very similar to yours, John."

"I'd like one of those, if I may," said Jack.

"And I'd like to have one like yours, Bert," said Charles. "If you don't mind, that is."

Bert selected two of the watches and handed them to the Caretakers. "Remember," he said as he placed the watches in their open hands, "Believing is seeing."

"Believe," John, Jack, and Charles said together.

"Don't go yet," Bert said quickly. "I have something else for you." He handed each of the companions another watch.

"Spares?" asked John. "In case we lose the first one?"

"No," Charles said, understanding. "These are for our own apprentices, aren't they?"

"Exactly," said Bert. "There may be a time when you will want to know, without doubt, that someone will be there to come to your aid—as I have always counted on you. You'll choose your apprentices when you give them the watch.

"But be very careful about whom you choose to give them to," he continued. "They are the only means of telling whether or not someone is a true emissary or apprentice of the Caretakers. They cannot be duplicated and cannot be bought or sold—only earned.

If they are stolen, they will crumble into dust. If they are sold, they will crumble into dust. If they are used for evil purposes, they will crumble into dust. But if they are cared for, and used properly, they have the potential to become much, much more, as the wearer earns the right to learn of their powers.

"But if nothing else, value them for being what they are—a symbol that the wearer belongs to the most honored and honorable gathering of men and women who have ever drawn breath.

"So," he said in conclusion, "choose wisely, and choose well, whom you give them to. Your very life may depend on it."

"So if Kipling is in league with Burton," John said as they returned to the conservatory, "his watch probably crumbled to dust."

Bert nodded. "That was all the evidence we needed that the wrong choices were being made, and we had a cuckoo in our midst."

As they approached the conservatory, they could hear the noises of a heated discussion taking place. Quickening their pace, they rushed into the room and found that a new arrival had come to Tamerlane House.

"Ransom!" Jack exclaimed. "It's very good to see you!"

"You made it!" said Ransom with obvious relief. "When I lost the Yoricks, I tried jumping back to this time, but it took a few tries to nail the date. It's all been a botch of things from start to finish."

"We're just happy to see that you made it away in one piece," said Charles.

"Yes, yes," Ransom said distractedly. "It's good to see you alive and well too, all of you. I'm sorry if I'm a bit brusque, but something terrible has happened. I have to show you, right now."

"Whatever you need," said Chaucer, gesturing broadly. "Please."

Ransom cleared a space on the table and hefted a small case onto it. He popped open the twin latches on top and spread it open to reveal a curious device. It had coils and lenses, and two sets of frames that held slides in front of a turntable.

"It's called a Hobbes stereopticon," Bert explained as Ransom assembled the machine. "You can use a lens built into the side of the case to record events, and then it replays them for you later."

"A camera *and* a projector," said Jack. "Very nice."

"Better than that," said Bert. "It projects images and sound in three dimensions, and you can walk through them to observe a scene from every angle."

"Do you have somewhere I can plug this in?" Ransom said, holding up the cord. "I used up the batteries making the recording."

Jakob Grimm took the cord from Ransom and scrambled under one of the tables, searching for an outlet. "Got it," he called after a moment. "Give it a go, Ransom."

The philologist flipped a switch on the back of the stereopticon, and suddenly an incredible light show blazed to life. As Bert had said, the projection was displayed in all three spatial dimensions, filling the room. It was the coastline of a massive island, reduced to the size of a play set—except the tin soldiers were real, as was the battle they were witnessing.

Because the projector was on the table, the ground level of the film was at the Caretakers' waist level. And so, as they walked around examining the scene, they looked like leviathans wading through the channel.

There was a great deal of destruction evident past the coastline. Fires raged, and in the distance, they could see buildings being toppled. According to Ransom, it got worse.

"The island is called Kor," he said, looking back at John. "Do you know it?"

"It's one of the oldest and largest in the Archipelago," John said. "But what would cause all this destruction?"

"This is a declaration of war," stated Ransom. "And a message to us all. If Kor can fall so easily, then it bodes ill for the rest of us. But there is something else."

He pointed to several small objects on the surface of the water that disappeared as they watched. "Seven ships," he said grimly. "Seven ships—and an army comprised of children—caused all this damage."

"This is not an event in the future history," said Twain, "but a continuation from one *past*."

"Agreed," said Bert. "This *must* be the Winter King."

"Were those ships what they appeared to be?" John asked with a rising feeling of dread. "Surely they couldn't be. Not here. Not *now*!"

"The Dragonships lost in time," said Jack. "From the Underneath, in 1926."

Ransom grimaced. "I can't say for certain, but I believe so. And I think he's put them to use in places other than in the Archipelago."

"Then why wait so long to begin the war here?" asked Jack. "The Summer Country has been at war for years—what was he waiting for?"

"He hasn't just been waiting to make a move in the Archipelago," said John. "He's been planning to conquer them *both* all along."

• • •

"This must be discussed with Artus and Aven," Bert said as he paced the floor. "We need to go to Paralon."

"That's a good idea," said John. "We need to see what Artus's plans are. He needs to know, if he doesn't already, that the war has finally come to the Archipelago."

"I'm sorry, John, but you must remain here," Chaucer said, almost apologetically. "As Caretaker Principia, there are responsibilities to attend to with the Gatherum."

"Rose and Quixote should also stay," said Bert. "Until we have a plan of action, it's safer for them here. But I'd like Jack and Charles to come with me, to advise the king and queen."

"Of course," Jack said. Charles also nodded his assent.

"Do you want to go by Trump?" Ransom asked. "It's easily done."

Bert shook his head. "I need to take the *White Dragon* in for repairs and restocking," he said. "From the looks of things, we'll need more armament as well."

"Fine by me," said Jack. "I could use the fresh air."

It took only a few hours to make the preparations to leave in the *White Dragon*. Ransom went on ahead to announce their impending arrival, while Jack and Charles said their good-byes to their friends and the Caretakers.

"We'll be back soon," Jack promised Rose. "Artus and Aven will help us sort things out, you'll see."

Charles pulled Quixote aside. "Just a caution," he said softly. "We were surprised by Kipling. I don't want to be surprised again, so stay with Rose. If there are enemies here, they could be anywhere."

"I understand," said Quixote. "I shall guard her with my life."

Bert, Jack, and Charles boarded the *White Dragon*, and, with a last wave, they lifted off into the air.

The airships were faster by far than the original seafaring-only ships had been, and it was only a matter of hours before they were over familiar waters.

It was a pleasant day, and Jack and Charles spent most of their time enjoying the trip, rather than rehashing the earlier events and the terrible situation in England. There would be time enough to do that soon.

Charles did a double take as he thought he saw something in the sky just ahead. He shaded his eyes and took another look.

"Bert!" he exclaimed. "We're steering right into a flock of enormous birds!"

Bert laughed and rushed past the confused Charles to the railing. "They aren't birds," he said, waving his hand in the air. "They're our royal escort!"

The cluster of birds suddenly split apart and flew into formations that spiraled around the *White Dragon*. It was then that Charles realized they weren't birds at all—they were flying children.

For several minutes the ship was surrounded by shifting patterns of laughing, aerodynamic children—no, young adults— most of whom Charles had last seen on an island called Haven.

Three of the winged dervishes glided close, then landed smoothly on the deck.

The tallest of the three, obviously their leader, was dressed in tight leathers and laced boots, and she wore goggles that pinned down her light brown hair, which was sticking out in every direction. Her wings, long and majestic, were attached with a harness that crisscrossed her chest. She lifted up the goggles and flashed a dazzling smile.

"The first time I saw you," Charles said, beaming, "you had smudges on your face, and you weren't nearly as accomplished at flying. Also, you were shorter."

"It's wonderful to see you again, Charles," she said, embracing the only slightly taller man.

"It's wonderful to see you, too, Laura," he replied.

"That's Laura Glue," she chided him gently, "as if you'd forgotten!"

"I haven't forgotten, Laura my Glue," said Jack as he came around the cabin to give her a welcoming hug. "That was the most impressive display I've ever seen!"

"Aw, we was just fooling around," said the second flyer, a thinner girl with dark, spiky hair. "You should see us when we're actually *trying.*"

"Sadie!" Laura Glue admonished. "Discipline."

The girl snapped back to attention. "Sorry, Captain."

"Captain?" said Jack. "Laura Glue—are you the leader of this group, then?"

"I am." The girl nodded. "Captain of the Valkyries."

"That reminds me," said Jack. "I need to thank you for sending all those Lost Boys to the taverns and inns at the Crossroads to watch out for us. We would never have gotten Rose out alive if not for your boy Flannery." He craned his neck to look at several of the other Valkyries who had landed on the *White Dragon.* "Is he here with you? I'd like to thank him myself."

Laura Glue bit her lip and looked at her shoes. Sadie cleared her throat loudly, and Laura Glue looked up again. There were tears in her eyes.

"Three years ago, there was a skirmish with the Yoricks at one of the Soft Places," she said, her voice steady. "It went up in flames. Flannery didn't make it out."

"I'm sorry," said Charles.

"As am I," said Jack. "We left him only a few days ago, but to everyone else, we've been gone for seven years. A lot can happen in that time."

"A lot *has* happened in the last seven years," said Laura Glue. "Not much of it is good. They'll fill you in at Paralon. Artus is waiting to receive you."

She moved over to speak to Bert about other arrangements that needed to be made at Paralon, and Jack pulled Charles aside.

"One thing's for certain," Jack whispered. "When this is all over, and we've gotten back to the time we're supposed to be in, I'm going to make certain that Flannery is nowhere near that tavern, wherever it is."

"Changing a history?" asked Charles.

"Making a prophecy," said Jack.

As the crew of the *White Dragon* gently guided the airship to its customary spot in the Paralon harbor, a tremendous racket sprang up from the docks. It had the vaguest resemblance to music, but was more on the order of a collision of train cars that happened to be carrying musical instruments.

"The Royal Animal Rescue Squad," Jack explained to Charles. "I'd forgotten you haven't met them yet."

Jack went through the group of mammals and made

introductions, giving special attention to their friend Tummeler's son, Uncas.

"I have a speech prepared," announced Uncas. "Would you like to hear it?"

"A speech? In our honor?" said Charles, puffing out his chest. "But of course!"

"I think it's honor enough that you chose to write it," said Jack. "To hear it read aloud would only be anticlimactic."

"Oh, uh, great!" said Uncas brightly while Jack winked at the deflated Charles. "Well then, since it's on the way, would you like to come by the shop? We've now got the biggest operation on Paralon, and my son Fred would love to meet the great Scowler Charles."

"You don't say?" Charles said heartily. "Lead the way, Uncas."

The badgers' publishing enterprise, which had begun with Uncas's father's editions of poorly selling cookbooks, had grown exponentially with the release of the popular edition of the *Imaginarium Geographica*, then again with the abridged edition of the guidebook to everything, the Little Whatsit. But even then, the whole venture consisted of a single storefront and a backroom printing facility. It was nothing like the Herculean complex that Uncas was so proudly ushering them into.

The main building itself was the size of an airplane hangar, and was tall enough to have its own weather patterns—*indoors*. There were badgers of every size scurrying to and fro, very occupied with the business at hand. They were all smartly dressed in white shirts and frocks, and all wore black armbands.

"Grandfather Tummeler will be very sorry to have missed you," Fred said earnestly. "He still speaks of you often."

"Good old Tummeler," said Charles jovially. "How is he?"

"Well enough," Fred replied, "but quite far along in badger years. He's basically in retirement at a house Artus had built for him next to the Great Whatsit. That way, he can use it for research as often as he likes."

"Research?" exclaimed Charles. "Is he working on another book?"

"Several," Uncas said, handing a stack of papers to his son. "He's constantly offering revisions on the Little Whatsit, but he's also working on his memoirs. I think he's titled it *There and Back Again: A Badger's Tale*."

"Really!" said Charles. "That's extraordinary. I can't wait to read it."

"The title's a bit bland, though," said Jack. "We'll have to mention it to John. Maybe he can think of a way to improve it. He's very good with titles, you know."

"Uncas," Charles said, "what is the meaning of the black armbands? Are you in mourning for someone?"

On hearing the question, all the badgers nearby stopped what they were doing and, almost in a single motion, turned to look . . .

. . . at Jack.

"What?" said Jack, looking around at his feet as if he'd inadvertently stepped on someone's tail. "Did I do something wrong?"

Uncas hemmed and hawed and stuttered and stammered until Fred sighed and stepped forward to answer. "It's not so much what you done, Scowler Jack," he began, "as it is what you're *going t'* do."

Charles frowned. For Fred to both address Jack formally and

to lapse into the slipped vowels of the less-formal badger-speak meant it was a grave matter indeed.

"This isn't about the giants again, is it?" said Jack. "I told Bert—"

"No, no, nuthin' like that," said Fred. "It's just that . . . that . . . well, y'r an *Oxford* man, Scowler Jack!"

"As I always plan to be," Jack said with a trace of defensiveness.

"Well then," said Uncas morosely, "in th' Summer Country, in the year of our Lord nineteen hundred and fifty-four, y'r in for a *big* surprise."

"All this because I supposedly—in the future, mind you—take a post at Cambridge?" Jack whispered as he gestured around at the armband-wearing badgers. "Is it possible to feel guilt over something I don't plan to do, and won't do anyway for *years?*"

"That's an interesting question," replied Charles. "I wonder how the intention or non-intention plays into the concept of repentance."

"Repentance?" Jack sputtered. "But I haven't done anything! Or at least, not yet! And even then, at worst it's because I go teach at another university?"

"Not just another university," Charles said. "*Cambridge*. Not only have we been joking about it for all these years, but according to Bert, the only Caretakers who have ever really botched the job came from Cambridge, not Oxford. It's basically a cursed place, as far as these little fellows are concerned."

As if to punctuate Charles's point, a smallish badger intern carrying a bundle of ribbon markers stopped and looked at them, whiskers quivering.

Jack gave it a little wave, and in response the tiny mammal burst into tears and went running from the room.

"Oh, for heaven's sake," said Jack.

"I'd better do all the talking while we're here," Charles said, laying a comforting hand on Jack's shoulder. "Apparently I don't do anything controversial at all in the fifties."

The great palace at Paralon was still recognizable, as it was a massive edifice that would resist change or alteration—but the regal air that had permeated the entire island capital of the Archipelago had been replaced with something . . . *different.*

"Mmm," said Charles, inhaling deeply. "Smells like bureaucracy."

"I'm sure you meant to say 'democracy,'" said Jack.

"What's the difference?" Charles replied. "Either way, I suspect that Artus got in over his head."

"He's probably been reading too many American Histories, I'm afraid," said Jack. "There's a lot to advocate for, and I believe his ambitions are nobly based—but I think he may have been better off with his parliamentary-oriented monarchy."

Instead of the Great Hall, where visitors would normally have been received, the Valkyries led the companions to a large storeroom which had been converted into an office. Artus, the former king of Paralon, rose and greeted them warmly.

"My dear friends," he said happily. "It's wonderful to see you. I'm so glad you're not dead!"

"As are we," said Jack, "but we've apparently missed out on a lot of new developments, including, ah, fashion trends."

"Oh, yes, the armbands," Artus said with a sheepish expression on his face. "I'm sorry about that."

"Apparently the controversy that's fired up the badgers involves my future," Jack said, "or one of them, at any rate. We've accidentally leaped some seven years ahead of where—uh, when we were meant to be, so I realize that there will be articles of common knowledge to you that will be incomprehensible to us. But how is it that the badgers know things that won't happen for another decade?"

"It's the Time Storms," Artus explained. "They ebb and flow, and occasionally deposit something here that shouldn't be. It's all fallout from the destruction of the Keep of Time. So Bert has occasionally had to share something he knows about the future, so we don't completely derail it in the present."

"Is there any way, maybe something Samaranth or the Cartographer might know, that can keep the Time Storms from getting worse?" asked Charles.

"That's the problem," Artus said with a grimace. "They haven't gotten *worse*, they've gotten *better*. In fact, they've almost completely stopped."

"Pardon my ignorance," said Charles, "but wouldn't that be a good thing?"

"No," Jack interjected, realizing what Artus was getting at. "It wouldn't. If the fall of the keep and the loss of the doors are what threw a myriad of portals into time itself to the four winds, then the only way that they can be reined in again is—"

"Is if someone's repaired the tower," finished Charles, "and restored the doors."

"Worse," said Artus. "Someone may be building *another* tower altogether."

✦   ✦   ✦

As they talked, Artus ordered some food and drink to be brought in. A short time later Bert and Ransom joined them, and the philologist relayed the terrible news about Kor.

"This is awful," Artus said. "Kor was one of the islands fighting against protectorate status."

"I'm sorry," said Jack. "What does that mean?"

"The Senate has been preparing for an eventual attack by the Winter King," Artus explained, "by promising increased protective measures from the republic in exchange for oaths of fealty. It was a plan presented by a very influential man on the rise named Chancellor Murdoch."

"Chancellor?" said Jack. "Which land does he represent?"

"That's the strange part," said Bert. "No one seems to know. He appeared out of nowhere, with no history, no credentials that I can find, and yet all the primary leaders in the Archipelago—save for Artus and Aven—have embraced him and his counsel."

"It's surprising that I've never heard of him," said Jack. "I consider myself very well up-to-date on events in the Archipelago."

"We've also missed seven years," Charles reminded him.

"I'm hoping you might still know something about him," Artus said. "There's a belief that he might actually be a leader from your world."

"One of our people?" exclaimed Charles. "Here? That smacks of Burton's involvement, if you ask me."

"I hope not," said Artus. "The Chancellor is proving to be very popular—and in a republic, that alone can carry the day. Burton is already a thorn in our sides, but if a world leader from the Summer Country is becoming our best ally against the

Winter King, then I don't see how he wouldn't be involved."

"What does the Chancellor look like?" asked Jack.

"Our agents, particularly Ransom, have managed to acquire a few photographs of him," Artus said as he spread several pictures out on the table. "The one thing that's peculiar about him is that in all of the pictures, he's seen holding this spear."

"That looks very familiar," said Charles, "but I can't quite put my finger on it."

"I can," said Jack with a groan. "And I *have*. It's the spear we took from Mordred in Camelot. It was called the Lance of Longinus, but you'd know it better as the Spear of Destiny."

"Great Scott!" Charles exclaimed. "But what did *you* have to do with it?"

"John and I gave it to Chaz, when he became the first Green Knight," said Jack. "And every Green Knight since has carried it, including . . ."

"Magwich," Artus said.

"Well, now we know where that idiot Maggot went," Charles fumed. "He threw in with this Chancellor, and he gave him the spear."

"What's the connection between the Green Knight and the Chancellor, though?" asked Jack. "How would someone from our world even know about Magwich or the spear?"

"Here's your connection," Charles said darkly. "Look at this photo—the close-up in profile. Do you recognize him?"

"Yes," Bert declared. "I *have* seen him before!"

"The Red King," said Jack. "From the Clockwork Parliament! But I thought they'd all been destroyed after our first trip into the Archipelago!"

Artus was crestfallen. "So did we," he said. "Apparently, we were mistaken."

"That's not all we've overlooked," said Ransom. "Look more closely at the photo."

"Hmm," said Charles. "That's a puzzler."

"You see it, don't you?" asked Ransom.

"I think so," said Charles. "The light source is on the right, so all the people are casting shadows to the left. But the Red King, Chancellor Murdoch, or whoever he is—well, he appears to have *two* shadows."

"Lord preserve us," breathed Jack. "Now we know where the Winter King's Shadow went. It wasn't destroyed after all."

"The Chancellor isn't preparing the Archipelago to *fight* the Winter King," said Ransom. "He *is* the Winter King."

PART FOUR

The Town That Wasn't There

There were other familiar faces as well . . .

CHAPTER THIRTEEN
The Legendarium

Richard Burton was a man used to responsibility. What he was not used to was accountability, especially when the rules of the game he was playing suddenly changed.

"The last door was defective," he said gruffly. "I don't know what the problem was."

"Define 'defective,'" said the Chancellor.

Burton could always tell when the Chancellor was upset. There was a strange whirring sound emanating from his chest, and his neck made an odd clicking noise when he spoke. Not good.

"It didn't open into a time, it opened into a place," said Burton. "A small stone room that was completely empty. No exit, and no dragon. We've already discarded the door."

"Fine," said the Chancellor. "We'll be done soon enough anyway."

"What about the Caretakers?"

"They know where to look now," the Chancellor said, glancing at Kipling. "And they will be coming, make no mistake."

"Should I summon the others to return as well, before they're found out too?" Kipling asked.

"No," the Chancellor said after considering the question. "They may yet be useful where they are."

"You realize I can't go back. They'll be watching now."

"That's what we want," came the reply. "They'll be looking for you, and not watching their backs. That's how I was able to procure this." The Chancellor held up an object.

Kipling went pale. "How did you get that?"

The Chancellor laughed, and it was a harsh, grating sound. "Let's just say your report was useful, and two of your colleagues have finally redeemed themselves."

"The timing of the attack on Kor is no coincidence," said Artus. "The next scheduled referendum at the Senate is regarding whether or not to give increased powers to the Chancellor. And as the islands that have joined the protectorate remain untouched, while a powerful nation such as Kor is in flames, I have no doubt the motion will be overwhelmingly passed."

"When is the referendum scheduled?" asked Bert.

"Tonight."

"Can't you stop it?" asked Jack. "Or postpone it? Or something? You're the king!"

"An honorary title within the republic," said Artus. "I have more influence than power, and with the Chancellor's allies, I have far less influence than he."

"I'm guessing his allies include the Goblins and the Trolls?" asked Charles.

"The Goblins remain apart from the rest of us," said Artus, "but the Trolls were early participants in the protectorate."

"And this didn't set off any alarm bells for you?" asked Jack.

"Why would it?" Artus replied. "While war has run rampant in the Summer Country, we've had relative peace here—and the protectorate initiative has been taking care of the lands rather than invading them. We've been watching for an attack from the Winter King, not a fruit basket."

"He's attacked you now, though," said Charles. "Can't you use that against him?"

"How?" asked Artus. "The Chancellor will decry the attack and want to rally to Kor's aid! Anything I say, with only suspicion and photographs as evidence, will look like a personal attack."

"Not to mention that it will alert the Chancellor—uh, Winter King—whatever he is that we know what he's up to," Bert put in. "I have an alternate suggestion. We should consult Samaranth for advice. Outside of Verne or Poe, he'll have a better idea of what to do than anyone."

Reluctantly, Artus agreed. It felt a bit like cowardice, to slip away from the palace to plan and prepare, but it was the only sensible option if their beliefs proved true. "We'll leave shortly," he said as he threw the photos into a leather satchel. "I'll take some precautions here first, and I'll meet you at the badger's garage."

"I have other matters to attend to for the Caretakers," said Ransom, "but I'll stay close."

"Let's go," said Bert. "The clock is ticking."

Fred was more than happy to see the scholars again, particularly Charles. He took great pride in showing the Caretaker every part of the garage where the principles were maintained, while Jack and Bert outfitted a vehicle for the trip to see Samaranth.

"So, Fred," Charles said, "other than the family traditions of publishing and automotive care, tell me what else you've been studying these years past."

"As much as I can of just about everything, Scowler Charles," replied Fred. "I read what I can when I'm not working with my father at the press—although if it were up to my grandfather, I'd still be in cooking school."

"If it hadn't been for your grandfather, we would never have defeated the Winter King," Charles explained, "and if not for you and your father, Jack and John would never have been able to rescue Hugo Dyson."

"T' be fair, Scowler Charles," Fred said, "it was partially our fault Hugo got trapped in time t' begin with."

"Sure," said Charles. "And your willingness to acknowledge your mistakes, and to learn from them, is one of the main reasons I've decided to give you this."

Fred looked down. In Charles's hand was a silver pocket watch, emblazoned with a red dragon. The symbol of an apprentice Caretaker.

"A Samaranth watch!" Fred exclaimed, still unsure of what was happening. "But—but—Scowler Charles—you don't really mean t' give that t' me?"

Charles nodded. "I do. Jack has told me how much help you were to Hugo, and of how diligently you were studying to become a true scholar. So I know of no one who deserves it more." He placed the watch into the small mammal's trembling paw, then closed his fingers over it.

"You know what this means, and you understand the responsibility that comes with it. So don't disappoint me."

Fred was shaking with excitement. "I won't! I promise!" He

stopped and furrowed his brow. "Does this have to be a secret? Or can I tell someone? I mean, someones?"

"It's supposed to be a very secret thing," said Charles, "so just be careful about who you do choose to tell. I'm guessing your father and grandfather?"

The badger nodded. "Yes, Scowler Charles."

"That should be fine. And Fred—you're my apprentice now. You can just call me Charles."

"Thank you Scowl—I mean, thank you, Charles!" Fred said as he walked away in as dignified a manner as he could without appearing to want to run.

"Holy hell, lad," Charles called after him. "Run. Run and tell them!"

Without a backward glance, the badger broke into a dead run, his feet barely touching the ground.

In short order, Bert, Artus, and Jack had joined Charles and his newly appointed apprentice in a spacious six-wheeled principle called the Strange Attractor. Fred took the wheel and soon revealed himself to be an expert driver. The trip was innocuous enough, and the engine loud enough, that the companions could talk without being overheard as they traveled.

The first time John, Jack, and Charles met the great dragon Samaranth, he was the only dragon left in the Archipelago. All the other dragons had abandoned the lands and the service of the king, because he had proven himself to be unworthy to call on them.

Now Jack and Charles were again going to see Samaranth, and again he was the only dragon left—but this time, it was because Artus, as the king, had sent them away in the belief that as long as the dragons were always there to solve any problems, he and his people would never fully mature as a race.

"Of course I went to Samaranth first," Artus explained to Jack and Charles, "and when I told him what I planned to do, he was quiet for a very long time. Then, when he finally answered, he asked a question."

"What did he ask you?" said Jack.

"He asked if I had ever seen a baby bird that pushed past its parents and tried to leave the nest before it was ready. I told him I had. And then he asked if I knew what birds like that were called, and I said no."

"What did he say they were called?" asked Jack.

"Lunch."

"That's terrible," said Charles. "Is that all he said to you?"

"No," said Artus. "He told me that I was the King of the Silver Throne, and the dragons served at my pleasure and could be released from service by blowing a horn that he kept in his cave. He said it was very old, and then he said something I didn't understand—he told me it was from a time and place before he was a dragon."

"That's interesting," said Jack. "So what did you do?"

Artus sighed. "I blew the horn. Then I came back to the castle and formed a republic. Everything has been utter chaos ever since."

"Well," said Jack, "sometimes the magic works."

"And sometimes, you really wish it hadn't," said Artus. "I wonder if it's possible to unblow a horn?"

"It isn't possible to unblow a horn," Samaranth said disapprovingly. "You're intelligent enough to know that, Artus."

It had not taken the companions long to reach Samaranth's cavern, and once they were there, it took even less time for them to realize that he was not pleased to see them.

"The Caretakers have not remained steadfast in their jobs," he said in a raspy voice, "and the King of the Silver Throne has handled his stewardship with even less aplomb."

"We've dealt with every crisis we've been called to," Jack pointed out. "Minor and major. And we've always emerged triumphant."

Samaranth snorted one, twice, and then three times—and they realized he was laughing. "Triumphant? Really? With the Keep of Time nearly destroyed, the Morgaine and the Green Knight gone from Avalon, and a new power rising in the Archipelago who may in fact be the enemy you were brought to defeat to begin with? In what way do you consider that triumphant, little Caretakers?"

"We're learning the value of persistence," said Charles. "That's a start."

Samaranth sighed heavily and regarded the companions with weary eyes.

"That you are," he said, blowing out a thin cloud of smoke. "I'll tell you this much. The Prophecy you are meant to fulfill is true—and you have been in the midst of it since the first time we met.

"So, consider everything that has passed before now to be a test. A test of your worthiness to survive."

"As Caretakers?" asked Jack.

"As a king?" said Artus.

"No," Samaranth replied. "As a *race*."

"We'll meet the test," said Charles. "We just need to know if we'll be seeing it through alone."

"You aren't alone unless you believe you are," said Fred.

"The Child of the Earth speaks wise," Samaranth said to Artus. "Ask what you're here to ask."

Artus swallowed hard and took a deep breath. "Can I still summon the dragons?"

The great red dragon ambled over to one of the metallic compartments that lined the walls of the cave and removed a horn. It was stained ivory and curved in on itself like a lily.

"There's one call in it left," he said as he handed it to Artus. "Do not use it until there is no other option. Once the horn is blown, it will be useless to you. So choose your time wisely and well."

"It will bring back the dragons?" said Artus.

"It will do whatever you wish for it to do," said Samaranth. "The Horn of Bran Galed was one of the great treasures of the world. It was acquired by Merlin before he became the Cartographer, and it originally belonged to a centaur who was slain by Hercules. Most of those whose hands it passed through believed that its particular value lay in the fact that it would contain any drink one wished for. The truth was, it gave one *anything* one wished for, and stupid, stupid man-creatures wasted almost all of its wishes on ale and wine."

"So when you told me that blowing it would free us from our dependency on the dragons . . . ," said Artus.

"That's what it gave you, because that's what you wanted the most," said Samaranth. "The desire for independence. It's one of the qualities that makes you a good leader—but you also lost the ability to use the Rings of Power. Not because you were no longer worthy, but because you wished for it.

"Far too much has been made about royal blood meaning more than noble worth, and there is far too much concern about spells and summonings and process and prophecy. If you want something, ask. If you are willing to pay the price, to earn what you desire, then pay it, and take what is rightfully yours.

"Some of the Caretakers have touched on one of the great truths of creation," Samaranth continued, "and like all great truths, it is elegant in its simplicity."

"Believing is seeing," said Fred.

"So believe," said Samaranth. "Good luck, and farewell."

The drive back to the palace was much quieter, as each of the companions was digesting what the great old dragon had said. Of them all, only Fred was certain that the visit had yielded great results. None of the others were quite so sure. The Caretakers, including Bert, were stinging from the dressing-down Samaranth had given them. And Artus was told in so many words that he had essentially made a bad decision for good reasons. But the one thing they all understood was that there was still a chance to win—for all of them.

In his first years as King of the Silver Throne, Artus had proven to be surprisingly effective at governing the vast, eclectic kingdom that was the Archipelago of Dreams. A large part of his success came from his willingness to delegate to others who were more qualified in certain areas than he was. Another factor was his declaration of equal status for his queen, Aven. But the greatest part of his accomplishments came from the fact that he was unafraid to take risks and then stand behind them. There was little point in being responsible if one could not also be accountable.

As the Strange Attractor pulled up to one of the boulevards that led to the main part of the city, a badger jumped out of the brush next to the road and flagged them down.

"Uncas!" Jack exclaimed.

"Dad!" Fred shouted as he slammed on his brakes. "What are you doing out here?"

"You can't go into the city, and nowhere near the palace," said Uncas. He was obviously very upset—he'd twisted his hat into a knot.

"Why not?" said Artus. "What's happened?"

"The Senate convened early, and the Chancellor was granted sovereignty over the entire Archipelago!" Uncas cried. "He started by putting out a call to have you arrested for instigating the attacks on Kor!"

"And so it begins," Artus said, his face darkening.

"This is a put-up job," exclaimed Jack. "You're being set up for a fall, Artus."

"What should we do?" Charles asked.

"Already in the works," Uncas said as he climbed into the back of the Strange Attractor. "We're to meet everyone at Halsey Cove."

"Who's everyone?" asked Charles.

"Y'know," Uncas said. "*Everyone.*"

Halsey Cove was an old, seldom-used port several miles south of Paralon proper. It was more archaic, but architecturally more elegant than the main seaports. It was also occasionally used for covert meetings of any kind. Ransom was standing at the head of the docks when they pulled up.

"I trust you heard there's a party being thrown in your honor back at the palace," said Ransom.

"I heard," Artus said. "I think I'll skip it."

"While you've been having tea with a dragon," Ransom said, grinning wryly, "I've been gathering a few friends."

The companions climbed out of the vehicle and realized that Uncas had been telling the truth: Everyone was indeed waiting.

Five of the seven great Dragonships of legend were assembled at the docks. Their captains, along with many personages and creatures who remained loyal to the Silver Throne, were waiting in formation for the king. And foremost among these were the queen, Aven, and her son, Prince Stephen.

The companions rushed forward and greeted them joyfully. Bert, Aven's father, embraced her with tears in his eyes. She hugged him tightly, then stood up straight to take Jack's measure as he was taking hers.

She had aged, as had he, but she was still the pirate girl he had adored, and she still had the mettle in her eyes that made her the greatest captain in the Archipelago.

"Hello, Jack," she said, embracing him tightly.

"Hi, Aven," he said, smiling. "It's good to see you."

"Well, um, yes," said Artus. "Jack, Charles—you remember our son, Stephen."

Both men took turns shaking Stephen's hand—and reeling. They'd known Artus at an age younger than this, and he was always a hero at heart—but Stephen was a heroic figure in every sense of the word.

Artus had been thrust into the role of king as a young man, after a childhood that had consisted of being raised by three witches who occasionally dropped him down a well; one remarkable journey to become a knight and slay a dragon, which had turned out successfully at the time, but which became less so as years went by; and then a sudden revelation that he was the heir to the throne of the entire Archipelago. It was all very heady and would have been hard to process for anyone. For someone who preferred to be on an equal status with his own subjects, and who preferred his friends to call him "Bug" when in private, it was nearly impossible. But he had managed to survive, and to prosper.

His son, Stephen, on the other hand, was born to authority, and he proved to be a stunningly effective commander. He was the perfect synthesis of leader, explorer, and inventor. It was he who first proposed that all the legendary Dragonships be converted into airships. And under the watchful eye of the shipbuilder Ordo Maas, and with the permission of the Dragonships themselves, he performed every conversion himself.

Thus he had a personal rapport with every Dragonship that was second only to those they had with the captains who piloted them. This was more impressive when one realized that he had spent the last years of his childhood as a brainwashed prisoner of the King of Crickets, who was really the Winter King's Shadow in disguise.

As a young man, he had been impressive enough with his noble features and proud bearing. But as an adult, Stephen cut a majestic figure. He wore a leather vest and trousers that mimicked those of the Valkyries, but he also wore the symbol that marked him as a man of legend: the horns and pelt of the Golden Fleece. Together with the mighty double-edged ax he wielded, there were few men in any world who would not pause at his arrival.

"He's the first mate on the *Green Dragon*, under the new Captain, Rillian," said Artus.

"I don't think I know him," said Jack, looking around at the group.

"He's a unicorn," said Uncas.

"Really?" said Jack. "The only ones I've seen were those poor beasts in the Winterland. And what that Wicker Man had done to them," he added, shuddering. "Awful."

"Unicorns?" Fred asked. "Oh, you mean the Houyhnhnms. The larger ones, probably pulling a cart, or some such."

"There are unicorns *smaller* than horses?"

Fred laughed at this.

"You human scowlers," he said, "have always gotten that wrong. Unicorns aren't another name for a horse with a horn. It's a classification for *any* animal with one. In fact, most unicorns are mice. It's just that no one ever really notices the ones *here*"—he crouched low and waved at the ground—"because they're always looking for the ones up *here*." He stood on tiptoe and pointed upward.

"So this Captain Rillian . . . ," Charles began.

"Pleased t' meetcha," said a voice from below. Charles bent low and shook the unicorn mouse's paw. "And I you, Captain."

"Ho, Caretakers!" said a tall, graying centaur. "Are we up to picking a fight?"

"Charys!" Jack exclaimed, clasping arms with the centaur. "It's a pleasure to see you again!"

"The pleasure is mine, Caretaker," Charys replied. "I very much enjoyed those books you wrote. Traveling to other planets, oh ho?" The centaur laughed and clapped him on the shoulders. "What an imagination you have!"

"What books was he referring to?" asked Charles as the centaur trotted over to shout some orders at another group arriving in the cove. "When did you write about space travel?"

Jack shrugged, bewildered. "I haven't the foggiest. It's something I've been toying with, and Ransom certainly sparked some interesting ideas. But I'm a blank slate."

"That's the annoying thing about time travel," said Charles. "You always feel like you're late to the party, even when you aren't."

There were other familiar faces as well: Eledir the Elf King; Falladay Finn, of the Dwarves; and the Valkyries, led by Laura Glue.

"We have everyone," she said to Aven and Artus. "Everyone still loyal to the Silver Throne. We're almost ready to go."

"Are you abandoning the Archipelago?" Jack asked in astonishment.

"No," said Aven. "We're moving the base of operations for the true government to a safer place."

"We're consolidating our power," said Bert, "and we're going to do it in the Nameless Isles."

"Is this a coup?" asked Laura Glue. "I think we're starting a coup."

"We might be at that," said Aven. "We're only waiting for one more ship to arrive."

"Oh, yes," said Artus. "Of course."

"He came through with one of the Time Storms a year ago," said Artus, pointing out into the cove. "I think you're in for a real surprise, Jack."

Just past where the *White Dragon* was moored, the surface of the water had begun to bubble and roil about. A ship was surfacing. A very familiar ship.

The great, gleaming bulk of the *Yellow Dragon* rose up out of the water, and the port hatch lifted. A man both familiar and not stepped out onto the hull and crossed his arms defiantly.

Charles looked on in wonderment, while Jack reeled with the shock of the sight before them.

The man was scarcely out of his teens, if that, but his manner and bearing—and his arrogance—were instantly familiar.

"Speak, and be recognized," called out Uncas. "Who be ye, and where be y'r allegiance?"

"My allegiance is to my ship and crew," the youth replied, dropping off the ship onto the dock, "and to the Archipelago and those who serve her. And as for me," he finished, jabbing a thumb at his chest, "I am the seventh son of the seventh son of Sinbad himself, and I'm here to pick a fight."

He strode over to Jack and stuck out a hand in greeting. "Nemo is my name."

The gatekeeper was a blind man . . . covered in tattoos . . .

CHAPTER FOURTEEN
Abaton

Geoffrey Chaucer called the Gatherum of Caretakers to silence, then addressed the first order of business. "This is one of the reasons we required you to stay at Tamerlane House," he said to John. "We are the historic Caretakers of the Imaginarium Geographica, but we are also past our times. Outside of these walls, we can influence very little, and for too short a time.

"But you are still young and vital—and you are the current Caveo Principia. The Principal Caretaker. And so while we may debate, and offer opinions and counsel, the ultimate decision must be yours."

"Which decision is that?" asked John.

"Whether or not," Chaucer said evenly, "Richard Burton is right."

The concept stunned John into silence. Right about what? About the Archipelago? Were they actually considering the position of their enemy as being more worthy than their own?

"I understand what you must be thinking," Charles Dickens said. "After all, I was the one who recruited him as my apprentice. But ever since your first clash with him, we have been debating whether or not there might not be some merit to his point of view."

"Secrecy has been the mandate," added Twain. "It always has been. But there comes a time when we must acknowledge that the horse may have left the stable long before we barred the doors."

"What do you mean?" asked John.

"These," Hawthorne said, tossing a copy of Tummeler's *Geographica* on the table. "They're everywhere."

"Everywhere in the Archipelago," John corrected. "We were very clear about that. Tummeler was more than happy to comply, and I know Artus was keeping an eye on his operation."

"That's part of the problem," said Chaucer. "This move Artus made to turn the kingdom into a republic has only made his affinity for the ways of our world grow stronger. We fear that an embargo may not be sufficient."

"Copies are bound to slip across the Frontier," said Irving, "and we no longer believe that Artus would see that as a threat to the Archipelago."

"Wasn't the Silver Throne established to unite *both* worlds?" John asked. "Under the rule of Arthur?"

"That was the original plan, and one of the reasons to have Rings of Power in both," said Chaucer, "but that was effectively ended when Mordred returned and killed Arthur. His heirs were able rulers, but they constrained themselves to rule in the Archipelago, not in the Summer Country. And as the years passed, the divide simply grew broader."

"And now," continued Twain, "we fear that Artus may seek to reestablish a foothold in the Summer Country. And if that happens, even in the attempt, he will compromise everything that is here."

John leaned back and steepled his fingers in front of his face. "If it's as risky as you say, then isn't the debate about Burton moot?"

"Burton cares less about rule and authority than he does about the welfare of the Archipelago itself," said Dickens. "He was, and is, an explorer at heart—and he simply wishes to share his discoveries with the world."

"That's something I've often wondered about," said John. "If Burton believes so strongly that the truth of the Archipelago should be known, why hasn't he spread copies of the *Geographica* far and wide a long time ago? All he'd have to do to expose all of us is tell the truth—so why bother with the cloak-and-dagger machinations and plotting?"

"For the same reason that Houdini and Conan Doyle chose discreet silence," said Twain. "Without the permission of either the dragons, the king, or the Caretakers, Samaranth would hunt them down and roast them otherwise."

"Which alludes to my point about Artus," said Chaucer. "Our oath of secrecy was to protect the Archipelago as well as the atlas itself."

"It seems to me we've strayed far afield from our point," said Twain, "which is that as the *Geographica* becomes more widely known, it becomes far less rare—and less dangerous."

"There are still many things within the actual atlas that are secret," said John. "We certainly didn't allow Tummeler access to *those.*"

"There will always be secrets, just as there will always be mysteries," said Chaucer. "But stories will go on regardless. All we are really given is the opportunity to shape how the stories are told."

"There is one great difference between them," a soft voice

said from somewhere above. Poe was watching, listening.

"Mysteries are meant to be solved, to be discovered. But secrets are meant to be kept, to remain hidden," he said, "and sometimes one doesn't discover a secret was actually a mystery until it's too late."

"What is it?" asked Twain. "What's happened?"

"The book," said Poe. "Someone has stolen the Last Book."

The entire room was pin-drop silent for a few seconds before it exploded into an uproar. Caretakers were yelling at one another, and yelling for order, and one or two were simply yelling.

"That's done it," said Irving. "We're done for."

"Someone should be flogged," said Shakespeare.

"It was bound to happen," said Defoe.

"Will everyone please be quiet!" said Chaucer.

Suddenly a shot rang out, and the entire room went silent again.

Mark Twain blew the smoke off the barrel and pocketed his small silver gun.

"A gentleman never fires a pistol unless it's to defend a lady's honor or to quiet a herd of braying jackasses," he said. "Luckily, since Lady Shelley and Miss Dyson are among us, I got to do both at once.

"We like to pretend that we're civilized and organized," Twain continued, "but when we're taken by surprise, we suddenly fall apart like clay soldiers. We have the Caretaker Principia with us, and the Grail Child. The Prophecy will be fulfilled—as long as we don't derail it ourselves."

John stood up to better take advantage of the momentary

lull. "Samuel's right. We need to organize, and I think the most important concern isn't that the book is gone, but that it was taken at all."

"I concur," said Chaucer. "We still have an enemy in our midst."

"Well," Grimalkin said as he appeared in the center of the table, "you'll have plenty of help discovering who he is. There's an entire armada pulling into the harbor."

John flew to the window. "Well, this is a fine how-do-you-do," he said to the other Caretakers. "It seems the Dragonships have come to the Nameless Isles."

"Which ones?" asked Twain.

John pursed his lips. "All of them."

It took the rest of the day to receive the new arrivals, which was still extremely expedient, considering Tamerlane House had never had so many guests at once.

The flight from Paralon had happened quickly, and so the only provisions the refugees had were what they had had onboard the ships. Bert, Twain, Defoe, Hawthorne, and John took charge of assigning quarters to the newcomers, and the other Caretakers began converting the conservatory into a war room. A meeting of the king and queen, the ship captains, and the Caretakers would have to be held as soon as possible.

Charles, on the other hand, had a plan of his own—which Jack was only too eager to share in. At present, there were at least three conversations Jack had managed to avoid on the trip to the Nameless Isles, and if he could delay them longer still, all the better.

"You heard about the book?" Charles asked as he, Jack, and Fred walked to the Pygmalion Gallery.

"Yes," said Jack. "We keep ending up one step behind! I wonder if Kipling had something to do with it?"

"I was thinking the same thing."

"What would be helpful is if we knew where Kipling went," said Jack. "I can't get past the feeling that if we'd said something when we got here, we might be a lot further along." He opened the doors to the gallery, and the three of them walked in.

"I wonder if they'll keep his picture here now that his portrait is just a landscape?" asked Charles.

"I think we ought to just burn it," Jack said irritably. "He won't be returning to Tamerlane House now that we know what he is, so there's no further use for the painting."

"Maybe there is," said Charles, running his hand across his head. "I have a strange idea, but I believe it will work."

"What do you mean?" asked Jack.

"We're going to try taking this battle to the Chancellor's doorstep," Charles called back as he took the stairs two and three at a bound. "Fred, find Bert and bring him upstairs to the atelier. Jack, find Ransom, and bring him up as well. We need to talk to Basil Hallward."

"It *is* possible," Ransom mused after Charles had explained what he proposed to do. "Difficult, perhaps. But not impossible. What do you think, Basil?"

Hallward shrugged and chewed on the end of a brush. "It was a different painting," he said. "When I created Kipling's portrait, it was different."

"So he had to have already been liberated from the real portrait beforehand," said Charles, "and when Bert thought he was bringing him out, he was really just stepping through the Trump. It's quite ingenious."

"Remind me to be impressed later," said Jack. "My question is, can you duplicate the painting as a Trump for us?"

"I don't see why not," said Hallward. "The only real criteria is that it has to be a real place, somewhere, and I have to know exactly what it looks like. And this place must exist, or else he couldn't have gone through."

"And if he can," said Bert, "what then?"

"If we have a Trump," said Charles, "Fred and I can go through and discover where their base of operations is. At present, they don't know where we are, and we don't know where they are. I'd like to shift the balance in our favor."

Bert considered this a moment, then nodded. "Just one thing," he said sternly, "no adventuring. Reconnaissance only. Learn what you can and come back. But don't take any risks."

"Fair enough," said Charles.

Together the group of men and the badger went into the Pygmalion Gallery, where Hallward set up a makeshift easel in front of Kipling's picture.

Ransom gave Hallward one of the blank Trumps, and slowly, carefully, the artist duplicated the scene depicted on Kipling's portrait. "That should do it," said Hallward. "It's already dry, if you'd like to give it a whirl."

Charles held the Trump up in front of him and concentrated on the picture. Slowly it began to expand, and in moments it was large enough to step through.

"Are you sure you don't want any of the rest of us to go with you?" Bert asked.

"You can't spare the resources," said Charles. "And besides, Fred and I are basically reprising another successful espionage partnership. His grandfather and I made quite the team."

Fred beamed. "That you did," he said proudly. "May our venture be as successful."

"Very well," said Ransom. "I'll keep the card open here on this end. If you have any trouble, come running. But remember, Charles . . ." He let the sentence trail off.

Charles nodded. "I understand. If the portal is discovered, you'll have to close it."

"We've opened it this time," Ransom said, "but I don't know if we can do it again. Time is of the essence, Charles."

The two men shook hands, Ransom shook Fred's paw, and Charles thanked Bert and Hallward for their help. And then he and his apprentice stepped through the portal in search of the Town That Didn't Exist.

In his own explorations, Charles had once come across a place in Germany where a narrow alley between a distillery and a seed merchant actually led to an entire district outside space and time.

The entire community seemed sickly and poorly maintained, with faded whitewash on the houses and holes in the cobblestone streets. The seasons themselves were confused in that place, and the trees were barren even in springtime.

He had always planned on exploring it at greater length, but others in the area had stumbled on it and ransacked the hidden village. Not long after, a series of grisly murders occurred in all the nearby German towns, and people whispered that it was the vengeance of the dark spirits who dwelled within.

It was only then, at the moment he was passing through the Trump, that he recalled that the townsfolk who claimed to have seen the spirits described them as men with oversized bird skulls for heads.

He tried to contain the shiver that rolled up his spine, and only just managed to disguise it as stretching before Fred noticed.

"Are you worried?" asked Fred.

"Not in the slightest," said Charles.

"Good," said Fred. "So am I."

There was a signpost pointing to Abaton that stood just before a half-crumbled gate. The gatekeeper was a blind man, dressed in a loincloth. Every inch of his body was covered in tattoos—some pictorial, but most were words and random markings.

He perked up as he heard them approach. "What business have ye in Abaton?"

Charles sighed. It was not good espionage to declare your intentions. "Our own, if it's all the same to you."

"It's my job to ask, no need to be twisty about it. Sign your names, and enter."

"Sign?" said Charles.

"With the stylus," said the man. "On my skin. I am the keeper of the gate, and all who enter and leave must sign."

"Certainly," said Fred. He took the steel-pointed tool from the man's hand and quickly scribbled two names, which flared with silver fire. As they watched, the writing turned blue, as if it were changing ink.

"Thank you," said the tattooed man, and promptly went to sleep.

"Just a word of advice," Charles began.

"Oh, the names?" said Fred. "Don't worry—I didn't use ours. That might get us into trouble."

"Very perceptive!" Charles said, surprised. "Whose names did you write?"

"Harry Houdini and Arthur Conan Doyle," said Fred.

"This is already a great partnership," Charles said as they entered the town.

It was a pastiche of a town that seemed to have been assembled from a dozen cultures. There were gabled roofs topped with elaborate weather vanes sitting side by side with Turkish domes. The overarching theme was vaguely eastern European, but that might have been an impression generated by the age of some of the structures. The very air was ancient here. And although it was dressed up in familiar garb, that was just the wool covering the wolf underneath.

"There are stories," Charles whispered, "of a German village called Germelshausen, which fell under an evil spell cast by a witch. I've also heard of a similar tale from Scotland, about the Brig o' Doon, in Bobby Burns country, where Tam O' Shanter raced to safety across a stone bridge to escape from a village full of witches."

Fred swallowed hard. "An awful lot of references t' witches, Scowler Charles," the little badger said. "I hope this village in't like those villages."

"You and I both," said Charles, hitching up his belt. "Nothing to do but follow the path and see where it takes us."

As it was, their path led them right past a bakery, which was filled to overflowing with cakes, and pastries, and puddings, and on and on and on. It was a culinary wonderland in the middle of a virtual medieval village.

"Grandfather would be sorry he missed this," Fred said, reaching for a muffin from a cart near the door.

"Don't," warned Charles, grabbing Fred's paw. "I don't think it's wise to eat anything here. I've read far too many stories about travelers being trapped in places just because they ate a morsel of food—and if it's all the same to you, I'd rather be able to get home!"

"No problem, boss," said Fred.

"This also smacks of a witch's gambit," said Charles. "The minute you set foot in the gingerbread cottage, you suddenly find you're in an oven being roasted for dinner."

"Good call," Fred said, pointing up.

In the sky above them, silhouetted against the apricot sky, was a gaggle of witches—but Charles commented that they were wholly unlike any witches he had ever seen.

"How many have you seen?" asked Fred.

"Practically none," said Charles, "but I've read a lot about them, and these don't fit any of the descriptions."

The witches were not on brooms—they were riding bicycles. Each one was sitting upright with ramrod-straight posture and was wearing a dour gray dress, topped off with a black shawl and a pillbox hat.

The bicycles were as average as any he'd seen, except for the fact that they flew. Each one had reflectors on the front (for safety, he assumed) and a small wicker basket behind the seat. They bobbed and wove exactly like a flock of birds, each following in formation behind the others.

Charles and Fred ducked down an alleyway to stay out of sight, splashing through some puddles and tripping into a laundry line as they ran.

The witches were gradually moving southeast to northwest. They had nearly moved away from Charles and Fred altogether when one of the last witches in the gaggle pulled away from the group and stopped, hovering in the air above them.

She squinted her eyes and turned her head from side to side, then lifted her head up to the air and sniffed, then sniffed again.

A smile spread across her face, and she looked down directly at Charles and Fred's hiding place.

"Oh, no," said Charles. "She can smell us."

"You mean me," Fred groaned. "Wet badger fur is a curse—a curse, I tell you!"

"This way!" Charles yelled. "We'll try to lose her in the alleys and switchbacks."

No sooner were the words out of his mouth than he ran headfirst into a solid brick wall. Fred plowed into him a second later, and they both ended up sprawled in a heap.

Charles had led them into what was a blind alley. There were a few open doors on the adjacent walls, but the wall at the end was too high to scale.

"That's an unexpected turn of events," said Charles. "I don't think we can outrun her now!"

"We'll get you, my lovely boy," the witch cackled, "and make a fine pie of your dog!"

"I'm not a dog!" Fred shouted. "I'm a badger!"

The witch swooped down with terrifying speed and swung something at Charles as she passed.

He threw himself aside just in time, but she caught his sleeve. He rolled over as the witch spun about for another pass, and he realized that the elbow of his jacket was in tatters.

Rather than brandishing a wand, the witch was wielding a long, razor-edged fork.

"Oh, come on," Charles groaned. "A fork? What kind of a witch are you?"

"The kind who eats lovely little children like yourself!" she screeched as Charles again threw himself aside, protectively shielding Fred.

"Children!" Charles huffed, jumping to his feet. "I'm no child! I'm an *editor*! With *tenure*!"

The witch just laughed in response—a sound that was like grinding metal gears. She made another lightning pass that reduced Charles's jacket to a ragged mess.

"Curse it," Charles exclaimed. "There wasn't supposed to be any fighting. We're the espionage division, for heaven's sake!"

The witch continued to laugh as she came around again, but this time she wasn't targeting Charles. She was aiming at Fred.

Charles threw himself in front of her just before she ran down the little mammal, and the bicycle bounced violently off of his back. It knocked the wind out of him and only irritated the witch.

"Fred! Run!" Charles shouted. "I'll buy you some time and keep her attention on me!"

"I'm not leaving my partner!" Fred yelled back. Then he turned and dashed inside one of the houses.

"I didn't really expect him to go," Charles said under his

breath. "That was just something you're supposed to say."

The witch stopped laughing as she realized that she'd just lost track of one of her quarry. She rode the bicycle more slowly now, and a dark rage settled over her face.

"I can catch you anytime I want," she said with menace as she brandished the fork, which was tipped with crimson.

My blood, Charles realized. This was not going at all well, and it promised to get worse.

"I enjoy the game," the witch said, "but now it's time to finish it."

She dropped down to a height just level with Charles's head and hovered in front of him.

"You aren't going to escape," she said, grinning wickedly, "and neither will your dog."

"He's a badger, actually," said Charles.

"Did you really think you could defeat me? Was that your plan?"

"Not precisely, no," Fred responded as he appeared in a nearby doorway. "The plan was to get you to come closer and hold still."

Before she could react, Fred threw a handful of a thick, cream-colored substance at her. It struck her in the face and stuck like glue.

The witch shrieked in fury and wheeled the bicycle about. She let go of the handlebars to clutch at her face with her hands, and the bicycle spun crazily around, finally flipping end over end, completely out of control.

The bicycle crashed into a wall and plummeted to the ground. The witch fell off it just before it struck, and she rolled several times before she finally came to a stop against a barrel. She didn't move.

"Betcha no dog can do *that*," Fred said, wiping his paws and smirking. "Stupid witch."

"What was that?" Charles asked, flabbergasted.

"You said I couldn't eat anything, but you didn't say I couldn't use the food as a weapon," said Fred. "There were no muffins in there anyway. So I used the next best thing. Tapioca pudding."

"Fred," said Charles, "I'm completely impressed!"

"It's not as good as a poke in the eye with a sharp stick," said the little badger, "but it'll do in a pinch."

Charles and Fred had finished binding and gagging the witch, whom they hid behind a bushel of potatoes in the cellar of one of the houses. She only narrowly avoided being put into an oven.

"I still say we should have flipped the coin for three out of five," Fred grumbled. "She wouldn't have given us that much of a chance."

"That's what separates her from us," Charles said in admonishment. "We try not to eat anyone else."

"Oh, I wasn't going to eat her," said Fred. "But she would have made a nifty chunk of charcoal."

"At least she provided us with transportation and a disguise," Charles said as he pulled the shawl over his shoulders. "What do you think?"

"You make a pretty good witch," said Fred.

"Thanks a lot," said Charles. "If anyone asks, you're a dog."

"That's very insulting," said Fred.

"Hey," said Charles. "If I have to go in disguise, then so do you."

"Fair enough."

"How do you think this thing works?" Charles asked, examining the bicycle.

"It's not mechanical like the principles," Fred said, crouching to examine the gears. "I think it's purely magical."

"Oh, excellent," said Charles. "No risk there," he added with obvious sarcasm.

"Unless you've got a better idea, this is our best means of seeing the entire area at once," said Fred. "Time is of the essence, remember?"

"Okay," Charles said as he straddled the bike and lifted the lid on the wicker basket. "Hop in, Rover."

"This is very humiliating," said Fred as he clambered into the basket.

"Better than taking on another one of the witches, or something worse," said Charles. "Hold on—I'm going to attempt a takeoff."

He started pedaling and found he had to hold the handlebars tightly to counter the wobble from one of the bent wheels. He had no idea if a damaged wheel on the ground would have any effect on the contraption's ability to fly.

It didn't. With a few shaky hops, the bicycle bounded into the air. Pedaling furiously, Charles had cleared the rooftops in a matter of seconds, and soon they were high enough to see all of Abaton.

They were still on the eastern edge of the town, which sprawled all across the hilltops and into the valley below. They could see clusters of flying bicycles, but none near enough to cause immediate alarm.

There were several fires burning throughout the town, and the smoke obscured much of the sky. But it was clearer to the west, and Charles and Fred realized in the same instant that the western edge of the valley was where they needed to go.

There, in the distance, was the unmistakable form of a tower, stark and black against the twilight.

It was the Keep . . . remade as a patchwork lighthouse . . .

CHAPTER FIFTEEN
The Construct

The council of war at Tamerlane House looked as if a library of fairy tales had collided with a library of literary biographies, and someone had turned the result into a full-color, three-dimensional frieze.

The king and queen sat opposite Edgar Allan Poe at one end of the table; Charys, the centaur, sat between Mark Twain and Charles Dickens; Rillian, the unicorn mouse, sat on the table in front of Washington Irving; and Stephen, in full Golden Fleece regalia, sat next to his mother across from Geoffrey Chaucer. The Valkyrie Laura Glue, her wings discreetly folded behind her, was standing behind John and Daniel Defoe, and the improbable young Nemo stood next to her; while the Elf King Eledir, the Dwarf leader, Falladay Finn, and several surly fauns stood behind the rest of the Caretakers. It was, to put it simply, a remarkable group.

"Geoff," John said, still assimilating the recent events, "where should we begin?"

They had already decided to conceal the covert operation Fred and Charles were engaged in. If there was still a traitor among the Caretakers, serving him a play-by-play summary of their own efforts wouldn't be helpful.

The Last Book was already a secret from almost everyone—and so it would be difficult to express the concern the Caretakers were feeling at its loss.

Thus, once Bert, Artus, and Aven had addressed the group and detailed the events that had occurred on Paralon, the next order of business became the Prophecy itself.

"We believe that the Chancellor has spies within these walls," said Chaucer, "and so we must prepare for the inevitable. We will be attacked. And I believe that it will happen sooner rather than later."

"I concur," said Bert. "To move so in Paralon itself, he must be exceptionally confident."

"With good reason," said Artus. "He's been amassing power and influence for a long while. His allies will be our former allies—and so this will not be a war of armies. It will be a last stand."

"What Artus is trying to so cheerfully get across," said Aven, "is what my father was explaining earlier—this is not a new battle, as far as the Prophecy is concerned. This is the endgame."

"Oh, that was much more cheerful," said Defoe. "We have the Caretakers and the knight—when do we acquire the weapon the girl is supposed to use against the Winter King? Or Chancellor? Or whatever we're supposed to call him."

"The Shadow King," said Poe. "The Winter King is no more, and the Chancellor is a fiction. We are dealing with a Shadow King, and we will prevail. I have seen it."

"How do you know this?" asked Eledir.

"Because," said Poe, "in the future, there are still pistachio nuts."

"I'm going to assist Quixote and Rose," said Bert, "in their efforts to acquire the weapon. Artus and Aven have asked Jack to assist the captains in fortifying the Nameless Isles in preparation for the

Shadow King's move against us. And John and Stellan are going to continue in the effort to learn more of what our adversary is planning."

"We should have someone trying to suss out other spies," Defoe said with a sideways glance at Jakob Grimm. "Whoever they might be."

"That's a good idea," said Chaucer. "Will you take charge of that, Daniel?"

Defoe nodded. "I will."

"Excellent," Chaucer said. "Then for the moment, we've work to do."

Jack realized that being in charge of the war preparations meant that he was going to have to speak to the young Nemo. The appearance of the youth and the gleaming Dragonship was not as unusual to those in the Archipelago as it was to him. There had been numerous events caused by the Time Storms that had changed many things in the lands. But this was a harder thing to process. After having caused the older Nemo's death during the great battle at the Edge of the World, Jack made sure to visit Nemo's grave every time he'd come to the Archipelago, and he always had plenty to say. But now, with a young Nemo in the very next room, alive, he realized that he couldn't find any words.

Jack's musing was interrupted when a strong hand clapped down on his shoulder.

"When first we met," Charys said, "you were a student who was playacting at being a warrior. Now you are a teacher. And as a descendant of Charon himself, I can truly say there are few callings more noble."

"A teacher, yes," Jack replied. "But still playacting at being the warrior, I'm afraid."

At this the centaur grew serious. "Not playacting, Caretaker. Your deeds are well known throughout the Archipelago, and your bravery and skill are without question. The Far Traveler himself told me that you were a soldier of note in the Summer Country as well. Is that true?"

Jack nodded. "It is. But I'm afraid I didn't fare much better there than I did here. I still failed to protect the ones who depended on me."

"We are all here of our own choosing," Charys countered. "None among us has been coerced, or compelled against his will. Nemo knew what he was doing, and he knew, as do I, the day of his death."

"I know, and I accepted that, long ago," Jack said with a fleeting glance over at the young captain he was avoiding. "But I was hardly prepared for . . . for *this*."

"I have some of my own troops to attend to," Charys said as he wheeled about on his hind legs, "but consider this, Caretaker: What if you are the one who makes Nemo into the warrior he becomes? What if this is the opportunity to teach him what he needs to know to truly be a good man?"

"But for what?" Jack said, protesting. "We know what happened to him in the end."

"If for no other reason," Charys called back over his shoulder, "teach him well, so that when the time comes in his own future, he will be prepared to pass on what it means to be a man . . .

". . . to *you*."

❖   ❖   ❖

Charles and Fred landed well short of the tower. They concealed the bicycle in a thicket a few hills to the south of it, then stood up to take stock of their target.

Charles let out a long, slow whistle. It was the Keep of Time, remade as a patchwork lighthouse comprised of doors, rough-hewn stones, and creaky scaffolds. The space between the doors was only broad enough to allow one to open without compromising those adjacent to it, and there were few landings on the stairways—as if the opportunity to pause between doorways were an unthinkable folly.

Unlike the authentic keep, wherein the stairways were on the interior and the doors opened out into whatever time they were anchored to, this construct was exactly the inverse. The structure was built as a hollow tower, and the doors were then inserted into frames, which allowed them to open inward.

"That can't be safe," Charles murmured. "It's practically insane."

"Why?" asked Fred.

"Because all of the doors are linked to some point in the past," Charles whispered. "Just harnessing that kind of energy is almost impossible to conceive. But at least in the real keep, the doors opened out—that let each portal have its own space, so to speak. But if the doors open inward . . ."

"There's no space," said Fred. "They'll all be jammed in together."

"That's my worry," said Charles. "I don't think anything good can come of this."

The tower was all but impossible to approach. It was positioned high enough that any two guards could see everything approaching in any direction, and that would have been hard enough to bypass. The tower's scaffolding was a beehive of activity, with workers shoring up the base, adding to the top, and building new frames for doors to be set into.

Even worse, two more men approached the tower from the west, dragging another door behind them. Charles had briefly entertained the idea of disguising himself as a laborer, but there was also the possibility of running into Burton, who would easily recognize him. These two new arrivals tripled the odds of that happening.

"Houdini and Conan Doyle," Charles whispered. "The rogue Caretakers."

"I've heard tell of them," said Fred. "That's why I signed their names when we got here—although just mentioning them makes Bert very sad."

"I don't doubt it," said Charles. "They're worthy men—they've just made some very poor choices."

They watched as the Magician and the Detective carried the door to a frame that was built in a nearby field and placed it upright. Another man was called over from the tower to examine it, and Charles shuddered in recognition.

"And there he is," he hissed. "Burton. All the players but one have come to the stage."

Burton opened the door and looked inside. From their position, Charles and Fred couldn't see what he was looking at, but he seemed to declare it satisfactory, as two other workers came over to help carry it up to the top of the winding scaffolding.

"Do you think they're arranged the same way as they were in the real keep?" Charles wondered aloud. "Oldest at the bottom, and getting younger as they rise?"

"That would make sense," said Fred, "if they have been harvesting them as they fell. They would want to fix each door in place as they brought it here."

"I agree, apprentice," said Charles. "We've got to get over to that tower for a closer look. They're building it for some purpose, and we must discover what it is."

"Someone's coming this way," said Fred, pointing.

A very familiar-looking figure came clomping along the cobblestones. He was muttering to himself and walking with a strange, clumsy, high-footed gait.

As he came closer, they could see why. Bags, which were leaking sand in copious amounts, were bound around each of his feet and were tightly bound mid-calf. With every step he took there was a whumping sound and a small cloud of dust.

The figure stepped under one of the lights, and Charles swore softly and rolled his eyes in exasperation.

"Why am I not surprised in the least?" he said under his breath. "If there's something shifty or untrustworthy to be done, it's a level bet that Maggot is somewhere about."

Fred squinted to see better. "The Green Knight, you mean? He's a maggot?" He frowned. "He doesn't look like a maggot."

"You'd be surprised," Charles replied. "There's nothing under that armor but slime."

"Then how did he get to be the Green Knight?"

"It's supposed to be a penance."

Fred looked over the crates again. "Well then, he's doing it wrong."

Charles grinned. "We'll fix that. Follow me."

✦   ✦   ✦

The Caretaker and his apprentice slipped silently along the tree line just on the outer edge of Abaton's southernmost wall, mirroring Magwich's movements along the cobblestone path. When he came to an entrance into the town itself and turned his back to them, they leaped out and seized him, dragging him back into the bushes.

At first Magwich thought he'd been grabbed by a witch and an overly large familiar, but then Charles pulled off the hat and shawl and revealed his identity to the hapless knight.

"Eeep!" Magwich shrieked. "What—what are you doing here? You aren't supposed to be here!"

He stopped and looked at Charles more closely, puzzled. "You're dressed like a witch," he said, fear giving way to curiosity. "What's *that* all about?"

"I'm in disguise," said Charles.

"It works for you," said Magwich.

"Oh, shut up," Charles fumed. "How were you able to leave Avalon?"

In answer, Magwich pointed to the bags strapped to his feet. "In point of fact, I haven't left, not really. These bags are full of beach sand from the island. That means I can go anywhere I want to. I'm finally free of that stupid, empty, lonely island!"

"Your job wasn't done, Maggot," said Charles. "You abandoned your post."

"What post?" Magwich retorted. "After the Morgaine left, there was nothing left there to guard."

"You're wrong," said Fred. "There was a lot left."

"What is he chattering on about?" asked Magwich.

"Where's the spear?" Charles asked. "The spear that has been carried by all the other Green Knights in history?"

Magwich's jaw dropped open, and his eyes grew wide. "I—I couldn't say," he finally answered. "I must have lost it."

"Lost it, or sold it?"

"I wouldn't sell it!" Magwich exclaimed. "Burton would have had my head if I'd—"

Too late he realized his slip.

"He isn't too bright, is he?" asked Fred.

"That's a major understatement," said Charles. He grabbed Magwich by the breastplate and pulled him close. "Listen, Maggot," he said in as threatening a tone as he could manage, "we need to know what's going on here. We need to know what Burton's doing with the tower, and with the spear. And we need to know right now."

"You can't scare me!" Magwich retorted. "I have rights, you know. And when the Chancellor finds out what you've done, there'll be consequences, I promise you!"

"The Chancellor will never know," said Charles, drawing him closer. "Do you know what happened to the last Green Knight who tried to leave Avalon?"

Magwich gulped and swallowed hard, shaking his head.

"He set foot on a boat," said Charles, "and his arms and legs caught fire. And then his chest exploded."

Magwich's eyes were huge.

"Then," Charles went on, "insects began to nest in his chest cavity, where they laid eggs. Eventually the eggs hatched into worms—and the worms burrowed their way up his neck and into his head, and he got to watch the entire time. And the last thing he saw before he perished in terrible agony was the worms eating into his eyeballs. That's what happened to him."

"I—I don't believe you!" Magwich stammered.

"It doesn't matter if you believe me," Charles said with finality, "but if you don't tell us what we want to know, we're going to take those bags off your feet, and you can find out the truth for yourself."

Magwich paused to consider whether he was serious, and on cue, Fred reached out with a sharp claw and snicked open one of the straps that held the bags in place.

"All right, all right!" Magwich yelled. "I'll tell you everything!"

And he did. It took only a few minutes, but when he was through, all the blood had drained out of Charles's face.

"We've got to get back right now," he said to Fred. "This is too important to wait."

Fred tied Magwich's hands and legs and gagged him. They threw him over the handlebars of the bicycle and tied him down; then Fred climbed into the basket as Charles began to pedal.

It was much harder to take off with the added weight, but Charles did not want to risk leaving Magwich behind. It took several tries, but finally they became airborne. Once they were at altitude, it was much easier to navigate the bicycle, and they set course for the Trump portal that lay past the eastern gate of Abaton.

"Uh-oh," Fred said as he peered through the weave of the basket. "There's trouble a' comin."

Flying straight toward them were three witches, also on bicycles.

"I hope the disguise works," said Charles.

"So do I," said Fred. "I don't have any more tapioca."

The witches stopped in midair and greeted Charles. "Hello, sister," said the first witch. She pointed at Magwich. "What have you got there?"

"Uh, lunch," Charles said in a terrible falsetto.

"Lunch?" said the second witch. "He's a Green Man. You can't eat a Green Man, even in Abaton."

"We're going to use him to start the fire," said Charles.

"That's just asking for trouble," said the second witch. "The rest will burn *us* out if you do that!"

"Hey," said the third witch, who had flown around to look at the wicker basket. "What have you got here?"

"It's, ah, my dog," said Charles.

"Woof," Fred said helpfully.

"It's the ugliest dog I've ever seen," said the witch. "It looks more like a badger."

"That's very rude," said Fred.

"Oh dear," Charles said before the witches could react. "Hold on tight, Fred!"

Pedaling as if the devil himself were at his heels, Charles put the bicycle into a steep dive and aimed for the eastern gate. He had almost reached the tattooed man when Fred pointed out that the witches were right behind them.

Charles grimaced. Of course they were. The witches were better bicyclists than he was—or at least they were much more experienced—and they weren't carrying a badger with lousy self-control and a Green Knight made of wood.

The bicycle careened past the gate, and they could finally see the portal, hanging in the air just ahead.

"Hang on," he said again. "We're going to come in hot!"

Without slowing, Charles aimed the bicycle straight for the portal and went screaming through, crashing hard against the opposite wall of the gallery in Tamerlane House.

He staggered to his feet. "Ransom! Somebody! Close the Trump, quickly!"

Ransom ran in from the anteroom and took hold of the Trump just as the witches were coming into view. Rapidly the illustration began to shrink; in moments it was the size of a card again, and Ransom placed it in the pages of a book.

All the Caretakers were summoned, along with Aven and Artus. The still shaken Charles hurriedly explained what he and Fred had been doing, and why the Green Knight was bound and gagged.

Jack and Dickens dragged Magwich off to lock him in a closet, and John brought a kettle of hot tea for Charles and Fred as the other Caretakers arrived in the gallery.

Once they had regained their breath, Fred and Charles took turns relating what they'd seen in Abaton, giving special emphasis to the tower of doors.

"What are they doing with it?" John exclaimed. "What can they be using the doors to do?"

"That's the worst part," said Fred. "The Chancellor's using them to find the dragons one by one."

"Good luck with *that*," said Jack. "What's he going to do? Poke them with the spear?"

"He's discovered a use for the spear that no one ever anticipated, no one ever dreamed . . . ," Charles said, his voice trailing off. "There's just . . . there's no way to . . ."

"What is it, Charles?" demanded Jack. "What is he doing with the spear?"

"He's using it to sever shadows," said Fred. "*Anyone's* shadow."

"So he's creating another army of Shadow-Born, then?" asked Jack. "We've dealt with that before."

"Not like this, Jack," said Charles. "*Any* shadow. From any creature, whether it walks—or flies."

It took a moment for Jack to realize what he was being told, and when he did, his eyes widened in disbelief. "You can't mean . . . How? How is that even possible?"

"We don't know how he's doing it," Charles said, rising and pacing. "We just know that he is. He's using the Spear of Destiny. Somehow, Chancellor Murdoch is severing the shadows from the *Dragons themselves.* And the army he is building with them will be unstoppable."

. . . an apparition . . . her gown floating in the water . . .

Chapter Sixteen
The Broken Sword

"There is a Ring of Power here, in the Nameless Isles," said Bert. "It's not made of massive standing stones, as the others are. This one is closer to a fairy ring, in that it can be used only to summon a single entity—the Lady of the Lake.

"You have the authority to use the ring," he told Rose, "and Quixote has the right to request a boon. So only the two of you should go, if she's to appear at all."

"One more thing," said Chaucer. "There is a guardian. He may or may not let you pass. It's our hope that he will. But tell him your request, simply and honestly, and I believe that he will see you through to the Lady."

"It's low tide," Bert said. "You should be able to walk to the upper crescent island. You'll find the guardian and the Ring of Power there."

They watched as the girl and the old knight walked out of Tamerlane House and toward the northern part of the island.

"Will it be dangerous for them?" asked Chaucer.

"No," Bert replied with a sad smile. "As a great poet once said, 'It ain't nothin' but a family thing.'"

◆　◆　◆

The guardian was tall and bearded, and his hair was white, with two streaks of gray. He was dressed simply in a tunic and leather breeches, and he carried a black staff.

He started when he first heard them approach, then relaxed when he could see them more clearly, and he even smiled as they stepped into the circle of firelight.

"Greetings, niece," the man said, rising from where he was tending the fire. "What brings you to the island at the top of the world?"

"Niece?" Quixote exclaimed, startled by the unexpected greeting. He had fully expected to have to answer a riddle, or perform a feat of skill to be allowed to approach.

"Don Quixote," Rose said in introduction, "this is my uncle, Taliesin the Lawgiver."

Taliesin bowed his head in greeting. "It is simply Taliesin these days. I no longer deal with laws, or those who would see them broken. I am more than content to spend my days here, tending the fire and guarding the circle."

"So it's true," Rose said. "From here, we can summon the Lady of the Lake?"

"Yes," he said. "She may be summoned here. But I fear you may not like the reception she gives you."

"Why is that?" asked Quixote. "I have met her before, and found her to be most gracious."

"I have heard of you, O Riddle Master," Taliesin said with a lopsided grin, "but I was speaking about the Grail Child. I have come to terms with her existence, but my sister has not."

"What did you come to terms with?" asked Rose. "Have I offended you in some way?"

Taliesin shook his head. "Not you, my dear, but your father."

"I know what he is," said Rose. "I hope that I've learned better lessons than he did."

Taliesin gave her a long look, then gestured for them to sit by the fire. "Do you know," he asked when they were seated comfortably, "how Arthur died?"

"I don't," said Rose. "Not really, other than knowing that Mordred was involved."

"Mordred was always on the fringes of the kingdom, waiting for his chance at vengeance," Taliesin said. His beard glowed red from the fire, and his eyes sparkled as he talked. "But it was not Mordred alone who caused Arthur's downfall. He was betrayed by one of his own knights, his most trusted and loyal friend."

"Lancelot," said Quixote, nodding. "I have met this knight."

Taliesin looked surprised at this, but simply continued his story. "There had been decades of peace in both worlds, thanks to Arthur. It was, in every possible way, a Golden Age. And then Lancelot fell in love with the queen, Arthur's wife—your mother, Guinevere. He became consumed with the idea of being with her, of having her to himself. And so he conceived of a plan to see Arthur, his own best friend, killed on the battlefield—and he arranged with Mordred to do the deed."

"D-did my mother participate in this plan?" Rose asked.

"She did not help, but she knew about it—and she did nothing to stop it until it was well in motion," said Taliesin.

He paused, and poked some embers from the fire with the staff. They sparked and danced in the air.

"Mordred was successful in his revenge," Taliesin continued. "Arthur was slain. Together with her sons, Artigel and Eligure, Guinevere removed his body to Avalon. Lancelot was banished for his part in the murder, and Mordred was cut off completely from entering the Archipelago.

"Artigel assumed the Silver Throne and began to draw a curtain of secrecy over the whole Archipelago, to ensure that Mordred never found his way back. And that was the beginning of the separation of the two worlds.

"Because of the contention between our sibling-cousins, Merlin and Mordred, our family has known little else but suffering and grief," said Taliesin. "Only Thorn, who became the Arthur, has ever brought a glimmer of light into our circle. And even he was born only because Merlin forced himself on Nimue, who became the Lady of the Lake. She raised him to be a good, strong, and noble man—and then he was killed by your father's hand, and your mother's betrayal. So can you understand, young Rose, why she might not be so eager to speak to you?"

"I do understand," Rose answered, "at least as much as I am able to. But I must try, nevertheless. Many people are counting on it."

"Very well," said Taliesin. He looked at Quixote. "Are you prepared for the challenge?"

Quixote nearly fell off his rock. He composed himself and stammered something that sounded like an acceptance. Would it be a trial of skill? Or a battle of wits?

"If you can answer my question, you may pass," said Taliesin. "How long is a rope?"

"Eh . . . What?" said Quixote.

Taliesin chuckled and waved his hands. "I but jest. It's a joke I heard from a bird once. Of course you may pass." He stood up and gestured to them. "Come this way."

He led them up and over a small, grassy rise, then down to a hidden cove. It was more placid than silent, and was unremarkable: just a sandy beach, a few grasses, and the occasional petrified log. Then they saw it.

It was a small ring of standing stones, which glittered in the light of the rising moon. A miniature Ring of Power.

"I will leave you to your business," Taliesin said. "Do you know what to say?"

Rose nodded. The old man shifted his staff to his other hand, clapped Quixote on the shoulder, and walked back over the rise.

With an encouraging nod from Quixote, Rose stepped inside the ring and began to speak.

> *By right and rule*
> *For need of might*
> *I call on thee*
> *I call on thee*

> *By blood bound*
> *By honor given*
> *I call on thee*
> *I call on thee*

> *For life and light your protection given*
> *From within this ring by the power of Heaven*
> *I call on thee*
> *I call on thee*

At first she was afraid it hadn't worked—that she had done something wrong, or, worse, that she simply hadn't been worthy enough to speak the summoning.

Then a ripple appeared on the placid surface of the water in the cove, then another, and another.

A greenish blue light began to emanate from somewhere below—far deeper than the water actually seemed to be. Then she appeared.

To describe the lady as an apparition would not have done her justice. The folds of her gown floating in the water, twinned with the long strands of her auburn hair, gave her a spectral appearance, but as she rose higher and broke the surface, she was revealed as a creature of flesh and bone. But whatever else she appeared to be, she was not to be toyed with.

Her eyes were stern and cold, and her bearing was haughty. She glided closer to the shoreline, her feet never losing contact with the water.

"Who has summoned me in the old way?" she asked, barely containing her fury. "Who has called the Lady of the Lake?"

Rose knelt in the sand, careful not to touch the water. "I have," she said simply. "I am Rose Dyson, daughter of Guinevere."

The Lady moved closer. "I know who you are," she said coldly. "Tell me why I should not take you now and drag you into the deeps of the sea to drown."

"I gave my lifeblood once to save your son," Rose said softly. "Would you take it again, just to avenge him?"

The Lady retreated, just a little, and the mask of anger slipped, then fell.

"Would that I could," she answered. "Your kin have always been a vexation to me."

"Your kin as well, milady," Rose reminded her, "and I cannot say I disagree with you."

The Lady smiled at that—this girl was an odd mix, she thought. Confidence and boldness, but coupled with an openness that made her hard to dislike.

"Why have you summoned me, child? You may not like the answers I have for you, whatever you ask."

"I summoned you because I could," Rose answered, "and I do have many questions, but there is someone else here who would speak with you."

With that cue, Quixote strode forward next to the ring and removed his helmet.

"Greetings, milady," he said, bowing his head. "It is good to see you again."

"As it is good to see you, brave sir knight," the Lady said. She moved forward almost to the water's edge and pulled gently on his shoulders, permitting him to rise. "I have often thought of the great service you did for me, so long ago. It is among my fondest memories."

"It is one of mine as well, milady," said Quixote, "and that is the reason I have come. I seek a boon."

Her eyes flared up briefly before she softened again. "Of all who seek me out to ask for favors," she said, "only you have the right to do so. What do you seek?"

"Milady," Quixote said, "we seek the return of the sword Caliburn."

The Lady drew back a few feet, then drew back again, holding her hands to her chest. "My son's sword?" she exclaimed. "You wish me to give you the sword of Arthur?"

"We do."

She shook her head. "It is shattered. It is useless to you."

"Surely there must be a way to repair it?" Quixote asked. "It is a matter of the gravest importance."

"You are speaking of the Prophecy, are you not?"

He nodded. "I am."

The Lady seemed to shrink in on herself at this. "The only thing more destructive than limitless ambition," she said, "is a Prophecy, and the fools who follow it."

Turning, she sank into the water and disappeared. For a moment Quixote and Rose were worried that they had offended her, but an instant later she rose back through the water and approached them again, arms outstretched.

In one hand she held the hilt, in the other, the blade. She handed them both to Quixote.

"Thank you," he said gratefully. "Now that we have the sword, we can repair it and—"

"Repair it?" said the Lady. "It cannot be repaired by any smith in the Archipelago or in the Summer Country. It was forged in a time before the age of the Old Gods was over, and none remain who can match the work."

"There must be someone," said Rose. "Taliesin, perhaps?"

"If it were only that, then it might be possible," said the Lady, "but this sword was not shattered by force—it was shattered by a breaking of the Old Magic. And only by Old Magic may it be restored.

"There is only one way to repair Caliburn," she continued, with a tone in her voice that defied argument. "Only he who broke it may restore it. Only Madoc."

"Madoc!" Rose exclaimed. "My father? But he may be the very enemy we are fighting against—or at least, an aspect of him."

"I told you that you would not be so happy to hear the answers I had to give," said Nimue.

"I am not sad," said Quixote. "I asked for a boon, and you granted it. We needed this sword, and you gave it to us. We needed to know how to restore it, and without seeking more for yourself, you shared the secret with us. There is nothing that has happened here today that has saddened me."

"Just remember," Nimue said as she turned and began fading back beneath the water, "do not make the mistakes your forebears made. Do not sacrifice that which you want the *most*, for that which you want the most *at that moment*."

"And do not forget," she said, almost gone.

"Only Madoc may repair Caliburn. Only Madoc."

"But he's dead—isn't he?" asked Shakespeare. "The great Dragon dropped him over the waterfall at the Edge of the World."

"His Shadow survived, and plagues us still," said Bert, "so we believe that somehow, somewhere, he must still be alive."

The war council had been reconvened to decide what to do. They had the sword—but making it whole seemed impossible.

"There's no way to even find him if he lives," said Defoe. "No one's ever gone over the Edge of the World. No one who has returned, that is."

"That's not exactly correct," said Twain, "is it, Professor? It is indeed possible that Mordred—pardon, Madoc—survived, and it's equally possible to find where he is."

"What does he mean?" John said, turning to his mentor.

"It's very simple," said Professor Sigurdsson. "Rose must find Madoc, and I must accompany Rose as her guide. There is no other alternative."

The room went silent, as every Caretaker to a man looked over at the professor.

"That makes sense," John said reasonably, not realizing how much more gravitas was evident in the faces of everyone else. "You certainly have the training, and the experience, and if I were in your place, I wouldn't want to miss a chance for one last adventure."

Defoe let out a bark of a laugh and was elbowed in the ribs by Hawthorne. The professor responded only with a smile that was more melancholy than admonishing.

"That's more true than you realize, John," he said, clapping his protégé on the shoulder.

"Have we missed something?" Jack asked. Charles shrugged and looked at Twain, who merely observed the three companions and puffed on his cigar.

"Rules of time may be broken," said Professor Sigurdsson. "Rules of space may be broken. But not together, and not at the same, ah, time, so to speak. Bent, sometimes, in the rarest of circumstances. But not broken."

"There are limitations," Bert explained. "It's one of the reasons that this place has been kept such a secret. Yes, using Verne's technology it is possible to do as we have done, and summon personages from the past to dine, and discuss, and determine the fate of the world. But the price they pay is that this is all there is—none of them may pass beyond the threshold of Tamerlane House and live."

John sank back in despair. "Then we're handicapped before we start."

"Seven days," came a voice from the upper floor, ghostlike and ethereal. "One may pass outside this door, but unless he crosses back before the end of seven days, he will vanish back into the ether."

"Is that true?" said John, looking at Bert, then the professor.

"I'd trust in Poe," said Bert. "It is his house, after all, and much of what Jules learned was based on his writings. If he says seven days, then you can plan on it."

"You can't do it, Professor," John said, already anticipating his mentor's decision. "We'll find some way to communicate your instructions, to transfer the information they need to navigate to them without sending you in person. There must be some other way."

"It's a bit odd, isn't it?" said Charles. "We have the ability to travel around in time, and into alternate dimensions. We can summon people from the dead. And we're at an impasse to save the world because no one thought to install a telephone system in the Archipelago."

"Actually, we tried," Bert replied. "Nemo was keen to do it, but we could never get all the lands to agree to hook it up. And when you add to that the peculiar weather patterns, the temporal shifts, and mermaids who had a tendency to chew up any cables strung underwater, the result was the lostest of lost causes. The badgers have set up a rudimentary version, but it's not much more advanced than a telegraph, I'm afraid."

"There is no other way, John," the professor said. "Other than Bert, I'm the only one who has ever traveled that far west—at least, the only one willing to act as a guide."

They all knew from the professor's hangdog expression that

he was thinking of his old friend Uruk Ko, the Goblin King.

The Goblins were among the most ancient and noble races in the Archipelago, and Uruk Ko and Stellan Sigurdsson had shared a love of adventure and discovery that had culminated in an unprecedented journey. But when the first war with the Winter King took place, Uruk Ko chose to side with Mordred. And after they were defeated, he closed the borders of the Goblin lands to all outsiders.

"We can persuade the Goblin King to do it, somehow," John pleaded. "It's worth trying, and better than you going to a certain death."

The professor laughed heartily at this. "My boy, I have already suffered a certain death, as you put it. Anything from here on out is just gravy."

"But you're *alive* again! It's such an opportunity!" John cried. "We can't just waste it!"

The professor took his young study—who was now nearing the age he had been when he died—firmly by the arms and looked into his eyes.

"John," Professor Sigurdsson said gently, "the reason we were given the chance to come here, now, to this extraordinary place, was to discuss the gravest of crises at the most crucial time in history. Only we Caretakers, gathered here in this way, have the means to decide the future of all that exists. And it seems I am to play a significant role in that. There is nothing wasted in this, John. Not for three days' sake, or three thousand years. It is not wasted. And you should never think it so."

Suddenly a wild idea crossed John's mind. "Hallward!" he exclaimed excitedly. "If the journey takes longer than seven days, can't he just paint another portrait of the professor?"

Bert and Stellan looked at each other, then at their protégé. "No," Bert said after a long pause. "He can't. Didn't you notice, among the Elder Caretakers, that one significant member was missing?"

John chewed on his knuckle and thought, and suddenly realized that there had been one more canvas in the gallery—but one that was only a pastoral background, with no portrait.

"Dante," he said at length. "It can only be Dante Alighieri. His is the missing portrait, isn't it?"

"Yes," said Bert.

"I just assumed he'd been liberated earlier for some reason. What are you telling me, Bert?"

"He was one of the earliest portraits Jules arranged for Basil to paint," Bert explained, "mostly so that we could glean from him more details regarding the Underneath at Chamenos Liber. Dante decided he wanted to actually go there, and he was with the Lost Boys when the time limitation had passed. They reported back to us that he simply faded away into bits of light and dust.

"The others who were here promptly reentered their paintings and only ventured out again after much cajoling. But when they remained as they were, we realized the confines of Tamerlane House were the only limitation to their existing in perpetuity."

"Hang on a minute," said Charles. "If the Caretakers Emeritis can't leave without risking disintegration, then hasn't Kipling just cut his own throat? He certainly won't come back, but if he doesn't, he's doomed."

Bert screwed up his face a moment, considering. "I don't know," he said finally. "We've never tried sending any deceased Caretakers through a Trump. Not because it hadn't occurred to us, but because to have persons who should be dead running around in the open could change too many things. Plus, it scares the horses."

"Can't you go, Bert?" said John. "You wouldn't be at risk the way the professor would be, and you said yourself that you were the only other one who'd ventured that far."

"He might," said the professor, "but he's needed here, more so than I. And I cannot captain the *White Dragon*."

"But—but there has to be some way," John began.

The professor shushed him with a gesture. "Our forces are few, and those of our enemy are many," he said, smiling. "We must use the resources we have to the fullest capacity—and when it comes down to it, I can be the most helpful by doing this."

"But you'd be risking your life!" said John.

"We're all risking our lives, John," the professor reminded him. "And anyway, all I'm risking is my second go-round. I'm willing."

The rest of the Caretakers murmured their agreement and thumped the table for emphasis, and John resigned himself to the fact that this course was indeed the most practical. "All right," he said. "That sounds like a plan."

PART FIVE

Beyond the Edge of the World

The old knight . . . moved the Scarlet Dragon . . . over the edge . . .

CHAPTER SEVENTEEN
Strategies of War

"**We have to destroy it,**" said Artus. "We have to destroy it now."

The rest of the collective at Tamerlane House were in agreement. The new Tower of Time in Abaton needed to be destroyed.

"He can't reach the dragons without the tower," said Bert, "and until we have the means to fight the spear, this is our best means of attacking him."

"I agree," said John. "There's no way of knowing how many Dragons he's gotten to already—so we should be prepared for anything."

A stealth team was assembled to go back through the Trump into Abaton. No Caretakers were included other than Jack and Charles—it was too great a risk to send them through to an unknown region. If a mishap occurred, it was possible for the still living to find a way to return. The lives of any Caretakers who had come through one of the portraits would be limited to a week if they could not get back.

Charles and Fred were the guides, and Jack was the commander of the small group, which included Stephen, Nemo, three of the Elves, and Laura Glue, along with five of her Valkyries. The latter six were included in the event the witches were still hovering near the entrance to Abaton.

The Elves were coming along specifically to guard Magwich. Charles suspected that his involvement might be necessary at some point, and as reluctant as he was to include the traitorous Green Knight, he couldn't discount the possibility that he'd be needed.

At first John objected to Laura Glue's inclusion—until Aven diplomatically reminded him that she was a veteran warrior and was already older than he had been the first time he went to war.

Artus, Aven, Charys, and the other ship captains set about deploying their small armada along the inner borders of the ring of islands in preparation for the pending attack. There was no way to know how large an army to expect, nor did anyone know what they might do if the Dragon shadows arrived. There was no way to defeat the Dragons themselves—and to combat the shadows was unthinkably terrible.

"That's why we have to repair Caliburn," reiterated Professor Sigurdsson. "It's the only possible way."

"Do you think it will restore the Dragons?" asked John. "Basically reverse the effects of the spear?"

The professor shrugged. "I've no clue. We simply have to trust in the Prophecy and do the best that we can."

"I'll take Rose, the professor, and Quixote to Terminus in the *White Dragon*," said Bert, "where they will be able to continue on using the *Scarlet Dragon*. I'll return as quickly as I can."

John didn't say it, but he knew what they were all thinking: In the coming conflict, one more Dragonship might make little difference, if any.

"Let's go to it, then," said John. "There's no time to waste."

+   +   +

"How many poets does it take to change a lightbulb?" asked Twain.

"I give up," said Swift. "How many?"

"Three," Twain replied, cackling. "One to curse the darkness, one to light a candle, and one to change the bulb."

"What's a lightbulb?" asked Shakespeare, scratching his head.

"Samuel, Jonny, leave William be," said Bert. "We're trying to save the world here, remember?"

"Sorry," said Twain. "I'm just trying to keep ourselves distracted while everyone else is being productive."

"Pardon," said Hawthorne, "but has anyone seen Jakob? I can't find him anywhere."

"That's not a good sign," said Defoe. "I'm starting to wonder if we haven't discovered who the traitor is who stole the Last Book."

"Jakob is a good man," said Bert, "and I trust him."

"Well enough and fine," Defoe said, rising. "I'm going to go look for him just the same."

The passage into Abaton went as easily as before.

The skies were clear—wherever the witches had gone, they weren't waiting about for a scholar and his dog.

They passed through the gatekeeper by signing with the names of members of the Imperial Cartological Society.

"As a precaution," Charles had advised them, "just in case anyone's checking."

In short order they reached the vantage point where they could observe the tower without being seen—but unlike before, there were no workers milling about.

"This doesn't bode well," said Charles.

There were several dozen Yoricks congregating at points all along the base of the tower, and among them, dressed as he had been at Tamerlane House, was Kipling.

"So he really is a traitor," Jack said, his temper rising. "He's mine."

"Agreed," said Stephen, "if we can get there at all. We don't have enough warriors with us to take on all of those Un-Men."

"I wonder," said Fred. "Would you call them a flock of Yoricks, like birds? Or something else?"

"They knew," Stephen whispered. "They knew we were coming. It's a trap."

"How could they know?" said Charles. "No one saw us! And Kipling didn't know we'd been here!"

"Maybe they realized I went missing," Magwich sniffed. "I'm very vital to their plans, you know."

"There's how they knew," Laura Glue said, pointing.

The tattooed gatekeeper was standing in front of Kipling. His arms were raised, and he was turning around, giving the rebel Caretaker a full view of the fraudulent signatures.

"Drat," Charles exclaimed. "I thought it was a clever idea."

"So what should we do?" said Stephen. "If we leave to bring reinforcements, they might do the same."

"I say we simply attack," said Nemo, rising. "We're all warriors here, are we not? Then let's have a battle!"

"Sit down!" Jack whispered, pulling the young captain off his feet. "You'll get us all killed!"

"Are you afraid to fight?" Nemo scoffed. "Perhaps you ought to stick to your books."

"I'm not afraid," said Jack calmly, "but I'm not stupid, either. You should learn that a good plan beats a swift attack."

"So what do you propose?" said Stephen.

"We brought the Valkyries along as defense against the witches," Jack said. "I think they'll serve us better as a distraction."

"But the bird-men," Nemo began.

"Are flightless," said Jack. "They can't fight what they cannot reach."

Torches were lit, and Jack's plan was put into motion. The Valkyries were sent aloft, and almost instantly they caught the attention of the Un-Men.

Laura Glue, Sadie Pepperpot, Abby Tornado, and Norah Kiffensdottir each took a compass point above the tower and hurled the torches into the scaffolding. Then, as one, they flew to the north.

As Jack had hoped, Kipling sent half the Yoricks up into the tower to douse the flames, while he led the other half in pursuit of the cackling Valkyries.

"Nonny, nonny, nonny!" Norah called down. "Stupid birds!"

"Discipline, Norah," said Laura Glue. "If you're going to taunt them, remember to stick out your tongue."

"Sorry," said Norah. "I forgot."

"Aren't you worried about the Valkyries?" asked Nemo. "What about the witches?"

"They'll be fine," said Stephen. "Laura Glue can outmaneuver any bicycle ever made, flying or not."

"Now," said Jack, "we finish the job."

Suddenly Magwich let out a howl and threw himself over the

bushes, past his surprised guards. "Chancellor!" he cried out. "Wait for me! I'm coming!"

"Nothing to do now but follow that idiot," said Charles as he grabbed a torch. "Let's go."

The small group ran after the Green Knight, who was losing sand with every footfall. They caught up to him just as he reached the tower.

"Magwich, you fool," Charles exclaimed as the knight started to climb the steps. "We're going to burn it down! Come back here!"

"I'm not coming down!" yelled Magwich. "One of these will open for me! I know it!" But every door he tried was locked.

"What do we do?" asked Jack.

"He made his choice," said Charles, "and we have none." He thrust the torch into the lumber at the base of the tower.

Once the flames caught the first planks, the rest of the base burst into flame in a matter of minutes. In no time at all the entire tower was a raging inferno of blue flame.

"Look at that thing burn," said Fred. "You're really good at setting fires, Charles."

"Thanks," said Charles. "It seems I have a special knack for destroying Keeps of Time."

The Valkyries circled back around just as the others reached the Trump portal. By now, the flames from the burning tower could be seen from many miles away.

"We lost them," said Laura Glue. "They'll not catch us before we're long gone."

"Excellent," Charles said as he stepped through the portal. "With the exception of Magwich, this couldn't have gone better."

Jack felt the same way—but as he was preparing to step through the portal himself, he glanced back to where the gatekeeper had been . . .

. . . and he saw Kipling, who waved, then stepped through a Trump of his own.

The war council cheered at the news of the successful raid against the tower, then despaired as Jack told them what he had seen.

"They have been a step ahead of us the entire time," Defoe complained. "They knew about the raid, and after it was carried out, Kipling waves at you?"

"It could simply be an act of chivalry," said Spenser. "Acknowledging the victory of a superior opponent."

"I'm not feeling all that superior," said Jack. "Just a bit weary."

The Caretakers were left to debate the next course of action, while Jack and Charles joined Artus on the large island to the south to help prepare their defenses.

"There are a number of people on the ships I don't recognize," said Charles. "Are these all vetted allies?"

"Each and all," said Artus. "The reason some are a bit unfamiliar is because some of them came through in Time Storms just like young Nemo. The person who conceived of and trained the Valkyries came through to the Underneath, actually, during our battle with the King of Crickets. Amazing woman."

"Would her name be Earhart?"

"Yes," Artus said, surprised. "Do you know her?"

"By reputation only," said Jack, "but she's a good match for Laura Glue."

"That explains why Falladay Finn has been ignoring us, then," said Charles. "He must have come through from a point before we met."

"Mmm, no," Artus said, shaking his head. "That's the same Falladay Finn—he's just in a particularly bad mood. We found we can't just summon armies and allies willy-nilly, like picking fruit from a bowl. We've had to be much more precise than that."

"Precise how?" asked Jack.

Artus grinned. "If Mordred can pull allies from out of the past, then so can we. Come and take a look."

He opened the hold of the *Blue Dragon* and revealed a giant clockwork man. It was covered in silver and carried a great ax.

"We call him the Tin Man," said Artus, "but really, his name's Roger."

"I thought you were done with clockworks," said Charles, "after the Parliament fiasco."

"Shh," said Artus, closing the doors. "He's sleeping, and I don't want him to hear you.

"This fellow's not exactly a clockwork," Artus continued. "He's more of an old friend who's managed to, ah, enhance his physicality."

"Fair enough," said Charles. "We'll take all the allies we can get."

"I heard how things went on the raid," Aven said to Jack as Charles and Artus continued to check the ships. "Stephen told me. I think you handled Nemo well."

"He's headstrong, and he just won't listen," said Jack, exasperated. "I'm not really sure what to do with him."

"He sounds very much like a young man I once knew," Aven said, raising an eyebrow. "He didn't listen much either."

"That's an angle Charys already tried," said Jack. "I'm certainly not the same person I was, and neither is Nemo."

"That's right," Aven replied. "You aren't. You're an experienced, mature teacher—and he's a spoiled youngest son of royalty, who thinks he's invincible."

"I just don't know how to talk to him, Aven," Jack said. "How can I, when I'm the reason he ends up dying?"

"Maybe because you must, if for no other reason," she said. "It hasn't been any easier for me. Nemo will one day become Stephen's father, and I know he will die. And Stephen knows it too, having never known his father at all. But now, here, we all three have the chance to say things unsaid, and to help this spoiled boy fulfill his own potential.

"My father always talks about how even in time travel, we are always moving forward," she continued, "so consider all this talk of Charles's and Ransom's about causality, and timelines, and different dimensions. What if one of the reasons Nemo took an interest in you then was because you've taken an interest in him now?"

Jack rubbed his chin. "Charys said something similar," he murmured. "You may both be right."

"There's a reason the centaurs have been the great teachers of the ages," Aven said as she walked out of the room, "and there are reasons why both you and Artus come to me when you need advice."

She walked away toward the *Yellow Dragon*, leaving him alone.

◆ ◆ ◆

The *White Dragon* eased slowly down to the beach on the southern shore of Terminus, which rose over the westernmost edge of the sea. Bert disconnected the harnesses that had bound the *Scarlet Dragon* to the larger vessel and turned to his companions.

"You know how badly John wanted to come, Stellan," Bert said, almost as an apology.

"Yes," replied Stellan. "I know it. But he would have wanted to continue past the Edge, and he has other responsibilities to tend to."

"You must lower the *Scarlet Dragon* into the water," Bert explained, "and go over the edge as if you were a twig caught up in the current. Only then, once you are over and falling, may you deploy the chute, and then unbind the balloon and rotors."

"Isn't that awfully risky?"

"There's nothing about this venture that isn't risky," Bert replied, "but it's the only way past the falls. We've tried to sail airships at altitude, but we always get forced back. The only way over . . . is down."

"It's quite a dilemma, isn't it?" a voice said into John's ear. He sat up straighter in his seat and spun around. A cat's head was grinning at him and floating in midair above his chair. "This business of saving the world."

"Grimalkin," John said, sitting back. "You startled me."

"I seem to be good at that," said the cat. "It's a Cheshire thing."

"Is it also a Cheshire thing to be trusted?" said John. "No one here worries much that you appear and disappear at will."

"I'm trusted, because I'm bound," said the cat. "Do you see my collar? It's a Binding."

"I thought Bindings were spoken spells, involving True Names and blood."

"They are—so consider how terrible a creature I must have been to require a physical binding as well."

John gave Grimalkin a quizzical look. He really wasn't sure whether the cat was just playing with him, or whether the words spoken were serious. "I'm not quite sure what to make of you."

"That's why I trust *you*," the Cheshire cat said, grinning. "You aren't hasty in your judgments."

"I should be quicker to speak, though," said John. "If I had, we'd have caught Kipling. And we might be further along than we are at resolving all of this."

"Things are not always as they appear," said Grimalkin. "An ancient Elder God may appear to be a cat, or vice versa. But which is which depends entirely on when you look."

"What does that mean?"

The cat shrugged. "I can't explain. If I did, I wouldn't be a cat."

John sighed. "You're worse than Samaranth."

"I'll take that as a compliment," said the cat. "If I wasn't, then I'd feel undistinguished. He is still just a young creature, after all."

"Samaranth?" John said in surprise. "He's the oldest creature in the Archipelago. He's even older than Ordo Maas."

"I was ancient when Ordo Maas was still chasing young desert girls in the Empty Quarter," said Grimalkin, "and I was with him on his first voyage into the islands, during the flood. It seems to be my fate to be present whenever someone does something that alters the composition of the world."

"Is that what I'm about to do?" asked John. "Change the world?"

"What do *you* think?" asked the cat. "Would you be doing all these things if not for the Prophecy? Or would you be doing the things you believe to be right, even if they were in spite of it?"

"I don't know what to think," John said miserably. "I don't know who to believe."

"Decide what you want to do," the cat said before vanishing completely. "Then do *that*. There's no other way to move forward—with anything. If you don't believe in yourself first . . . then no one else will either."

With a final wave to his old friend, Bert signaled to the crew of the *White Dragon* to take the ship aloft. He pointed the ship to the east, and it began to pick up speed. In moments it was gone.

"That's it," Rose said. "We're on our own."

"Clears the mind, to have solitude," said Archimedes. "Relative solitude, that is."

"I agree," said Professor Sigurdsson. "We are each appointed to our tasks, and that should be sufficient."

"I concur!" Quixote exclaimed. "I am thy protector, Milady Rose. The good professor is our guide. And Archimedes is, ah . . ."

"I'm the muscle," said Archie.

"Methinks I miss your meaning," said the knight, "but I admire your resolve. Shall we be away?"

"No time like the present," said the professor. "Rose?"

There was nothing more to be said. Rose gave assent with a simple nod of her head. The old knight adjusted the trim and moved the *Scarlet Dragon* forward and over the edge of the falls.

❖ ❖ ❖

"It is time," said the Shadow King.

"I concur," said one of the others. "We may have lost the tower, but they still have no idea how to discover the spies within their own house."

"Indeed," said the Shadow King, "we know where they are hiding, and we will take the battle to them, and end this, once and for all."

He unrolled a sheet of what appeared to be leather, but was pliable, pale, and . . . *moist?*

"This map will tell us where we need to go," said the Shadow King. "Its previous owner was reluctant to supply it to us, but all things come to pass, given time."

"Have you converted them all, then?" said Houdini. "All of the dragons?"

"Enough," said the Shadow King. "One remains elusive, but only because I cannot find his True Name."

"You can't just sneak up on him?" said Houdini. "*I* could sneak up on him."

The Shadow King didn't answer, but instead shot the Magician a withering look. Houdini lowered his head and stepped back.

The Shadow King looked down at his new map, which was leaving a red puddle on the ground. "It was clever of them not to include this in the atlas," he murmured. "When we find these islands, I will make certain that the world knows just where they are."

Burton blinked. "Hasn't that been the goal of the society all along?" he asked. "To open all the borders and reveal all the secrets? Why else have we been doing all this for you, if not to usurp their power and change the world in the way it's meant to be changed?"

"The goals of the Imperial Cartological Society are of interest to me," said the Shadow King, "so long as they serve my own. Don't forget your place, Burton."

"But Mordred," Burton began.

"*I am not Mordred!*" the Shadow King hissed. For a moment longer, the explorer and the clockwork king stood looking at one another. Then Burton dropped his eyes.

"Good," said the Shadow King. "Anyone else?"

No one spoke.

"Then it is time for the Wars of the Worlds to begin."

The Shadow King and his minions left the Great Hall of Paralon, but Burton lagged behind, pensive.

Kipling turned at the doorway. "Coming, Sir Richard?"

"After a moment."

Kipling paused. "You aren't having second thoughts, are you? About your support of the Chancellor?"

Burton's eyes glittered. "You've had them yourself."

Kipling raised an eyebrow. "Come, Burton," he said, gesturing with his hand. "We should talk."

"You want to talk about what I think?"

"No," replied Kipling. "I want to talk about what you *believe*."

CHAPTER EIGHTEEN
The Descent

"The Elves have annexed Abaton as one of their territories," said Artus, "and with my blessing. All in all, I'd say we've achieved a great victory. We destroyed the tower of doors into time that was giving the Chancellor his power, and we've taken over his base of operations. Not too shabby."

"Of course, he still has control of the rest of the Archipelago," said Jack, "and Lord knows how many Dragon shadows at his command."

"It's a start," Artus said defensively.

"I still believe it was the right course of action," said John. "Having access to his secrets was going to do little good if he could still cause damage by using the doors and the spear. Now he's lost one of his tools."

"I just wish we still had eyes and ears in his camp the way he seems to have them in ours," said Artus.

"Pardon the interruption," said Defoe, "but there's some sort of commotion going on outside."

"Is it an attack?" John exclaimed, bolting from his chair. Was it possible for the Shadow King to retaliate so quickly for the raid on Abaton?

Resting amid some coral . . . was an oval-shaped frame . . .

"It's another Dragonship," Artus said, pulling aside the curtains for a look. "Have we had another Time Storm?"

Jack groaned inwardly. Dealing with two *Yellow Dragon*s was already more than he could handle even without Nemo. Adding a third was impossible to even contemplate.

"I don't think so," John said. "This one looks like it's come voluntarily."

The others crowded around the windows for a look, and Bert was unable to contain the cheer that left his lips.

It was the *Indigo Dragon. His* ship.

"But if the *Indigo Dragon* is here," said Charles, "then that means . . ."

Nemo and several of the Elves marched a prisoner up the steps to the front door of Tamerlane House.

"Greetings, Caretakers," Burton said. "I seek asylum with you here in the Nameless Isles."

The roar at the top of the falls was deafening, but Rose and her companions soon realized that it was only the sound of the endless sea crashing against the rim of the world past Terminus that produced the noise. In a normal waterfall, that sound is reflected, amplified, and added to by the water thundering against the rocks below. But as the little craft dropped farther and farther away from the crest of the falls, they realized that falling water produces no sound, only a gentle susurration, as if it were wind blowing through willows.

It took just moments for the light to recede as well. Above and past Terminus was only darkness, so the only light was that which spilled over the top of the waterfall.

Quixote and Professor Sigurdsson quickly released the parachute, which slowed their fall with a violent jolt, but instantly settled them into a much more comfortable and controlled descent.

A few miles down, there was no light at all save that which they'd brought with them: a silver lantern, fastened to the fore of the boat; and a portable tallow lamp and three candles that the professor had persuaded them would be necessary to complete their task.

Archie's eyes cast a faint greenish glow when he turned away from the light of the lanterns. "We've still picked up a great deal of speed," he said pointedly. "Shouldn't we try to deploy the balloon before we're moving so fast it's simply torn away?"

"We've gone past the Edge of the World," the professor said. "I don't know if physical laws apply. In truth, I don't even know if this is water we're seeing fall, or air we're passing through, or if we only think it is. I just know that we have to keep going down."

"Well, at some point 'down' will end, correct?" said Archimedes. "You know what they say—it isn't the fall that kills you, but the sudden stop at the end."

Quixote and the professor exchanged blinks and rapidly unpacked the balloon. It took no time at all to inflate, and it rose up underneath the parachute, which would serve as a sheath.

Their descent slowed enough that even with no warning, an impact at the bottom would cause minimal damage to the boat. Thus prepared, they settled in to pass the time, and wait.

Professor Sigurdsson pulled a small book out of his pocket and read by the light of the lantern. Quixote, ever vigilant, kept at the prow, watching the darkness. And Rose and Archie stayed busy playing games of logic and inventing word puzzles.

After a while, Rose fell asleep as the professor continued reading—so it was Archimedes and Quixote who were watching out as the light came up below them.

They woke Rose, worried that an impact was imminent, but the diffuse light that surrounded them was part of the very atmosphere some several miles above the bottom of the falls.

"Professor," Rose asked, "what time is it?"

"Oh, we're making good time, my dear Rose. Worry not," he replied. "Just sit back and try to enjoy the ride. I'm sure we're having a better time of it than Mordred did."

The waterfall was ever present, but was more visible now. The *Scarlet Dragon* kept a wide expanse between itself and the falling water, just in case there were any surprises, or other falling objects.

The noise began again, but to nowhere near the degree that they had expected. The water roiled where it struck the earth below, and foam and spray rose up hundreds of feet into the air. It would have—should have—been louder, but there were no rocks or crags for the water to crash against. It simply fell into a smooth basin that rose up to transparent shallows.

The professor guided the *Scarlet Dragon* over the spray and then down to the water, where he instructed Quixote to deflate and store the balloon and parachute.

"Wouldn't it be faster to continue flying?" asked Rose.

"Faster, perhaps," the professor answered, "but we have no idea where Mordred—I mean, Madoc—is, if he survived at all. We need to be closer to the islands if we're to discover what's become of him."

"I thought speed was our first priority."

He shook his head. "Our first priority is success. Speed will be a luxury to indulge in after."

They had expected to find all manner of detritus along the bottom of the waterfall, but there was nothing to be seen. It was as if they'd crossed over into a pristine world where no human or creature had set foot.

"Apparently, people have taken the warnings seriously," said Quixote.

"That's why we put it on the maps," said the professor.

After promising not to fly out of sight of the *Scarlet Dragon*, Archimedes lit out to do a little exploring. He was gone only a few minutes when he returned, jabbering excitedly.

"A ship!" he squawked. "I've found another ship! Well, most of one, anyway."

"How do you find 'most of' a ship?" asked Rose.

"Part of it is there, and part of it is not," Archie replied. "You've obviously been spending too much time with those idiots at Oxford."

Archimedes was correct—not a mile away from the falls, on a due west heading, was a ship. It had been badly wrecked and lay in the shallows, with various pieces scattered in the waters nearby.

It was elegantly simple in its design, and several times larger than the *Scarlet Dragon*. On one side, the painted letters peeling from the effects of weather and age, was the name of the vessel: the *Aurora*.

"My old ship!" the Professor exclaimed. "I'd always wondered what happened to her!"

"You left her here?" Quixote asked.

"No," replied the Professor. "We took her back to Paralon, but that was many years ago. Apparently someone tried to duplicate our voyage to the End of the World. But when we went, it was through the Southern Isles, not here."

"There is an End of the World in the south as well?" Quixote said in surprise. "How can that be?"

"It's a curious cartological principle," the professor replied. "If you are standing on the top of the real world at the North Pole, every step you take in any direction will be south. Similarly, the world ends in the same way no matter which path you take to reach it."

"How did you get it down here, Professor?" asked Rose. "Was it an airship too?"

"The first of them, I believe," the professor said proudly. "It was a creation of my old friend, Uruk Ko, the Goblin King. Of all the races in the Archipelago, theirs was the most technologically advanced. They had been testing airships for decades before Ko and I decided we wanted to undertake this journey."

"The ship," Rose said. "There's no dragon on the prow."

"Oh, it wasn't a Dragonship," the professor said. "Those were not to be used on a foolhardy exploration such as ours. It was built solely for the journey we took—and it came back in one piece. It was the first time Bert and I had the opportunity to really become friends, and it is one of my fondest memories."

"But aren't all the ships similarly equipped with balloons and sails?" Quixote asked. "I understood that to be a recent development."

"After the old *Indigo Dragon* was rebuilt as an airship, Prince Stephen initiated the program to convert them all," said the professor. "He was the only one brave enough to propose doing it to all the Dragonships themselves."

"I wonder why they were here?" said Rose. "That's very sad, to have come all this way down the waterfall only to wreck so short a distance away."

"It weren't a wreck," a faint voice said from somewhere ahead of them. "It were a dread sea-beastie, and the crew never even saw it coming."

The voice had come not from the *Aurora*, but from the wreckage just below the surface.

Resting amid some coral and sea plants was an oval-shaped frame with the portrait of a well-to-do pirate under a piece of heavy, curved glass. It was halfway hidden by some of the undersea flora and seemed to have gone down with the *Aurora*, judging by the amount of silt that had accumulated around it.

"I am Captain Charles Johnson," the portrait said, looking up through the water. "Who is it that you be?"

"I am Don Quixote de la Mancha," the old knight said, bowing deeply, "and these are my companions, the lady Rose, the teacher Archimedes, and the Caretaker Emeritus Professor Sigurdsson. We are on a quest."

Captain Johnson sneered. "Caretaker Emeritus?" he said to the professor. "I didn't realize Caretakers could retire."

"How is it you know of the Caretakers?" Sigurdsson said in surprise.

The portrait blinked. "Are you daft, man? I'm trapped in a painting of myself on the other side of the waterfall at the Edge of the World. I didn't just fall here by accident, you know. Of *course* I know about the Caretakers. I know that you, Professor, are the only one of their number who has ever come over the waterfall—just as I know I was betrayed and left here by one of your predecessors."

"Really?" said Sigurdsson. "Which one?"

"That snake-in-the-grass Daniel Defoe," said Johnson. "He and I were training as apprentices to Cyrano de Bergerac, along with my best friend, a silversmith named Eliot McGee. Cyrano had his eye in particular on Eliot, whom he thought might make a suitable apprentice for the Cartographer himself."

"He was a mapmaker?" the professor said.

"One of the best," Johnson replied. "His father, Elijah, had been approached by a pirate to help him create a map to his own hidden treasures, and he was so successful at it that McGee became the de facto mapmaker to all the pirates in the Caribbean. Elijah trained Eliot in the discipline, and it was then that Daniel and I made his acquaintance."

"What had distinguished you, if you don't mind my asking?" said the professor. "Why did Cyrano seek you out?"

"I was compiling a history of the pirates," Johnson replied. "Basically, as an audition to become the Caretaker after de Bergerac."

"'*A General History of the Robberies and Murders of the Most Notorious Pyrates*,'" said the professor. "I know it well."

"Really?" Johnson said, beaming.

"Yes—but I thought Defoe wrote it. *Everyone* thinks Defoe wrote it."

"Arrrgghhh," the portrait growled. "I hate that! He stole it from me, every jot and tittle!"

"To be fair," Sigurdsson said, "most of the editions carry your name—everyone just thinks it was a pseudonym for Daniel Defoe."

"Daniel Defoe murdered me in 1723," Johnson stated. "He

and Eliot were working on a companion book they called the *Pyratlas*. It was to be Eliot's audition to become the Cartographer's apprentice, and with me having my own book, Defoe was going to be shut out altogether. So he had me killed, and published the book himself."

"That's very interesting," Sigurdsson said as he made a shushing gesture to his companions out of Johnson's view. No point in antagonizing the fellow by letting him know they'd just had dinner with his old-friend-turned-adversary. "So how is it you came to be here, in this, ah, state?"

"Apparently, at some point Defoe betrayed Eliot as well, and faked his own death to go into the Archipelago," said Johnson. "In the years that followed, Eliot's son, Ernest, had also become a mapmaker, thus continuing in the family trade. What Defoe only discovered later was that the McGees had been hiding secret clues to the pirate treasures in duplicate maps—maps that young Ernest subsequently burned. A few survived, but not enough that Defoe could use them to find the treasures without consulting a second book I had been writing, which I called *The Maps of Elijah McGee*.

"Somehow Defoe had discovered a process to resurrect the dead by way of painting their portraits—so he commissioned one of me to ask me the whereabouts of the book. The minute I could speak, I spit in his face."

"You can spit?" said Archimedes.

"Well, I could make the gesture," said Johnson. "As long as he knew my intent, it didn't matter if I couldn't really spit. Anyroad," he went on, "after he realized I couldn't be coerced, he sold me to someone who'd just stolen one of the Dragonships—the *Indigo*

Dragon, I think he called it—so I ended up in the possession of actual pirates. Ironic, isn't it?"

"That would be a correct assessment," said the professor. "Did any of these pirates have names?"

"Most of them flat-out ignored me," Johnson said, "except when they needed something. So I never got more than the occasional name, like 'Coleridge' or 'Blake.' But I did catch what they called themselves as a whole—they said they were part of the Imperial Cartological Society, and that they'd been commissioned by royalty. That makes them privateers, which is as bad as pirates in my book."

"I agree," the professor said, looking somberly at his companions. They were all thinking the same thing: that Defoe, who was among the Caretakers Emeritis, was in league with Burton—and they had no way of telling anyone at Tamerlane house. "Did any of them survive the, ah, sea-beastie attack?"

"I couldn't tell you," said Johnson. "After the first blow, I ended up where you see me—and my peripheral vision isn't what it used to be."

"I'm impressed that you even made it this far," said the professor.

"We used your own notes, Professor," Johnson replied. "Yours, and those of someone called Bert. They were given to the society by someone called Uruk Ko."

Professor Sigurdsson lowered his head. That was the hat trick. If the Goblin King had aided the Imperial Cartological Society, the Goblins had to be in league with the Winter King's Shadow.

"The notes," he said suddenly. "Did any survive the wreck?"

"I doubt it," said Johnson, "but I can recall most of what was written on them. They had to do with the precautions, I believe."

"Precautions?" asked Quixote.

"There are seven islands that must be crossed," said Johnson. "You cannot simply bypass them. Each one is akin to a gate, and gates must be entered properly."

"I remember," said the professor. "We've come prepared."

"That's good," said Johnson, "since we weren't. We didn't take the cautions seriously, and as a result, the *Aurora* was lost."

"Professor," Rose whispered, "you have one of the pocket watches—is it possible to release Captain Johnson from the portrait?"

"An interesting thought," said the professor. "Let's find out."

They explained what they wanted to try, and Johnson responded with considerable enthusiasm. Archimedes retrieved several scraps of cloth and timber from the wreck, and Quixote fashioned a sort of sling-on-a-pole to scoop up the portrait.

It took only a few tries for him to succeed, but when they had the picture onboard, their expressions fell.

There was no place on the frame to insert the watch. Johnson was trapped within.

"That's all well and good," he said. "I've gotten used to it, anyway."

"It may be for the best," said the professor. "There's a time limit unless you're at a particular location. And that would literally ruin your week."

"Will you still take me with you, anyroad?" asked Johnson. "I'm really tired of seeing the same fish and coral day after day, and there's only been one other person come over the falls since I got here, and he died straightaway. He's just over there, to the right."

Quixote steered the *Scarlet Dragon* over to where Johnson had indicated, and sure enough there was a skeleton, facedown in the water. It could not have been there very long, as the coral had not yet begun to form around the bones, and scraps of his clothing that had not yet rotted were still floating about.

"I think this is Wilhelm Grimm," the professor said sadly. "He must have displeased his master."

"And he was simply dropped over the waterfall?" Rose exclaimed in horror. "If he died, then what hope do we have of finding Madoc alive?"

"Your father is a man of unusual mettle," said Sigurdsson, "and I suspect, as Samaranth probably knew, that just dropping him over the falls would not be enough to kill him. The same might not be true for mere mortals like myself."

"No, look," said Quixote, pointing. A dagger was lodged firmly between two of the skeleton's ribs, next to its spine. "He was killed, then discarded. Truly, an ignoble act."

"Do you think it was Burton who did it?" Rose asked quietly. "Or someone else?"

"Whoever it was, my dear child," the professor said, turning her away from the sight, "this person is past worry. The troubles of this world are no longer his."

"Pardon," said Quixote, "but that is a strange platitude to hear from someone who is himself dead."

"I am a Caretaker," Sigurdsson replied. "The troubles of this world *are* my business."

No one spoke any further, and Quixote adjusted the sails, pointing the little craft to the west.

Standing among the ruins was a man, dressed in rags . . .

CHAPTER NINETEEN
The Ruined City

The portrait of Charles Johnson struck up an immediate friendship with Archimedes, who was fascinated by the tales of pirates and privateers. Their Golden Age, which had been documented by Johnson, Defoe, and the McGees, was an era that the owl had missed completely when Jack and John had brought him into the future with Rose.

"You actually hid clues to the treasures in the maps themselves?" Archimedes asked. "Ingenious!"

"It was Ernest's idea," said Johnson, "because of his connection to the Empress Josephine, and Napoleon's hidden fortune."

"You're more interesting than most portraits I'm acquainted with," said the owl.

"Thank you," said the captain.

With Johnson thusly preoccupied at one end of the boat, the professor, Quixote, and Rose were able to discuss their concerns with a bit more privacy.

"The *Aurora* belonged to the Goblins," said the professor. "If Burton was able to procure it from them, along with my notes, it's all but certain they are in league together."

"What worries me more," Quixote mused, "is what Johnson

told us about Defoe. That isn't the behavior of a Caretaker."

"It isn't," said the professor, "but we shall just have to trust in the Caretakers' ability to look after themselves. We have a hard enough task of our own."

"Heads up," Johnson called. "We're approaching the first gate."

The first of the seven gates was a lighthouse.

"That's rather small for an island, and rather odd for a gate," said Quixote.

"It's a most important one," said the professor, "and one I'm guessing the society disregarded."

"I tried to tell them," Johnson said, sighing, "but they wouldn't listen."

"What must we do?" said Quixote.

The professor picked up the tallow lantern. "Simply take this to the room at the top and replace the lantern that's there."

Quixote looked at him in surprise. "That's all?"

The professor nodded. "That's all. But hold fast to the empty lantern. It's our receipt, so to speak."

"On whose account?"

"This is the land of the dragons," said the professor. "Somewhere up there in the darkness, they're watching. And somewhere here below as well. The lantern is marked with the letter *alpha*, and replacing a light in the lighthouse is a show of our good intentions."

"Sort of like leaving the milk out for the faery folk, or the brownies," said Rose. "I think I understand."

Quixote hopped from the boat to the narrow steps of the lighthouse and quickly ascended the steps. While the others waited, they scanned the waters around them for any signs of life, and it was Johnson who found it.

"Oh, dear," he moaned. "Look."

They looked in the direction Johnson was facing and saw a rising swell of water. Something massive was swimming just under the surface, and it was coming toward the *Scarlet Dragon*. It grew closer, and larger, and the professor was just about to suggest deploying the balloons on the boat when a brilliant beam of light cut through the gloom above their heads. The light shone in two directions: one beam back toward the waterfall, and the other forward to the west.

The swell disappeared.

"Whew," said Johnson, as Quixote descended the steps with the empty lantern and rejoined them. "That was excellent timing."

"I'm sorry it took as long as it did," Quixote replied. "I forgot to take a match. Fortunately, someone had left some behind."

He held up a small brown coin purse. "There were a few matches inside, along with some coins and a few pebbles," he said. "We got lucky."

"The luck is accidental," the professor said, taking the small purse. "I must have left it there myself. I've been wondering what happened to it for decades.

"Here, look," he said, examining the contents. "This round black quartz is actually the tear of an Apache princess that I found in Arizona. And this"—he held up a small white stone—"I took from a stream in France that is said to cure all ills and heal all wounds."

"And the coins?" asked Quixote. "Of what significance are they?"

"I kept those in case I needed to buy an ale," said the professor. "This adventuring life is hard work, and it makes one very thirsty."

With the offering to the dragons made, they sailed on toward the next island gate.

"Professor," Rose asked suddenly, "do you know what time it is?"

"I'm not sure if time works the same way here as it does up top," the professor replied. "Worry not, dear Rose. We'll get there, by and by."

"But professor," Rose started to say.

"There," the professor interrupted, pointing. "The second gate!"

The next island was wildly overgrown with foliage and was almost perfectly divided down the middle by a large swamp.

"Anything dangerous here?" asked Quixote.

"The usual," said the professor. "Ligers and tigons, and the occasional gorilla, who will leave you be if you throw the names of books at them."

"Throw books?" asked Rose.

"No," said the professor, "just the names. They're usually content with those. The only creatures to watch out for here are the crocodiles—they fly, you know."

Sure enough, the moment the *Scarlet Dragon* moved into the swamp, the air was suddenly filled with winged crocodiles. They swooped and wove as if they were a great flock of leathery cranes, flying south for the winter.

It took only seconds for them to focus their attention on the tiny boat and its edible occupants, and they changed their formation to envelop the *Scarlet Dragon*.

Before the others could react, the professor reached into a satchel and flung a handful of small objects into the air. The crocodiles immediately dispensed with the formation to chase the treats. Professor Sigurdsson threw two more handfuls for good measure, and soon all the flying crocodiles had retreated into the jungle.

Rose peered inside the satchel. "Lollipops?"

"Indeed. The crocodiles here are fond of lollipops," the professor explained, "and I made certain to raid the store of them Bert keeps onboard the *White Dragon* so that we'd be prepared."

"I don't think it likely that you carried many lollipops on your first voyage here in the *Aurora*," said Quixote, "so how did you discover the crocodiles' weakness for them?"

"Completely by accident, I assure you," replied the professor. "As we were fighting them off, one of the crew was yanked overboard—and it was in watching the crocs tear the poor devil to pieces that we realized what they were really after."

"The lollipops," said Rose.

"Just so," said the professor. "He had a penchant for them. Claimed it kept him from eating too much, as he hoped to keep his weight down. Ironic, isn't it?"

"This is not a gate where we must pay a toll to get through," the professor said at the third island. "To pass here, one must simply resist the urge to take something."

"How do you mean, professor?" asked Rose.

"I'll show you," he said, "but this is a place we'd best cross in the air."

He and Quixote deployed the balloons, and the little craft rose into the air.

The island was small, and unremarkable in most respects. It had palm trees, sandy beaches, and a few gently rolling hills. And in the center was a large, glistening lake.

"Look," he said, pointing over the edge of the *Scarlet Dragon* at the water below.

The lake was filled with gold.

Not just raw ore, or coins, but every manner of object one could think of: fruit, and fish, and mugs, and swords, and on and on—all made of the gleaming yellow metal.

"A pirate's repository, perhaps?" asked Quixote.

"No," said the professor. "Death. The waters here bring death. Look farther."

All around the edges of the lake were larger golden masses, which the companions had at first assumed to be simple piles of gold. But they weren't—they were people.

"The water turns everything it touches into gold," said the professor, "including those who seek to take some of it for themselves."

Quixote was holding Johnson so that he could also see the spectacle below. "Look!" the captain said. "There's one of those sorry privateers!"

Professor Sigurdsson looked more closely, then lowered the *Scarlet Dragon* a few yards.

"Hmm," he said. "That's William Blake, unless I miss my guess. Surprising—I would've thought he had a stronger will than that."

In a few more minutes they had passed over the lake, and the professor said it was safe to drop back into the waters past the western beach.

* * *

According to Johnson's memory of the professor's notes, the next island gate had a name. "It's called Entelechy," he said.

"Both are," said the professor. "The island, and its queen. They share the same name—although it's more politic to refer to her as 'the Quintessence.' As far as I know, she's Aristotle's goddaughter, and so is at least two thousand years old."

"Finally," said Rose. "I'll get to meet someone my own age."

Entelechy was a prim and proper island, with a well-kept harbor and several soaring towers of blue stone. They stopped at the dock and left Archimedes and Captain Johnson to guard the boat. The professor led the others to a great turquoise-tinged reception hall.

The Quintessence was seated on a throne at the head of a magnificent banquet table. She was perhaps twelve feet tall and had all the presence of a giant. Her gown billowed around her immense chair, and her hair was piled high above a glittering crown.

"Great Quintessence," the professor said, bowing. "We seek passage through your gate, if you please."

"Come closer," she commanded, "that I may better see you."

A curious look of . . . happiness appeared on the queen's face as she watched the professor. She considered them all, briefly, then turned back to Rose.

"You have the look of the Old World to you, girl," she said. "I may allow you to pass. Who are your forebears?"

"My father's father was Odysseus," she replied.

"Ah," said the queen. "I might have guessed. You are familiar to me. And your mother's parentage?"

"No one you'd know."

"Hmm," said the queen. "And you?"

Quixote bowed. "I am the lady's humble protector," he said simply.

"I see," said the queen. "And you?"

"I am a simple traveler," said the professor, "seeking out what beauty there is in the world."

"And what have you found?"

"If seeking beauty was my only goal, I should be happy to stop here," said the professor, "but we have other needs, and thus must go on."

The queen smiled. "That's an excellent answer," she said, smiling. "I believe I will let you pass, for a price."

"There's not much left to barter with," Quixote whispered to the others, "only the candles!"

"Those are for a different gate," said the professor. "Name your price, milady."

"Will you give me a kiss?" the queen asked, bending down so he could reach her.

"I shall," said the professor. And he did.

"Ahh." The queen sighed. "I have missed that—it was as nice as before, so long ago. It does grow lonely out here, you know," she said with a look of sorrow on her face. "There have been few other visitors of late.

"Another descendant—or was it an ancestor?—of Odysseus passed this way not long ago, and I allowed him through, because he knew my godfather."

Rose and Quixote were silently thrilled by this—the first proof they'd had of Madoc's survival, and passing.

"There was another," said the queen, "but he was rude, and a bit delusional. I let him pass, but I kept one of his arms."

"We really ought to be going," said Quixote, his eyes wide. "Begging your pardon."

"You won't stay to dine with me?" said the Queen.

"We really must go," Rose concurred.

"So we must," the professor said. He bowed deeply and kissed the queen's hand.

She bowed her head in assent, and the companions returned to the boat. Shortly after, they were again underway.

"I don't know what to say, Professor," Rose said with a broad smile. "That was an impressive display of personal charm."

"Thank you," replied the professor. "Bert used to refer to it as my 'shield of charisma.'"

"She seemed to remember you," said Quixote, "and very fondly at that."

"And now you know one of the reasons that Bert could not be your guide," said the professor. "The Queen of Entelechy would never have allowed him to pass."

"Why not?" asked Rose.

"Because," explained the professor, "when we came here before, the first words out of his mouth were, 'You're the largest woman I've ever seen in my life!'"

Both Johnson and Quixote groaned. "A terrible mistake," said Quixote.

"Awful," said Johnson.

"I don't get it," said Rose.

"You're still very young," Quixote told her, "but I will tell you what my grandfather wisely told me. Never, ever mention a woman's size, or her age. Women are timelessly young and eternally beautiful."

"Always?"

"Yes, always," Quixote and Johnson said together.

"That's part of the reason it took Bert eight hundred thousand years to find a wife," said the professor. "No tact."

The fifth gate was a trio of tall, spikelike rocks standing only yards apart from one another. The professor lit the tallow candles and instructed Archimedes to place the first one atop the center stone, the second on the stone to the right, and the third on the stone to the left.

"That's it?" said Quixote.

"That's it," said the professor. "We may now pass."

"What would have happened if we hadn't placed the candles there?" asked Quixote.

The professor shivered and drew his coat closer. "I don't even want to think about it," he said. "I've been dead for a quarter century, and the idea *still* gives me nightmares."

After the fifth island gate, they passed into what must have been night. The haze was replaced by complete darkness, and then, eventually, a night sky full of stars.

"Do you recognize any of them, Professor?" asked Rose. "I don't see any of the constellations!"

"I don't believe those are stars, per se," said the professor in a hushed voice. "I believe those are the *dragons* themselves."

It was a sobering, fantastic thought: that they were actually somewhere underneath thousands upon thousands of dragons—and so, the companions slept.

In a few hours, still under the night sky, they came to the sixth island.

Broad, with no hills or cliffs on the beaches, it was not a small island, but it had been completely overbuilt with temple after structure after edifice, until it was practically a city. And the city must have been deserted for countless years, because it was all but ruined.

The crumbling remains were more ancient than those they'd seen on Avalon, and even more ancient than the islands of the Underneath.

Standing among the ruins was a man, dressed in rags and clutching a book. He was staring up at the stars.

"Ah, me," said the professor quietly. "It's the last of the society pirates."

They pulled the *Scarlet Dragon* onto the beach, and the professor took a few steps toward the man, who had not yet acknowledged their presence.

"Hello, Coleridge," said the professor.

The man looked up at the mention of his name. He squinted at the boat on the beach, then at the passengers who were now standing in front of him.

"Sigurdsson?" he asked eventually. "Is that you? What are you doing here at the end of all that is?"

Rose wrinkled her brow at the question, but Quixote's discreet touch on her arm signaled her not to speak. This man should be dealt with by the professor.

"This isn't the end," the professor said, his voice calm and soft. "This is just one more stopping place."

"Dreams come true here, you know," said Coleridge. "I've seen it happen. But no one told me . . ."

His voice trailed off, and he turned away again.

"No one told you what?" the professor asked.

"Nightmares come true here as well," said Coleridge.

"Are you all right?" asked the professor.

"She took my arm," Coleridge said simply, "but she let me go past. I had to come here. I had to see . . ."

"Come with us," said the professor. "There's no reason for you to stay. Do come. Please."

The emaciated figure turned to look at him. "I cannot, for it may yet change. And there is nowhere else to go. There is nothing further. This was the last place in the world. This was the great city I saw in my vision, and it's all a shambles. Destroyed."

"You know it was once great," said the professor. "You know how it began."

"I did not know how it ended," Coleridge said, looking up at the sky. "I did not know."

He did not turn around again. The professor motioned for the others to get on the boat, and they sailed around and past the city.

"What a sad man," said Quixote. "What happened to him?"

"On this island, dreams do eventually come true," said the professor, "but true things are also real, and real things eventually fade. What we saw was the end of his particular dream."

"What was this island called?" asked Rose.

The professor smiled, but it was a melancholy smile. "Xanadu," he said. "It was called Xanadu."

The waters after the Ruined City were placid, with no indication of currents or tides. Above them, disturbingly, the stars began to go out—but soon they realized it was because the light was coming up again. Strangely, it appeared that the sun was rising in the west—until they realized that it was not the sun at all, but the last of the seven island gates.

The island, emerald green with a thick blanket of grasses, was smaller than the last, and had no structures on it—only a ring of standing stones.

A Ring of Power, virtually identical to that on Terminus, save that the stones were larger.

They were pristine, and spread far enough apart that the areas between were paved with smooth stones. In the center was a long stone table draped with a crimson cloth, and seated at the table was a tall, silver-haired man.

As the companions approached, he rose to greet them. His tunic was also silver, shot through with crimson down the left side of his chest, and he was almost as tall as the Quintessence had been.

"Greetings," said the professor. He introduced himself and the others, then asked if the tall man had a name.

"I am a star," he said with an air of haughtiness, "or at least, I once was. I think I may be still, but it is difficult to say. However, when I was still in the sky, those who worshipped me called me Rao."

"Is this a Ring of Power?" Rose asked. "Like the one used to summon the Dragons?"

Rao frowned. "Dragons? I know of none here who may be called to this place, save that I call them. And I would not deign to call Dragons, for they would not come for one such as I."

"A Dragon would not come at the call of a star?"

"One, perhaps," said Rao. "He would not look down upon me

as the others might, for not having ascended. He himself chose to descend to the office of Dragon for the sake of a city, so he is, as you might think, different."

"What was his name?" asked Rose.

"Samaranth," said Rao. "But enough of this. Will you settle the dispute?"

"What dispute is that?" asked Quixote.

"There is a dispute between some of my children," said Rao. "Have you come to arbitrate for them? To judge which is in the ascent, and which must descend?"

"We have not come to judge anyone," said the professor. "We have merely come seeking someone who may have passed this way. He is called Madoc."

Rao's eyes narrowed. "None come here save that they fell. Are you saying you have come seeking one of the fallen?"

Before the professor could answer, Rose stepped forward again. "Not everyone must fall, great star," she said, bowing her head respectfully. "We have come here of our own accord, and we did not fall. We flew."

"Hmm," Rao mused. "This I see, Little Thing. But take a caution—others before you have chosen a similar path, and fared the worse for it. Flying is not always ascending."

"Are you one of the fallen?" Rose asked.

Professor Sigurdsson winced. That was not a question he thought would get a good response from a former star.

Strangely enough, Rao looked at her with gentleness, and even touched her head. "I was not," he said. "I had not yet ascended, and thus did not have to choose. But soon, soon."

"If I may," said the professor.

"Little Thing," Rao said bluntly. "Why have you come here?"

"We seek passage beyond your island," said the professor, "in search of the man Madoc. May we pass?"

"You may not," Rao said blithely. "None may pass save that one must stay. That is the Old Magic, and the old rule."

"Then I offer myself," said the professor. "I will stay, so that the others may pass."

"No!" Rose cried. "You can't!"

"That, dear Rose, is the other reason Bert could not come," he replied. "Years ago, we turned back when another star made the same request. And we both knew it would be made again. A life for the passage. That's the rule."

"But we need you!"

"No," he said gently, "you don't. You needed me to get you to your father—and you're nearly there. Quixote is your guardian—I was merely your guide."

"We still have to convince him to repair the sword," said Rose. "We can't do that without you."

"Rose," the professor began.

"I'll stay," said a voice behind them. "I'll do it."

It was the portrait of Captain Johnson. "I'd be willing," he stated, "if the fact that I'm essentially an oil painting doesn't count against me."

"Can you arbitrate?" asked Rao. "Will you arbitrate the disputes of my children?"

"I witnessed more than seventy pirate trials," said Johnson. "I could give it a go, I suppose."

"Little Thing," Rao said, "this is acceptable to me. You shall stay, and the others may pass."

Rose took the portrait from the boat, kissed it quickly, and handed it to Rao.

Quickly, before the star could change his mind, the companions hurried back to the boat and put her to sea.

"Thank you, Captain Johnson," Rose called out.

"Farewell, Captain," Quixote said.

"I'd rather have left the Caretaker," said Archimedes. "There's an entire *houseful* back in the Archipelago."

"Remember," Johnson called out, his voice growing faint as the island vanished behind the mist, "don't trust Daniel Defoe!"

CHAPTER TWENTY
The Bargain

"**Absolutely not,**" said Dickens. "It's the most insane thing I've ever heard of in my life."

"I concur," said John. "He's caused us more grief than almost anyone except for the Winter King himself, and he almost single-handedly brought about the Winterland when he tricked Hugo Dyson through that door. Letting him have asylum here, in Tamerlane House . . ." He paused and took a deep breath. "Well, it's just unthinkable."

"I think it's worth at least a debate," said Defoe. "He knows a great deal about the Shadow King's plans."

"Because he was his chief lieutenant until just a few hours ago!" said John. "We should consider him a prisoner of war, not a refugee seeking asylum."

"I think he should be flogged," said Shakespeare.

"But just yesterday," Chaucer pointed out, "weren't we debating whether or not his beliefs about the Archipelago and the *Imaginarium Geographica* were in fact superior to our own? That alone should change our perception of him."

John rubbed his temples. This discussion was not progressing

In one hand he held a hammer. The other was not a hand at all . . .

in a reasonable direction. "All right," he said finally. "Bring him in."

Richard Burton entered the conservatory, flanked by Nathaniel Hawthorne and Daniel Defoe. He grinned and nodded at John as he took a seat at the table.

"You should realize, Burton," John began, "that none of us here trusts you in the least."

"I don't trust you any more than you trust me, John," Burton said, "but desperate times make for strange bedfellows, and you don't have to trust me—just my motives."

"Which are?"

Burton raised his hands and smiled. "The same as they've always been," he said simply. "No more secrets. My goals and those of the Caretakers have seldom been far apart—we just differ in how we approach them. But I've realized that the goals of the Chancellor are not mine—and whatever he is, he is not the man I would willingly serve. I believed he was. I was wrong."

"Would you be willing to give us the information we need to defeat him?" asked Chaucer.

"I will share what I know," said Burton.

"We haven't yet decided whether to give you what you're seeking," said John, "but we're considering it. In the meantime, you're not to be left alone at any time. Either Charles and Fred will be with you, or Defoe and Hawthorne."

"Fine."

"You won't be allowed to go near the docks," John continued. "You must not leave Tamerlane House under any circumstance, and your men must remain within the bounds of their quarters. No exceptions."

"Agreed."

"Very well," said John. "Do you have any questions?"

"Yes," said Burton. "Where's the kitchen? I'm starving."

Charles, Defoe, and Fred took the first shift watching Burton, as the Caretakers continued the debate; and the kitchen was as secure a room as any other in Tamerlane House.

"You're eating quite heartily for a prisoner of war," said Charles.

"Asylum seeker," said Burton, "depending on which way your friend's wind blows."

"Has anyone seen Jakob?" Hawthorne asked, peering around the corner. "I was supposed to help him with some notations an hour ago, and his cat is looking for him."

"There's a hall of mirrors in one of the rooms here," Defoe said. "I think he wanted to go have a look at them, maybe see if there are any trapped princesses or lost treasures in them."

"Very well," said Hawthorne, sighing. "I'll tell Grimalkin."

"What the devil are you eating, Burton?" asked Charles.

"Aardvark," he replied, chewing. "Will you have some? It's delicious."

"It looks a bit greasy to me," said Charles. "Where did you get it? It isn't something the Feast Beasts usually bring out for the banquets."

"Oh, we brought them ourselves," Burton said. "We didn't want to impose on—or expect—your hospitality. The northern lands are crawling with them, and they're easier to hunt than a baby deer."

"How's that?"

"Well," explained Burton, tearing off another piece of flesh with his teeth, "do you know the old joke about how you can hunt deer with an apple and a hammer? Aardvarks are even less trouble than that, mostly due to their sensitive natures, and the fact that they're very slow."

Burton leaned over the table and spoke in a conspiratorial whisper. "To catch an aardvark," he said, grinning, "all you have to do is find one, then start insulting it."

"Really?" said Charles.

"Yes. Instead of running away, it gets offended and sits down, whining about how no one likes it and everyone just wants to be mean to aardvarks."

"And then what?"

"Then, WHAM!" Burton exclaimed, slamming his fist to the table. "We wallop it with a hammer and marinate it in garlic and butter."

"That's positively barbaric," said Charles.

"I *am* a barbarian," said Burton, stroking his scarred cheeks with a bowie knife. "And besides, what else are aardvarks good for?"

"Good point," said Charles.

The loss of their newfound friend was sobering to all four of the companions. In an unfamiliar place, Captain Johnson had been a comforting voice of reason and tact. Granted, being an oil painting, he had less to lose overall, but a life is a life, Sigurdsson told them, and his sacrifice was as meaningful as anyone else's would be.

Past the island of the star, the waters grew still, but they remained cloudy, so it was difficult to estimate their depth. There were no other islands in sight in any direction, and only a smudge of color on the horizon, which hinted at thunderstorms. Other than continuing in the direction they were going, there was no strategy or plan of action they could employ. There was not even an expectation, said the professor, of what they might encounter next.

"Haven't you been here before?" asked Rose.

The professor shook his head. "Remember, we only got as far as the star. When we had to leave someone behind just to go on, Bert and Ko and I decided that we'd gone far enough, and returned to the Archipelago."

"So," said Quixote, "we are truly journeying into an unknown region. This is truly the quest to end them all."

"I know it's just a turn of phrase," said Sigurdsson, "but that really isn't a comforting thought."

"Professor," Rose said gently. "Can you tell me what time it is?"

Professor Sigurdsson opened his mouth to reply, then saw the look on her face and stopped. He turned back to look out over the water and sighed. "Third time's the charm, eh, Rose?" he said quietly.

He reached into his pocket and removed his silver pocket watch. Flipping the lid open, he took a quick glance and snapped it shut again, swallowing hard as he did so.

"How long have we been gone, Professor?"

"It took less than a day for Bert to fly us to Terminus," he said matter-of-factly, "but more than a day to descend the falls. And from the time we discovered the *Aurora*, we have traveled for two full days. All told, we've been gone for just over a hundred hours."

Rose closed her eyes as she realized what that meant. They

were past the halfway mark that would allow the professor to return to Tamerlane House and the safety of the Pygmalion Gallery.

The professor reached an arm around her shoulders and gave her a comforting squeeze. "No time to worry about the trip back when we've yet to reach our destination, hey? Let's see to that first, and we'll worry about the rest when we have to."

"Wall ho," Quixote called out.

"Land ho, you mean," said Archie.

"Land is land and a wall is a wall, and I know the difference between them," Quixote retorted. "Look."

In the near distance, what they had assumed to be storm clouds on the western horizon was now revealed to be more substantial than clouds, and taller besides.

It was, as Quixote said, a wall.

As high as the waterfall at the world's edge had been, the wall was tall, and it stretched away in both directions, north and south, to the vanishing point on each horizon.

"I wonder what's on the other side?" Professor Sigurdsson mused, squinting as he looked up for a glimpse of the wall's summit. "I wonder if there's a way over?"

"This is how people are chosen as Caretakers of an atlas like the *Geographica*," Quixote said to Archimedes. "They can't escape it. It's in their blood."

The wall was so massive that even once they had sighted it, it took another two hours to reach the base. It stood on a narrow beach that was perhaps thirty feet wide and, as far as they could tell, ran the length of the wall. It was as if an infinite barrier had been placed on an equally infinite sandbar.

They pulled the *Scarlet Dragon* into the shallows and clambered out to examine the wall. It was made of stones that were placed so closely and precisely that Quixote could not get his sword point between any two of them.

"Impressive," he said with grave sincerity. "I would not have believed such a wall was possible."

"I can't find a top," called Archie, who was spiraling back down to the others. "I could fly higher, but the air was getting too thin to keep me aloft."

"Is this the end of our journey, Professor?" asked Rose. "If we can't get over it or through it, then how do we go on?"

"It is the end of all that is," a voice said from farther down the beach. The words were spoken calmly, but were tinged with menace, and perhaps . . . fear?

The companions turned around to see a man standing about twenty feet behind them. In one hand he held a hammer. The other was not a hand at all; his arm ended in a hook, which was tarnished and rusty. He was heavily bearded, and his clothing was in tatters. And on his face was a look that was almost indescribable, a mix of fury and what might be relief.

"Hello, Father," said Rose. "It's nice to finally meet you."

There was none among them, other than the professor, who might say how the fall over the water's edge had changed the man called Madoc.

Rose had seen him only once before. At the time he was known as Mordred; he had just tried to kill her uncle Merlin, and had lost his hand to her cousin Arthur. Quixote had also never seen him, but knew of him only through stories about the Winter King, as his enemies had called him. Archimedes had known him when he was still called Madoc, but that had been many centuries earlier. Only Professor Sigurdsson had seen him as the man he was now—and that was moments before Madoc, Mordred, the Winter King, had killed him in his study.

Madoc's hair and beard were long and greasy. His arms were thick and corded with muscle, and he watched the new arrivals with suspicion. Slowly he paced back and forth across the width of the sand, never taking his eyes off them. Finally he decided to speak—to the owl.

"Hello, Archimedes," he said. "You're looking well."

"You're not, Madoc," Archie replied, lighting onto Quixote's shoulder. "You look like you've been hit by a train."

"Actually, I was dropped over a waterfall," said Madoc, "but the net result is probably the same."

"How did you bypass the gates, then?" asked the professor. "And once below, why didn't you try to return to the Archipelago?"

"I was compelled," Madoc said, "and I remain so. I briefly thought of trying to repair that ship, the *Aurora*, but I was unable to even pause to appraise the vessel's damage. I may have been swimming, or walking, or otherwise moving perpendicular to the waterfall, but make no mistake—I was always falling, and am falling still."

"Until you reached this wall," said the professor.

"Yes," said Madoc. "Until I came here. As far as I can determine, it is endless. I spent years doing nothing but walking, first in one direction, then the other. After a while, I began to hallucinate. I dreamed that as I slept, all my progress was undone, and I had been returned to the place I started. Even if that had been true, there was no way to know for certain.

"It's impossible to climb—believe me, I've tried. I wasted a year on *that*. Then I considered trying to dig my way through, but other than this," he said, holding up his hook, "I had nothing that was capable of even scratching it. I built a forge and created several tools, using metals I've scavenged from the beach, but they've all proven too soft for the stone as well. That was almost two years ago. I've spent all of my time since planning my revenge."

The professor started, and Madoc laughed.

"I'm only joking," he said to the old Caretaker. "Really, though—what were you expecting me to say? That I've had time to reconsider my choices, and I've turned over a new leaf?"

"I'm pretty sure that's a lie," said Archimedes.

Madoc rolled his eyes. "Of course it's a joke, you stupid bird," he said, more exasperated than irritated. "I used to be the villain of the story, or hadn't you heard?"

"Actually, you still are, after a fashion," said Sigurdsson. "Or at least, your Shadow is."

"Now you have my attention," Madoc said, sitting cross-legged in the sand. "Tell me."

The companions sat on the sand across from Madoc, and Professor Sigurdsson told him everything that had happened in the quarter century since the conflict on Terminus.

Several times the professor nearly paused in his narrative, concerned that he might be sharing something that would better remain a secret—but each time he reminded himself that without Madoc's help, they would not be able to defeat the Shadow King. And while they were still a long way from being friends, or even friendly enemies, Madoc was at least listening to what they had come to say.

"We need your help, Madoc," the professor said. "Show him, Rose."

She walked back to the *Scarlet Dragon* and retrieved a bundle, which she placed on the sand in front of Madoc. Slowly, carefully, she folded back the oilcloth to reveal the shattered remains of the sword Caliburn.

"We need you to repair the sword, Father," Rose said simply. "Can you do it? Please?"

Madoc stared at the sword for a long moment, as if he couldn't comprehend what he was seeing. His face was inscrutable, and Quixote and Sigurdsson exchanged worried glances. What did this mean, that he didn't react at all?

Suddenly Madoc fell to his knees, dropped his head into his hands, and began to shake violently.

Quixote was about to step forward, and Rose was reaching out a hand to comfort him, when they realized together that Madoc was not sobbing.

He was *laughing*.

He laughed so hard that he could not speak, could not stand. Tears ran down his face as he erupted in a paroxysm of laughter, choking, sobbing, guffawing, all at once.

"If you only realized, child," he choked between spasms. "If you only understood how important this object was to me, once . . ."

"We do understand, Madoc," Sigurdsson began.

"You understand nothing!" shouted Madoc, his anger rapidly sobering him. "Nothing!

"My brother was the one who wished to conquer the world!" he cried. "I only wanted to do what was right! But each time, he forced his way ahead and did as he wanted—only I paid the price!"

"He paid a price too, Father," Rose said. "He was imprisoned in the Keep of Time, never to leave. And it was his own son who banished him there."

Madoc blinked at her, as if he didn't understand. "Arthur?" he said. "Arthur banished him?"

"Yes," said Rose.

"He—he never said," Madoc began. "Even when I returned to Camelot, if he had only told me . . ."

"Would that have changed anything?" asked the professor.

Madoc grew cold again. "No," he said, his voice edged with hatred. "He took my hand, and then he took my wife. He deserved everything I brought down on his house."

"All you've ever brought down is darkness, Madoc," said the professor. "And that darkness has continued to fester and grow, until it now threatens to cover two worlds. And you still have the ability to choose the right thing."

"It's too late for that," Madoc said, shaking his head. "After what was done to me—"

"Spare me," said Archimedes. "You were always the rational one, Madoc. But nothing you've said is rational in the least. So Merlin wanted to conquer the world, and sacrifice his own son in the process. You defended the boy, then lost your hand trying to kill your brother. And after all that, you set out to basically subjugate everyone else who has ever lived. And you failed at that. So why don't you show some of the mettle you used to have, and just do the thing you know to be right?"

Madoc glared at the bird and trembled a little, but then he steadied himself and spoke. "All right."

"All right, what?" said Archimedes.

"It's very simple," Madoc said. "I will do as you ask, and repair the sword. But I want you to do something for me."

"I'll consider it," said Rose. "But I cannot promise anything."

"This is not a negotiation," said Madoc. "This is a barter. I am the only one who can give you what you want, and so I am asking you for something I want. You either say yes, or you say no. Whatever happens now is entirely up to you."

"What is it that you want, son of Odysseus?" said Quixote. "Ask, and we shall consider."

"As I said," Madoc repeated, "it's very simple. I'll repair the sword, and you can go back and defeat whatever evil it is that my Shadow has perpetrated. But when you are victorious, I want you to return to Terminus and drop a door from the Keep of Time over the waterfall."

"You want us to provide you with a means of escaping your prison, you mean," said Professor Sigurdsson. "I don't know if that will be permitted."

"I'm not asking for escape," said Madoc, "or else I'd be demanding to return with you now. I know that there are lines no one will cross for me, and if nothing else, I don't relish the idea of encountering Samaranth again anytime soon. All of which is why I'm asking for the door—any random door will do. It won't be a means of escape so much as a sort of parole."

"Freedom is freedom," said Quixote.

"I say we agree to it," said Archimedes, who had continued listening and observing during the entire discussion. "I've actually known him longer than any of you, and honestly, I always liked him better than the other one."

At the mention of his brother, Madoc winced, as if the words stung. But he said nothing.

"Even if we do agree," said Quixote, "where do we find a door from the keep?"

"If this is successful," the professor said, "then we will have recovered all of the doors that are being hoarded by Burton. We can have our pick of them."

"And if you're not successful?" said Madoc. "What then? I will have done this service for you for no benefit to myself."

"Once you would not have asked a boon for yourself, to do something that cost you so little and helped so many," the professor replied.

Madoc regarded him with a rueful stare. "That was a different time, and long past. Don't try to sway me with what cannot be reclaimed."

"I've read the Histories," the professor said. "I know as much about you as any man, save for my protégés, and I know the caliber of man you once were."

Madoc brandished his right arm, which bore the tarnished hook. "It was your students whom I have to thank for this," he said, waving the hook in the air. "And also for making me the man I am now. And that you cannot change."

"Will you take my word of honor?" Quixote said suddenly. "My word, as a knight, that whatever it may take, we shall deliver you one of the doors?"

Madoc tipped his head back and laughed. "I might, if you were a real knight," he said brusquely. "Go back and play your little games with windmills and shrubberies and fat, useless squires. There's nothing for you to promise here."

"My word then," offered Sigurdsson. "As a Caretaker of the *Imaginarium Geographica.*"

"A bit more appealing, but no," said Madoc. "Not that I doubt your sincerity, but from what I can gather you appear to be dead—and dead people have a way of living down to one's expectations."

"Then will you take *my* word?"

Rose stepped between the knight and the professor and laid a comforting hand on Madoc's hook. He started to protest, but after a moment lowered it. Rose took his other hand in hers and looked up at him, her face serene.

"I am your daughter," she said softly. "I am the child you never knew, who was raised by someone you claimed to love. In her name, and on her blood, which also runs in my veins, will you take my word that whatever we must do, we will somehow find a way?"

At first, as she spoke, Madoc would not meet her gaze. Then, slowly, he lifted his eyes to look at her.

"Green," he said quietly, "flecked with violet. Her eyes were not violet."

"But yours are, Father."

He looked at her a moment more, then, almost imperceptibly, he nodded. "Your word I will take."

"Then we agree," Rose said. "If you will repair the sword, we will give you one of the doors from the Keep of Time."

PART SIX

Reign of Shadows

"Show them what it looks like when a hope is fulfilled . . ."

Chapter Twenty-One
The Return

It was not by accident that it began in Oxford.

The darkness that began to spread over the cities of Europe covered England first, then moved east.

The Allied forces had been assured that it was all according to some greater plan—but calls to the Chancellor went unanswered, and it was no comfort to them when they received reports that their enemies' strongholds were also being plunged into darkness.

It had been unsettling enough to receive the strange reports of ships manned by children that appeared and disappeared, mounting raids against friend and foe alike before disappearing into the mists. But this strange darkness was worse, because it had been foretold. It was worse because it was darkness with form, and with purpose.

One by one, the cities of the world were made dark by the shadows of the Dragons.

Hank Morgan watched numbly as the shadows covered Oxford, then London, and Paris, and Berlin, and Cairo, and Amsterdam, and Tokyo, and Rome, and on and on.

He returned to the Kilns in Oxford and looked around at the tumbledown wreck the cottage had become in the last seven years.

Reaching behind a cupboard, he retrieved a hidden Trump and quickly began to sketch in the details of a destination he'd been told never to draw.

A few moments later he stepped through the card to Tamerlane House.

With Quixote and Archimedes' help, Madoc soon had the forge glowing hot. He had several rough but still incredibly inventive tools, which could be attached to his hook for a multitude of uses. Once the coals were turning white with the heat, he waved off the knight and the owl and went to work.

Rose watched from the sand not far away, while Professor Sigurdsson was content to sit in the boat and read. "It's John's book, you know," he said in explanation. "I'd like to finish it before the trip is over."

Rose knew what he was avoiding saying, and she resented slightly that he was not more direct—but at the same time, she was a little bit grateful for the lie.

Quixote quickly realized that the work Madoc was doing was far beyond his own experience, and he wisely kept his distance. But Archimedes was a different story. The sword, and its original creation, were not so far removed from his own time, and from the culture that had created him.

He offered a word of advice now and again, and eventually Madoc offered him a modified apron to wear to protect him from the showering of sparks, and Archie took an active role in restoring the sword.

Rose watched this in wonderment. Archie had been Madoc's teacher before he was hers. He had been present when her mother fled Alexandria, during the first betrayal. And now, here he was, centuries later, helping Madoc to create the weapon that would destroy a piece of himself.

Archimedes did not judge him, and was no more or less critical than he was with anyone else. *Is that because he's mechanical, and not truly alive,* she wondered, *or is there something more? Is it perhaps because he knew Madoc before he was Mordred, before the betrayals— and is helping the man he was, not the man he is?*

Is there a difference? And is the difference in the man I see, or in how I choose to see him?

She also looked back at the professor, reading in the *Scarlet Dragon*, and wondered what had motivated *him*. This trip would very likely cost him his existence—an existence that was essentially a second chance at life. But he had risked it to seek out the very man who had killed him, to ask for his help. Why? How could he have believed it was even possible? And yet there Madoc was, doing the very thing they needed the most.

Rose suspected she knew what her uncle John would say if he were here: *This is what it means to grow up, to learn why we do the things we do and make the choices we make. It just comes down to how much you believe in something, and doing it, and not worrying about the outcome.*

Come to think of it, she reconsidered, that was more along the lines of what her uncle Jack would say.

Madoc worked for one hour, then two, then four. The sweat was pouring off him in rivulets, and his arms had gone brown with the heat.

Again and again he flipped the sword with the tongs and

hammered away at it as if possessed. Slowly, ever so carefully, the pieces of the sword began to coalesce into a whole again.

Finally he swung the hammer high over his head and struck the last blow.

Tossing the tongs to Archimedes, he dropped the hammer in the sand and walked over to the water's edge.

He stood there for a long moment, examining the glowing red metal. Then he bowed his head. "Thank you, Nimue. Forgive . . ."

Madoc knelt and plunged the sword into the water.

A cloud of steam issued up and enveloped him, and for a moment he was completely enshrouded in the whiteness. But then it evaporated, and he rose to his feet.

Madoc turned around to face the others. In his hand, he held the gleaming black sword Caliburn.

He clenched his jaw. "This is what I wanted," he said numbly. "This is what I fought for, what I . . .

"Here." He flipped the blade around to offer the hilt to Rose. "Take it. I no longer want it—not when I know what it's already cost me, and everyone else who has touched it. Take it."

But Rose merely stood there with her hands at her side.

"You have the sword Caliburn in your hand," she said. "You have a Dragonship. You could return and take the throne if you wish. You could defeat your own Shadow easily—and then you would be master of the world."

Archimedes let out a squawk, and Quixote stared at the girl in astonishment. Was she suddenly insane?

Madoc met her eyes, trying to read what he saw there. She was inscrutable, and worse, there was no guile in her. She was really offering him the sword and the ship.

"Madre de dios," Quixote muttered.

"Choose," said Rose.

"I shattered this sword the first time," Madoc told her evenly, "because I truly believed that was my destiny. I return it to you now, whole and unbroken, because I know that it is not."

"That," Rose said as she took the sword from his hand, "is why you were able to hold it at all. And that, if nothing else, means there is worth in you still."

Quixote raised his eyes heavenward in a silent prayer, then held his hand out to Madoc. "Thank you."

Madoc looked down at the outstretched hand, then turned his back to the companions and strode over to the forge to start breaking it down.

"What if you need to use it for something else?" said Archimedes. "Shouldn't you leave it be?"

"I won't use it again," Madoc said as he continued his dismantling effort. "Once you've repaired the sword of Aeneas and Arthur, everything else is just metal."

It took only a few minutes for Rose, Quixote, Archie, and the professor to ready the *Scarlet Dragon* for the return voyage home. They wrapped the sword in an oilcloth and secured it under a crossbeam in the prow. Then they went to say good-bye to Madoc.

He had finished dismantling the forge and had strewn the pieces all across the beach. He was standing with his back to them, forty or fifty yards away—far enough that he couldn't feel them behind him as they prepared to leave, but not so far that the echoing properties of the wall wouldn't conduct their farewells.

"Thank you, Madoc," said Archie. "Farewell."

"I am grateful to you," said Quixote, "and we shall not forget our promise."

"I forgive you," said the professor. "This visit has been far more enjoyable than the last time we met."

"Good-bye, Madoc," said Rose. "Good-bye, Father."

Madoc did not turn around, nor acknowledge that he had heard them.

The four companions boarded the *Scarlet Dragon* and inflated the balloon. In seconds it was aloft and pointed east.

The *Scarlet Dragon* flew rather than sailed, because on this trip there was nothing to search for but the horizon. The little ship sped along through the gloom and mist as quickly as they could compel it to go.

It was difficult to estimate time or distance, because there was no real day or night here—it was all varying degrees of light and dark.

Every so often, one of them would glance over at the bundle under the cross-brace, as if to reassure themselves that they had really done it, that the sword was there, and whole. Once Rose offered to unwrap it, but Quixote placed his hands on hers and shook his head.

"It is not a frivolous thing, to be displayed for our amusement or comfort," he said. "You will know when the time is right, and you will hold it as it is meant to be held."

"Also," said Archimedes, "you might drop it over the edge. And that would be a bad, bad thing."

"We don't want to spoil the trip now, do we?" said Professor Sigurdsson.

"Professor," Rose began to ask—but she could not find the words to finish the question. It didn't matter. He knew what she wanted to know, and his answer was that he refused to turn and look at her.

"Faster," Rose whispered to the *Scarlet Dragon*. "We must go faster."

It was difficult to tell, there in the twilight of the place past the Edge of the World, if the ship was flying any faster because of her prompting, but she felt it was, and that gave her hope.

Their altitude was such that they could not see the waters below, and had no way of knowing if they had passed most or all of the islands. Their only hope was an eastward course—and speed.

The professor fell.

He did not faint, but suddenly his legs would not hold him upright in the boat any longer.

Rose and Quixote knelt next to him and sat him upright. "Are you all right, Professor?" Rose asked. But she could read the answer on his face. He was pale—but not from exertion or anemia. He was beginning to become slightly transparent. Ethereal.

He was starting to fade.

"No, no, no, no," Rose said, squeezing his hand. "We're almost there, Professor! You have to hold on!"

He tried to stand, but it was too difficult, and he slumped back down. "Here," Quixote said, folding the professor's coat into a pillow. "Lie down a moment. Gather your strength."

"I fear my strength has all but left me, Don Quixote," said

the professor. "I just wish it wasn't so dark out here. I suppose it's all right for the Dragons, but I really prefer the sunshine."

"Really, Professor?" Rose asked, anxious to keep him talking. "Tell us about it."

"It was among my greatest joys of living," Professor Sigurdsson said weakly. "That may sound odd for someone who lived in London, but in my youth, I often traveled to sunnier climes. I had just hoped, when my time finally came, that I would be able to expire in some golden field somewhere."

"There is such a place," Quixote said quietly. "I have seen it, and it is the most wonderful place. There is indeed a golden meadow, the most glorious you can imagine, filled with grasses and flowers that cover every inch of earth. And just beyond is a castle made of crystal, where the great heroes of history may go when they have earned their final rest.

"I am certain," he went on, laying a hand on the professor's forehead, "that there is a place there for you, my noble friend. And there are three beautiful women who watch over the heroes, so that if any have lost their way, they can help them find the road to Paradise."

Tears filled Rose's eyes, and they ran down her cheeks and dripped onto the professor's face. "Don't worry, my dear," he said, consoling her. "Things have happened the way they were meant to. I got to see my dear friends one last time. I was able to make peace with the man who murdered me. And I got to be a hero one final time. There is nothing more I could have asked or expected in this world or any other, and truly, I am content."

"A light!" Archimedes shrieked. "I see a light!"

The companions looked past the prow of the ship to see

what had gotten the owl so excited—and then they became excited themselves. There was indeed a light.

The edge of the waterfall was in sight.

Rising swiftly out of the darkness, the light that spilled over from the Archipelago created an artificial horizon—but it was still distressingly far away.

"We're going to make it, Professor," Rose said, gripping his hand. "I know it."

But he shook his head, and touched her cheek. "My dear, we might—just might—make it to the surface again, but it will be too long a journey back to the Nameless Isles for me to survive. You must accept this."

She bit her lip and nodded, then hugged the old man tightly, for she knew it would be her last opportunity to do so.

"Is there anything I might do?" Quixote asked.

"Just one thing," the professor answered. His voice was little more than a whisper now. "I don't want to go while I'm lying here on my back. Will you help me to stand?"

"Of course, my friend."

Together, Quixote and Rose lifted Professor Sigurdsson up until he was on his feet, but he was already too weak.

"It's all right," he said, slumping in their arms. "I can meet my fate sitting."

"You shall not!" said Quixote. "Not while I am with you. By God, you will stand!"

The knight stood next to the professor and pulled his arm around his own shoulders. "I will be your legs," Quixote said. "I shall be your strength."

"The light!" Archimedes called. "We're almost high enough!"

Rose threw aside the parachute to lighten the ship and wring out every ounce of speed. "We're nearly there, professor!" she exclaimed. "You're almost home!"

"So nice," the professor murmured as the first rays of light struck his face. "I can almost see that meadow, Quixote."

"As I knew you would, my friend," the knight said through his own tears. "You will never be in darkness again, only in the light of a glorious, endless day, where every sleep is brief, and at every waking you shall rise up to meet the sun."

The light swept over the little craft as the professor's eyes closed, and his body began to shimmer and fade. In moments he had burst into an explosion of light and joy, and tears, and then he was gone.

There was no time to mourn the loss of the professor. The *Scarlet Dragon* had reached the limits of its endurance, but a respite was within reach, if they could only reach the water past the falls.

The wind-battered Dragonship rose to the crest of the immense waterfall and edged its way over, just barely skimming above the surface. They made it several yards in before the ship started to flounder—but the current was still an immediate danger.

Off to the left, not a mile away, was the island of Terminus.

"There!" Rose exclaimed excitedly. "If we can make it to the island, we may be able to repair the ship!"

Quixote was doubtful that anything could salvage the *Scarlet Dragon*, which had been pushed well past its limits, but after all they had endured with the journey down to find Madoc, and the terrible sacrifice made by Professor Sigurdsson, he was not about to dampen the girl's unflagging spirits.

"We'll make it," he said encouragingly. "Upon my word as a knight, we'll make landfall, my dear, dear girl!"

The knight grabbed the tattered remnants of the balloon and wrapped a rope around the tears. "Ho, Archimedes!" he called out over the roar of the falls. "Take one of the starboard lines and give us a pull!"

Between the port propeller, which was functional but sputtering badly, and the strength of the clockwork owl, the ship skipped slowly across the surface of the water. When it dipped too low, the tremendous current yanked the boat downward, but Archie and Quixote resolved to hold their course. In a matter of minutes, the little craft settled safely onto the sandy beach that lined the southern shore of Terminus, and the balloon finally deflated completely.

Rose and Quixote staggered from the boat and collapsed among the sand and grass. Archie joined them, for once too drained to go circling about.

Rose propped herself up on one elbow. "We can't rest here too long," she told her companions. "We have to find a way to repair the *Scarlet Dragon*. Everything depends on our getting the sword to the king."

"But how, my lady?" Quixote asked without raising his head. "There is nothing on this island but grass, and rocks, and a gravestone."

"Not quite," a voice said from over the low hill behind them. "There's also a friend, who is very, very happy to see you here safe and sound."

Rose and Quixote sat up in astonishment, and Archie let out a squawk of happiness. Just coming over the rise of the hill toward them was a man they had not expected, but were not surprised to see.

"'Believing is seeing,'" said Ransom.

"'Believe,'" answered Rose. "It's wonderful to see you, Mr. Ransom."

"As I told your uncle Jack, dear girl," Ransom admonished, "call me Alvin."

Ransom had with him a small store of food and water, and had even remembered to bring a wind-up mouse for Archie, so the four friends sat down and had an impromptu dinner, while Rose and Quixote took turns telling Ransom about the journey over the waterfall.

His face grew dark when they related what had befallen Professor Sigurdsson.

"He is one I would have liked to know better," Ransom said after offering his condolences. "I have heard great things about him, especially tales of his younger days. He was renowned as an archaeologist and had many adventures even before he was recruited as a Caretaker."

"He did as he told us he would," Quixote said, "and he paid the price he knew must be paid. Now it is for us to make certain it was not a sacrifice made in vain."

"How is it you're here on Terminus, Mr.—Alvin?" asked Rose. "It is, after all, the last place in the entire Archipelago where anyone might go."

"I found my way to the elusive Inn at the World's End," Ransom said as a broad smile spread across his face, "so I was able to sneak in a drink or two before coming here to wait for you. The passage through the Trump requires quite a leap of faith, and when I did get there, I found the place packed. Some sort of metaphysical funeral was going on outside. I asked the innkeeper, and all he would say was that a dream had died. Odd, but a nice tavern nevertheless."

"You came here for us?" Rose exclaimed. "Why? How did you know?"

"There are friends and allies waiting for you all along the edge of the falls," said Ransom, pointing to the water's edge. "Every vessel that wasn't commandeered into battle with the Shadow King. Boats, bottles, bathtubs—whatever would float. I'm not a fan of boats myself, so I elected to wait for you here—where they'd have brought you anyway."

"But why?" Rose repeated.

"In case your quest succeeded," replied Ransom. "We needed a way to get you to the heart of the war as quickly as possible. And since it's partly my fault all this happened, I volunteered to be the one to take you back." He paused. "You were successful, I take it?"

"Oh!" said Rose. "We forgot to show you!" She bounded over to the *Scarlet Dragon* and pulled out the sword, which was still wrapped tightly in the oilcloth.

Reverently she unwrapped it and held it up to the light. The black sword was gleaming and unbroken.

Ransom whistled in appreciation. "Now that's a sword. Let's get you back to Tamerlane House. There's no time to lose."

"Back?" Quixote said, scanning the beach. "Did you bring one of the Dragonships?"

"Better," said Ransom. He opened up his jacket and removed the Trumps. "Remember the ones I reserved in case of an emergency? Well, if the End of the World doesn't qualify, I don't know what does."

At that moment several voices called out to them from the water, and they turned to see a flotilla of small boats and rafts converging on the beach. They were occupied by fauns, and a few badgers, and several old men and young boys from the various islands. All those who were not able to fight in a battle had come here to risk their lives anyway, to be of service to the one who could bring hope to the Archipelago. The hopeful and anxious looks on their faces said everything the companions needed to know.

"Show them," said Ransom. "Show them what it looks like when a hope is fulfilled and a dream comes true."

Rose stood and slowly held the sword high over her head. The response was a wave of cheering and sobbing and chanting of her name. Everyone in the boats was filled with excitement and joy—and, as Ransom had said, hope.

"If you've recovered enough of your strength," said Ransom, "we need to get going. There are a great many people waiting for you back in the Nameless Isles."

"I thought you weren't supposed to create a drawing of the islands there, to keep it a secret?" said Rose.

"All the secrets are out," said Ransom, "and all the cards are on the table except one—and that's you. If this doesn't work, there won't be any place left to keep a secret."

"Is it really that dire?" asked Quixote.

"It is," said Ransom. "But look at all those out there, in the boats. They believed, and here you are. Others believe in you too."

"And believing is seeing," said Rose.

"That's the grand thing about dreams," Ransom said as he held the card up to the light. "Some may eventually pass on, but there's always another one to take its place."

Chapter Twenty-two
Pax Terra

"So the endgame has begun," said Twain. "The Shadow King is making his move to conquer the Summer Country."

"I believe so, yes," Hank Morgan said, nodding. "Otherwise, I wouldn't have taken the risk of crossing directly here."

"It was a flaunting of the rules," said Spenser.

"Says the man sitting next to *Richard Burton*," Morgan shot back.

"The boy has a point," said Burton.

"It was the right call," said John, "and Ransom will hopefully soon be putting the Trump to even better use. But the question remains as to what we should do now. We can't possibly fight a war on two fronts, in two worlds."

"Maybe we can," said Artus.

"What do you mean?" asked John.

Artus held up the horn Samaranth had given him. "It still has one call in it, remember? What if I used it to call the Dragons? Do you think they'd come?"

"I don't think it would help," said John. "Remember those whose shadows became Shadow-Born? They were little more than

A tearing sound ripped across the hilltop . . .

wraiths, drained of life. I think the Dragons might be the same."

"It's worth a try, isn't it?" asked Twain. "If the dragons have any strength at all, it's only a blessing to our side."

"Actually, that wasn't what I was thinking at all," said Artus. "I've already given up the Dragons for lost. But I think they—or at least, their shadows—might still be summoned by the horn."

"Forgive me if I missed something," said Hawthorne, "but aren't they under our adversary's control?"

Burton chuckled. "That's exactly his point, you idiot."

"Burton's right," John said, looking at Artus with admiration. "I think it might work, Artus."

"What might, John?" asked Jack.

"The Horn of Bran Galed will summon the Dragon shadows— and draw them all away from the Summer Country," said John. "It might make our job harder here, but at least for the moment, it would spare the rest of the world."

The Caretakers looked at one another, then nodded their agreement, and the King of the Silver Throne walked outside, put the horn to his lips, and blew.

The note was clear and pure, and took long moments to fade.

"What happens now?" asked Jack.

"We wait," said Artus. "The last time, I—"

Suddenly, without warning, the skies went dark all around the Nameless Isles.

Swirling up like an impenetrable fog, the darkness rose on all sides, leaving only a small circlet of open sky above the ring of islands.

"Is it an eclipse?" Nemo asked.

"I wish it were," said Jack through clenched jaws. "Do you see what I'm seeing, Charys?"

The centaur nodded grimly. "I fear there is no way to strategize, no way to rally for opposition like this," he said, wheeling about. "All we can hope for is a quick, noble death."

"What is it?" Nemo asked as Charys trotted away to organize the captains of the Dragonships. "What are you both so afraid of?"

"That's not just darkness," Jack said. "It's *shadow*. And it's not just any shadow. It's the shadows of the *Dragons*."

"What can we do?"

"We fight as long as we can," Jack said, "and pray for a miracle."

"Why hasn't the darkness covered the sky completely?" John said. "Why haven't the Shadows simply fallen down and overwhelmed us?"

"It's why I built Tamerlane House here," said Poe. "This grouping of islands is among the oldest lands on the Earth, or hadn't you noticed? They form a giant Ring of Power. The original rings were built by the giants—but they modeled them after this place. The shadows cannot come in, but neither can we leave."

"And in the meantime, the armies of the Shadow King will sweep through and devastate us," said Charles. "Wonderful."

"We have our own armies," said John, "and I have faith in them. We just need to hold out until Rose can return with the sword."

Burton laughed. "Do you really believe that that's going to help?"

"You've chosen your side, Richard, whether or not we've accepted you back," said Twain. "Our fate is now yours—so if you have something useful to contribute, now's the time."

"I'll tell you what I can," said Burton, "although it may be too late. He is bringing an army you cannot fight."

"Cannot defeat?" said Charles.

"No," said Burton. "Cannot *fight*."

"Shadow-Born?"

"No. He took the cauldron only so that it could not be used against him," said Burton. "The Spear of Destiny is more compelling, and easier to use. All he need do is speak one's True Name, and bind them, then he can take the shadows with the spear. Using the doors of the keep, we could catch the Dragons unawares, and with the shadows of the Dragons, he has no need of anyone else's."

"But if the Dragon shadows cannot cross into the Nameless Isles," said John, "then it's a stalemate."

"Aren't you listening?" Burton exclaimed, pounding his fist on the table. "Stupid little Caretaker. Years ago I warned you, and still your vision is too small.

"Once you have been defeated, his conquest of the Archipelago will be complete, and the shadows of the Dragons will sweep across the Frontier and back into the Summer Country. But he won't need them to defeat you, because he has an army you cannot fight."

"The only enemy a man cannot defeat by combat is himself," said Shakespeare.

"Finally the idiot savant speaks wise," said Burton.

"What are you talking about?" said John.

"This," Burton said, rising to his feet. He strode to a curtain and threw open the shutters. "Look and see for yourselves. Your enemies have arrived."

The Caretakers crowded around the windows and looked in the direction Burton was pointing.

A Time Storm was forming out over the water. The clouds roiled about, flashing with lighting, as seven shapes emerged and entered the Nameless Isles.

"Oh, no," John whispered. "It isn't possible."

"I've been waiting for them all these years," said Burton. "I'm surprised you haven't been."

Out on the edge of the harbor, in front of the defensive line of Dragonships, seven more ships drew up close and stopped.

They weren't just ships—they were the Dragonships *themselves*, brought out of the past by the Shadow King and led by a fourteen-year-old Stephen and the half-clockwork sons of Jason of myth.

"And thus is the history fulfilled," Bert murmured. "If Stellan and the others don't return soon, this is truly the end for us all."

On the large, outermost of the Nameless Isles, Artus despaired.

"Are those what I think they are?" he said grimly.

"Yes," Jack said, stunned. "Those are the ships we saw in the Underneath, and attacking Kor! But how could he do this? How did he bring them here?"

"It doesn't matter," said Artus, summoning Laura Glue and the Valkyries. "We can't fight them. They are our own children. The best we can do is try to hold them back long enough for—"

"I know," said Jack.

"Spread the word," Artus told Laura Glue. "All ships to the air, where they cannot follow us. And those of us on the ground should be instructed: defense only. No child is to be harmed, if we can help it. They are being compelled, and their wills are not their own."

"Consider this," Jack said as Laura Glue sped off. "When they returned to us during the conflict in the Underneath, after being pulled away in Time, they were battered and bruised, but unharmed. This was when they were pulled *to*. Things may yet turn out in our favor."

"Or it means that they wiped us out here," said Artus. "Whatever happens, we'll hold them, won't we Jack?"

"We will," Jack said, gripping his friend's shoulder.

There was a stirring of a westward breeze in the Pygmalion Gallery, and Rose, Archimedes, Quixote, and Ransom stepped through the portal from Terminus.

"What must we do now?" asked Rose.

Ransom went to the window and looked up at the sky.

"I just pray we haven't come too late," he said. "The Shadow King is here."

"Archie," Rose said. "Get to Bert and the Caretakers, right away! They need to know about Defoe!"

Obediently, Archimedes flew from the room.

"We have to go outside," Rose said to Quixote. "I don't know what's to be done, but we need to get to the king or queen."

"According to the Prophecy," said Ransom, "the sword is for you to use."

"It never occurred to me to ask," said Quixote. "Do you even know how to use a sword?"

"The one good thing about British boarding schools," Rose said as they left the gallery, "is that the better ones all teach fencing.

And I wouldn't be my grandfather's heir if I hadn't taken first place in the competition."

"John!" Hawthorne shouted from down the corridor outside the conservatory. "Come quickly! Hurry!"

John and several other Caretakers rushed out to see what the matter was. It was Jakob Grimm. Hawthorne was half carrying, half dragging him down the hall, trailing blood.

"It's how they found us!" Hawthorne said as they pushed open a door to one of the spare rooms. "They took Jakob's map off his back!"

"I'm sorry!" Jakob cried through the tears and mucus running down his face. "I didn't want to bring them! I fought it, as hard as I could! But then they took what they wanted anyway, and it's all for nothing!"

"What is, Jakob?" asked John, getting his arm under the poor man's shoulder to help Hawthorne place him on a settee. "What's for nothing?"

"The Shadow King promised," Jakob sobbed. "He said if I cooperated, he would let my brother live. And I resisted!"

"If he promised something like that," said Chaucer, "then I suspect your brother is already dead."

Jakob collapsed in a heap of shuddering sobs as the Caretakers and several of the ravens began tending to his terrible wound.

"Grimalkin and I found him in one of the upper rooms," Hawthorne said, looking appreciatively at the Cheshire cat that had appeared at their feet. "Somehow, a spy is still among us."

"How are they getting in?" John asked, pounding a wall in frustration. "We've sealed off the gallery and posted guards at both ends. Is it possible there is another Trump hidden inside the house somewhere?"

"Doubtful," said Twain. "There are very few of those sheets unaccounted for, and even fewer people trained in making them. So unless you know someone with a magic box that people can just pop in and out of, I'm at a loss."

"Magic box!" John exclaimed, snapping his fingers. "You're a genius, Samuel!"

"Was there ever a doubt?" Twain called out as John tore from the room. He looked down at Grimalkin, who was missing his torso. "What did I say?"

John burst through the doors of the conservatory. "Jamie!" he said, panting from exertion. "When you died, who handled your estate?"

"My boys, of course," Jamie replied. "Why?"

"For your personal belongings, certainly," said John, "but what about items relating to the Archipelago?"

Jamie shrugged. "I had practically nothing left there in London," he said. "Only a few papers, and the old wardrobe—and I left those to you, Jack, and Charles."

"That's what I was afraid of," said John. "Because we jumped forward in time by going through the Trump, we weren't there to claim anything."

"But the wardrobe is still useless without the second one," said Jamie, "and it's—"

"Safely in Paralon?" John finished. "Under the control of the Senate, and the new Chancellor?"

"Oh, my stars and garters," said Jamie.

At that moment, Archimedes flew into the room.

"Archie!" John exclaimed in shock. "You've come back! Is the professor—"

"No time, no time!" the owl squawked. "I know who the traitor is!"

Quickly Archimedes related to the Caretakers what he had learned from Captain Johnson, and as he spoke, they became more and more resolved.

"We must talk to Poe," John said. "Right away!"

The new Dragonships commandeered by the children pulled onto the beach, and the spellbound young warriors began to pour from the holds.

"There are thousands of them!" Charys cried. "How can we do this? How do we fight children?"

"We don't," said Jack, looking quickly around the island. "There!" He pointed behind them to one of the cliffs. "They can't hurt us, and we won't have to hurt them if we reduce the size of the target."

The other allies on the ground quickly realized what Jack was referring to, and under the cover of the airships, they swiftly retreated to a narrow isthmus between the cliffs. As Jack had hoped, the masses of children followed.

Once on the other side, the allies would only have to deal with a narrow trickling of the children, rather than all at once.

"How did you learn to do that?" an astonished Nemo asked.

Jack grinned. "*You* taught me how to do that," he said. "About a quarter century ago."

"We'll still have to fight them," said Charys. "It's unavoidable."

"Not completely," said Jack. "Artus! It's time for your secret weapon!"

Artus nodded and grinned, then he signaled to the Elves. They lowered the *Blue Dragon*'s enormous bulk and opened the hold.

The Tin Man jumped out with surprising agility, and without any instruction, he rushed forward to the narrow pass. Between his bulk, and the gentle sweeps of his ax, he managed to effectively block the advance of the children.

Many stopped, but those who pressed forward received only bruises, and the worst injuries were broken bones.

"That's incredible!" Nemo declared. "You're winning the battle without having to fight!"

"Not winning," said Jack. "Delaying. That may be the best we can do."

"That is the least you can do," said a chilling voice beside them. Jack and the others spun around in time to see Kipling and the Shadow King step out of a Trump portal and onto the hilltop. Kipling held a sword, and the Shadow King carried the Spear of Destiny.

"Get into the airship," Artus said to Nemo and Jack as he stepped forward and drew his sword. "Protect Aven."

"We're not leaving you," Jack began.

"I know that!" said Artus. "But we have to hold on! I believe! Do you?"

"Yes," said Jack, as he eyed Kipling. "I believe." But he didn't climb into the ship, and neither did Nemo or Stephen.

"Stay clear of his reach," Jack warned. "He has the spear, and we don't have anything that can defeat it. Not yet. All we can do is try to hold him off," he finished grimly, with a silent prayer.

"Come, let us reason together," said Artus.

"No reasoning, no discussion," said the Shadow King. He glanced up at the Dragon shadows circling overhead and smirked. "You may have delayed my plans for the Summer Country, but that is all you have done—delay. There is nothing to discuss but your defeat. And you have nothing that can overpower my spear."

"I don't have to defeat you myself," said Artus. "I just have to hold you back long enough for Rose to get here, to do what she's destined to do."

"I've read your Prophecy," the Shadow King hissed, "and it means nothing to me."

"It means something to *him*," said Kipling, "and you shouldn't underestimate that."

"Kill him," the Shadow King said. "Kill him now."

"You know," Kipling remarked, "I really don't think I'm going to be able to do that."

The Shadow King looked at him in confused fury. "What about that order didn't you understand?" he shouted. "Kill him!"

"What about my refusal didn't you understand?" said Kipling. "I'm not a violent man, and I detest war." He dropped the sword to the grass. "I quit."

"You forget what I promised you, Caretaker," the Shadow King said as he touched a contact on his chest and a circlet of mist began to swirl behind him. "You forget what I can do, whom I can return to you."

Kipling paused, and started to look back. In the swirl of mist, a face began to appear—a young man, a soldier.

Kipling steeled himself and bit his lip. "I haven't forgotten. I've just managed to keep the things that are truly right ahead of the things that I want for myself."

"Your son, Kipling—"

"Is dead."

With a snarl, the Shadow King released the contact, and the young soldier vanished.

Kipling walked around the reach of the Shadow King and stood behind Jack. "Greetings, Caretaker."

"I don't understand," Jack hissed, "but I won't argue with your choice."

"I see," said the Shadow King. "There are more traitors than I knew, here in the Nameless Isles."

"Not traitors," Artus said, turning to smile at Kipling, "just friends. And that's how I know we're going to win."

"You won't," the Shadow King replied. With a single motion, he thrust the Spear of Destiny through Artus's heart before anyone could cry out a warning. "I'm not going to take your shadow, boy," he rasped. "I'm just going to end your life."

"Ah, me," Artus said, looking down at the spear sticking out of his chest. "Aven, I—"

The King of the Silver Throne dropped to his knees, then fell over on his side, dead.

When Defoe stepped out of the wardrobe secreted away in the uppermost room at Tamerlane House, a contingent of Caretakers was there to greet him.

"Well, this is a fine how-do-you-do," he said, "to borrow a phrase. How in Hades did you find me out?"

"Traitors are themselves easily betrayed," Poe said softly.

"Friends may quarrel, and the bond may remain unbroken. But a traitor can have no friends who will not eventually side against him."

"I can see that," said Defoe. "You welcomed Burton into your midst easily enough."

"Don't take my name in vain, Daniel," Burton said as he strode into the room. "I knew there were more moles about, but I thought you'd at least have been brave enough to be up-front about it."

"Says the original traitor," Defoe spat. "Physician, heal thyself."

"Oh, I'm feeling just fine," said Burton. "I finally realized that there was a price too high to pay to achieve my goals. It serves no one and nothing to seek after truth as an ally of evil."

"You got cold feet, you mean."

"I came to my senses," said Burton, "and you've let the Shadow King's hunger for power color your judgment."

"Chain it," Poe ordered, pointing at the wardrobe. "I'm guessing wherever the other one is, we'll find Houdini and Conan Doyle."

Defoe just glared at him.

"That's answer enough," said Poe. "We'll strand them, and retrieve them when this is finished."

"It'll be finished soon enough," snarled Defoe.

"I agree," said Poe. "It will."

"I'll take responsibility for the Detective and the Magician," said Burton. "They're my apprentices, not the Shadow King's. They'll be penitent enough, I think."

"You didn't bring them with you," said John. "Why?"

Burton grinned. "Self-preservation first. I *am* a barbarian, after all."

Suddenly Defoe ripped a mirror from the wall and smashed

it against Archimedes, who'd been perched atop the wardrobe. The owl screetched and flapped his wings, scattering silvered glass all over the Caretakers. John shouted to Bert, and together they calmed down the bird, who was ruffled but unharmed—but the distraction had served its purpose. Defoe had disappeared down one of the endless hallways.

"Never mind," said Poe. "We've cut off his means of escape. We'll find him later."

"If Archimedes is here," said Bert, "does that mean Stellan and the others are too?"

"Not Stellan," said Poe, looking at his watch. "It's been too long."

"We must mourn later," Bert said, grabbing John's shoulders. "We have to find Rose!"

"I agree. I've had enough of debate," said John. "We're going out to join the battle."

The Tin Man, staunch as he was, was being overrun.

The masses of children were finally proving too much, so others of the allies, still under the instruction to delay and not harm, tried to aid his efforts.

The Valkyries were the most effective of the allies' forces, because they were more mobile and flexible than any of the other groups. But they were also the most vulnerable, because they couldn't wear armor and still fly—and any blow that could knock them out meant a fall to the death, unless one of their companions caught them.

The warrior children started hurling stones with slings when they realized their closest enemies were airborne. Sadie Pepperpot had taken a terrible blow to her shoulder, and her left arm was hanging nearly useless at her side. Several others were also injured.

The Tin Man started to pull back, and the others realized that combat with the children might be inevitable.

Stephen cried out when the Shadow King had speared Artus, and he rushed forward, but Jack held him back.

"Look!" Jack cried out. "There! Down the hill!"

The companions, keeping one eye on the Shadow King, edged away from him and risked a glance to where Jack was pointing.

It was Ransom, Quixote, and Rose. And she was holding Caliburn. The sword was whole again.

On the opposite side of the beach, John and Bert had landed and were coming forward at the same time.

Across the bottom of the cliffs, Charles was leading Charys, Falladay Finn, and Eledir to where the fallen king lay in the grass. And Aven leaped down from her airship to stand next to her son.

"Now we're going to finish this," Aven said, drawing her sword. "You can't take all of us, demon."

"I don't need to," said the Shadow King, indicating the children in the pass. "They can."

His words were confident, but the companions noticed that he had not taken his eyes off Rose—and the sword.

"We're going to get him," Stephen called up to Laura Glue, reaching for her. "Can you give us a little more time?"

"We'll keep them off you as long as we can," gasped Laura Glue, swooping down to take his hand.

"Thank you," Stephen said. He gripped her hand tightly for

a moment, as words unspoken passed between them in a long, lingering glance. Then she pulled free and rose into the air like a shot.

"Valkyries! To me!" she called out with a loud, trilling battle call. "Norah! Sadie! Abby Tornado!" The Valkyries, aided by the centaurs Charys had summoned, were holding the pass, if barely.

Rose and Quixote reached the top of the hill.

"I don't believe it!" said Charles. "You did it!"

"It's a fraud," the Shadow King hissed. "This is your last chance to surrender."

"No," said John, as he and Bert topped the hill, "it's *yours*."

Rose looked at Artus's fallen body and winced. Then she looked up at Stephen and offered him the sword.

"You brought it back," Stephen replied. "It's yours to wield, just as the Prophecy said."

"There is no Prophecy!" the Shadow King said as he took another step back. "I don't believe!"

Rose drew the blade across the palm of her hand, leaving Caliburn's edge slick with her blood.

The winds of the Time Storm suddenly increased and began to howl around the island, as high above, the shadows of the Dragons circled, waiting.

"What are you doing?" the Shadow King whispered, his voice full of menace. "What do you think you are doing, girl?"

"I'm fulfilling my destiny," she said. Her voice was barely audible over the howling winds. "I'm going to heal my family. I'm going to heal my father."

"I *am* your father!" the Shadow King spat. "Give me the sword! Give me Caliburn! It is mine! It always was!"

"You are *not* my father," Rose said calmly. "You are the darkness in his soul, which he chose to set aside. You are the strength, which takes no responsibility, and the will, which has no desire but to consume. You are his spirit, and when you have joined with him once more, it will be his choice what kind of man he is. Now, and forever."

She leaped forward and pressed the tip of the sword against the Shadow King's armor—right at the point where it curved into shadow.

The Shadow King froze in place. Caliburn had trapped him in the shell of the Red King.

"What are you doing, girl?" he screamed. "Stop! Stop this! Release me! I command you!"

"That's exactly what I intend to do," said Rose. "I'm going to release you, from everything." With both hands, she drew the sword across his chest, making a lopsided figure eight. The point of the sword never left his armor, and where it passed, it left a mark of blood.

"I Bind you, Shadow," she said softly, not caring if he or anyone else could hear. "With the mark I have chosen for myself, I Bind you."

Then, as the Shadow King continued to scream, she spoke the words:

> *Shadow of my father*
> *By right and rule*
> *For need of might*
> *I thus bind thee*
> *I thus bind thee*

By blood bound
By honor given
I thus bind thee
I thus bind thee

For strength and speed and heaven's power
By ancient claim in this dark hour
I thus bind thee
I thus bind thee

Rose stepped back and lowered the black sword to her side. On the Shadow King's armor, the infinity symbol she had drawn glowed briefly with a blue fire, then faded.

"Let me see who's really in charge," said Rose. "Show yourself, King of the Shadows."

A tearing sound ripped across the hilltop as a thick, dark form pushed its way out of the Red King's body. It had no face, only roiling hatred that crackled in the air.

"That's good enough," she said, gripping the sword with both hands. "I just wanted you to see my face."

Rose swung the sword through the middle of the dark form, and it shattered apart, screaming, at the touch of Caliburn.

"Now," she said to Stephen, "avenge your father, as I've avenged mine."

"Gladly," Stephen said. He stepped forward as the Shadow King's body howled in dismay.

"I'm sorry!" the frozen king cried. "I—I didn't mean for all of this to happen!"

"Good or evil," Stephen said, clenching his jaw, "that's the first thing you've said that I really believe."

He swung the ax and cleanly lopped off the Shadow King's head.

A burst of sparks and flame shot out of the neck as the body dropped to its knees, then fell over onto its right side, unmoving. The head went spinning down the hill and bounced several times, before at last coming to rest against a petrified log.

The body had only its own shadow. The second shadow had been destroyed by the touch of Caliburn.

Charys approached the spot where the head had fallen and looked down. Nothing remained of the countenance of the Shadow King—all that was left was the original clockwork once called the Red King.

"This is all very unorthodox," the head of the Red King said. "Is the Parliament out of session?"

"It is now," said Charys. He reared up with his forelegs and brought them smashing down onto the head, which exploded into gears and wheels and wires.

At that moment, all the Timelost Dragonships and the thousands of spellbound children crusaders, including young Stephen, vanished.

A cheer rose up from the hovering airships and the allies alike.

"The clockwork!" Bert said in amazement. "It was a giant Anabasis Machine, like the pocket watches! That's how he was able to manipulate the Time Storms to capture the children and the ships!"

"That machine is no more," Charys bellowed, "and I think all debts have been settled!"

"Not entirely," a voice called out from farther down the rise.

"There are still other claims to be made, and I'm claiming the Archipelago as my own."

It was Defoe. And in his hands he held the Spear of Destiny.

He looked at John and smirked. "You should act more swiftly against those you discover to be your enemies."

"Don't be a fool, Daniel," said Bert. "You cannot do this!"

"I think I can, and I shall," said Defoe. "We've often searched for the means to make the Society dominant over the Caretakers, and I always believed it would be in the service of Mordred. But I realize now that it was my destiny all along to do it myself."

"Rose has Caliburn, Daniel," said John. "You're outmatched."

"Ah, I think not, young Caretaker," Defoe replied. "I have the shadows of the Dragons. And that makes me the victor, even before the battle is begun. You are trapped here in the Nameless Isles, and I get the rest of creation. That sounds like a fair exchange."

"Overconfidence was Mordred's downfall," said John. "It will be yours, too."

"It's hard to be overconfident when I control all the Dragons," said Defoe.

"Oh, I wouldn't say all of them," Bert noted, looking up. "You missed one, Daniel."

With a terrifying rush of speed and a sickening crunch, Samaranth dropped out of the sky and crushed Defoe beneath his feet.

"I learned my lesson about banishment last time," said Samaranth. "This is now done and done."

The battle was finally over.

＋　＋　＋

"Why didn't the Shadow King go after you?" Jack asked the Dragon. "I'd have thought he would have made certain to get you first."

"He tried," said Samaranth, "but he could never find my True Name to bind me. His mistake was in believing it was in the book. It wasn't."

"Where is it?" asked Jack.

"That would be telling," said Samaranth.

"We saw something similar happen in the battle with Peter Pan," said Jack, referring to the destruction of the Shadow. "How is this time different?"

"Dissipated is different from destroyed," said Bert, "and silver pixie dust is different from the sword of the gods. The Shadow is gone. Forever."

"That begs an interesting question," said Charles. "The Shadow could not survive if the owner was dead—but what about the reverse? With his Shadow destroyed, what will happen to Madoc?"

But Bert didn't answer. He smiled grimly, then strode off to find Aven to move Artus's body. The king had been the only casualty.

Jack wondered if Bert hadn't answered his question because he couldn't . . .

. . . or because he *wouldn't.*

"Answer my question," said John. "Which side are you on?"

Kipling's only response was to reach into his breast pocket and pull out a silver pocket watch. A pocket watch with a red dragon on the cover.

"How did you get that?" John exclaimed. "Haven't you turned traitor?"

Kipling smiled. "I got it in the usual way, and no," he said blithely, "I have not become a traitor."

"The Shadow King had Defoe and poor Jakob in our camp," said Bert with a weary smile, "but we had Kipling in theirs."

"Don't worry, lad," Kipling said. "We'll explain it all to you by and by. Just know that everything's gone as it was supposed to go."

"Everything?" John said, looking at Artus's body, which they had moved to the deck of the *Blue Dragon*.

"Yes, John," Bert said sadly. "Everything."

John gestured skyward at the shadows. "The Shadow King created this terrible army, and he never even used it."

"He tried," said Kipling, "in the Summer Country. But we summoned them away, then defeated their master. We *won*, lad."

John smiled bitterly. "It just seems to have ended too quickly."

Kipling whirled around, eyes flashing. "Were you hoping for a bigger battle, John? A valiant, vain struggle against foes we could not possibly defeat? That would have made a very dramatic story—for anyone who survived to tell it. But can't it be enough that we won? That our enemy was beaten, and only Artus paid the ultimate price? You were a soldier once," he continued. "How many deaths did you have to witness to make you hate war?"

"One was enough."

Kipling nodded. "I lost my son, and my world changed. If a million more had died in grander battles, it would have made no difference to me—it was already more of a burden than I could bear.

"No," he finished, looking at the sky, "what great things we did today were done despite the terrible cost. But they would not have been made greater had the price we paid been more terrible still."

Kipling clapped John on the shoulder and turned away. "We don't always get the ending we hope for, lad," he called back, "but if we work hard enough to earn it, we sometimes get the ending we deserve."

"So my ancestor was your cousin, hundreds of years ago," Stephen said. "Does that make you my aunt?"

"That's probably as close as anything," said Rose, as she looked up at the still dark skies. "What do we do now?"

"How do we go about freeing the Dragons?" Jack asked Samaranth. "The Shadow King didn't create them the same way he did the Shadow-Born, so I'm guessing the cauldron is going to be of no help."

"You guess correctly. The Dragons are not creatures such as yourselves," Samaranth said slowly, his voice a low rumble. "They cannot be restored with a magic jar, as you did with the Shadow-Born. For a Dragon, its shadow is too intrinsically a part of its being to be severed. So when the Shadow King was cutting into them with the spear, he was not merely severing their shadows—he was ending their lives as Dragons upon this Earth. And he was only able to do that much because he knew their True Names.

"Rose can do nothing now but release the spirits that are left."

"They'll die?" said Rose. "I can't do that! I won't!"

"You must," Samaranth said sadly. "They cannot return to what they were. All we can do now is liberate them."

The Caretakers and the others on top of the hill circled

around Rose in support, as she slowly realized that it was indeed her responsibility.

The sword suddenly felt a great deal heavier as she realized that in some way, she had known all along what she would be asked to do.

"All right," she said finally. "What must I do?"

"You know the words of Summoning," said Samaranth, "and this entire group of islands is a Ring of Power. Summon them here, and then you'll be able to release them."

It took a very long time.

... Hallward was just completing the varnish on a painting.

CHAPTER TWENTY-THREE
Justice and Mercy

The funeral for Artus was small. Later, there could be a full ceremonial service on Paralon so that the entire Archipelago could mourn. But for now, only the three Caretakers and Bert, Aven and Stephen, Rose and Quixote, and the Dragon Samaranth were present as the king's body was lowered into the earth.

He was buried opposite the grave of Nemo, on Terminus. Both graves were within sight of the ring of stones.

"This is where he wanted to be buried," said Aven. "He said that this was the place where he grew up."

"I thought he'd always lived on Avalon," said Charles.

"Not that kind of 'grew up,'" said Jack. "This is where he stopped being a boy and became a man. It's where he became a king, when he summoned the Dragons."

"He fulfilled his destiny," said Aven. "He was the last king of the Archipelago, the last to sit upon the Silver Throne. And he honored his calling more than anyone could have imagined."

"The first time we met," said Samaranth, "he had a bucket on his head, a wooden sword, and a deep desire to become a great knight. I knew, even then, what his destiny was to be, and so I encouraged him the best that I was able."

"This may be an indelicate time to address this," said John, "but do I understand you correctly that Stephen will not be assuming his father's place on the Silver Throne?"

"The Silver Throne will be kept," said Stephen, "and I'll keep the title of king, if only to continue to manifest the changes my father began."

"It's going to make for a fragile peace," said Jack. "The races of the Archipelago are still as fractured as ever—and the first real unifying personage they've ever had turned out to be a despot. That'll be hard to overcome."

"A fragile peace is what we've always had," said Stephen. "I don't think it was any different with a republic than it was with a monarchy. Mother told me there was a Parliament of Kings guiding the lands before, and it really wasn't any more successful at preventing wars and conflicts than we've been these last decades."

"So what are you going to do?" John asked.

Stephen grinned and shrugged. "We're going to pick up the pieces and start all over again," he said wryly. "Just because we're terrible at making it work in practice doesn't mean the principles aren't still sound in theory. That's what my father believed, and it's the reason he sent away the Dragons in the first place. As long as we always had a fallback position, we were never truly committed to the battle."

"Can the Dragons be reunited with their shadows and made whole again?" asked John. "We're going to be returning to our proper time, before these events all took place. Is there a way to save all the Dragons whose shadows were taken as well?"

Samaranth looked away for a long while without answering, and when he finally did turn to face the companions, they were shocked by his expression. As long as they had known him, Samaranth had always appeared ancient. But this was the first time he had ever appeared . . . *old*.

"They are finally free—free of a choice I compelled them to make aeons ago. I believe they should remain so.

"The Dragonships remain ships, but they are no longer living and cannot cross the Frontier. They lost their lives when their shadows were taken. Those that may have escaped the Shadow King in the past will never return to this place, now or ever. And those lost cannot be restored.

"I am now in fact as well as name the last Dragon," said Samaranth, "and you are, as a race, now well and truly entirely on your own."

"Defoe survived?" John exclaimed when they returned to the Nameless Isles. "But we saw Samaranth crush him to death!"

"Correction," said Bert. "We saw Samaranth crush him. He was *already* dead. Now he's just a bit more disorganized and upset than usual. But no," he finished, sighing, "he didn't die."

"What's to be done with him, then?" asked John. "He's far too dangerous to just be released or banished. And I doubt anyone would consider making him the Green Knight. After Rose's report, and after what happened with Magwich, it'd be foolhardy in the extreme to release someone as willful and resourceful as Daniel Defoe."

"The Caretakers Emeritis have penalties of their own," said Bert. "I don't think there's any way he can escape what's planned for him."

"Fair enough," John said. "And what of Burton?"

"That's going to be a matter of some debate," Bert replied. "Poe for one believes him. We weren't exactly winning when he chose to defect—which lends credence to his claim that he and certain other members of the Imperial Cartological Society did indeed have goals more noble than world domination."

"Pull the other one," said John.

"Don't ascribe to evil what can be attributed to well-intentioned stupidity, John," Bert cautioned. "Burton caused more damage than Defoe, but at the end, he wouldn't betray his ideals. For Defoe, the cause was just a means to an end, which was to gain power over others. That made him a stronger ally for the Shadow King, and a weaker man than Burton. But rest assured—everyone pays a price for the choices they make, no matter what their reasons were."

"Burned alive?" Charles exclaimed. "That's a terrible way to go, even for Maggot—er, Magwich. I can't say I'm sorry that . . ." He paused. "Oh, curse it all." He sighed deeply. "As despicable as he was, there was something I *did* like about Magwich. Maybe it was his constancy."

"His constant whining, his constant lying, his constant cowardice," said Jack. "Is that what you mean?"

"Pretty much, yes," said Charles. "There was less pretense about him than almost anyone I've ever known. I think I might even learn to miss the old bugger."

"I can't believe you just said that," Jack said.

"I'm a bit surprised myself," said Charles.

"Then you may find this cheering," said Eledir, the Elf King. He approached the companions and handed a small bag to Charles. It was filled with soil and tied around a small, slightly charred plant.

It had only three offshoots, and the leaves had only just begun to bud. In the center, at the top, was a curiously shaped bulb.

"Several of my captains discovered this as we were sweeping the field," Eledir said. "I meant to give it to Samaranth, but I overheard your discussion, and I think it more appropriate that you have it."

"Well, uh, thank you," Charles stammered.

The King of the Elves gave the Caretakers a staunch salute, then spun about and walked away to finish gathering his people and return home.

"Imagine that!" Charles said. "The Elf King gave me a plant. I wonder if it symbolizes something in his culture."

"You'll have to bring it along when you move to Oxford," said Jack. "It'll look good in the window. I wonder what kind of plant it is?"

"Oh, no," John said as he rushed over to his two friends. "I thought Eledir was going to give it to Samaranth." He sighed heavily and rubbed his temples. "It's too late to refuse it now. Eledir would only get offended."

"Refuse it?" asked Charles. "Why would I possibly want to refuse it?"

In answer to his question, a strange, high-pitched whistling noise emitted from the plant. The companions leaned closer to hear better.

"Oh, for heaven's sake," said Jack. "It's talking."

And indeed it was: "Help meee . . . ," the plant said in a tiny, tinny voice. "Help meee. . . ."

Charles's mouth dropped open. "I'm cursed. Cursed, I tell you."

Jack let out a loud guffaw. "Now I have indeed seen everything.

Charles, old sock," he said, patting his friend on the back, "you've just become the proud owner of a Magwich plant."

There were a few more good-byes to be said. Aven and Stephen prepared to return to Paralon, and the other captains and kings went off to their respective lands. But some farewells were more difficult than others.

"Ho, Jack," said Nemo.

"Ho, Nemo," Jack replied. "What's to become of you now?"

"I have to go back," he said, casting a furtive glance at Aven, and a more lingering and direct one at Stephen. "I have a future to live, and many things to do. And," he added with a grin, "a young soldier to teach."

"You still have a lot to learn," Jack said, clapping him on the shoulder. "But you are already becoming the man I knew and admired, and I have no doubt you'll get there, in time."

"Literally so," said Nemo. He held out his hand. In it was a silver pocket watch. "Bert instructed me in how to use it, and when I return to my proper time, I'm to turn it back over to him."

"You don't want to keep it?"

Nemo shook his head. "I'm the captain of the *Nautilus* and the heir of Sinbad. I'm meant to be sailing in the Archipelago, not through time."

"Fair enough," said Jack, offering his hand. "Be well, Nemo."

They shook hands, and the young captain strode away. He did not look back.

Quixote noted that one other friend in particular struggled with saying farewells.

Uncas was finding it difficult to adjust to the idea that Fred was an apprentice Caretaker—and to the fact that his son was going to probably have the kind of adventures he had only dreamed about.

"I believed myself too old for adventuring," Quixote said to the little badger, "but apparently, I was mistaken. There may be a few more journeys left in these old bones yet."

"I wish you luck, brave sir knight," Uncas said glumly, while trying to appear pleased for him. "I guess I'm going to go back to work at the press. Scowler Charles said I have the temperament to be a fair editor."

He chewed thoughtfully on a paw. "I wonder if he meant 'fair' as in 'just,' or 'fair' as in, I won't be really awful at it?"

"I'm sure he meant the latter," Uncas's son Fred said in consolation. "You've been a mainstay there for years. Editing might be the next natural step."

"With which," Quixote said, "a journey of a thousand miles may be taken. But as always, it is for you to choose the direction."

"And which direction are you going?" asked Fred.

"A knight must needs have a squire," Quixote proclaimed as he knelt before the badgers, "and at the moment, I find myself sorely lacking." He leaned closely to Uncas and pointedly raised an eyebrow.

"Well," Uncas said thoughtfully, "we could help you advertise, put up flyers and whatnot. Maybe we could get Aven t' sponsor a competition or summat, like a contest for a maiden's handkerchief, except you'd be the handkerchief. But not a maidenly one," he added quickly. "More like a manly kind of handkerchief."

Fred rolled his eyes heavenward and elbowed his father in the back. "He's talking about *you*, Pop. He wants you to become his squire, right?"

Quixote nodded, and Uncas's eyes grew wide with the realization of what was being offered to him.

"Y'—y' mean, go with you? On adventures, and heroic quests, and, uh, adventures? Do I get a sword?"

"A dagger, perhaps, would better suit one of your stature," Quixote replied. "But you get a hat with a feather in it."

"And a horse?" said Uncas. "I get to ride a horse?"

"Actually," said Quixote, "I know of an ogre who has a donkey that might be just the right size and temperament for you."

"What's the donkey's name?"

"Donkey," said Quixote.

"That's perfect!" Uncas said, hitting a fist into his other paw. "I can remember that! But . . . ," he continued, his expression suddenly sorrowful, "I have responsibilities here. I mean, the press . . ."

"Will do just fine without you, Father," Fred said hastily. "You've trained me well, and it practically runs on its own, anyway."

"True, true," Uncas said. "But I'm the seniormost member of the RARS. I can't possibly deprive them of my wisdom an' guidance an' . . . uh, smartness."

Fred continued to press the point that this was a great opportunity, but it wasn't until a dozen other badgers who'd heard of Quixote's offer rushed forward to reassure Uncas that somehow the Royal Animal Rescue Squad could struggle along without him, that he finally acquiesced.

"All right," Uncas said to his son. "As long as you'll be able to muddle through on your own." He turned to Quixote. "It would be my privilege," the little mammal said as he bowed deeply, "to become the squire to the great knight, Don Quixote Enchilada."

"De la Mancha," said Quixote.

"Gesundheit," said Uncas.

"We have one last matter to attend to," said Poe. "Caretaker Principia? If you'll come with me."

"Of course," said John.

Poe led John to the atelier, where Basil Hallward was just completing the varnish on a painting. Even from across the wide room, the visage was impossible to mistake.

On the easel was a portrait of Daniel Defoe.

"Are you crazy?" John said to Poe. "We'd just gotten rid of him, and by his own choice, essentially! Why do this now?"

"He was a Caretaker once," said Poe, "and we look after our own. We could not let him die the final death, when we had the means to prevent it."

"By creating a new portrait?" asked John.

Poe shook his head. "By creating the *first* portrait. And the last, for him. The other portrait was a fake, very much like the one we created for Kipling to use. Defoe had prolonged his life through other means. He had never truly been among those Caretakers in the gallery."

"And no one noticed the painting wasn't one of Basil's?"

"It was close enough to fool us all," said Poe, "because it had been painted by Basil's teacher—William Blake. He'd created other portraits, such as the painting of Charles Johnson, but never one of Defoe."

"Good," said John. "Two Defoes would be twice the trouble."

"By a strange quirk of the Pygmalion resins," said Poe, "they can be used for a person only once, and never again. So this picture cannot be duplicated. And he will never again leave Tamerlane House."

"That's good for you lot," said Defoe's image. "If there were more of me, I'd already rule the world."

"Oh, do shut up," said John. "You aren't going to put him in the gallery now, are you?" he asked Poe. "Even being turned to the wall seems too light a sentence, considering you've already saved his life, so to speak."

"No," Poe said, lifting the still wet painting off of the easel. "I have something else in mind for him."

With Defoe cursing all the while, they carried the picture down endless corridors and flights of stairs until they were in the basement, which seemed to be a repository of unused furniture.

Poe walked straight to a tall grandfather clock and moved the hands to midnight. The clock chimed and swung open to reveal a door, and more stairs.

Underneath was an immense cavern, which was chill and dark. Offshoots of the tunnels led in every direction, with the largest carrying the scent of salt water.

"Does that lead outside?" John asked.

"Yes," said Poe, "but the entrance is guarded by a forty-foot-tall flaming red bull. No one comes in or out without my permission—and even then, it's a crapshoot."

The cave had been built out with brick walls that formed dozens of rooms, as if someone had tried to impose a sense of order on the chaos of the cavern.

Poe moved down several levels until he came to a shallow niche, where he placed the painting.

"You think putting me down here is a punishment?" Defoe sneered. "Someone's bound to come exploring and find me."

"They won't after we're through," Poe said, as he picked up two trowels and handed one to John. "The mortar's in that canister. I'll fetch the bricks."

"You are not seriously considering this," Defoe exclaimed as John and Poe laid down the first row of bricks. "This is barbaric."

"Well," said John, "I have been accused of worse."

"But—but you're Caretakers!" Defoe said, eyes grown wide with panic. "You're supposed to help people."

"That," said Poe, "is precisely what we are doing."

The wall was almost complete. John spread the mortar on the last row, and Poe put two more bricks in place.

"Stop!" Defoe shrieked, having dropped all pretense that he was not bothered by his situation. "You *can't*! John, don't do this!"

"Ironic," said John. "That's the last thing I remember someone saying to *you*."

"For the love of God!" Defoe screamed as Poe slid the last brick into place. "For the love of—"

Then, nothing. It was a good wall.

"There's another irony for you, John," Poe said, wiping his hands on his trousers. "Everyone thinks I wrote that story as entertainment. No one ever realized it was actually an instruction manual."

"You promised *what* to *whom?*" John said in astonishment. "Absolutely not."

Rose had finally been able to reveal what she had promised to Madoc in return for restoring the sword—and she chose to tell the three Caretakers in the presence of her uncle, the Cartographer, in his room atop the Keep of Time. It was an appropriate place to do so, she said, because she had made a second decision in concert with Aven and Stephen—to release the Cartographer from the keep.

"It was the only way," said Rose. "He would not have repaired Caliburn otherwise."

"You didn't see what happened when Hugo Dyson went through one of the doors," said Jack, his face flushed with emotion. "The entire world changed into the domain of the Winter King. We had to traipse through two thousand years of history just to fix it—and that was all mostly by accident. Do you know what kind of damage he can cause if we give Mordred himself the means to go into the past?"

"I agree," said Charles. "He went into exile, and that's where he should stay."

"I gave him my promise," Rose said firmly. "And so did Professor Sigurdsson," she added, looking askance at John. "And we didn't give that promise to Mordred, we gave it to Madoc."

"It's the same person," said Jack. "What difference does his name make?"

"Jack," said Bert mildly, "of all of you, I would have thought you would be the most receptive to the idea of giving the door to Madoc."

"Me?" Jack said in surprise. "Why?"

"Because you alone have had the experience of getting a second chance you never expected to have."

"You mean Nemo," said Jack, nodding. "I've considered that. It's a strange loop to be caught in—to know I'm still the one responsible for his death in his future, while having had the chance to teach him, to mentor him, in my present creates conflicting feelings I don't quite know how to process."

"It's very simple," said Bert. "Your actions now redeem your actions then. Nemo knew his part and valued you for what you would one day become—a good man."

"How can we do any less for Madoc," John said, "considering it's in large part *our* fault that he became the man he is today?"

Throughout the entire discussion, the Cartographer had remained silent, observing but not offering any opinion either way. Rose stepped over to his desk and laid a hand on his arm.

"You knew him best, Uncle Merlin," she said plaintively. "What would you choose?"

The Cartographer looked at her for a long moment, then swallowed hard. "I—I have no right to suggest a course of action here," he finally said. "I betrayed him at every turn, and if we're laying our cards out on the table, I have to take as much responsibility as anyone for the evil he's done."

"What would you choose?" Rose repeated, more firmly this time. "You cannot answer badly, Uncle. And whatever you say, it won't change my decision to free you from the keep."

"That's the reason I hesitate," the old man replied. "If we are discussing justice, then he should stay, as punishment for his crimes. But if so, should I not continue to pay for mine, and also his, which he committed because of what we made him into?

"But if we are discussing an act of mercy, which you are offering to me, then would it not also be an act of mercy to offer freedom to him as well?"

"There are no longer any Dragons to compel you to stay," said

Rose. "None save for Samaranth, and I think he'd agree with my decision."

"Then . . . yes," said the old mapmaker. "If you are asking, I would choose freedom for myself—and for Madoc."

The keep trembled, and below them they could hear the muffled sounds of stones ripping away from the walls.

"You'd best hurry," said the Cartographer. "There are only a few doors left."

Quickly the Caretakers raced down the stairway to where a door was hanging precariously from a half-fallen archway. They grabbed it just as the stairway below was starting to buckle, and then secured it onboard their own airship.

"Good enough and done," said John.

"Yes," Jack said, grimacing. "Heaven help us all."

"What will you do?" Charles asked as they returned to the Cartographer's room.

"For centuries I have made maps based on the descriptions of others," he replied. "I have long wished to return to the journeys I abandoned so long ago in my youth, and I think that's exactly what I'm going to do."

"Would you like to take anything with you?" asked Rose.

He looked around the small room of Solitude, which had been his only home, and shrugged. "I brought very little with me, and there's little here I wish to keep."

He bent down and retrieved a black scabbard from behind his chair. "Here," he said, handing it to Rose. "Give this to your cousin Stephen. It belongs with his sword, anyway."

The Cartographer gathered together a few rolls of parchment, some bottles of ink, and several pens, and wrapped them all together in a large sheet of oilcloth.

"That should do it," he said as another rumble shook the remains of the tower, "and just in time, from the sound of things."

"Then it's time, Rose," John said, stepping back.

Rose used a small knife to cut into her palm, which she then placed against the old man's forehead as she began to recite the words of power:

Myrddyn, son of Odysseus
By right and rule
For need of might
I thus free thee
I thus free thee

By blood bound
By honor given
I thus free thee
I thus free thee

For strength and speed and heaven's power
By ancient claim in this dark hour
I thus free thee
I thus free thee

As she spoke the last word, the lock on the door popped open with a quiet click. It would lock no longer.

The Cartographer was free.

They stepped out into the tower, onto the last landing that

remained, then down to the awaiting airships: the companions onto the *Indigo Dragon*, and the Cartographer onto the *Scarlet Dragon*.

Both airships descended, then pulled away from the tower as another rumble shook a few stones free.

"Farewell," John called out. "May the wind be at your back, Myrddyn."

"Oh, hell's bells, lad," he said over his shoulder as the *Scarlet Dragon* picked up a crosswind, "call me *Merlin*."

Their task completed, the companions laid a course for Terminus one last time. They had one errand to complete, and then they could at long last return home. None of them chose to look back. None of them were even tempted.

And so, no one was watching at the isles called Chamenos Liber when the last stones fell from what was once the Keep of Time. The final door never fell, but simply swung open as the archway around it crumbled. The sky darkened for a moment, as the future became the present, then vanished into the past.

Chapter Twenty-four
The Notion Club

"You realize, you cannot return to the Archipelago," Bert said with obvious remorse. "It may be impossible for you to do so now. At least," he added, "for the next seven years, anyway."

When all the loose ends had been attended to in the Archipelago in 1943, the companions had returned to Tamerlane House, where Poe activated all their pocket watches as functional Anabasis Machines. He then instructed them in the use of the time travel devices, and after Ransom delivered them back to the Inn of the Flying Dragon, John, Jack, and Charles returned to 1936.

"You went back only minutes after you originally left," said Bert, "so Ransom had already led the Yoricks away. And without Rose, they will have no reason to return to Oxford."

That had been the most difficult decision—to leave Rose at Tamerlane House, where she could continue her education under Poe and Jules Verne.

Bert had arranged for them to meet again a week later at the Inn of the Flying Dragon, and he and Ransom brought Rose and Fred with them.

"You can meet her here whenever you like," he said, handing them a card with a drawing of the inn. "And with the Trump,

"Greetings, Caretakers and company," said the stout, bearded man ...

you can contact her if a need arises. But you cannot return to the Archipelago. Not until after the point you left in 1943."

The companions were stunned. "But we're the Caretakers," said John. "How are we to look after the Archipelago if we can't go there at all?"

Before Bert could answer, the mop boy brought a tray of drinks to the table.

"Thank you, Flannery," Jack said, smiling. "It's good to see you again."

"It's good to see you too, sir," the boy said as he put the tray of drinks on the table. He bent closer so that only Jack could hear.

"I just wanted you t' know," Flannery whispered, "Mr. Ransom spoke t' me as you'd asked, an' he warned me about the you-know-what in the you-know-where that you-know-who told you about. And I'll be nowhere near there then. I'm going to finish school on Prydain."

"Really?" said Jack. "On Prydain? That's exceptional, Flannery. What do you plan to study there?"

The boy stood up and took the now empty tray. "Music. I plan to learn to sing, and play an instrument or three, and tell stories in epic songs. The next time you see me," he said proudly, "I won't be mopping up at a tavern—I'll be Flannery Flem the Bard."

Jack winced, as did Charles and John.

"You know," Charles offered, "if you do plan to study on Prydain, you might want to consider changing your name ever so slightly to something more local."

"Change my name?" said Flannery.

"All performers have a stage name," said Jack. "Like Houdini, and . . . well, other performers."

"I'll do it!" Flannery said. "Thanks!"

"You cited *Houdini?*" Charles chided as he lifted his ale. "What kind of example does that set?"

"Says the man raising a Magwich plant," said Jack.

Charles spit out the ale he'd just drunk. "Good point," he said, coughing.

"You knew," John said to Bert. "You and Verne knew how this would go. So why not just take Rose to Tamerlane House to begin with?"

"It was necessary," said Bert, "because it would have been impossible to hide Rose otherwise. To some, she is all but invisible. But to those who know how to look, she shines like a beacon. There was nowhere and nowhen in space and time where she could be safely hidden—so we arranged for her to skip ahead in time to the point where she would be needed most. The point the Shadow King never wanted her to reach. But more important, we needed the three of *you* to skip ahead in time as well."

"Why?" asked John.

"Because," Bert answered, "according to a future History, you already *had.*"

"Did you know?" Jack asked, looking at Ransom. "Did you know the Trump would move us in time as well as space?"

Ransom shrugged, then shifted uncomfortably in his chair. "I, ah, suspected it was possible, but I couldn't have said for sure. We were whistling in the dark, really. Making things up as we went along. Hank has more of a knack for time travel than I, and Rappaccini's daughter is better at spatial concepts. But yes, I did think merging the two was possible. We'd just never tested it before, nor assessed the risks."

"I don't think it would have worked," Charles remarked, "if it hadn't been for that old man in the infinite white room."

"We have some associates looking into that," said Ransom. "We don't know who he is, but we do suspect you're right, Charles. Somehow he aided you. We just can't tell how. Or why."

"The old man's technique may work," said Bert. "Using a Trump twice. But we have too few agents to have risked anyone in a test."

"As you did with us," said Rose.

Bert sighed. "Yes. We had to try it. And the theory *was* sound."

"That was a dangerous way to test the theory," John said, casting a watchful eye at the girl, "given Rose's importance."

"But won't that danger still exist now?" said Jack. "If she's there, in the Archipelago where she can be discovered, won't the work we accomplished be undone?"

"The work has already been done," said Bert, "but your concern is also ours—so Jules plans to take her Elsewhen to continue her training."

"Elsewhere?" asked Charles.

"No," said Bert, signaling to Flannery for more drinks, "Else*when*. And Tamerlane House is as safe as . . . well, houses. At least in the Archipelago."

"We still have a lot of questions," said John. "Almost all of them about the Caretakers. I just can't seem to keep the rules straight—but I suspect in part it's because you haven't yet told us what all the rules are."

"Secrets make you sick," Fred commented.

"Didn't Freud say that?" asked Charles.

The badger shook his head. "Beats me if I know. I figured that out watching Magwich."

"All the secrets are out now," said Bert, "and the Prophecy has been fulfilled. There's no need for more secrets, so ask what you will."

"So we have to stay in England, while all of this unfolds, without changing anything," said Jack. "How is that resolving the war that will come?"

"You already *have*," said Bert. "When Ransom sent you into the, ah, 'future,' you changed the events that needed changing. So there's no need to do it again. But if you try, if you alter anything now, and in the coming years, you risk the very victory that you've already won."

"But there will still be a war," said John. "We know it's coming, and we know how and where it's going to start. Shouldn't we try to do something about that? Isn't it the right thing to do?"

Bert sat down across from John and clasped his hands together in thought. After a moment, he looked up and answered. "That's how a man should think, John, yes, and it's to your credit that you would take such a large thing upon yourselves. But there is, as always, a greater canvas to consider, and the matter of free agency among the rest of humanity."

"Haven't we already tampered with that," said Jack, "and more than once? We've gone back in time two millennia when it was necessary. Wasn't that considering the greater canvas and taking away the free agency of two thousand years' worth of the entire world?"

"You didn't initiate that," Bert replied in soft rebuke, "you were responding to the actions of our adversaries. They put the causes into play, and your job was to make sure the effects preserved the free agency of the world. Had you not done so, we would be living in Albion still, under the rule of the Winter King."

"But things will change anyway," said Charles. "Jamie's wardrobe, for example. Burton only got it because we supposedly weren't here to claim it. How do we deal with that?"

"You must remove yourselves from any and all dealings with the Archipelago, and anything associated with it," said Bert. "To take care of the future, you have to become invisible in the present. Throw yourselves into your work. And try not to think about altering events—else we risk changing the result we wanted all along."

"That's a terrible answer," said Jack.

"There's something else, Bert," said Charles. "We've spent a lot of time in the company of seemingly dead men—some who have eluded death via the portraits in Tamerlane House, which I understand. But there are others, like Burton, who never had a portrait painted but are still walking about. Are they traveling in time, like yourself, or have they managed to avoid death by some other means?"

Bert tipped his head back and laughed. "By my bones, Charles, you've quite a mind! And you're more right than you know.

"There are indeed several ways of defying death, but very few that are moral, and fewer still that are honorable."

"How do you mean honorable?" asked Jack.

"Death has little to do with sorrow," said Bert, "although that's what we feel when someone dies. The veil between this life and what comes after is surprisingly thin. Life persists. Consciousness persists. Spirit persists. It's only those of us on this side, who don't see it firsthand, who feel sorrow.

"Life is about the fulfillment of one's duty, and for most, their duty extends past what we know as 'death.' But for some, such as the Caretakers, there is a need to have them here, in this life, after their allotted time has passed. And so Basil paints the portraits in the gallery. But only the one time, and only under the limitations of Tamerlane House.

"There are other ways that allow more freedom—but the reasons to choose one of those methods must be carefully examined, as must one's motives for wanting to do it at all."

"That's why the option of a portrait or one of the other methods hasn't been used to bring back Artus or Nemo, isn't it?" asked Jack. "Neither of them would have chosen to do it."

"That's why. There are certain costs, and other drawbacks to having made such a choice. But it *is* a choice. And in their cases, they had done the work they had been here in this life to do—and it was their time to go forward and continue their work in the next life."

"And what about Professor Sigurdsson?" asked John. "Why couldn't he choose another option, and live on?"

Bert and Ransom exchanged pensive glances, as if they'd expected this question to come, sooner or later.

"As I said, there are several ways for a person to survive past death," Bert began. "The one preferred by the Caretakers Emeritis is the method you have already seen: the creation of the portraits by use of the Pygmalion resins. But there was also another means available to the Caretakers, which was discovered long ago by our first renegade."

"Dr. Dee," said John.

"Yes," Bert said, sighing. "Dee discovered a method for creating a new body, a virtually immortal body, into which one can 'move' upon death. It's basically willing a new self into existence. The Tibetans call this creation a *tulpa*, and the strength of the creation depends only on the will of the creator. And Caretakers are very strong-willed.

"Roger Bacon scorned the process and disavowed it as a tool of darkness. But some, like William Blake, embraced it and taught the method to others, such as Burton, who has made spirited use of it. He went back in time to recruit his allies in the Imperial Cartological Society before their own deaths occurred, and before portraits could be painted. Most of his recruits were either not yet full Caretakers, or like Doyle and Houdini, not yet dead when he got to them. Only one actual Caretaker has even gone through the process upon his death—and it was at the request of Poe and Verne that he did so."

"Kipling," said Jack. "It was Kipling, wasn't it?"

"It was the only way to ensure that he was accepted into the enemy camp," said Ransom. "It was a heavy price to pay, but he did so willingly."

"How is virtual immortality a heavy price?" asked John. "It sounds like an easy decision to me."

"That's because you're going to live for several more decades," said Ransom. "You and Jack both have plenty of life ahead of you, so it's not a test of your convictions to suggest a way to live forever."

"It is, as with everything in life, a choice," said Bert. "The Caretakers decided long ago that to meddle in the world past our allotted spans was not the ethical choice. As residents of Tamerlane House, through the use of the portraits, we could advise, and counsel, and be a living repository of information for those who came after. But we would not walk about messing around in the affairs of a world we were not meant to be in."

"*You* do," said Jack.

"I haven't died yet," said Bert, "but when I do, I shall join the others in the gallery. Stellan chose to live at Tamerlane, and then to die, finally, on Terminus. And he did so as a hero, John. Do not begrudge him that."

"There was no portrait of Poe in the gallery at Tamerlane House," said Charles. "What does that mean?"

"It means it's his house," said Bert. "He doesn't need a portrait, because he's never actually died."

"There was another one missing," Jack said. "Jules Verne. He died many years ago—but he seems to be pulling all the strings from backstage on everything that's happened. Is he a portrait, or a tulpa?"

"He'll answer that for himself," said Bert. "He should be along shortly. It was he who requested this meeting."

"You said there were other ways to survive death," said John. "Could none of them be used to help the professor?"

"I'm sorry, lad," said Bert, "but none that I know of. Had he been a tulpa first, as Defoe was, we might have created a portrait. But as he was a portrait first, there were no other options. And as Poe told you, the resins can only be used once, so his portrait cannot be recreated. I am truly sorry, John. For all of us.

"What I was referring to by mentioning other methods was other Caretakers, like Bacon, who never needed a portrait at all. He still serves the Archipelago, in his own fashion. You met him in the battle, I believe."

"Bacon?" Jack exclaimed. "I met Roger Bacon? When?"

"He saved your life, and Nemo's beside," said Bert. "Charys calls him the Tin Man."

"I thought that was just another clockwork," said Charles.

"In a way, he was the *first* clockwork," said Bert. "The only difference is, his mind remains inside. All he needs is the occasional spare part, and he can keep wandering the Archipelago until the end of time, if he so wishes."

"That's why the Shadow King was frightened by him," said John. "He saw what he was trying to be, but with, you know, less evil."

"We all learned lots of lessons there," said Bert. "That's one benefit of traveling to your own future, and making the trip part of your past."

"So are all the members of the Imperial Cartological Society immortal?" asked John.

"Only virtually," said Ransom. "They haven't aged, from what we can tell—and while they *can* be killed, it's much harder to manage, as you saw when Samaranth stepped on Defoe. So it's more like they have a second life."

"A very resilient one, and without the restrictions of the portraits," said Charles thoughtfully. "It would be very tempting."

"Everything has changed now," said Ransom. "Hopefully the members of the society truly are more misguided than traitorous."

"Why didn't Jakob Grimm's watch dissolve?" John asked suddenly. "We know he was a traitor, even there, in Tamerlane House."

"The magic that governs the watches is not one of mere cause and effect," Bert replied. "It is attuned to the desires of your heart. Jakob did what he did out of a sincere belief that he was doing what he must to save his brother."

"Even to the point of aligning himself against the Caretakers?" Charles said. "That's a long stretch."

"Jakob has paid his price," said Bert. "And it was more than just the physical damage he suffered. He knows he chose poorly, and he will have to overcome that. And regaining his self-worth will not come easily."

"I'm still unclear what Kipling's role was," said Jack. "Did he switch sides, as Burton tried to do? Or was he your man all along?"

"When we realized that there were traitors among the Caretakers, we seeded Kipling among them so that we would have a means of keeping track of them. The Shadow King found the means to quite seriously tempt him and make it appear he had betrayed us—but we discovered that someone else was already feeding pages from the Last Book to the Shadow King."

"The True Names of the Dragons," said Jack.

"Precisely," Bert replied. "Kipling realized that once Poe revealed the details of the Prophecy and our plan of action to the Caretakers, the traitor would probably try to steal the book itself and get it to his master."

"So Kipling went first, to draw attention to himself?" asked John.

"Again, precisely," said Bert. "If Kipling went, then all the Caretakers' attention would be on him, and any other defection would be much more difficult. It also gave him the opportunity to give Burton the nudge he needed when it was evident that the Shadow King cared more about conquest than anything else. And Burton was still more Caretaker than traitor."

"But Defoe stole the book anyway," said Charles. "That was

the one action that devastated the Dragons and nearly lost the entire conflict."

"Yes," said Bert, "and he covered his betrayal well. Kipling never suspected him, nor did any of the rest of us. But Kipling was still in a position where he could continue to report to us, and then, when the time was right, betray the Shadow King. If he'd uncovered Defoe's true allegiance sooner, before he'd taken the book itself, then it would have been too difficult for Kipling to follow after without arousing the suspicions of all the Caretakers."

"So you knew where Abaton was all along," said John.

"We didn't know, but we suspected," said Bert. "Defoe provided Hallward with the image for the painting, and Poe told him to go ahead and paint it. We didn't know *where* it was, just that it went *somewhere*. We weren't sure how to follow up Kipling's actions, until Charles made his suggestion to duplicate Defoe's painting as a Trump. That proved to be the perfect solution in more ways than one."

"All of this started when Kipling tried to capture us here," said Charles. "What would have happened if he had succeeded then?"

Bert grinned. "He wouldn't have. He just needed you to believe he might, so you'd go along with Alvin. His only real problem was making sure the effort looked good so the Shadow King would never suspect he had a cuckoo in his nest."

"Who planned this bit of espionage?" asked Charles. "It seems to have been a very deep game."

"Who else?" said Bert. "Jules is called the Prime Caretaker for a reason. And Poe has perceptive abilities that are far and away the best I've ever witnessed, in any era. Outside of we three, only Chaucer and Hallward knew."

"I knew," said Grimalkin, who was gradually appearing on John's shoulder, "but then again, cats always do."

"I think you've been adopted," Bert said, winking at the cat.

"He's quite unusual," John said, reaching up to scratch the cat's ears. "I wouldn't mind keeping him."

Bert chuckled. "I was talking to *you*, not the cat."

"I'll trade you," said Charles. "I'll give you the Magwich plant for the cat."

"Don't do it, John." Ransom laughed. "You end up with Magwich in 1945 anyway."

"Why is that?" Charles asked. "Do I finally get tired of him?"

Bert scowled at Ransom, as all the blood drained out of the philologist's face.

"Not exactly," Ransom finally managed to stammer. "John gets him because Jack wins the coin toss at your funeral."

"Ah," said Charles. His face betrayed no emotion, but his hands trembled as he set down his beer. "I see."

"When we met," said Ransom, "I said I had come to protect you, Charles. And that was true. Protecting Rose was my primary objective, but you were also in danger. And in some versions of the histories, you did not survive 1943."

"Oh?" exclaimed Charles. "Well, uh, well done, then. I think."

"It's one of the reasons I requested the assignment from Verne," said Ransom. "Of all of you, Charles has a particularly resonant influence on the different dimensions. He seems to be a key figure in all the worlds, and that makes him—in whatever form, or whatever he's called—worth looking after."

"So in some, he's called Chaz," said Jack.

"And in others, something else?" asked John. "Alvin, perhaps?"

Ransom smiled. "Some things aren't just coincidences," he answered. "And some things are just what they appear to be."

"Well, thanks for spilling the beans," Fred said, scowling at Ransom.

"You weren't supposed to know," Bert said to Charles. "No man needs to know the day of his death until it's upon him."

"Nine years is close enough," said Charles. He raised an eyebrow at Ransom. "That portrait Hallward was working on at Tamerlane House," he added with a sudden realization. "It wasn't you after all, was it? It *was* my portrait."

Ransom bit his lip and nodded.

"Sorry, old fellow," Jack said supportively.

"I'm not dead yet!" Charles retorted. "And from what we've been discussing, maybe I won't have to be."

"What are you thinking?" asked Bert.

"Well," said Charles, "what if I was to suggest that I didn't believe my duty would be fulfilled by 1945? What then?"

Bert nodded, as if he was expecting to have this particular discussion. "Come with me," he said, rising. "Let's discuss this privately. I think you'll be relieved and more than a little surprised by what I want to suggest."

"I'll hold down the fort here," said Fred. "Me and Rose, that is."

Rose winked at the little badger. "I'll have Flannery bring over more Leprechaun crackers."

"Y' sure know the way to a badger's heart, Miss Rose."

"Bert never really answered my first question," John said to Ransom. "Communicating with Rose by Trump is one matter, but how are we supposed to fulfill our responsibilities as Caretakers if we aren't allowed to return to the Archipelago?"

"It isn't a certainty that you can't return, not yet," said Ransom. "You resolved a terrible conflict—but you did so in the future. We want to make certain that that future is preserved in this and every other dimension it touches, and so for the time being, we have to move forward as we already have. And that means we must act as if you were not in the Archipelago again for seven years."

"That would apply here as well, then," said John, "because we were completely removed in time. But records still existed of our accomplishments here in Oxford, so somehow, we *were* still present."

"That's his point," said Fred. "The records we had of you *then* are of the deeds you'll perform *now*, and over the coming years. That's what you're meant to do. But here, and not in the Archipelago."

"Time does move in two directions," said Ransom, "but the lives we lead only move forward. That's how a 'Charles' from one world can become the Green Knight in this one."

"And how a 'Charles' from another can arrive here to protect the one we already have, eh, 'Alvin'?"

"Precisely," said Ransom.

"At any rate," John said reflectively as he lit his pipe, "it *is* only for seven years, after all. We went longer than that between our first two visits. And in a way, we've already been there anyway."

"This is making my head spin," said Jack as Charles and Bert returned to the table. "I can't keep track!"

"Jack," Ransom said, "were you able to spend much time with Poe while you were at Tamerlane House?"

Jack shook his head and grabbed a handful of Leprechaun crackers. "Not much, I'm afraid. After the initial Gatherum, I went off to Paralon, and then everything went to hell after that. So it was mostly John who was there, and he was usually locked in a debate with the Caretakers Emeritis."

"So you never got to discuss any of the other *Geographicas* with him?"

Jack choked on a cracker and washed it down with a gulp of ale. "*Other Geographicas?* What the devil are you talking about, Ransom? The whole point of the last quarter century of my life has been to protect the one, unique atlas—and now you're suggesting that there are *others?*"

"The *Imaginarium Geographica is* unique," Ransom replied. "To *this* world, anyway."

Jack started to sputter a response when Ransom shushed him. "Later, later," the philologist said. "There's someone just about to join us whom I think you're all going to want to speak with."

"Greetings, Caretakers and company," said the stout, bearded man who had just entered the Inn of the Flying Dragon. He was elegantly dressed in a manner more dapper than stylish, and he had a twinkle in his eyes. "I'm Jules Verne, and it is my great pleasure indeed to finally meet you all."

John, Jack, and Charles were stunned into silence. After all that had happened, not just in recent days, but over the last twenty years, they were unprepared to meet the man who seemed to have been the architect of everything they had experienced.

"Let's order a round of drinks, and an assortment of foodstuffs, and get caught up," Verne said as the door opened behind him and three more figures entered the inn. "But first I'd like to introduce you to the last three gentlemen I've invited to our little gathering. I believe you've all made their acquaintance before."

Fred let out a yelp of surprise, and Rose pursed her lips. Bert and Ransom said nothing, for they had expected this—but John, Jack, and Charles were slack-jawed with astonishment. Behind Jules Verne were Harry Houdini, Arthur Conan Doyle, and Sir Richard Burton.

"Greetings, little Caretakers," said Burton.

"What is this about, Bert?" John said, rising. "What are they doing here?"

"I was waiting until Jules arrived to tell you," Bert said placidly. "The Caretakers Emeritis have reached an accord with the leadership of the Imperial Cartological Society."

"'But how was the play otherwise, Mrs. Lincoln?'" Charles commented drolly. "The enemy of my enemy is my friend, eh, Bert?"

"Not enemies," said Verne. "Differing philosophies. We have managed to persuade Sir Richard that complete and unfettered openness would be disastrous."

"But," said Burton, "Poe and the others have conceded that total secrecy has not been the Archipelago's salvation either. So we have agreed to compromise."

"Compromise how?" asked John.

"Sir Richard, Sir Arthur, and, ah, Harry, have agreed to abide by Poe's request that no unauthorized information about the Archipelago will be made public. In exchange, we have agreed to formally sanction the establishment of the Imperial Cartological Society. They will no longer operate in shadow, so to speak. And we need not fear being exposed, because the eventual goal of the society under the Caretakers' purview is to open the knowledge of the Archipelago to all those who prove worthy of it. As it was, once, a long time ago."

"Your apprenticeship program writ large," Burton said, nodding at Fred. "Just imagine—where you are now three, there could be thousands of Caretakers, sharing the secrets and wonders—"

"And responsibilities," said Charles.

"That won't just happen overnight," said John.

"No," said Bert. "It may take a generation or three to implement, but we believe it *is* possible."

Jack slapped his forehead. "And who's to be in charge of this grand endeavor? We probably shouldn't set it up at Oxford—that would be pressing our luck, with John and I teaching there, and Charles having joined the Inklings. Too much risk of exposure."

"It wouldn't be set up at Oxford," said Houdini.

"Then where?"

"Uh-oh," Fred said to Rose. "Here it comes."

Burton grinned wickedly. "Cambridge."

"And the other shoe finally drops," Jack said, leaning on Charles. "I think I'd rather find out when I'll die."

"I'm not convinced," said John, eyeing Burton and the others. "Will this change our future?"

"There will be time enough to explain that as we sup, young John," said Verne, sitting down. "But in this, you may rest assured: There will be time enough for *everything*."

Epilogue

Madoc stood looking at the door, considering. His daughter had kept her word—but he had fully expected that. It was not in her nature to be deceptive, although he was certain that the others advising her had argued mightily against it. After all, he was indirectly responsible for all of the trouble that had occurred back in the real world—both in the Summer Country and in the Archipelago. And to be honest, he was surprised to find himself still alive.

It had been proven that a Shadow could not persist if its owner was deceased. And he had long known that he and his Shadow could exist, even function, with great capacity, independently of each other. But he was not sure, not until the recent events had taken place, that he could survive the destruction of his Shadow.

Apparently, he could.

He felt it, the moment it happened, as if an imperceptible weight were taken from him. He had long ago cast it away by choice, so he felt strangely mournful to realize it was now gone for good. Even that had been his own doing, since he gave them the means to defeat the Shadow after naming a price he never believed they'd pay.

And now, standing before him, was the means to end his exile. The Dragons were gone. No one would know where or when he might go if he stepped through the doorway—and they fully knew the kind of consequence that might occur if he changed the past.

The thought gave him pause. They would know. He could create great chaos, no matter where or when he went. So why would they have allowed Rose to drop the door over the waterfall? What possible argument could she have made, that would have persuaded them . . . ?

And then he knew.

Redemption.

She had argued that the chance for his freedom would also be a chance for redemption. And for a moment, the thought made him seethe—but that passed as he considered the door, and his choice.

Even after one has fallen into the abyss, it was once said, redemption still might be found in how one chooses to accept the consequences of one's actions. To some, even the smallest act of nobility carries within it the seeds of redemption—but was his choice to repair the sword noble, or selfish? Or did Rose hope that the noble act might come in the future?

Whatever the motivations, Madoc reasoned, the door ensured that there would be a future for him, even if it lay somewhere in the past. He took a deep breath and opened the door. Sunlight steamed through from a distant horizon, which framed a seaport and a bustling marketplace. The styles of dress were unfamiliar to him, but he would adjust and adapt, as he always had.

As Madoc stepped through, pulling the door closed behind him, the lingering notes and cheerful lyrics of a song being sung on the other side echoed past him and into the void: "Yankee Doodle went to town, riding on a pony, stuck a feather in his cap and called it . . ."

Then the door was closed, and the Deep was silent once more.

Author's Note

Since the release of the first book in the Chronicles of the *Imaginarium Geographica*, the aspect of the story that has drawn more reader interest than anything else is the idea of the atlas having had Caretakers before John, Jack, and Charles.

The previous Caretakers (or Caretakers Emeritis, as they prefer to be known) were what justified my conceit of presenting this particular trio of authors as the guardians of this most valuable book. If H. G. Wells and Jules Verne could be Caretakers, then why not Sir James Barrie? And if he could be a Caretaker, then why not Dickens, Poe, Twain? And from there it was easy to make a list of authors, scientists, thinkers, and creatives who might have been so inclined to take the offer to explore and document an imaginary world.

Some were obvious choices (Shakespeare); others, like Schubert, a bit more oblique. A few, such as William Blake, were good choices creatively, but temperamentally more suitable as comrades-in-principle to Richard Burton. This was the basis for the rival organization, the Imperial Cartological Society, and for a corresponding list of almost-Caretakers, failed Caretakers, and could-have-been Caretakers.

The differences between those who were chosen and those who washed out became the core of this book. It was less often a matter of good versus evil as it was a differing of philosophies—and sometimes it was a difference of degree only. This realization is what prompted me to create a subset of the Caretakers: the apprentices. I wanted to be able to examine more formally the characters who were in that position of deciding what they really believed. I wanted to have them face situations that were morally and ethically cloudy, so that when their choices were made, it would be with full knowledge of the decision, and with full responsibility for the results.

All of this was to help refine what I believe is a Thing That Is True: that it is less important to become a Great man than it is to be a Good man who aspires to serve a Great cause.

This book was also much more complex, due in part to the time travel aspects. The real-life counterparts of John and Jack wrote time-travel stories that are more obscure than their greater fantasy works; and Wells and Twain were well known for theirs. So it was inevitable—and a lot of fun, to boot. But, as was underlined by Charles's discovery near the end of the book, time does pass; people do grow older (mostly). And my Caretakers are aging. So the next most ardent questions are these: Who are the Caretakers that follow John, Jack, and Charles? And are there Caretakers today who look after the *Geographica*?

To these, I can only answer that I've already dropped hints about other modern-day Caretakers: men and women with names like Ray, and Madeleine, and Lloyd, and Arthur. The apprentices, and the new status of the ICS, are also markers of where things might go; and the prominence of Rose Dyson in this book should not be underestimated. At some point in every story, real and imagined, the students become the teachers as the torch is passed on to a new generation. In a manner of speaking, everyone who reads these books and shares these stories has become an apprentice Caretaker, in spirit if not yet in fact. And as for the Principal Caretakers themselves, I've already written how they can be identified: They carry the silver watches with the red Chinese dragon on the case. . . .

Just like mine.

James A. Owen
Silvertown, USA

Check out a sneak peek of the next book in
The Chronicles of the Imaginarium Geographica

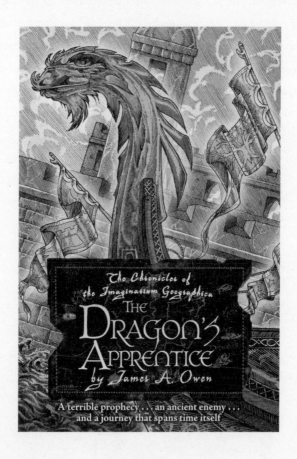

Available now

Twilight had just fallen across the sky when the ghost pirate appeared at the base of Magdalen Tower. At first it seemed as if the ghost was on fire, but that was only a trick of the light. It was already quite dark along the cobblestone walk that crossed beneath the tower, so the light that emanated from the ghost filled the courtyard with an unearthly brilliance.

Eleven people were passing the tower in the moment that the apparition appeared. Three were professors who had seen many ghosts in Oxford, and so gave it no notice. Two more, also faculty at Magdalen, felt similarly about pirate costumes, and merely sniffed their annoyance as they passed, assuming as they did that it was some sort of student mischief. Four more were actual students, who reacted with surprise, awe, and no small amount of fear, and they scattered into corridors adjacent to the tower.

The last two people who witnessed the ghost's appearance were Caretakers of the *Imaginarium Geographica*, and a ghost pirate was at least as interesting as some of the other fantastic things they had seen, so they moved closer to have a better look.

John had arranged to meet his friend Charles at the base of

Magdalen Tower so that they might walk together to their friend Jack's private rooms there at the college, and they met just as the sun was setting. It was in that moment that the apparition had appeared.

Even if they hadn't been Caretakers, a ghost would have been nothing to cause them alarm—Oxford had long had a reputation of being a haven to spectres and spirits of all kinds, and as long as they didn't disrupt the business of the university, no one made a fuss. Even in the midst of the Second World War, it was also good for tourism.

"I didn't think I'd ever actually see this fellow," John whispered to Charles. "I've heard about the Old Pirate for years but never had the pleasure of seeing him in person, uh, so to speak."

"How many other ghosts have you met here?" asked Charles.

"Ah, none, I'm afraid," John admitted, "although I haven't exactly sought them out, either."

"Well, why not?" Charles retorted as he approached the ghost, hand outstretched. "They could prove to be really helpful to my writing, you know. Worth asking, anyroad."

The ghost simply stood there, hunched over, staring into the darkness as the Caretaker introduced himself. "Well met, old fellow. My name is Charles."

Suddenly the ghost began to move, jerking about awkwardly, as if it were a puppet in a penny nickelodeon. It seemed as if speaking to it had engaged it in some way. Charles dropped his hand. "Are you in distress?" he asked the ghost. "Why are you here?"

The ghost stopped, then turned and focused its rheumy eyes on Charles, who took full stock of it for the first time. The spectre had presence and looked as if it stood in bright sunlight—but it was transparent, ethereal.

By appearance, it was certainly a pirate, no doubt, but an ancient one, many, many years old. His hair was long and straggly, and the clothes he wore, once fine, were tattered with age. His hands were shaking, and his head twitched nervously. But his eyes were piercing, intense—and, Charles thought with surprise, oddly familiar.

"Caretakers?" the ghost said with a trembling voice. "Be ye Caretakers, here, at Oxford?"

Charles and John exchanged surprised looks. This was no run-of-the-mill ghost. Not if he knew who they were. Then again, there had been stories of the Pirate Ghost appearing in this spot for two centuries, and no one had ever reported that he spoke at all, much less that he had mentioned anything about Caretakers.

"Who is asking?" said John, stepping forward. "Who are you looking for?"

"Jamie?" the ghost answered. "Jamie, is that you?"

John sighed. "The only one of us who ever quit," he said to Charles, "and he's the one everyone asks for in a crisis."

"No," the ghost said, shaking his head. "Ye be John, I think. Ron John Tollers, unless I miss my guess."

John stepped back in surprise at hearing a mishmash of his nicknames. "That—that's right," he said. "I'm he. Do I know you?"

The ghost spread its arms and smiled. "In another life, another time," he said, his voice weary, "I was your friend Hank Morgan."

"Good Lord," said John, glancing again at Charles, who was equally stunned. "We can't even walk across Oxford without stumbling into an adventure."

The old saying about absence making the heart grow fonder is over-rated, John had thought to himself as he prepared to go out earlier that afternoon. *Absence doesn't do anything except create longing, and an ache that cannot be remedied until the waiting is through.*

He and the other Caretakers of the *Imaginarium Geographica,* Jack and Charles, had been waiting for seven years for a chance to return to the Archipelago of Dreams. In earlier times, they had gone for longer periods without visiting, but there had been less urgency in those days—and maybe that was what stirred John's unease. That, or the fact that they'd been forbidden to return. *We never truly know we want something,* he thought, *until we've been told we can't have it.* Or perhaps it was the dark days of war covering the earth that made him long for the escape of the magical lands in the Archipelago.

Whatever it was, the price they'd had to pay for a victory in the future was steep. They'd jumped forward in time and defeated a terrible enemy, before returning to the time where they were meant to be. But to ensure that the victory remained certain, they had to stay away from the Archipelago, so as not to risk changing the outcome that had already happened.

They hadn't realized how hard it would be to wait through most of the new Great War that had swept the Summer Country.

The Darkness of the shadows was hardest to bear. In those days when the shadows of the Dragons swept over all the Earth, John in particular struggled mightily against the impulse to act.

"We *are* acting," Charles and Jack would remind him, "and we have. By waiting. We know that this is a battle we have already won, John. We just need to do our duty—and do nothing. Nothing but wait."

Now, however, the waiting was almost over. The clock had caught up with the past, and the future was about to become the present again. And they could finally return and fully take up their mantle again as true Caretakers.

John had put on his jacket and looked at himself in the mirror. He was finally feeling the years of his life—and not just because of the Wars. He had now been a Caretaker for longer than he had not. It was one of the roles that defined him—and yet it was still one of the greatest secrets he kept from all but a few. *Until,* he thought with a smile, *the new calling of Jack's comes to fruition. If that works, well . . .*

Everything could change. Everything.

He had kissed his wife and children good-bye and stepped out the door.

It was less than an hour later that he and Charles began their conversation with the Pirate Ghost of Magdalen College.

"Hank!" John exclaimed. "What's happened to you? You look so . . . so . . ."

"Old?" Morgan replied with a cackle. "Two centuries of waiting will do that to a man."

"Waiting for what?" asked Charles.

"For you," the ghost replied simply. "I was waiting for you, Good Charlie, and Ron John, and Jack-Jack the Giant Killer. I was waiting for the three of you." He narrowed his eyes. "Where be Jack, anyroad?"

"He's finishing a discussion," said John. "We, ah, we weren't exactly expecting to see you, Hank."

"And why should ye?" Morgan retorted. "I've only been appearing in this same spot for two hundred years, give or take."

"No need to be snappish," said Charles, "but you never spoke to anyone before now."

"Because no one has ever spoken t' me!" said Morgan. "It only works if *you* speak first."

"What are you talking about?" John said, clearly puzzled. "You've lost me."

"No time, no time," said Morgan, waving his hands. Then, he laughed, wheezing. "Or just enough, I suppose. Yes—it was just enough.

"Listen to me," the ghost insisted with a new urgency in his voice. "You must build the bridge. Shakespeare's Bridge. You can't get back without it. But the bridge won't work without a trump."

He stopped and pulled one of the familiar silver watches from a broad pocket. He flipped it open and grimaced. "I've told them," he murmured to himself. "The loop should have closed."

Charles gripped John's shoulder, and looks of worry creased both men's faces. They were missing too many pieces of a far bigger picture here.

"Hank," John began, "perhaps if we—"

"You must build Shakespeare's Bridge," Morgan said again. "It's the only way! The only way for you to—"

He stopped and looked down at his watch, which had begun ticking. "Oh, thank God," he murmured as he adjusted the dials on the device. "You've finally managed to make a new—"

In midsentence, Hank Morgan vanished.

"Oh my stars," said John. "What just happened here, Charles? What did we just see?"

"Nothing we can sort out on our own," Charles replied as he looked around the courtyard. Morgan was indeed gone, and whatever his cryptic message had meant, it was apparently all they were getting. "Hank's supposed to be joining us at dinner later at Tamerlane House, anyway. We'll just take it up with him then. Maybe it's some sort of joke. To welcome us back?"

John shook his head. Whatever else the ghost was, it was no joke. The age, the hard years that weighed on their old friend, were real. And that meant the warning was too.

"Let's go," he said, spinning away on his heel. "Jack will be waiting for us."

"What is it?" Jack asked his friends as he ushered them into his rooms. "What's happened?"

He knew by their demeanors that something was amiss. John went straight to the cupboard to fetch glasses for a drink, while Charles wearily draped himself in one of the chairs. "I'm not sure how to begin," Charles said. "Let's just say we've been having a little chat with a ghost."

"Really?" said Jack, smirking, as John handed him a snifter of brandy. "Which one?"

"The Old Pirate," Charles replied. "You know, the one that appears at the base of the tower."

"Good Lord," said Jack after a moment. "You're serious, aren't you?"

"Quite," John said, sitting next to Charles, "but that's just the start of it."

Over the next several minutes, and a round of drinks, John and Charles related to Jack their experience with the ghostly Hank Morgan. When they had finished, he sat back and rubbed his forehead.

"Amazing," Jack said. "Two centuries is a long time to wait to deliver such a cryptic message."

"I got the impression that's all he could give us in the time he had," John noted, "relatively speaking, that is."

Charles rubbed his chin, deep in thought. "I think it's more than that," he mused. "He said it only works if we spoke to him first, remember? I think that ghost may not have actually been Hank, but some kind of avatar that could speak only when spoken to."

"A recorded message?" asked Jack. "And interactive, to boot? That's some trick."

"Exactly," said John. "Who else but Hank would have the skills to pull it off?"

"Manipulating space as well as time," Jack said, pacing the width of the room. "Not too many, I think. Alvin Ransom, probably. Rappaccini's daughter, maybe. Verne. Bert. Possibly Kipling. That's about it. There are others, associates of the Cartographer, who might have the skills, but they wouldn't have the need to send a message so indirectly. Not now."

"Associates?" Charles asked. "You mean apprentices, don't you?"

"Not necessarily," replied Jack. "Several of them were, but others ended up joining with Burton's Imperial Cartological Society."

"Ah," Charles said as he leaned back in his chair, crossing his legs. "I see."

The Imperial Cartological Society had operated as a sort of shadow organization to the Caretakers Emeritis. Comprised of rejected Caretakers, former Caretakers, and those men and women of history who might have been Caretakers in another time and place, the Society was dedicated to spreading knowledge of the Archipelago of Dreams and all its secrets—by any means possible.

It was only after the Society was subverted by the Shadow King that there was a split among its ranks, and the de facto leader, Sir Richard Burton, brokered a truce with the Caretakers.

The Society would not attempt to spread knowledge about the Archipelago without the involvement and approval of the Caretakers Emeritis. And in return the Caretakers, under Jack's supervision, agreed to start a formal educational program at Cambridge in order to begin creating a greater awareness of the Archipelago among those who proved worthy to know of it.

It was an imperfect alliance, and it was likely to go through a succession of growing pains. But a tentative peace was better than war—and they had all already had more than enough of war.

"I'll just say it, then," John said, rising to his feet. "Shouldn't we consider that this could be some sort of trick of Burton's? He's done it before."

Jack dismissed the question with a wave of his hands. "Not using Hank, no," he said. "And besides, he's sitting at the Caretakers' table, so to speak. There's nothing he can gain through deception that hasn't already been offered to him on a silver platter."

"We can just bring it up with Hank when we get to Tamerlane House," Charles said, stretching as he rose to stand with his friends. "After all, it can't be much of a crisis Hank was warning us about. Not if he had to go walking through two centuries just to deliver the message. Another day shouldn't matter that much."

"Speaking of walking," said Jack, "we should start heading for the Kilns. That's where Ransom is expecting to take us through, and besides, I want to check in with Warnie and see if Mrs. Morris has shredded Magwich yet."

"Mrs. Morris?" Charles asked. "I thought your cat was a he."

"Morris *was* a he," Jack replied, "right up until the point she had kittens. It's been Mrs. Morris ever since."

"You have kittens? Charles asked. "I hadn't seen any."

"Oh, we don't let them roam the house," said Jack. "We keep them in the storeroom with that stupid talking shrub."

"I really do appreciate you taking him on," Charles said apologetically. "He and Michal were getting on horribly, and I had enough trouble with her already after I explained about the map tattooed on my back. Apparently, wives like to be consulted about that sort of thing."

Jack shrugged. "Maybe I ought to put him at Cambridge," he mused, "make him the centerpiece of the new Imperial Cartological Society. Sort of a living cautionary tale about what happens when an evil henchman turned green knight mismanages his chance at redemption."

"Does it really count as a secret society if everyone knows it exists?" Charles asked.

"As I have begun to plan it," said Jack, "it is most definitely *not* going to be a secret society. It's more like an invisible college. Those who know about it don't talk, and those who don't know don't care."

"I think that's half the reason the Caretakers Emeritis worked out a truce with Burton and the others," said John. "The number of people on the planet who would even give a flying fig about the Society is going to be roughly the same as the number of people who can be trusted to know about it."

"I still think we should have drawn straws," Jack complained. "No one warned me that being the Caveo Secundus would mean going to Cambridge."

"That was Burton's call, not to base it here," said John, "and besides, once we get you into a proper appointment there, you'll have a good shot at redeeming the whole University."

"It's strange how far apart we once were with Burton," said Charles. "We got the jobs he wanted, and he went renegade because he thought he could do it better. And now we have nearly identical goals. A bit chilling, that."

"We've been very bad at the job, by my accounting," said John. "After more than two and a half decades, the separation between the Archipelago and our world is more pronounced than ever. Sometimes I feel as if all we are doing is treading water."

"Holding the line," Jack echoed.

Charles let out a heavy sigh. "Our victories do seem to be becoming hollower and hollower, don't they?" he mused. "Of course, it doesn't help that we've had to put down the Winter King—Shadow King—Mordred. . . ."

"Madoc," said Jack.

"Whatever his name is, three times," said Charles. "Hopefully now he's contented enough not to come back around looking to conquer or subvert or whatever it is that's the fashion for dictators these days."

"We've seen the last of him," said Jack. "And time will prove we've made the right choices all along."

"That's what worries me," Charles countered. "Whatever else we decide to do now, the possibility remains that everything we know—everything we have done—may be completely wrong."

The Caveo Principia inclined his head in acknowledgment. "It's possible," he said. "I just get the impression that we're still being trained, being tested. That we have not fully been given the mantles of Caretakers."

"Well," Jack said jovially, "if they haven't made up their minds about us after almost a quarter century, then either they're very indecisive, or they're very, very selective."

John shook his head. "I don't know which one of those would be worse."

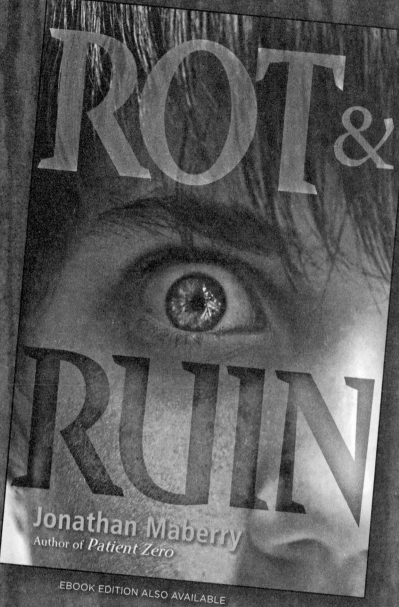